Ad

"I was consumed by the savage mysteries of Cameron's harsh and haunting fantasy world. A story of love and loss as searing as the desert heat."
—Diana Peterfreund, author of *For Darkness Shows the Stars*

"Harrowing and heartfelt. The intricately realized world of *Island of Exiles* crackles with harsh magic and gripping suspense."
—A.R. Kahler, author of The Immortal Circus series

"*Island of Exiles* is imaginative, bold, and as electrifying as a Shiara storm."
—Lori M. Lee, author of *Gates of Thread and Stone* and *The Infinite*

"A beautifully wrought fantasy filled with magic, rebellion, and romance, plus a strong, butt-kicking heroine to root for!"
—Lea Nolan, *USA Today* bestselling author of *Conjure*, *Allure*, and *Illusion*

"Erica Cameron's *Island of Exiles* is a remarkable achievement: a fantasy world so richly imagined, so finely detailed, and so strikingly original, even the most incredible elements feel totally real. The energy of the desosa will tingle along your skin as you race through this amazing book, and at journey's end, you'll long for the sequel so you can immerse yourself once more in the mysteries of Itagami!"
—Joshua David Bellin, author of the Survival Colony series

"*Island of Exiles* has everything I've been looking for in a fantasy— powerful characters, magical powers that make me itch with envy, and a spoken language that is as intrinsic to the story as it is beautiful."
—Amber Lough, author of *The Fire Wish* and *The Blind Wish*

ALSO BY ERICA CAMERON

ISLAND
OF EXILES
THE RYOGAN CHRONICLES

ERICA CAMERON

Entangled Publishing, LLC
2614 South Timberline Road
Suite 109
Fort Collins, CO 80525

Entangled Teen is an imprint of Entangled Publishing, LLC.

Visit our website at www.entangledpublishing.com.

Edited by Kate Brauning
Cover design by Anna Croswell
Interior design by Toni Kerr

ISBN: 9781633755925
Ebook ISBN: 9781633755963

Manufactured in the United States of America

First Edition February 2017

10 9 8 7 6 5 4 3 2 1

To Mom, for everything.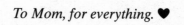

Beyond the desert's burning sun,
Beyond the perilous sea,
The verdant shores of Ryogo wait
When Shiara is done with me.
Miriseh bless the life I've lived,
The battles I have won,
And send me on to Ryogo
When death can't be outrun.

— **Blessing of the Miriseh, a prayer of Sagen sy Itagami**

CHAPTER ONE

I press as close as possible to the sandstone wall of the ravine, trying to shove my whole body into the narrow strip of shade on the rising slope. A few feet below, Rai does the same, pulling the canteen of water from the pack strapped to her thigh, loosening the atakafu cloth covering her mouth and nose, and sipping slowly. The sight makes my mouth feel drier than ever.

My hand falls to my own thigh pack, and I toy with the ties holding it shut. There isn't much water left in my canteen, and I don't know how much longer we'll be enduring the brutal, dehydrating heat of the desert sun. The hunt has been longer than we expected and far trickier than it should be.

Pulling my hand away from the temptation, I search the path above us for any sign of our prey. There isn't anywhere else the teegras could have gone once they entered the ravine, but we haven't spotted a single trace of them since— Wait. There.

"Rai, look." My murmured words are muffled by the

atakafu, but it's enough to draw her attention to fresh claw marks on the red sandstone.

She's already put the waterskin away, so she lifts the atakafu back over her nose and cautiously climbs until she can see the marks for herself. The corners of her round eyes crinkle with a grin as we cautiously hike up the steep ravine, moving as silently and steadily as we can.

We've barely gone thirty feet when the wind shifts. The gust presses my tunic tight against my body and nearly rips my hood off, but that's not what makes my pulse falter.

The desosa, the elemental energy in the air, has sharpened. It's carrying the tingling burn of electricity, but this is the wrong season for a typhoon. The first storms shouldn't hit for another moon.

"Do you feel that?" I don't look at Rai, keeping my eyes on the sky instead.

"No. What— Khya!" She tries to grab my ankle when I turn away from the narrow path; I pull myself up the wall of the ravine instead. "What are you doing?"

"Trying to figure out why the desosa just changed." Shifting my weight and ignoring a sharp rock that cuts into my bare feet, I look for a handhold that will get me to the top of this wall. I need to see the horizon.

"Rotten, obstinate, idiotic desosa mages," Rai grumbles as she follows me up the wall.

"*You're* a desosa mage." She's a kasaiji; she uses the ambient energy surrounding us for her fire magic just as much as I use it for my wards.

Rai grunts. "You know I can't feel it like you can."

"Then you'll have to shut up and trust me, won't you?" I place my feet carefully to avoid disturbing loose rocks. If the teegras are closer than we think, attracting their attention could be deadly. Those vicious scaled cats are a danger only for my squad. If I'm right, what's rolling in off the northern sea will threaten every man, woman, ebet, and child in the city. It'll threaten *Yorri*.

Testing the scents in the air is always harder through the filter of the atakafu, but I breathe anyway. On the wind, there's a heavy scent of salt and brine.

We're too far inland for the smell of the ocean to be this strong.

Miriseh save us. Even the briefest of storms will flood the area in minutes. Trapped here, the high walls of the ravine mean death.

At the narrow ledge near the top of the rock wall, the wind tugs at my hood and flattens the bottom of my tunic against my thighs. I stay low and pull Rai up after me.

"Why are we risking making ourselves dinner?" Sunlight glints off the iron blade of the tudo strapped to Rai's back, and it brings out the rich red undertone to her brown eyes. Before I can answer, her head snaps up, her gaze pointed north. "Oh."

Bellows and blood, I wish I had been wrong.

The barren plain is drenched in light, soaking up the heat from the sun and releasing it in waves that distort my vision. At high noon, there should be at least one pack of teegras roaming, their red scales glowing like embers. There should be colonies of mykyn circling above us, too, waiting to pick the bones of the teegras' abandoned kills.

The expanse is empty. The animals have dug deep into their dens or hidden in their caves by now, fleeing the coal-black clouds about to make landfall.

"Bellows," Rai breathes. "It's too early for a typhoon."

The desosa's needling prickle flares, cutting enough to make me flinch. A bolt of blue-white lightning rips the dark mass of clouds in half. The thunderclap that follows is distant, a sound I feel more than hear. Despite layers of cloth and padded armor, the hairs on my neck and arms rise.

This storm will rip apart everything in its path.

"We need to find the others." I'm glad Yorri hasn't earned the right to train outside the city. My younger brother is safer inside Sagen sy Itagami. Only the city's tall, thick walls and the network of caves underneath it will protect us from this.

If we can reach it in time.

No. Not getting back to the city alive—back to Yorri alive—isn't an option.

Rai lowers herself over the ledge and reverses the climb. I slide down with far less care, my bare hands and feet gathering scratches and scrapes, and Rai does the same before pushing away from the wall six feet above the floor of the ravine. As soon as our feet hit solid ground, we run, cutting through the maze of trenches and boulders toward the rendezvous point.

The gusts are almost strong enough to lift my feet from the ground, but running with the wind gives us the speed we need.

When we turn into a narrow pass, the gale comes at us crosswise, sending my loose hood flapping. I keep my feet. Rai grunts when her shoulder slams into a solid wall. She recovers but falls behind, more careful now.

I push faster.

Ahead is the mouth of the wider canyon, the red-and-gray rock walls almost a hundred feet high—our rendezvous point. Nyshin-ma Tyrroh is there with Nyshin-pa Daitsa, his second-in-command, and Nyshin-ten Ryzo, the command trainee a breath away from a promotion. Tyrroh tenses as soon as he spots me. I yank the atakafu away from my mouth.

"Storm!" I call. Protected from the gusting wind and unable to see the ocean, neither one of them could have noticed the impending danger yet. "Typhoon from the north."

Tyrroh pulls a horn from his belt, brings it to his lips, and blows three quick blasts. When Rai and I reach Tyrroh, pausing for breath just off Ryzo's broad shoulders, I search the horizon for the return of the others.

I can't keep still.

We have to wait for the rest of the squad, but the longer it takes for them to return, the more likely it is we'll all be caught by the typhoon. I shift from foot to foot. I itch to *run*. To fight. The brine-laden wind blasts into the canyon, heightening the sting of the desosa. It pelts the edges of my mind like hail. Drawing in power that unstable is risky. I have a tudo blade strapped to my back, but what good is a blade against wind?

Nyshin-ma Tyrroh eyes the horizon like an enemy he has to defeat. A ravine may be the deadliest place to get caught, but the open plain between the Kyiwa Mountains and the Itagami mesa won't be much safer. We're several miles away from the city, and the clouds loom closer every second.

Animals can be outsmarted. Enemies can be fought. Storms can only be survived.

Even the strongest mages and fighters in the clan are helpless in the face of a storm, and I hate that. I hate the fear chilling my skin and clouding my thoughts, and I hate that I can see all of those fears reflected in Nyshin-ma Tyrroh's eyes. "Go now, Khya. Take Rai and run."

I look toward Itagami. That way lies safety, and leaving now might get me there before the worst of the storm strikes. Staying, though... If the desosa remains this sharp, this dangerously electric, it'll be stupidly risky to channel that power into my wards.

It'd be safer for Rai to make it back to the city before the storm hits, but it doesn't matter, because she won't go back alone. She definitely won't go back without Etaro. Risk or no, neither of us will abandon our squad if there's a chance we can help protect them.

The safety of the clan comes before our lives.

Yorri is one of the only people I'd ignore that conviction for, though Rai and Etaro are tied for second, but running ahead to get back to Itagami first won't make it any more likely that I'll arrive alive. My best chance is with the squad, and their best chance is with me.

I shove my panic aside, squaring my shoulders and planting my feet. "I'm not leaving you all behind."

Tyrroh has been my commanding officer for more than a year. This is the first time I've dared disobey an order. He nods once, his dark eyes crinkling at the corners like they do when he smiles. That smile falls as the other six squad members appear over the rise. I fix my hood and reknot my atakafu to keep it in place over my mouth. As they approach at a run, I ready my wards; the invisible shield won't save us from the wind, but it may at least keep us from literally losing our heads to a barreling piece of debris.

Nyshin-ma Tyrroh barks orders, and the squad forms a tight column behind Rai and me. When we move, we move fast.

The first mile is protected by a narrow canyon, then the south wall tapers off to nothing. As the blasts of wind grow stronger, I watch the air as much as the ground, ready to deflect rocks carried by the currents of air. Soon—too soon—we have to turn east and leave the shelter of the high stone walls.

Each step becomes a battle. There's still daylight, but the normal blinding brightness of the desert at noon is gone. The storm will have swallowed the sun by the time we reach the narrow, winding path up to Itagami's gates. Even in daylight, that path is treacherous. But in the dark while fighting the wind?

I dig my feet into the hard-packed ground and push faster.

Someone shouts, but it's distant over the rush of the wind. How far back have they fallen? I look. Tyrroh is dragging Etaro up until ey is on eir feet again.

My stomach flips when Etaro cradles eir arm. Did I miss a piece of debris? I pay more attention to the sky, but I don't stop running. I might've been able to prevent whatever struck Etaro, but nothing I'm capable of will help the ebet now.

The Itagami mesa is dead ahead of us, and the fires in the watchtowers are beacons guiding us home. It's a safe haven that the Miriseh carved out of the rock for our ancestors, but it's too far away to do us any good.

The clouds are almost over our heads when the desosa flares again, the power so electrified by the storm that it nearly burns me. So electrified that it nearly burns cold.

Blood and rot. I've felt this before.

Years ago, Yorri and I stood on the north wall of the city to watch a storm, the wind whipping our skin like a lash. An arc of lightning had streaked through the sky, striking the exterior wall not twenty feet from where we stood.

It's happening again. Siphoning as much of the dangerously strong desosa into myself as I can bear, I bring up my wards and dive for Rai.

Miriseh, bless me; I hope this works.

Lightning tears through the sky, the flash sunlight-bright. It strikes exactly where we'd been standing. Even warded, the heat is like standing inside a forge. It's agonizing. Almost too much. I bite back a scream and grit my teeth, pulling in more of the unstable desosa to reinforce the magic.

Never draw power from unstable desosa. You'll burn out. Overload. Die.

My training master's warnings roar through my mind.

Too late. I've already ignored them all.

The lightning disappears, leaving only the rumbling, echoing thunderclap behind. My vision is washed out in red-tinged white light. I lose hold of the desosa. My wards drop.

Hands wrap around my shoulders. Someone hauls me to my feet.

"*Move!*" Tyrroh orders, gripping me by the waist and keeping me upright when my knees buckle. Two of the others do the same for Rai, pulling her forward.

I did it. She's fine. We're both okay.

A deep breath is barely enough to clear my head, but I manage to find my stride again.

We've almost reached the bottom of the path to the city's gates when the clouds unburden themselves on the sunbaked desert of Shiara. Sheets of water drench us to the skin as we run up the winding path cut into the sandstone.

The higher we rise, the stronger the wind gets. My hood fills with air and flies back off my head, pulling so hard it chokes me. Someone almost goes flying off the ledge. Rai tows them back just in time. I tuck my hood into my tunic as I press against the wall, moving as quickly as I can while hugging the stone.

The wet rock is slick under our feet. I slip, catching myself on the cliff. Wind rips strands of my dark hair from the twin braids keeping it tight to my scalp. Pieces stick to my forehead and cover my eyes. I wipe them back and keep moving.

Two hundred yards to safety.

Someone else gets too close to the edge. The gale rips them into thin air, but Ryzo catches their wrist.

One hundred yards.

All the muscles in my legs burn. Rai falls. Tyrroh barely catches her tunic in time to save her.

Fifty yards.

Ever-more-frequent lightning strikes light up the path, gleaming off Itagami's iron gate. The guards at the gate are shouting. Though the words are lost, the message is clear: Run, run, *run*.

I sprint, diving under the protection of the wide stone archway. As soon as the last of the squad is inside, the guards heave the massively heavy iron doors shut. The gate's groaning protests are lost to the storm, but the *thud* of it locking reverberates through my chest.

Miriseh bless it, we made it back alive.

Laughter bubbles up from my chest, relief leaving me light-headed and exertion leaving me too weak to stuff it away. Closing my eyes, I collapse against the wall of the archway until I can trust my unsteady legs to support me.

Stepping into the open, I pull my atakafu away from my mouth and turn my face to the sky, opening my mouth and swallowing as much cool, fresh water as I can. If we're lucky, this will replenish all of the pools in the underground caverns. Off-season rain is so rare that even the shortest of unexpected droughts leaves us teetering on the knife's edge. This storm might've nearly killed us, but it also might give Sagen sy Itagami enough water for us to survive another half a year.

"Ryzo! Get Etaro to Hishingu Hall for healing. Everyone else retreat to the undercity," Tyrroh bellows. I watch Ryzo help Etaro into the city, biting my lip. I should have been paying more attention. If I'd been faster, more alert, Etaro wouldn't have gotten hurt.

"Move, Khya!"

I jump, yanking my attention away from Etaro, and follow the squad.

The undercity is so massive I've gotten lost in its network of caves more than once, but Itagami couldn't survive without it. Partly because of things like the iron and crystal mines, the mushroom farms, the bathing pools, and the small spring of fresh water. Mostly, though, it's because of days like today. The undercity is our escape when a tornado, a typhoon, or a dust storm tears across the desert. Wind may keen and wail as it whips through the crevasses in the rocks, but the damage can't reach us here. We're safe.

As safe as we can ever be.

When we reach the caves, I turn toward Yorri's usual hiding spot. Rai stepping into my peripheral vision stops me. Her hand is raised to silently ask permission to touch, and she's staring at me with bone-deep relief in her expression. Water drips over her round face and into her eyes, but she doesn't seem to notice it. The fingers of her raised hand twitch and I nod. Only then does she place her hand on my shoulder.

"Thank you, Khya." She pulls me into a hug, and I don't have the strength to fight the embrace. I don't want to, either. If I had been but a hair slower, that strike would have left blood burned into the scorch mark the lightning left behind.

"Don't stand in the way of lightning." I hope it sounds

like a joke and not a plea, but I don't know what I'd do without her. Rai and Etaro are the only reasons I don't drive myself to distraction during most of our long shifts on the wall. Clearing my throat, I disengage from her clinging hug. "Next time I might not be there to ward you."

Rai laughs, running a trembling hand over her face. What can I say to bring her back to herself?

"Nyshin-ten Khya, a word." Tyrroh's timing is wonderful. I want to hug him for keeping me from saying anything too unbearably sentimental. Rai smiles at me and inclines her head to our nyshin-ma before she leaves.

"Every time I think you can't surprise me, something like this happens." He's almost smiling at me, and I suppress the urge to shift under his penetrating stare. His hood has been pushed back and his atakafu unwrapped. Rich brown skin worn by the sun, scarred by battle, and wet from rain gleams in the firelight. "This squad owes their survival to you."

I bite the inside of my cheek, trying not to grin. Nyshin-ma Tyrroh does not impress easily. To have him in my debt? It's a heady thing.

"Didn't your blood-parents have a second child?" Tyrroh's words catch my attention. It's not surprising that he remembered; more than one child from the same set of blood-parents only happens with sumai bond pairs. He looks pleased when I nod. "Miriseh bless us. If they have even half your instincts, they'll be a gift to the ranks."

More than one person has joked that if our blood-parents had a third child—unlikely as it is—they would have ended up with one offspring of each sex. Whether another child had been born ebet to round out the set or not, I doubt it would have mattered. I can't imagine a third sibling fitting in the bond I have with Yorri.

This time, I let myself smile at Tyrroh. This time, the expression is a lie.

Tyrroh inclines his head with the same respect Rai had shown him and then leaves, headed for the bathing pools. Though I'm sure Tyrroh means well, his words have started an avalanche inside my head.

What moon cycle is it? We're three moons away from the rainy season, so that means... Bellows and blood. I'd known it was coming up, but I hadn't realized just how soon it was.

Yorri will face the herynshi in one moon.

Reminding myself that this is a rite of passage every child of Sagen sy Itagami faces doesn't warm my chilled skin. It doesn't slow my stuttering heart at all, because the herynshi is the night the Miriseh decide if we'll have the full rights and honors of a nyshin, linger with the city guards as an ahdo, or spend our lives toiling in obscurity as a yonin. There's no comfort thinking that the fourth outcome is rare. There's never comfort in death.

Surviving Shiara's deserts takes iron, will, and magic, and sometimes even those aren't enough. It's why the Miriseh use the herynshi to test our skills, and it's why the magic-less yonin don't ever leave Itagami.

I found my magic when I was twelve. Our blood-parents Anda and Ono both discovered theirs at fourteen. Yorri will be sixteen in one moon cycle, and there's been nothing. Not a single hint of power. But if he can't display his power at the herynshi, he'll spend the rest of his life as a yonin, working in the mines, the farms, the forges, the kitchens, the nursery, the—

No. Shuddering, I try to breathe.

A hand locks around my arm, and Yorri spins me around. His dark eyes search me for injury, and I find myself doing the same to him.

Though he's a year younger than me, he's taller now, his nose level with my forehead. When we were little, people had a hard time telling us apart. Both of us have the same lean build, sharp features, brass-flecked brown eyes, and dark curls. Yorri's hair has grown longer than he usually wears it, long enough to cover the tips of his ears and brush the top of his neck; it's almost as long as mine.

"I wasn't sure you'd make it back in time." Yorri's voice is shaking. From fear? Relief?

"I'm fine. My legs feel like they're made of overworked leather, but I'm fine."

It's cooler in the undercity, where the sun can't warm the stone, and I'm soaked to the skin. That's why I shiver. Not because there's only one moon cycle until…

I force a smile, trying to reassure both of us.

Lips pursed, Yorri tightens his hold on my arm and turns toward the bathing pools. "Come on. We need to get you warmed up before you get sick."

Every few seconds he glances back at me, as though to make sure I haven't disappeared. That familiar action, and the concern that goes with it, both soothes and unsettles me. It's his empathy, his sometimes overflowing mercy, that has held him back his whole life.

The faintly steaming water filling the massive cavern always smells of sulfur, and it's unsurprisingly crowded with citizens carefully wading into the waist-high water. On the wide ledge surrounding the central pool, piles of tunics and pants to be cleaned are growing fast as every man, woman, and ebet strips to the skin, naked except for the band of leather around their left wrists, the one that bears the wardcharm showing their citizen class.

I watch them as Yorri and I soak in the warm water.

Their battle scars are slashes of pink, white, and beige against varying shades of brown. The marks are badges of battles Itagami's nyshin and ahdo citizens have survived. Will Yorri ever bear similar scars? He won't if he truly doesn't have magic. They'll never let him out to earn any.

Clean and no longer shivering, I walk toward the ledge, cautiously maneuvering around the others.

"Thank you," I murmur to the yonin who offers a drying cloth when I step onto the ledge that borders the pool. The taller one standing behind offers a jar of oil that we dip our fingers into and rub into the leather cuff on our wrists, keeping it from cracking when it dries. They nod acknowledgment when I give them a small smile, but say nothing.

Wiping my skin dry, I head for the shelves of clean clothes and take a breast band, a loincloth, a pair of the wide-legged pants that bind tight from ankle to calf, a high-necked sleeveless undershirt, and a long-sleeved hooded tunic. Yorri holds out an atakafu for me, already knotted to fit loosely around my neck since I don't need to wear it over my face in the undercity.

"Ready?" He places the circle of nyska cloth and silk over my head. When I nod, he leads me into the tunnels of the undercity, turning away from the central cavern where most of the clan congregates during the rains. There's a narrow alcove that's close enough to the clan to hear orders, but far enough away to make us feel alone.

It's a hideaway we've used for years, not a secret by any stretch of the imagination, but a space small enough no one else ever bothered squeezing themselves into it. It's where Yorri keeps the odd little treasures he collects, things no one else in the clan has any reason to want or need. He used to store them in the doseiku dorm, but the other trainees kept mistaking his projects for misplaced junk. It's all safer here.

"Sit," he says once we're settled into the familiar space. "Do you want one braid, two, or many?"

"Two." He kneels behind me and cards his fingers through my damp hair, pulling the short strands tight. My eye catches on an unfamiliar shape, something that looks like a tangled mess of scrap metal the size of two closed fists. Did he make another puzzle?

I reach forward, trying not to move my head. Catching one of the metal pieces with the tip of my fingers, I drag it closer. The pieces are interconnected in a pattern a lot more complicated than the last puzzle he created. I couldn't solve that one. This one looks impossible.

Yorri's nimble fingers quickly separate my hair, plaiting it into a pattern that lies tight against my scalp. I can't ever recreate his braids; they're almost as complex as his puzzles.

I idly turn his creation over in my hands, but my mind isn't focused on untangling the linked metal. Tyrroh's words and my own worries are taking up too much space.

"You're quiet," he says a few minutes later. "Even for you."

I run my thumb along one of the puzzle's curved edges and shrug.

Yorri has always been different. His hands and his mind are as quick as a lightning strike, but when he has a weapon in his hand, something holds him back. He's slow to take advantage of a moment of weakness or a mistake. He never seems to understand how to predict that moment when his enemy's guard is down and he can strike a killing blow. He leans toward mercy, and mercy has put him flat on his back staring at the tip of a sword more times than I can count. Mercy is weakness. Hesitation means death. He cannot give in to either if he means to make it through the trial as a nyshin.

No matter how much I want to, the herynshi isn't a fight I can save him from. Everyone enters alone, and the rank they're placed in is based entirely on their merit. For doseiku who've already found their power, it's our chance to impress the Miriseh with our skill and control. The Miriseh push those who haven't passed their own limits, giving them one last chance to escape the drudgery of life as a yonin, but the chances are good that if a doseiku walks into that ordeal with no power, that's exactly how they'll walk out of it.

The thought forms slowly, trickling into my head in bits and pieces until I'm holding my breath at the idea. Stupid and dangerous.

Yorri secures the end of the second braid and moves to sit against the opposite wall, watching me carefully as he does. His head is cocked and his stare intense. It's strange to think that we were never supposed to know each other like this—blood-siblings aren't usually placed in the same nursery. We're close enough in age that we trained and learned and practiced together for most of our lives. I've watched over him as best I could since he looked at me when he was five years old and told me, with absolute certainty, that I would be one of the kaigo council members one day. Since the day one of the yonin nursemaids smiled at me and said, "You take very good care of your brother."

Your brother.

Yorri had been *mine*—the first and only thing that had ever belonged to me more than the clan—and I promised to protect him; I swore it on blood before I knew how tightly those vows bind. Now, imagining life without him opens a sinkhole in my stomach, leaving me gasping and hollow. Now, he's the only thing that I value above what's best for Itagami. Above the future position in the clan I've imagined for myself since I first learned the legends of the Miriseh.

They came to us from Ryogo, from the haven we all ascend to when death finally takes us. For centuries the immortal Miriseh have protected and guided us, passing on their wisdom and showing us how to live honorable, loyal lives to earn a place in the afterlife. They gave up paradise to lead the clan, so in return we do what we can to serve them.

Now I'm actually contemplating risking our lives and a dishonorable death. I'm risking our chance at Ryogo just to hope that Yorri won't have to face the herynshi disadvantaged.

"I'm in."

His voice is so low and his lips so still that, for a second, I'm not sure he spoke. Then one of his eyebrows rises; he's waiting for a response.

"In what?" I ask, my voice just as quiet.

"Whatever trouble you're planning."

"How do you know I'm planning anything?"

The corner of his lip quirks up. "You may be able to hide it from everyone else, but I know you, Nyshin-ten Khya. I know that look."

"It's a bad idea. Dangerous." I look at him now, needing to know he's marking my words. "And it might not work. It might not be worth the risk."

It definitely won't be worth it if it doesn't work.

"I already said I was in. You can't change your mind now. Besides, if *you're* willing to risk trouble, then it has to be trouble that's worth getting into." Even in the dim light cast by the oil lamps, I recognize that look. Merciful my brother may be, but he's still *my* brother. Our stubborn streak runs deep and strong.

Groaning, I drop my head back until it thunks against the stone behind me.

After a moment I meet Yorri's eyes. He relaxes and smiles.

"You'll conveniently forget you said that as soon as I try to drag you into my plans."

"Probably," he agrees easily.

"Rot-ridden pest." I shove his legs away with the flat of my foot, but I can't erase my smile. "Show me how to solve that ridiculous puzzle before I lose patience with you and leave."

Yorri rolls his eyes, but he's grinning when he takes the puzzle from my hands and starts explaining how he pieced it together. It's comfortingly familiar, something we've done together ever since we were kids, but it's not enough to stop the thoughts and plans and fears spinning in the back of my head like a tornado. My brother is so lost in his explanations that it doesn't seem like he notices my tension.

But that's why I have to push him. I can't let him walk into the herynshi without magic, or he'll walk out of it as one of the yonin. He'll never rise through the nyshin ranks, following me higher until we can take our blood-parents' places on the kaigo council.

If I don't find a way to trigger his magic, I'll lose him to the undercity. Our lives will diverge, and that gap will eventually become impossible to bridge.

I cross my arms, tucking my clenched fists out of sight. Listening to Yorri verbally disengage the various pieces of his puzzle, I focus on my own challenge.

One moon. It might not be enough time, but, Miriseh bless it, it's all the time I have.

CHAPTER
TWO

When the walls of my barracks start to feel too close, I wander through the city, sticking to the smaller alleys instead of the main thoroughfares. On the wider roads I'd have to dodge nursery groups, formations of doseiku in training, and metal carts carrying food, weapons, or iron from the mines. The story of my squad's escape from the typhoon has spread. Everyone seems to want to hear it for themselves, but I don't want to repeat it. It's not as special as they make it sound. Any citizen would've done the same thing.

Five days after the storm, the city is finally returning to its usual rhythms. The yonin teams have finished sweeping the streets for debris fallen from the rooftop gardens, and I've seen far fewer hushed conversations with wary eyes cast to the sky.

"It struck without warning, but your strength and diligence ensured few lives were lost," Miriseh Varan told the clan the morning after the vicious winds faded and the desosa settled back into its usual soothing, constant vibration. "The Miriseh will see you through this like we've done for centuries."

And so it's been. The reports of damage have been given to the kaigo council, who serve the Miriseh and oversee the daily decisions—mission assignments, resupply requests, promotion approvals, and transfers. The kaigo sent squads to recover the fifteen citizens who died in the desert—drowned by flash floods or blown off heights by the wind. The bodies have been brought home to Itagami for saishigi rites. Repair orders for the base camps in the desert were given, but the first won't be carried out until tomorrow. Today the clan is focused on the herynshi—the ordeal I still haven't figured out how to see my brother through.

But in all honesty, what do I think I can do for Yorri in the span of a single moon that almost sixteen years of training and teachers haven't?

There is always a hint of brine and salt in the air over Sagen sy Itagami—not exactly a surprise since our mesa is practically part of the coastline of Shiara—but it's ten times stronger on the north wall. It's been especially strong in the five days since the daylong storm.

Between the edge of the north wall and the endless ocean is a strip of land barely long enough for me to lie across, and then there's a sheer drop of more than a hundred feet to the crashing waves and the rocky shore. Those red, beige, and gray rocks continue into the sea, jutting out from the water to break up the solid blue line of the horizon. The massive, black, barren isle of Imaku is the only one of them large enough to be an island in its own right.

Nodding to the ahdo team patrolling this section of the wall, I wait until they pass and then climb up the chest-high ledge of the exterior wall.

A stronger gust of wind strikes, almost unbalancing me. I bend my knees and shift with the motion it demands. That was how it happened with my magic, too. I found myself in a situation that demanded something of me—something *Yorri* demanded of me—and I figured out how to give it.

His mind was always a dozen places at once, never fully committed to anything. Not even training. One day, before he learned to channel his focus into a single task, Yorri was more distracted than usual. He missed a step—just a single step—and began to fall. Directly into the path of a zeeka sword. Someone had stumbled. Their swing had gone wide, into Yorri's training space. The blade would've struck his throat. I don't know if even the strongest hishingu in the clan would've been able to heal him if my wards hadn't burst to life, if I hadn't been able to deflect the blow.

Fear brought my magic out of me, fear and the overwhelming need to protect what was mine. The problem is that true danger, the kind that sparks soul-deep fear, isn't easy to recreate. It's even harder to create it in a way that isn't real. That's what the Miriseh use the herynshi for—to construct the convincing but controlled illusion of imminent death.

How can I put him in danger without actually risking his life? If I can pull it off, will it be enough? I shudder at the possibility. I've spent most of my life trying to keep him safe. Am I seriously considering purposefully endangering him for this?

The scar on his shoulder is the only visible reminder of the day I learned I was a fykina mage, the strongest class of ward mage. It could've been a death blow if I hadn't been there. What will happen to him during the herynshi if I don't intervene? He'll end up yonin. Or the first time he faces a battle as a nyshin or an ahdo, an enemy's blade will land the blow that I saved him from years ago.

I didn't purposefully aim myself this way, but coming to the north wall makes sense. This is one of Yorri's favorite spots in the upper city, and he's the puzzle consuming my mind.

The wind tugs at my hood and the end of my tunic. Because of the slits that rise to my hips, the back half flares out behind me like a mykyn bird's tail. It's not like the Kujuko-cursed wind during the storm, destructive and angry. This is the cool, playful breeze that carries the ocean with it. It reminds me of my brother when we were younger, constantly tugging at my tunic and asking me question after question. I only ever knew the answers to a portion of them, but he kept asking. Sometimes it felt like he thought if I didn't know the answer, it wasn't worth knowing. *That*, at least, he's grown out of.

I breathe the briny air and try to consider the options objectively. As objectively as I ever can when Yorri is involved.

Yorri, who was the first person to tell me that one day I'd be kaigo, just like our blood-parents, serving the Miriseh and earning high honors in Ryogo. I'd flicked him on the shoulder and said "Of course I will be," but his faith had been what convinced me I was right.

Yorri, who gets so excited he stumbles over his own words when he's explaining how he solved some new, impossible puzzle. He devotes himself with frightening fervor to anything that ensnares his arrow-quick mind, but sometimes needs reminding that the rest of the world exists.

Forget objectivity. It's worth the risk.

I am *going* to keep him safe, just like I always have.

"You're going to be late for the vigil if you stand here staring into nothing for much longer, Khya."

I tense, keeping my eyes on the angry, dark blue, white-capped waves. I'd heard the footsteps approaching, but several people had come and gone already and left me alone.

Tessen, however, never was able to keep his thoughts inside his head.

"I won't be late." I avoid looking at him until he moves into my peripheral vision.

He leans against the wall to the left of me, his forearms crossed on the ledge and his head tilted up. With his arms folded on the ledge and his body held slightly away from the wall, I can make out the lines of muscle under layers of cloth, all of it hard-earned—though I probably won't ever admit that to him. I don't look directly at him, but I turn my head enough to get a better look at his face.

He's taller than me, so looking down on him like this is strange. Seeing him without the hood and atakafu we always wear on duty is stranger. I don't think I've seen his whole face since he became nyshin over a year ago.

His thick eyebrows sit low over his deep-set eyes and the line of his nose is straight, because somehow he was always quick enough in training to avoid all but the most glancing blows to his face. The setting sun highlights the red in his terra-cotta skin and makes his oddly pale eyes flash. Usually they're limestone gray, but now they're paler than ever and gleaming almost as bright as the sunlight off the ocean.

"Shouldn't you be off training? Or guarding something?" I ask before he speaks.

"I am." He smirks at me. "I'm guarding the mad nyshin girl who's decided to perch on the walls and imitate a mykyn bird."

"I'm not planning on attempting flight." I wave my hand

at him, trying to brush him off. "You can go, Nyshin-ten."

His lips purse; I hide a smile. It was delightful discovering exactly how annoyed he got when I called him by his class and rank instead of his name. The flash of aggravation disappears quickly, replaced by his more usual sardonic smile. "Should I guess what has you lost in your own head the night of a vigil?"

"No. I don't have that much time."

"Then I won't guess. Only your brother puts that look on your face."

I look at him, expecting to see mockery in his eyes. There isn't any. He looks almost...serious?

"You're worried about his herynshi. Unless he's in trouble again? It's been a while. He's overdue."

"It's been a while because he doesn't have to deal with people who point out his every mistake anymore. Like *you*." Gritting my teeth, I bend to brace my hand on the ledge and jump down to where Tessen stands. At six feet, he's only an inch or two taller than me. Our eyes are nearly level when I square off against him. "You're one of the reasons he ever got in trouble in the first place."

"And you spent years trying to make him invisible." Tessen's lips thin, and the muscles in his jaw clench for a moment. "Even before you found your wards, you shielded him from everything. What he can do now that you're not there to monitor his every move should be all the proof you need."

"He would have *died* if I hadn't protected him." Nothing will ever convince me it was wrong to keep him alive. "You can't seriously be suggesting I should have let that happen?"

"No, that isn't— You don't even know what he's capable of! How long has it been since you've seen him fight? It's been—" He steps back, his lips pressed tight and his hands held away from his weapons. "Bellows, Khya. I didn't come here to fight with you. This isn't how this was supposed to go."

I blink. "What?" Tessen backing away from an argument? This has to be a trick. "How what was supposed to go?"

He shakes his head, a small smile quirking up the corners of his mouth. "I only came to ask if you'd dance with me tonight at the celebration."

He can't be serious...but there's not a single sign that he isn't being sincere.

I drop my gaze to hide the confusion that has to show on my face. My focus catches on the pendant gleaming against the undyed cloth of his tunic—a two-inch iron disc etched with crossed zeeka swords. Blood and rot, I hate seeing that around his neck. The zeeka is the symbol of the kaigo; the pendant is a symbol of their students.

Tessen is wearing the kaigo-sei pendant that should have been *mine*.

Out of the whole clan, the Miriseh and the kaigo only choose one nyshin-ten per year. His blood-mother, Neeva, is on the kaigo council. Being named a kaigo-sei isn't a guarantee of advancement, but it is a sign that the leaders of the clan are keeping an eye on you. The kaigo-sei are given extra training and have to face additional tests of magic, skill, and leadership. Not every nyshin named a kaigo-sei student becomes a council member, but no one who *isn't* a kaigo-sei will ever become one. I can still earn one—and I *will*, sooner rather than later—but it seems like they're already grooming Tessen to take Kaigo Neeva's place one day.

Rot take him, it was supposed to be me.

Swallowing the fruitless envy building in my chest, I raise my eyes to meet Tessen's again. "I don't make promises I don't intend to keep."

"But that's not a no, so I'll ask again tonight." He smiles, inclines his head, and then walks away whistling. I hate that sound, and I'm almost positive he knows that.

If I follow him down, he'll try to talk to me again, and I'll spend the entire walk to the courtyard trying not to strangle him with the leather cord of the kaigo-sei pendant. Growling under my breath, I turn in the opposite direction and run to the stairs at the northwestern edge of the city. The wasted time is worth it to keep myself from getting in trouble over Tessen.

I run down the steep steps and through the mostly empty streets. Bellows. It's later than I thought—almost everyone is gathered in the courtyard, holding vigil until the herynshi ends, until the Miriseh bless the new citizens and we see if the student or friend or lover we sent into the ring was strong enough to make it into the ranks of the nyshin.

For this vigil, and the introductions that come after and the celebration after that, the clan stands in ranks and formations. As a nyshin, I get to be part of the first class, but because I serve under a nyshin-ma instead of a higher ranking -co or -ri, our squad is pushed to the back of the nyshin.

As I wind my way through the ahdo squads I have to pass to reach mine, I spot Yorri. The doseiku stand behind the ahdo, and my brother is one of the oldest in the doseiku class now. He's easy to find in the center of the first line of trainees. I nod hello when his eyes meet mine, but my attention moves past him and the other trainees to the yonin standing along the rear of the square.

Their role within the clan is both necessary and worthy of respect, but anyone can farm, mine, cook, or clean. The work is without valor. Without honor or recognition. It means an entire life spent locked inside the walls of the city, often a life spent under it. That isn't the life I wanted, and it's not one I want for Yorri, either. I have to find a way to keep Yorri up here in the sunlight with me. Even if he doesn't venture into the desert to hunt or to help protect the borders, his quick mind would serve the clan so much better if he had the power to put his brilliant plans into action.

Trying to calm my racing pulse, I slip into place next to Rai and Etaro and focus on the bikyo-ko—the center of the city, the armory, the barracks for both the Miriseh and the kaigo council, and the focal point of the two main roads that divide the four zons.

The bikyo-ko isn't the tallest building, but it's the largest, stretching for at least a hundred square yards. The rest of Sagen sy Itagami is designed around this intricately carved three-story building and the courtyard in front of it—the only open space in the city large enough to hold all ten thousand citizens and doseiku. At some point, a talented ishiji used their stone magic to etch and then paint battle scenes into the once-smooth surface of the building, all of them depicting the legends of the immortal Miriseh and the clan's victories against the Denhitran and Tsimos clans. On every other building bordering the courtyard, the sandstone has been smoothed by wind and sand and rain, and only the symbols over the doorways adorn the otherwise bare walls.

Thud.

The sound reverberates in the air, echoing off the buildings. I look over my shoulder toward the road leading west. The sun has set, and Itagami's iron gates are closed for the night. The Miriseh and the new citizens have arrived.

At the head of the line approaching on the main road, Miriseh Varan and Miriseh Suzu march. Their hoods are dyed vibrant indigo, a color only the immortal elders are allowed to wear. Behind them, twenty-seven newly classed citizens march in three columns of nine while six of the Miriseh and eight of the kaigo council march in an honor guard on either side. I almost smile when I notice many familiar faces from my old training class standing in front, almost all of them ranked among the nyshin, but...

I look toward Yorri even though I can't see him from here. What will his position be in that procession when he faces the herynshi?

Rai snaps her fingers in front of my face.

Flinching, I spin in her direction. "What?"

Etaro is watching me over Rai's shoulder, eir narrow eyes crinkled with concern. Ey mouths silently, "Are you okay?"

I nod, and Rai jerks her chin toward the dais, whispering, "Then pay attention. I'm not doing laps of the wall because you got distracted."

When she tries to smack my elbow, I deflect her hand and roll my eyes. "Unless you're planning on sharing my bed tonight, keep your hands off."

"You wish," Rai whispered with a grin, puckering her lips and giving the air between us a smacking kiss.

Etaro huffs a laugh at both of us. They're right, and for more reasons than they know. I shouldn't—*can't*—let myself get distracted.

Varan and Suzu lead the group toward the bikyo-ko dais, traveling the path that runs down the center of the courtyard between squads. They climb the five steps, directing the columns behind them into position with small hand signals, and then stand in the center of the dais facing the clan. When they remove their indigo hoods, their dark hair picks up tinges of red from the firelight; their skin— normally the same pale beige as the sand on the narrow shoreline a mile from the city—has a similar red cast.

"In the eyes of the Miriseh, all who face the herynshi are blessed," they shout in unison, officially beginning the induction. One by one, Varan and Suzu introduce each nyshin and ahdo citizen by name and their new class-rank. "Welcome your new brothers and sisters!"

"Urah!" The clan raises their left hands, the wardcharms stitched to our leather cuffs glittering in the firelight—the yonin's circular iron disc stamped with the outline of a bare foot, the ahdo's small iron shield, the nyshin's miniature morning star, the kaigo's minuscule zeeka sword, and the Miriseh's iron and brass sun. They're symbols of our purpose within the clan, our standing, and our skill.

Our training master Ahdo-mas Sotra used to tell us that although victory should never be assumed, we would always be defeated if we believed we could be. Even though I don't yet know how I'm going to win, defeat isn't an option in this.

Varan's voice booms across the courtyard. "Tonight twelve have been placed within the safety of the yonin, and we ask that every citizen does their part to protect those who serve within the city."

I lift my right hand to my left wrist, running my thumb along the edges of my morning star wardcharm. In one moon, Yorri will wear one of these, too.

"The success of the night has been high," Suzu cries. "Celebrate the victory."

As soon as Suzu drops her arms, the drums begin. Iron

casks of ahuri wine are opened as circles of space, their boundaries marked by borders of gray limestone laid into the red sandstone, clear throughout the courtyard.

The tokiansu—the warrior's dance—is beauty, strength, grace, speed, and deadly skill melded into a glorious performance. I've only joined once since my herynshi a year ago. It didn't go well after I saw that my partner wasn't willing to take risks. It was disappointing and frustrating, and I walked away wishing I hadn't danced at all.

As much as I want to try it again, there isn't any citizen I trust to read me well enough. Yet. That will change once Yorri becomes nyshin, because we have years of practice behind us. Granted, we weren't supposed to be taking the tokiansu weapons into the undercity and teaching ourselves how to perform the complicated dances, but we did it anyway. And we got pretty good at it, too.

Until then, I can wait. Ill-matched partners often end with someone bleeding, which is one of the reasons sumai pairs are so good—the soulbond connects them in a way no one else can match. They know their partner as well as they know themselves, can predict moves with the flicker of an eye or the twitch of a finger.

Yorri and I aren't that, but we can definitely get through a dance without goring each other.

"Khya!" Etaro grips the sleeve of my tunic between eir fingers and tugs me toward the center of the square. Rai doesn't follow, already off to find a partner to dance with. "If we hurry, we might be able to get a spot at the inner ring."

"A spot for what?"

Etaro grins and keeps speed-walking, gracefully dodging people who aren't moving fast enough for em. "Trust me. I heard that— Just hurry up."

I hear the names before we're halfway there. My heart

skips a beat, and I no longer lag behind Etaro. Ey's right. I definitely want to watch this.

Kaigo Anda and Kaigo Ono grin at each other—both carrying a long, curved, narrow-bladed tudo sword—as they take the center circle. The rest of the clan holds its breath on nights when bondmates dance. It doesn't happen every moon, but it's happening tonight.

Sumai bonds run deep, but it means that when one of them dies, grief carves a permanent, unhealable wound on the other's soul. It's why so few people request the bond. Living unbonded and moving from one short-term relationship to another as the needs of life change is more common. And easier.

Many who are willing and able to bear children do eventually find a temporary khai partnership that meets the approval of the Miriseh, but that's more like a statement of intent than a true bond. There's no soul wound to recover from when an old lover dies, and on Shiara, death is the one thing that's inevitable. For everyone except the Miriseh, at least. My blood-parents risked it anyway.

"I need to find Yorri," I tell Etaro, rising onto my toes. We used to press as close as we could on the nights our parents danced, gaping from the sidelines as they twirled, ducked, and struck with gracefully unerring accuracy. "He'll want to see this."

"Fine, but hurry up or I won't be able to save you a spot." Etaro's smile spreads across eir sharp-featured face, lighting up eir dark, narrow eyes as ey wiggles eir way through the gathering crowd.

Though I'm searching the faces for Yorri, I spot Tessen first. He's bearing down on me with a determined stride, the fingers of his left hand striking his upper thigh in time with the drums of the dance.

Bellows. He was serious about asking again, wasn't he?

I cast a look at Anda and Ono, then lose myself in the crowd. Tomorrow I'll have to explain my disappearance to Etaro, but I'd rather face eir annoyance than Tessen's persistence.

Slipping through the press of people, I keep searching for Yorri. Some faces I recognize, others I don't—none are my brother.

A spot of stillness catches my attention.

Yorri stands near a side street leading into the Southwestern Zon, his hands balled at his sides and his shoulders tense as he stares into the shadows of the dimly lit alley.

Before I reach him, he leaves, skirting the more densely packed areas of the courtyard and moving toward the northeastern end of the bikyo-ko. He could be headed back to the doseiku dorm, but he looked upset. If he is, he won't want to spend the evening with the other trainees.

I walk straight for the main north road. The wide street is deserted tonight, so I'm able to run the mile and a half to the wall without obstruction. When I reach the small open space surrounding the staircase Yorri usually takes, it's quiet. I glance up at the wall. Did I beat him here or is he already up there? From this angle, I can't tell, but it isn't likely that he reached the wall before me. He had no reason to run.

Minutes pass, the only sounds the ocean, the wind, and the occasional orders from the ahdo-sa on the wall. No one is approaching the stairs. It doesn't sound like anyone but me is moving within a hundred yards of here. I look up again. Maybe I was wrong?

I shift toward the stairs. A light footstep against the

stone catches my attention. Seconds later, my brother appears out of the shadows of one of the nearby alleys. Yorri exhales heavily when he sees me, but he doesn't protest then or when I turn to follow him up the stairs.

It's odd for anyone to leave the celebration unless duty calls. It's stranger for Yorri to leave early if he doesn't have to. He loves the tokiansu, loves getting the chance to talk to our blood-parents, loves the revelry and the wine and the music. Tonight he left it all behind to come to the north wall and…pace?

I lean against the hip-high inner ledge and watch him cross the width of the wall. He's muttering to himself, I think. I can't make out the words. His steps get shorter, and his body gets tenser. His hands clench spasmodically, the motion almost like he's looking for the hilt of a weapon he's not wearing. But he's never instinctively reached for a weapon. What happened?

As soon as I straighten and reach out for him, he speaks. "Sanii was declared yonin."

"Sanii?" No one in the Northeastern Zon's training class was called Sanii.

Yorri's eyes flick away. "Sanii is an ebet from—" He snaps his mouth shut and shakes his head once. "It doesn't matter. I talked about em, but you haven't met. I wanted to introduce you two for moons now, but…" His eyes lose focus and his shoulders sag as he lifts one hand to rub his mouth. His voice trembles with barely concealed pain. "I thought there would be more time. I was so sure eir magic would be as strong as eir skill."

Sagen sy Itagami is far too densely populated for all of the trainees to fit in one school, but I do remember a doseiku ebet named Sanii who grew up in the Southwestern Zon. Almost a foot shorter than us, but exceptionally quick with eir hands. Wiry strength, large, intelligent eyes, a strong jawline that gave em a consistently serious expression. But how did I not know Sanii better if they were this close? I've never met em and, no, he *hasn't* ever mentioned—

Oh. He *has* mentioned someone named Sanii.

Breathing the brine-laden air, I force myself to think. And remember.

I've been busy with the squad, and he's been focused on the last moons of his training, and our free days aligned so rarely recently. The time we have gotten to spend together, I always wanted to hear about his puzzles and his training and our doseiku friends that I didn't get to see often. He'd talked about Sanii, but since I only ever had the vaguest idea who ey was, the stories hadn't stuck. I hadn't thought they mattered.

"Ey hasn't died, Yorri." I may not want my brother to live as a yonin, but it's not a fate that deserves a reaction like this. "If Sanii can't protect emself with magic, you know this is the safest place for em. The Miriseh are only trying to protect the clan."

"The safety of the clan comes before our lives." Yorri's face twists. He turns away, running his hands over his hair and muttering again as he walks.

When he faces me again, my heart stutters.

"No." I've seen that determination in his eyes before, but only when he's about to do something stupid. Like the day he attempted to rescue a baby teegra from the butchers. "Whatever you're thinking, Yorri, *no.*"

I expect my brother to fight, to insist I don't know what I'm talking about. Instead, he releases a long, slow breath, and all the tension in his body vanishes, leaving behind only sadness, a level of weariness I have never seen in his face before. "We'd planned to request a sumai bond after my herynshi."

My breath catches. A sumai? I had no idea my brother was that close to anyone but me.

How can you possibly do that? I want to shout at him. *How can you trust* anyone *with half of your soul?*

And why, in all the times Sanii had come up, would he never, ever mention this to me? If he's kept this secret—

No. It doesn't matter. At least, not now.

"How did you know em so well?" We met the doseiku from the other zons more than once over the years, but never often enough to develop a sumai-strength bond.

Yorri looks out over the water. "Ey liked to watch the ocean."

My brother has always been fascinated by the angry, endless expanse of water that surrounds us. I've always found the sight daunting. The waves are dark and dangerous, an impassable barrier and a tease in times of drought—so much water and all of it undrinkable without hours and hours of effort to obtain even the smallest measure of fresh water. And every year, at least five yonin die pulling in the fishing nets strung between the closest rocks. The currents are vicious and relentless, swallowing those who get caught in them, breaking them against the rocks, or bearing them all the way out to Imaku. That massive, black island is only a shadowy blot on the dark horizon now, but it's there, like a great black fist waiting to smash anyone or anything stupid enough to get too close.

Yorri has never been afraid of the water like I am. He likes the sound of the waves crashing on the rocks and rolling back. Did Sanii obsess over it in the same way? I can't believe it would be enough for either to have considered a sumai. Considering it he had been, though.

It's enough to make me wonder what else there is about my brother that I don't know.

Yorri has training sessions throughout the morning and afternoon, but tomorrow is my free day. I can train while keeping an eye on him from a distance, watching instead of protecting this time. Maybe I'll see whatever it was that Tessen hinted at earlier.

For now, the only thing I can do is rest my hand on my brother's back and my head on his shoulder, offering what little comfort there is to be had.

There are so few unbreakable laws in our world. A sumai between a yonin and anyone in the classes above theirs is one of those laws. Even a bond between an ahdo and a nyshin is looked at askance, but they're allowed. Not so with yonin. If Sanii is yonin, ey is untouchable.

Unless... *Oh, blood and rot.*

There's an exception. Yonin can bond among themselves.

Tonight Yorri may have found the motivation to give up fighting.

CHAPTER
THREE

Today I'll be spending more time with the doseiku class than I have since my last day as a trainee. It feels odd, like somehow stepping backward in my own life.

There are two separate sides to the yard, one for the doseiku and one for the nyshin and ahdo squads. I enter through the citizens' door, skirting the teams running drills and the nyshin-ma and nyshin-co shouting orders, and head for the long storage room that divides the two halves. I nod at those I recognize as I pass, staying out of the way but not hiding. The only person I'm avoiding is my brother. Yorri can't know I'm here, not if I want to see what Tessen hinted at.

From the practice weapons in the storage room, I take a curved, narrow-bladed anto dagger and strap its sheath to my belt, and then I reach for a zeeka sword.

"This isn't where I expected to see you this morning, Khya." Bellows. Tessen.

He'll be more insufferable than usual as soon as he figures out why I'm here. Swallowing a frustrated growl, I try to keep my expression indifferent as I turn to face him. I think that expression falters as soon as I see him.

How does he always look like he's just had a week of bed rest? Almost everyone in the clan is sleep-deprived and hungover the morning after a celebration. Never Tessen. I didn't even drink any of the wine last night, and I still feel—and probably look—like I downed half a cask.

He smiles, his eyes alight with amusement.

Oh, of all the blood-rotten things. How long have I been staring at him?

I try to keep my face from flushing, but this is Tessen. There's no way his basaku senses missed the way my pulse rate just jumped. I clear my throat and pretend I don't know that. "Me being here is no odder than finding *you* here the morning after a celebration."

Tessen shakes his head, his smile going tight. "I've been assigned to work with the third-year doseiku today."

My gaze falls to the kaigo-sei pendant, and the fingers of my right hand twitch, wanting to curl into a fist. Right. The early stages of a kaigo-sei's leadership training are working with small groups of doseiku. I'd been looking forward to doing that. I could do it well. I've already had years of practice working with Yorri.

"Then what are you doing talking to me?" I shift my weight, starting to turn back to the zeeka I was going to borrow for the day.

Tessen slides a step to the right, keeping himself in front of me. His expression is serious when he asks, "Why did you run last night, Khya?"

"I didn't *run*." I don't run, not like that. Retreat is necessary sometimes, but running is hiding, and hiding is cowardly. I am not afraid of Tessen. "There was something else I needed to take care of last night, so I left."

"I'm sure you found something to do after you left, but you didn't leave the center circle until after you saw me looking for you." He steps closer, his voice low enough that anyone else who happens to come through the storeroom would have to strain to hear him. "If you didn't want to dance, all you had to do was say no."

"As if you would've listened."

"I would've, I *will*, and I am. You're still not saying no." He smiles, his teeth bright against his russet-brown skin. "So I'll ask again next moon."

I roll my eyes and run my finger along the curve of my anto. "This is one fight you don't stand a chance of winning, Nyshin-ten."

"And yet not only haven't you said no, you're here on your free day, which means you might be listening to me about your brother after all." He shifts closer, his smile seeming warmer. "If it's all the same to you, I'll continue to hope, oh deadly one."

With a slight inclination of his head, Tessen winks at me and then disappears between the tight rows of stone shelves. There one second, and then gone.

Bellows. That boy might be bizarre, but he's undeniably fast. He's also smart, skilled, stubborn, and the strongest basaku mage the clan has seen in generations, possibly ever.

All of his senses are so strongly enhanced that he had to be sequestered in a near pitch-dark, solitary cave in the undercity for two full moons after he first found his power. Ahdo-mas Sotra told us that it had taken him that long to learn how to keep from being completely overwhelmed by his own senses; she'd also told us that two moons was far less time than any of the oraku mages—sensor mages who only have to adapt to enhanced sight, hearing, and smell—expected him to need.

I heard from an oraku who trained with Tessen that he once spotted a Denhitran raiding party almost a mile off. At twilight. There was another story about how he could pick a single conversation out of the noisy chaos of the celebrations every moon cycle.

Like Yorri and me, both of his blood-parents are still living—not necessarily a rarity, but certainly uncommon. Surviving more than thirty-five years in the ahdo or nyshin ranks is a sign of intense skill, power, or cunning. Tessen is the child of two of those survivors. I am, too, but even I have a hard time keeping up with Tessen when that deadly light gleams in his eyes.

He smiles more than anyone else in the city, but I've seen fury darken his eyes, turning them storm-cloud gray, and watched him move with as much speed and deadly grace as the iron-bladed fan he's named for.

We were almost friends once, but that was before his magic developed. He found his six moons before I did, and he usurped the promotions that were supposed to be mine. I might've been able to tolerate him better if he didn't treat everything like either a joke or an inconvenience. Especially all the honors and responsibilities he's earned— most of the time he acts as though they don't matter.

Rolling my shoulders to ease the tension in my muscles, I take a breath and let it out slowly. Only after I've shaken off most of Tessen's visit do I wrap my hand around the hilt of a decent-looking zeeka sword and head into the doseiku half of the yard.

Everything is so familiar; it's almost like coming home. The sun beats down on us through the open roof, and the clash of metal against metal rings through the air. It smells like sweat, dust, iron, and stone, and across the wide expanse, dozens of doseiku circle each other, all of them wielding weapons made to end—and also save—lives.

Yorri's training squad is on the south side of the yard and Tessen's squad is on the west, so I stay near the north wall where another group is running drills. I join them with permission from the training master, but only half of my attention is on the doseikus' movements and the corrections I give them. Every chance I can without drawing his eye, I watch my brother.

The first few moons after I became nyshin were completely taken up by the adjustments I had to make to my new role in the clan—moving into the squad's barracks, learning the signals and commands Nyshin-ma Tyrroh favored, and training with my new team every day we weren't on duty. My visits with Yorri those moons were short and usually focused on his puzzles or sitting on the ledge of the north wall, relaxing the way we didn't get to with anyone else. It became habit after that for our time to be more about talking than training.

Which means it's been more than a year since I've seen him with a zeeka in his hand.

At fifteen, Yorri was awkward and unsure in his movements, hesitating long enough in training bouts that he hardly ever won. He'd grown several inches that year, though; his longer arms and legs seemed to unbalance him. Now he has the muscle he needs to control his long-limbed body, and he moves with a fluid grace that wouldn't be out of place in the tokiansu. Each block or strike seems to land precisely where he intends it.

Blood and rot, was Tessen right? Yorri's skill has vastly improved in the past year. Because he grew into his height and became comfortable with his own body, or because I actually had held him back? Or maybe he held himself back while I was here, which isn't a theory I like any better.

Whatever the reason for it, this is good. I'll have a hard enough time coming up with death-defying yet somehow safe scenarios to scare the magic out of him. Training him to fight? I couldn't have done it in one moon.

Leaving one worry behind, I pay more attention to the group of ten-year-olds around me, helping one girl adjust her stance and showing an ebet the correct grip for eir anto dagger.

And then a furious shout splits through the yard.

Movements falter. Heads turn. I'm running across the yard, a chill crossing my skin. I've heard that sound before, but not for years.

A crowd has tightened around two fighters. I have to shove three people aside to reach the center of the circle. I'm already planning my attack when I reach the inside. And cringe. Aemon is strong. Not incredibly bright, but strong and brutal. He'll be tough to bring down if something has pushed him into attacking.

But… Am I seeing this right? I blink. The scene doesn't change.

Aemon isn't the one on the attack. Yorri is.

Heat flushes Yorri's cheeks a deeper shade of brown, but his eyes burn cold with rage I've never seen in him. He's wielding a short zeeka sword in one hand, its narrow, curved blade whipping through the air. His other hand grips an iron anto.

I can barely believe this is the same boy who resisted picking up even an anto dagger when we were children. Each move is faster and surer than I've ever seen from him, and each blow is millimeters from its intended target. None of them are blocked by Aemon's zeeka; it seems like they don't meet flesh only because Yorri doesn't finish the strike.

"Doseiku Yorri, stand *down*!" Ahdo-mas Sotra smoothly disarms Yorri, knocking his zeeka out of his hand with a deft twist of her own sword. Nyshin-ma Tyrroh is only a second behind her to restrain Aemon.

"Take it back, *now*," Yorri hisses at Aemon. There's so much fury in his eyes that I can't tell— Does he even realize Sotra is holding him back? If he doesn't stop fighting her grip, he's going to be in so much more trouble.

I rush to Yorri's other side, placing my hand on his chest, just below his throat, shoving him back when he tries to lunge for Aemon again.

Ahdo-mas Sotra catches my eye and nods before tightening her grip on Yorri. "Explain yourself, Doseiku Yorri," she demands.

Yorri stops surging forward, but I don't let him go. "He spoke ill of Yonin-va Sanii."

That display was over *Sanii*?

I'm glad my brother has found someone worth fighting for, but I've saved his life. I protected him for years, standing between him and a thrashing when his defensive skills weren't enough. More than a few times, I took those thrashings for him. How much less pain might I have suffered in our childhood if he'd managed to break through his mental barriers to avenge *me*?

"Who is Sanii?" Sotra asks.

"An ebet who serves the city with more honor than he'll ever know." Yorri swallows hard, deflating like a leaking waterskin. I slide my arm around his waist to give him something to lean on. "Ey would've been my sukhai if not... Eir herynshi was yesterday and ey..."

His voice isn't loud anymore, but the yard is nearly silent. People hear, and more than one of the doseiku watching repeats what they heard in a gasped whisper. It ripples through the audience so quickly and with so much genuine shock that the desosa reacts, rolling against my awareness like a ripple in the breeze.

Tyrroh's eyes widen, and he looks between Yorri and me. Whatever he's thinking stays inside his head. He outranks Ahdo-mas Sotra by a lot, but this is her domain.

"You were going to request a sumai bond after your herynshi?" She asks the question like she has to be sure she heard right. I can't blame her. I felt the same way when he told me. It's rare for anyone to request a soulbond. It's almost unheard of for it to happen at sixteen.

"I was. We *will* if I—" He closes his mouth fast when my fingers dig into his bicep, tightening so hard I might leave bruises behind.

No, I want to hiss into his ear. *Don't you dare think like that.*

"Is it true, Doseiku Aemon?" Sotra faces Aemon. Whatever he sees in her expression makes him shrink, his broad shoulders curling in. "Did you insult Yonin-va Sanii?"

For a heavy, tense moment, Aemon doesn't answer. Tyrroh frowns down at the doseiku and shakes him once, hard enough to make Aemon stumble. "Your training master asked you a question, Doseiku."

"Y-yes, Ahdo-mas," Aemon stutters, shame obvious in his face. "I...I said things I shouldn't have."

"Confession heard and witnessed." Sotra looks between Yorri and Aemon before she grunts and turns her attention to Tyrroh. "Nyshin-ma, would you take him outside? It seems like I need to find a way to reteach him what clan loyalty looks like."

"With pleasure, Ahdo-mas." Tyrroh shoves Aemon toward the exit without releasing his hold on the doseiku's arm and bellows, "March!"

As Aemon stumbles past, Yorri hisses, "*Never* speak to me again."

"Quiet! Don't think you're getting off without punishment, Yorri." Sotra hauls him to the north end of the yard. I follow a few feet behind them, as close as I think I can get away with.

Yorri's eyes narrow and his jaw clenches, but he stays silent, thankfully.

"Losing control like that—hurting another clan member— is absolutely unacceptable." Sotra releases him under the shade of the corridor ringing the open yard.

Yorri trips over a crack in the stone, but catches himself against the wall. When he turns to face Sotra's judgment, I almost believe the impassive resignation on his face. I might believe it if I didn't know him so well.

I hold my breath, waiting for her verdict. Miriseh, please let her be lenient.

"I know the provocation was harsh, but complete control over yourself and your reactions is the only way to survive," Sotra says. "You'll do an extra meditation hour after every training session until your herynshi, and for the next three days you're on restricted rations."

I release my breath. That's practically no punishment at all.

"And I am sorry there's a chance you might be separated from someone you care about that much, but if I hear or see you even hinting at willfully holding yourself back from your full potential, I won't let you out of my sight until you walk out of the city for your herynshi." Sotra stares Yorri down when he bristles. "We must all do our best to serve the clan, wherever that capability takes us. Do you understand?"

She doesn't bring up Kujuko, the empty realm that shirkers, cowards, and traitors are trapped in after death, but I don't think she needs to. That potential fate is not a possibility any of us forget.

Her posture doesn't relax until he drops his gaze and nods. "Good. Dismissed, Doseiku. Do *not* let this happen again."

My brother inclines his head, his wrists crossed at his chest, and then strides toward the stairs that will take him to the bathing pools. The crowd he leaves behind looks stunned, all of them watching Yorri with something close to awe on their faces—everyone except for Tessen, who's standing a few feet away. Tessen is the only one watching *me*.

Ignoring Tessen, I follow Yorri down to the undercity. The air carries the scent of water, and Yorri's steps echo off the walls; he's moving quickly. I pick up my pace to match his, but I don't catch up to him until we've reached the main level of the undercity. He glances at me when I step into place beside him, his jaw clenching and the tendons in his neck tensing, but he doesn't speak as we walk into the bathing cavern.

At this time of day, only a few dozen citizens and the yonin on laundry duty are here, scrubbing away desert dust and bloodstains, repairing ripped cloth, and reoiling cracked leather. None of them spare us more than a glance as we wash and dress in clean clothes.

Yorri tries to bolt as soon as his tunic is over his head. I run after him, fixing my clothes as I go. In a nearly empty tunnel, I reach for his arm. "Yorri, stop."

"I wanted to *kill* him." He pulls out of my grip, a shudder running through him, and stalks toward the stairs that let out closest to the north wall.

"Understandable. Even Sotra understood."

Yorri makes a wordless noise. It's not an agreement or a dissent, but at least it means he's listening. Probably.

"I'm glad you didn't go through with it, but the fact that you wanted to might be a good thing." I'm serious, but he scoffs. Anger, worry, and confusion churn my stomach and heat my face, making my next question sharper than I want it to be. "Would you *rather* be yonin?"

Yorri stops and turns, but his eyes lock on something behind me—the narrow, rapid stream running through the cave, or maybe the oil lamp guttering and dancing in the bracket on the wall. I take a long breath and concentrate on relaxing individual muscles, if only to give my mind something tangible to focus on. How can I put any of the thoughts spinning through my head into words that will make sense?

"You said you were in, that you'd go through with whatever plans I had, but that's not true if you're going to throw whatever potential you have away so you can spend the rest of your life down *here*." I run my hand over my damp hair, pushing the short strands out of my face, and exhale in a short, sharp gust. "If you're going to walk into your herynshi and actually *try*, you have to be willing to fight—to kill. The Denhitran soldiers aren't going to hold back. You can't either, not if you're going to survive outside Itagami's walls."

He looks at me, his dark eyes reflecting the firelight, but he doesn't speak.

Swallowing around the worry that's almost a solid block in my throat, I try to keep my voice even. He did well in the fight today, but the herynshi is going to be much, much more difficult. Kaigo Neeva's illusions are convincing; they left me with nightmares for weeks after my herynshi, though I never admitted that to anyone.

No matter what kind of foe she creates for Yorri to face, one thing will be true. "If you're not willing to strike, you've already lost. Do you understand?"

"Yes."

"And are you? Going to fight?"

Pain creates lines around his eyes that I hate seeing. He looks away, taking a shuddering breath. When he meets my eyes again, most of the pain has been pushed aside by resigned determination. "You're not the only one who would be disappointed if I gave up. Sanii would be furious if ey found out I let myself fail."

I close my eyes, the relief dizzying. That's a point in Sanii's favor. "Well, no matter what happens next moon, you'll have to introduce us. Ey sounds like someone I'd like."

He tries to smile, I think, as he runs his hand over his hair. The expression becomes more of a grimace than a grin, and the tug of his fingers through his loosely curled, dark hair reopens a small cut on his forehead. Blood is dripping sluggishly from the wound, so I take off the atakafu looped around my neck, put it in his palm, and guide his hand to the spot.

"You did good today," I say, pressing his hand against his head.

"Thanks." The tiny quirk to his lips looks rueful.

I pat his shoulder, and, as we turn toward the north wall where we can sit in peace for a while, I ask the question that's been burning up my mind since I shoved my way through the crowd to reach him.

"Where'd you learn to fight like that?" It really is galling to know that Tessen was right about Yorri, but my pride in my brother is enough to trump even that.

My brother smirks. "Where do you think? From watching you."

CHAPTER
FOUR

Yorri stands at the outer edge of the western wall,
his arms crossed and his gaze distant. Despite his
promise after the fight with Aemon, I've seen him
go distant like this too often the past few days. It's not an
expression that makes me think he's contemplating the
future—it looks a lot more like he's mourning the past.
Hopefully, in mourning he'll also learn how to let it go.

"Is there a purpose to us being here?" Yorri asks, finally
looking at me.

"Yes, but I'm not telling you what it is." I'm not sure the
plan to draw his magic out will work if he knows what I'm
trying to do. If what I have in mind doesn't work today or
over the next three weeks, then I can only hope that the
Miriseh can pull out of him what his training masters and I
couldn't. "You'll just have to trust me."

A shrug is all Yorri gives as a response. I take it as
agreement.

I don't have Neeva's rusosa powers, so the danger I
create has to be as real as it is controlled. For the first few

hours of the day, we balance on the outer wall, hanging over the sheer one-hundred-foot drop inches to our left. Weaponless, we run drills that test Yorri's speed and agility, but after a while it's clear this isn't going to come close to scaring him. He trusts his balance and knows his body. He doesn't fear the fall. Or, rather, he doesn't fear the fall enough.

It's time to add the threat of iron.

Leaving him with orders to practice, I collect my weapons from the barracks and then run to the training yard. I help myself to a zeeka, a longer tudo sword, and an anto dagger. No one does more than raise an eyebrow to see me leaving the yard with more weapons than anyone but a rikinhisu mage can wield.

Silence is a habit ingrained by training and nature, and when I reach the top of the stairs to the north wall I'm glad of my overcaution. Tessen is on the wall walking toward Yorri. I hide behind a wide square pillar.

I know he usually stifles his senses within the city— keeping them all at full strength would probably drive him mad—but there's still not much of a chance he didn't hear my footsteps. I haven't spoken, so maybe he wrote off my footsteps as one of the guards on the wall.

Keeping my breaths as steady and even as possible to avoid drawing his attention, I freeze. I don't want to deal with him right now.

"There are easier places to train," he says. "Safer, too."

Yorri scoffs. "What good will safety do me?"

"True." They're both silent for a moment before Tessen clears his throat. "Have you seen Khya?"

Blood and rot, what does he want now? Especially since he was named a kaigo-sei, he's been practically fought over for advice and companionship—in and out of bed. Why is he wasting time hunting me down?

"Not for an hour," Yorri says. "She went back into the city."

"After calling you reckless, probably. And you should listen. She's only trying to keep you safe."

"I'll keep that in mind, Nyshin-ten." The words are respectful, but the tone is much closer to how I usually talk to Tessen. "Did you need something from her?"

Tessen exhales. "I guess not. I'll be late if I don't leave now."

Yorri breaks the long silence, clearing his throat. "We'll see you tonight, then. I'm sure you'll be able to find Khya at dinner."

"And maybe she'll sit down to eat with me when kamidi lizards start flying like the mykyn." Tessen laughs, but it sounds wrong—tense and strained. Then he exhales, almost a sigh. "Be careful, Doseiku Yorri. I think your sister would find a way to blame me if you fell."

Yorri doesn't respond. I hold my breath, listening for Tessen's approach, but the footsteps on the stone seem to be fading, heading east instead of west. Peering around the corner, I see Tessen about to walk through the arch of the northwestern watchtower. Once he's out of sight, I come out of hiding.

Yorri's eyes widen. "If I'd known you were there, I would've let you chase him off."

"I don't seem to be able to chase him anywhere, even when I'm trying to." I lay the weapons out, and he chooses the zeeka. After moving the others out of the way, I unsheathe my own, climb onto the ledge, raise my blade, and face my brother. "Ready?"

I almost don't hear him when he mutters, "Miriseh bless it, I hope so."

We run drill after drill, sometimes coming within millimeters of tipping ourselves over the edge. Though Yorri's breath catches each time he unbalances—and he pales every time *I* do—nothing about him changes. The desosa in the air and the stone surrounding us don't change.

In other words, I failed.

It's taken two days to talk Nyshin-ma Tyrroh and Ahdo-mas Sotra into granting Yorri and me a pass to leave the city. As I walk to the training yard to collect the tokens, I half expect them to have changed their minds.

The yard isn't empty, but it's clear enough to spot Tyrroh and Sotra standing in the shade near the storage room. I approach quickly, then stop in front of them to bow to both. Even though I'm nyshin now, my old training master is one of the higher-ranking ahdo. Realistically, though not technically, Sotra still outranks me. Tyrroh probably always will.

"I'm only agreeing to this because your nyshin-ma assures me you can protect your brother," Sotra says. When I straighten, she's frowning. "I know you're strong, Khya, I've seen it for myself, but are you sure about this?"

"After what happened with Aemon? Yes, Ahdo-mas." Maybe it's wrong to use that incident as a reason, but it's not untrue. What happened proved why I have to push Yorri as much as possible for the next... Miriseh help me. Two and a half weeks. That's all I have left. Swallowing, I say, "I think time away from the city will help clear his head."

Though Sotra huffs, looking uncertain, she hands over

the token for Yorri after an encouraging nod from Tyrroh. He smiles at me when I take it, and from the glint in his eyes, I think he knows what I'm really trying to do. All he says is, "Don't go too far, Nyshin-ten. The ahdo-mas expects your brother back in one piece before sundown. And I expect *you* on time for your duty shift in the morning, so be careful."

"I'm always careful, Nyshin-ma." I smile when he snorts a disbelieving laugh and waves his hand at me, shooing me out of the yard like a troublesome bug.

I meet Yorri at the city-side door to the doseiku dorm instead of the one connected to the training yard. He's shifting restlessly, like he's a few seconds away from pacing, but he calms when he spots me.

"You got it?"

In answer, I toss him the iron disk. It's worth the effort of getting it to watch my brother rub his thumb along the engravings on either side. Like he's not fully convinced it's real.

The tokens that give citizens permission to leave Itagami without their squad aren't common. It's not just the risk of injury, it's the daily dangers of heatstroke, falling prey to the vicious teegras or the venomous kamidi lizards, or dying at the hands of a Denhitran raiding party. For a training master to give that permission to a doseiku is almost unheard of. Doseiku aren't allowed to leave the city until their magic develops and they can be placed with a mage for training.

We approach the gate, and Yorri's steps slow. The archway stretches fifteen feet across and at least twenty high, and the solid iron gate set into the stone is open, giving us a clear view out over the plain. Yorri stops under the shade of the wide archway, eyeing the ahdo guards as though they're about to pin him to the wall and rip the iron token out of his hand.

Brushing my fingers along the back of his clenched hand, I say, "Come on. We've got a lot to do before the sun gets too brutal."

Yorri presses his lips together, all other expression vanishing from his face. Which is for the best, because the gate guards look at us both askance when we hand over the tokens for passage. I outrank them, so they don't question me, but I'm almost certain they want to.

"Have the uniku spotted anything on the horizon?" I ask when they finish examining the tokens and pass them back. After that unexpected storm twelve days ago, I don't want to take any chances. There's plenty I can do to protect Yorri from a teegra or a kamidi. Even if we ran into a Denhitran or Tsimos raiding party, I could probably protect us both long enough for us to escape. I do not want to risk our lives against another storm like that last one.

"Nothing, Nyshin-ten," the gate squad's ahdo-sa commanding officer says. "And our strongest farseer is on the wall this morning. If there were any hint of a storm brewing, he's the uniku who would spot it."

Like they spotted the last one? I hold my tongue, though. The ahdo-sa may be a lower rank, but she's probably twice my age. I clear my throat and nod. "Thank you. We're heading southeast along the foothills of the Kyiwa, but we'll be back well before dark."

"I'll notify the next squad to watch for you. Miriseh keep you both," she says, crossing her clenched fists at the wrists and pressing them to her chest, but not completing the gesture with a bow. Yorri mirrors the gesture, but I simply nod and move toward the open gate.

I stop just before the outer edge of the wall and look at

Yorri. "Ready?"

"I'd better be," he mutters.

We adjust our atakafus, securing them over the bottom halves of our faces and making sure our hoods won't fall the first time we turn our heads. My fingers twitch, but I keep myself from checking Yorri's knots. He's the one who fixed all of my lazy knotwork for years. This is nothing for him.

I still want to check, though. I don't do it, but I want to.

And then we both cross through the gate, taking the first step away from Sagen sy Itagami.

Yorri has never been outside Itagami. He's never seen the way the sunlight reflects off the massive iron gates or the stark beauty of the Kyiwa Mountains at sunrise. He's spent his life protected by the mesa, and he spent a good portion of his early years in trouble for constantly asking the wrong questions at the wrong time—most of them beginning with *why*. I need him to see the city like I do, to know what he'll be protecting if—*when* he's declared nyshin.

When we reach a ridge half a mile from the mesa, I put a hand on Yorri's arm to stop him. Turning, we look back at Sagen sy Itagami.

In the early-morning light, the red sandstone almost glows. The mesa towers above the plain, a promise of safety from the dangers of Shiara. From the walls and the watchtowers, the guards have a clear line of sight for miles in every direction, and the steep, winding path leading to the gates is so exposed neither of the other clans has any hope of sneaking up on us.

Looking at all of this, Yorri's hands clench, but he doesn't turn away. Nyshin-ma Tyrroh has hinted before that I have the potential to become a member of the kaigo council one day, just like my blood-parents, and that his commanding officers would probably nominate me for the kaigo-sei soon. I want that—want it so badly it burns. Yorri is capable of it, too, of being one of the minds and hands responsible for keeping our home safe. All he has to do is reach for it.

Maybe I should explain it like that, explain why we've stopped and try to put what I see in him into words, but after several minutes, he looks at me and nods. Though there's grief in his eyes, I think I see resignation, too. And maybe determination to protect the city we call home— that Sanii calls home. Maybe he's realized that if he fights to keep Itagami safe, Sanii will be safe, too.

Miriseh, please let that be enough.

I turn toward the rocky cliffs and hills of the eastern end of the island.

"Why are we out here?" Yorri asks as we move. "Do you have a plan?"

"Yes. I'm going to teach you how to be silent."

Yorri raises an eyebrow. "You're going to kill me?"

I laugh, and then laugh harder when he rolls his eyes, barely able to suppress his smirk.

"Maybe I should," I taunt. "It might be easier."

After a decade learning to fight on the smooth, flat stone of the training yard, adjusting to the unpredictable footing of the desert terrain isn't easy. That's why teaching him how to silently cross this landscape is step one.

We start on the flat plain between the mesas east of Sagen sy Itagami because it's the easiest place to move and the safest—we're still within the territory protected by the wardstones and patrolled by the nyshin squads. The biggest danger here is accidental injury. A close second are the teegras. Not that enemy clans aren't a concern—the border is miles and miles long, and heat, age, damage, and interference can all eventually break through the wards— but they're lowest on my list and no part of my plan.

Although Denhitrans sneak through less than once a moon, and the Tsimosi appear no less than three times a year, it's rare that either clan manages to get within a mile of the Itagami mesa. Plus, if that happens today and they spot us, even from a distance, two good shots with a powerful ahkiyu longbow would bring us down in an instant. If they saw us before I saw them, I wouldn't be able to bring my wards up in time.

I want to bring Yorri face-to-face with at least one of the dangers the nyshin squads deal with out here, but not until he grasps the basics. Only after I start trying to show him those basics do I realize I have a problem.

I have no idea how to teach him something I do on instinct.

Everything crunches. Every rock could shift beneath your feet at any moment. Moving through this arid landscape is an art. I try to explain, but...

"You're not making any sense," Yorri grumbles. "Just do it. I learn better by watching."

If he was serious about learning to fight by watching me, I'd have to say he's right. I stop trying to teach and simply move.

As the hours pass, I realize I'm waiting for his old hesitance to hold him back. It doesn't. Sooner than I expect, he can follow me across the hard-packed ground and through the low gray-green scrubs without stumbling or starting a minor landslide. It's even more impressive to watch than the skills he used against Aemon because these abilities aren't fueled by grief and rage; this is skill and control. This is something he's working for.

The heat rises as the day wears on, but, thank the Miriseh, the faint breeze only carries the acrid scent of the stone and the vaguely sweet smell of the wild nyska shrubs. It's strong enough to stir up the dust coating the sandstone, but not enough to carry it away. The dust settles over my skin and infiltrates my nose and my lungs even through the covering of the atakafu.

During our brief rests, I tell him about the herynshi—what to expect and how to succeed. It's not something we're supposed to discuss with the doseiku who haven't faced that trial yet, but knowing what's coming won't necessarily change the outcome. Not for this.

We move up the sloping ridge to where the scrubs almost reach our waists, and the sweet smell grows stronger. It's densely packed here, the path more dangerous as we have to avoid the shrubs' sharp thorns, and the land harder to cross without leaving an obvious trail behind us. It takes him longer to pick up these tricks, but he's learning. His intelligence is just as much use here as his speed.

Skill hadn't been enough for Sanii, and it won't be for Yorri, either. No skill anyone can teach him will be enough to keep him from being placed yonin without magic. Just a glimmer by his herynshi. That's all he needs to be placed at least among the ahdo. I can't help hoping for something stronger than a glimmer, something strong enough to bring him into the nyshin.

When the sun is nearing its peak, I take Yorri toward a small oasis so we can drink and save our water for the trip back. The watering holes on the eastern end of Shiara are brackish but drinkable. They're also dangerous. We'll survive the water as long as the animals don't catch us. Silence and speed are key at the oases. This will be the first real test of Yorri's new skills and, if we're not alone here, the first potential moment of fear.

We approach one of the lushest areas on this side of the island, full of tall grass and the long, thin leaves of the nyska shrubs. Before we reach the water, I pull him behind an outcropping of rock and whisper quick instructions.

"If you hear something that sounds like the wind, but constant, run. If you hear a grumbling, freeze. The pira fish will make a meal of your fingers faster than you can blink. Snakes hide in the grass, and they can kill you with one bite. A teegra's claws are sharper than my sword; if they pin you, you're dead. We move in, take what we need, and then get out of there before anything else gets thirsty."

His eyes search what we can see of the oasis with a new wariness. "Or hungry."

"Don't fool yourself." I shift my weight, getting ready to run. "Everything on Shiara is hungry."

Heat, dirt, blood, death. Life is made of these things.

I mark time with taps of my fingers against his shoulder, counting down. My toes dig into the dirt beneath our feet, the heated rock searing my callused skin.

"Go."

We propel ourselves forward, flying across the low greenery surrounding the pool. The soft grass muffles sound, but that doesn't mean much when any shift in the breeze could call in every predator for a mile.

Vaulting over a boulder, I land on the bank of the pool and scoop the water into my hands. The pira circle below my shadow, waiting for me to give them something new to gnaw on. Luckily, they're as stupid as they are insatiable. I toss a rock into the other side of the pool; they shoot off to investigate. We have seconds before they'll be back. Yorri and I quickly scoop more water into our mouths and then back away with all our fingers intact.

I wanted to put him in some form of danger—I still do—but I can't help feeling relieved that we're leaving the oasis without facing anything more deadly than a pira.

Then I hear it, a rumbling that sounds like a rockslide in the distance. Oh, no.

A teegra cat and her mate stare at us from the opposite edge of the clearing. Their red scales ripple as they tense, and their pointed black tongues flick out to sample our scent on the wind, preparing for a rare, easy feast of human flesh.

"Yorri." I keep my voice low and level, hoping he can hear the underlying warning. He'd been watching the piras swarm, but he tenses as soon as he raises his eyes. My wards can keep us from getting shredded by the teegras' black claws, but they can't last forever. If he doesn't listen to what I'm about to tell him, I won't be able to save him. "Southwest. Forget silence. *Run*."

He turns and takes off. I draw my zeeka from the sheath on my back. The teegras pounce. I strike, using the force of the teegra's motion to drive the blade into its chest. The animal screams its fury and jerks, dark blood pouring from the wound. My sweat-slickened fingers slip off the hilt, and the blade is stuck in muscle and scale. I have to let my weapon go or be dragged into the pool with the thrashing animal.

I sprint after Yorri, scrambling up the slight incline. I find him too soon—he's moving too slowly. When he glances back and sees me, he picks up speed. His hesitation lets me bridge the gap between us. In seconds, I'm only a few feet behind him.

The teegras roar. Is the one I struck dying? I don't dare look back to check. Dead or not, teegras mate for life, and they don't take the loss or injury of their partner well.

There isn't much chance the vengeful beast will give up the chase after the wound I left one with.

We tear up a steep, narrow path in the rocks. The teegras' claws will let them follow us, but if we can gain enough distance over the rocks they might lose our scent. The wind blasts like a bellows fire across my eyes, and the sharpest edges of the rocks find the bottoms of my feet. Something slices. I might be bleeding. No time to wrap the wound.

What is pain when death bites at our heels?

I hear nothing behind us, but teegras go silent when they track.

Yorri hasn't had to outsmart them before, though. He starts to slow.

"*Run!*" I hiss as I fly past him. He falters, but then he's back in time with me and closing the small distance I gained.

Ahead is a wall of rock that will force us to choose a new direction. Veering southwest means running through the territory of those blood-rotten spitting lizards. The kamidi are massive and dangerous, but slow. If we head northeast, we might not find a place to stop until we're trapped between the ocean, the mountains, and a solid cliff wall. Is the teegra hungry enough to risk following us into kamidi territory? Bellows, I hope not. If it does, maybe today I'll get lucky and our animal enemies will finish each other off.

"West." The word comes out in a huff of breath, but Yorri must hear it. He turns southwest and keeps running.

We flash past ridges and jump over hidden crevices. I test the wind with every breath, trying to catch a hint of the scent of musk with an undertone of sulfur that always seems to surround the teegras, or the rotting flesh scent of the kamidi.

I hear nothing, see nothing, smell nothing, but that doesn't mean nothing is there.

Coming around a ridge, I freeze. My skin is already prickling from heat and sweat and fear, but that doesn't mask the moment the desosa shifts—the moment the energy in the air gains an edge of lightning.

No. No, no, *no*. Not again.

There's nothing for me to climb this time—the walls of rock are too smooth and too steep to climb in a hurry—but I know that scent. And from the look on Yorri's face when his eyes meet mine, I'm not the only one who smells it.

Rot take that Kujuko-cursed farseer. How could anyone who claims to be the strongest sight-enhanced uniku miss *this*? The only excuse would be if the storm has developed suddenly since we left at dawn, but that doesn't happen. Ever.

This isn't a danger I can control or fight. This isn't what I wanted.

"Another typhoon?" He asks the question with true, shaking fear in his voice. Yorri visibly trembles. From the strain of the run or fear of the storm? Whatever the cause, I hope he's strong enough to shove it aside and flee.

I was looking for something I could easily protect him from if things got out of hand. There isn't a single rotten thing I can do against what we're about to try outrunning.

"Drink now." I grind my teeth and nod toward the waterskin strapped tight to his side. "Once we start, we're not stopping."

He drinks as I explain the path we need to take. Then, I grip his shoulders and stare into his eyes. Blood and rot, he's going to hate everything I'm about to say. "If something takes me out, you need to keep going, Yorri. Do you understand? Do not stop. Not for anything."

His skin loses color, but he nods and straps the water-skin back in place.

We run, flying across terrain it took us all morning to cross. We run faster than when the teegras nipped at our heels. My lungs burn and my legs ache before we've crossed a quarter of the distance.

I push harder.

The desosa crackles, and there's too much of the ocean on the wind. It's becoming a gale with the power to hurl detritus. We blow past a congregation of kamidi. The lizards spit venom in our direction; we're well out of reach.

Tiny droplets of water strike the hard-packed ground. In minutes, these drops will become a deluge.

Caution is lost. Silence is gone. All we have is speed.

Growing wind, rumbling thunder, gathering darkness—I don't have to look at the sky to know time is running out. When the real rains start, the floods will be close behind. Those, we have no hope of outrunning. It may already be too late to reach the city. We're a mile away, within sight but too far out for anyone to help us.

A sharp blast of wind throws me off balance. My foot lands in a divot in the rock. My ankle twists. My knee pops. Agonizing pain streaks up my leg and across the entire right side of my body. I scream and crash to the rocky ground.

Yorri stops.

"Go!" I shove at his chest when he crouches next to me.

"I'm not leaving you." He kneels, his hands carefully shifting the rocks trapping my foot.

"Then we'll both die."

There's too much white showing in his eyes, but his jaw is set and determined. Fear doesn't stop him from shouting, "No, Khya. If you don't shut up and start helping me, *then* we'll both die."

He forces my arm around his shoulders and heaves me to my feet with more strength than I knew he possessed. Trying to put weight on my right leg is excruciating. The pain is so bad it turns my stomach and makes my vision blur. Yorri carries me onward, his steps too slow. He can't bear this much of my weight, fight the screaming wind, *and* move as quickly as he needs to. The full force of the storm is bearing down faster and faster. Fear and pain muddy my thoughts. I push it aside and hold as much of my weight as I can, counterbalancing him when the gale threatens to knock us off course.

We're more than three-quarters of a mile from the city. We won't make it. If he doesn't leave me here and run, we'll both drown.

"There!" I point to one of the smaller mesas. There's a protected ledge ten feet off the ground that might be safe. "Get me there and then run. You can come get me when the storm has passed."

I turn toward the mesa. Yorri shakes his head and grips me tighter, hauling me toward the city.

The desosa crackles against my mind. Lightning forms a fissure through the sky, blindingly bright and dangerously close. I bring up my wards. It doesn't stop the searing heat. I cry out. My good leg threatens to buckle. If I fall, I'll take Yorri down with me.

"You're being ridiculous." I pull my arm free and almost collapse.

Yorri is quick. His arm is around my waist before I crash to the ground. "Stop it, Khya. You'd never leave me behind. I am not going to leave you!"

He steps in front of me and wraps my arms around his neck. He crouches and grabs my thighs, hoisting me onto his back. The motion jars my right leg. Pain as searing as the lightning bolt shoots through me. I sink my teeth into my arm to keep from screaming.

Each step Yorri takes is agony, but he's moving faster now than he was with me strapped to his side. Not fast enough. Nowhere near fast enough.

This is *my* fault. I dragged him out here. And because of what? The fear he might be yonin? Stupid. Only bonding is banned between nyshin and yonin. Would I see him less? Yes. But I'd see him. I'd rather he was yonin than dead. Especially if he dies because of me.

"Please, Yorri. Please. You might make it alone."

He ignores me, jogging as quickly as he can over the open plain. Each step he takes feels like a struggle to stay on his feet. He's got to be exhausted and unbalanced by my added weight, but he manages. Somehow he manages.

How…how is he doing this?

Forcing myself to focus is a fight I almost lose, but then I feel it, the faint buzz under Yorri's skin. With each step, he stands straighter and moves faster. With each step, it seems easier for him to hold his ground against the wind. With each step, the buzz of the desosa gathering under his skin resonates quicker until it becomes a warmth as strong as a fire.

Then, with a slow exhale I feel but can't hear, Yorri *runs*.

At first his pace is close to what he might've managed alone, but he keeps pushing faster. The desert flashes by too fast for my pain-blurred vision. It's impossible. No one can move this fast while carrying a human burden and fighting a gale. Yet somehow he is.

Strength, speed, endurance, agility— Miriseh bless us. Kynacho. Yorri is a kynacho.

Relief leaves me so giddy I almost laugh.

Half a mile to safety.

Then the rains start. The clouds tear open, dumping water onto the parched, rocky terrain.

Yorri runs faster.

Quarter of a mile. I blink the water out of my eyes and look down. Through the pain haze I see the water swirling around his ankles. The plain is becoming thick and soupy; in certain spots, mud will soon swallow anything stupid enough to cross its surface, and no one but an ishiji can tell where those spots are until they're standing on one.

I do what little I can to ward us from flying rocks and debris, but today Yorri is the one saving me.

The roar of the wind is getting louder. A tornado? A flash flood? Or is this what the wind sounds like when you run faster than a storm?

Gripping him tighter, I silently urge him on. Faster, *faster*, or the plain will become impassible. Even for a kynacho.

Yorri digs his feet into the water and the sodden ground underneath and runs *faster*. I close my eyes against the pain and the force of his speed.

Nausea threatens. I hold my breath.

My fault. If we die out here, it'll be my fault. If we survive, it'll only be because of Yorri.

His body tenses. My eyes fly open when my body jerks. For a moment we've become mykyn, his jump so high and long it's as close to flying as I'll ever get. We land with a *thud* on the bottom of the path up to the city. Below us, the flood waters are rising, the natural dips of the plain becoming dangerously rapid rivers.

We made it with minutes, maybe seconds, to spare.

But that doesn't mean we're safe. Even Yorri's newfound strength can't last forever.

The wind is stronger with each foot we climb and it

feels like he struggles more to keep his feet. A swirling current of air knocks him away from the safety of the mesa wall. I lock my legs around his waist, screaming as pain bolts through my body, and grab an outcropping of rock with both hands. It keeps us from tumbling into the torrents of water below, but it's the last of my strength.

I can barely feel either one of my legs. My arms flop uselessly to my sides. I slide off his back and crash to the path. Yorri lifts me into his arms. Pain fills my body so fully that it's like there's no space left for me.

It's too dangerous, I want to tell him. *You won't be able to catch yourself if you fall.*

I don't think I manage a single word. Yorri wouldn't listen to me if I did.

Moving. Climbing. The roar of the wind and the warmth of Yorri's magic burning under his skin. Climbing. Faster.

And then something loud. Sharp. The clang of an iron bell. Or the crack of thunder. Something I recognize, but...

My blurry vision tunnels and I fall.

CHAPTER FIVE

'm not dead. I hope I'm not, anyway, because this isn't what I imagined Ryogo would look like. The Miriseh promised cool breezes and lush fields of green. Wherever I am now looks far too much like Hishingu Hall.

Closing my eyes again, I rub my cheek on the exquisitely soft mattress. The raised stone beds in the healer's ward are covered by feather-stuffed mattresses made of niora skin. Those furry cats from the southern mountains don't cross into our territory often. When they do, their russet skins go to the healers and the Miriseh. Whatever I did to need a healing, it's worth it for the chance to feel niora fur against my skin.

"I'd like to think you'll admit I was right about Yorri now," Tessen says. "Don't worry, though. I won't hold my breath."

"Yorri!" I gasp, sitting up fast. The pain in my leg is gone. How could I have forgotten what happened? The limb is stiff—bellows, my whole body is stiff—but nothing hurts when I turn to hang my legs off the side of the stone platform. Most of the beds in the hall are empty. The people I do see aren't Yorri. "Where is he? Is he okay?"

"He's fine. He came home in much better shape than you." Tessen takes a step back to give me room. "Luckily, there wasn't anything wrong with you that the hishingu couldn't heal. They were by not long ago and said you could leave when you woke up."

"Where is he, then?" I can't believe he'd leave me here alone unless something important kept him away. Maybe I can find Ahdo-mas Sotra and ask her where—

"Whoa. Stop, Khya." Tessen touches my arm, but he doesn't try to hold on when I jerk away. "He's with Kaigo Ono. It'll be another few hours at least before they're done categorizing his power and placing him with a mage for training."

Oh. I exhale heavily and lean against the next bed. That makes sense. That's exactly where he should be. More than that, it means that it worked. We made it back and Yorri is going to be a nyshin and everything will be fine. Maybe after the herynshi, they'll place him with my squad. The impossible strength and speed of a kynacho and the impenetrable wards of a fykina mage? Together we'd be unstoppable.

The thought makes me almost giddy. A smile spreads across my face. Tessen blinks and steps a little closer, his own smile softening. He opens his mouth to speak and—

"You're awake!" Etaro and Rai rush into the room, grins on both of their faces. They're coated in dust and splatters of mud. I can only assume they ran in here as soon as they were released from their shift. *Our* shift. Bellows. I missed it. The first one I've ever missed.

"What the bellows were you doing out there yesterday?" Etaro scans me quickly before hauling me into a crushing hug. I stiffen, the unexpected contact sending tiny prickles of alarm over my skin. By the time I take a breath and begin to accept the embrace, ey's stepped back, embarrassment and relief warring on eir face, the expression softening eir naturally sharp features. "Wasn't the last storm bad enough?"

"Khya has always had a death wish." Rai rolls her eyes and puts her hand on her waist, pulling her tunic tight against the wide curve of her hips. "She wants to see Ryogo."

"How can I resist paradise?" I shoot back at her. The taunt is old by now after a year together in Nyshin-ma Tyrroh's squad. She laughed the first time I mentioned the stories they told us about Ryogo and the afterlife when we were kids. It's a long-standing obsession, and she isn't the first one to tease me for it. When we were kids, Tessen used to laugh and say I enjoyed the stories we would get to hear while we ate more than the food itself. I glance at him now to see if that's changed, but... Where is he?

Oh. There. He's at the door, leaving without a single glance back.

"Are you going to tell us why Tessen was here?" Rai grins, her full lips stretching wide.

"What haven't you been sharing, Khya?" Etaro picks up the thread, eyes alight with the potential new gossip. "The boy was waiting by your bedside like a lovelorn sukhai."

"I was unconscious. How the bellows am I supposed to know why Tessen was here?" And I really don't. It seemed like he had been about to say something when these two arrived, but I can't begin to guess what it might have been.

"Well, what did he say, then?" Etaro asks.

"Nothing, really."

"Are you sure? Because you two were sitting awfully close," Rai adds.

"Of course I'm sure. I was there." I hope that'll be the end of it, but both of them are watching me expectantly. There's no way I'm getting out of this without explaining, so I do. It doesn't take long. "All Tessen did was remind me what happened yesterday and tell me where Yorri is."

Rai looks skeptical, but Etaro seems satisfied. Ey must be, because ey moves on.

"Speaking of your brother, he stopped by our barracks and asked us to check in on you." Etaro laughs and leans against the end of my borrowed bed, eir fingers running along the edge of the niora mattress. "As though we weren't planning on coming already."

"We didn't believe you'd survived until we saw the healers working on you last night." Rai runs a hand over her short, dark hair, brushing flakes of dried mud out with each swipe. Most of the time her eyes are wide, round, and extremely expressive. When she's trying to hide something—like fear or relief or worry—she squints. Exactly like she's doing now. "No one has ever seen a storm come up that fast."

"There wasn't any warning. It was on us even faster than the last one." Etaro's smile dims and ey shakes eir head, narrow eyes lined with concern. "Two squads of scouts were trapped between the city and the base camps. One of them lost *nine* and the other four."

"I heard all ten of the Miriseh and half of the kaigo have been in closed meetings since the storm struck yesterday and— Wait, the hishingu said you could go, right?" When I nod, Rai leads us out of the hall. There's no smile on her face, but her eyes are round again. She collects stories about the Miriseh the same way I obsess over Ryogo. "No one has seen them, and the nyshin-lu who assist the councils have been running through the city like mad for the last twelve hours."

With the brutality of that storm, a daylong meeting isn't surprising. Dealing with the damage, the repair orders, the lost supplies— Bellows, I get a headache just thinking about it.

I don't know how I'll ever learn enough to be responsible for ten thousand souls. I've only made myself responsible for one so far, and I mess that up more often than not. "Did the mines flood?"

"No." Etaro is walking backward in front of us, eir voice dropped to a whisper that's filled with confusion and worry. "The bathing pools are about to overflow, and the ishiji mages have to seal up some cracks in the stone of several buildings—there are leaks in more than one of the barracks—but the squads in the desert took the worst of the damage. Including the deaths in the city, we lost nineteen in that storm."

I'm afraid to ask if any of the losses were our friends. "Maybe that's why they're meeting. To figure out how to keep that from happening again."

Because that's what they do and what they *have* done since they arrived from Ryogo centuries ago. The Miriseh guide and protect the clan, teaching us what we need to know to thrive on Shiara and what we need to do to reach the haven of their world once we die, to avoid the emptiness and agony of an eternity trapped in Kujuko instead. Varan, Suzu, and the others have taught us—have *shown* us—how important loyalty to Itagami is, and how the only way the clan will survive is for each person to put their brethren's safety before their own. But that doesn't mean individual losses aren't mourned. The Miriseh have always done as much as they could to avoid preventable loss.

"I suppose." Rai's agreement seems disappointed by the rational explanation.

"Stop creating trouble." I smile to take the edge off the scold.

"Ugh, I know." Her nose crinkles. "Because Shiara provides us with more than enough," she intones, finishing the phrase everyone hears dozens of times growing up.

"Exactly." I smile and feel lighter than I have in weeks. Even if our trip to the desert went catastrophically wrong, it did work. It all but promised that Yorri will walk out of the herynshi as a nyshin in two weeks.

The only thing left to do is wait.

K nowing everything will turn out exactly the way I wanted doesn't make waiting any easier. It's still awful.

Yorri calls me down from my room the night before his herynshi. The doseiku don't have wardcharms, so they can't access buildings restricted to the citizen classes. Unfortunately, that includes the citizen barracks.

"It's almost time," I say when I meet him on the street. "Are you ready?"

I expect to see nerves. Fear maybe. Yorri's stance looks more weary than afraid, and there's resignation in his eyes. His shoulders are slumped and his eyes downcast. Tonight of all nights I expected Yorri to be nearly bouncing off the walls with energy, desperate to just get it over with. What I expected, or maybe what I'd hoped for, is definitely not what I see in my brother now.

His gaze turns north, lingering there for a moment before returning to me—a silent request to go to the wall. I nod, falling into place beside him, and we make our way through the streets. Neither of us has said a word by the time we're halfway there. Reaching out, I brush my fingers just above Yorri's elbow, raising my eyebrows in question. He shrugs and keeps walking.

It's not the first silent conversation we've had, but this one feels weighted with emotional undercurrents. The worry building in my stomach gets worse when we reach the top of the wall. Yorri stands with his hands on the chest-high ledge, leaning into the wind and staring out over the water. I watch him instead of the ocean and wait, pushing down the impulse to pelt him with questions. He'll speak when he's ready to.

But the silence stretches longer, long enough for the ahdo guards to pass us more than once on their rounds. They eye us curiously, but don't ask us to leave. Not that I thought they would. If they let us stay here when I had Yorri training on the wall's ledge while dual-wielding weapons, I doubt they'll kick us out for anything.

"Do you ever wonder if there's something else?"

I blink. "What do you mean?"

"Something else." He gestures toward the horizon. "Somewhere off Shiara and beyond what we can see—beyond Imaku. A place like Ryogo where the land doesn't hate us and we wouldn't have to fight for every breath, except you don't have to die to get there." His hands clench into fists on top of the wall, and his shoulders curl toward each other, but his eyes stay locked on the horizon. "Have you ever wondered about that?"

"I... What?" Something else? How could there be? Nothing can cross the ocean, and not even the strongest sensor's vision has ever seen anything on the horizon but more water. "No, I haven't. The Miriseh have been here for centuries. They would've told us if they'd heard a single hint of some other land."

"Just because they don't know about it doesn't mean it can't exist."

It's true, and they never have claimed omniscience, but that's not what I meant. I take a breath and turn, leaning my back against the outer wall so I can look over Itagami. "If some other land is out there—and I honestly don't think it is—it's too far away for us to reach. And expecting it to be anything like Ryogo is setting yourself up to be disappointed. Ryogo is a reward, and we're only allowed there with the blessing of the Miriseh. Besides, this is the world we have." I gesture to the city dug out from the mesa. "What's the point in wasting time wondering about something that probably doesn't exist and that we definitely won't ever see?"

Yorri's head drops and his shoulders shake. Is he... He is. He's laughing, but the sound is strangled. Pained. I want it to stop, but I don't know how to make it happen. I reach toward him, then hesitate. He sucks in air and it sounds like a sob. Reaching out, I place my hand on his shoulder, squeezing tight and hoping it's enough.

He slowly straightens, his eyes fixed on the horizon, but it takes a minute for Yorri's breathing to even out. "I don't..." Yorri sighs. He doesn't look at me. "I don't think I've said thank you enough for everything you've done for me. The last few weeks and—bellows, forever. My whole life you've looked out for me and I... Just, thank you, Khya."

"I don't want your thanks. You're clan, Yorri. This is what we do."

"I know." Yorri nods and finally looks at me. "But whether you want thanks or not, you have mine."

Thanks for protecting him when we were kids? Thanks for risking his life to force him into the nyshin? I wonder what exactly he's thanking me for. Maybe it doesn't matter. My brother thinks I've done something worthy of thanks, and somehow those small words feel like more than any rank or reward the councils could possibly bestow. It's something I want to wear like Tessen's kaigo-sei pendant.

My lip quirks up into a smile as the worry in my stomach settles. "You're welcome."

CHAPTER
SIX

'm glad I have to leave the city before dawn for a hunting trip the day of Yorri's herynshi; I think I'd have gone mad if the duty rotation had left me with nothing to do. Even now I should be focusing on the landscape of the plain, looking for signs of teegras, kamidi, or niora, and memorizing the way the landmarks and passages have changed because of the storms. Instead, I've been mentally tracking Yorri's progress all day.

Just after sunrise, one of the kaigo should've collected Yorri from the doseiku dorm and placed a mask over his face, allowing him to only see a small area directly in front of him. It's disorienting. How did Yorri cope with that? Better than I did, probably. He'd likely seen it as a puzzle, a mental challenge to beat. Knowing him, he'll come back and tell me he somehow figured out exactly where the cavern is, even though he could only see enough to keep himself from tripping.

The herynshi cavern is somewhere in the Kyiwa Mountains northeast of the city, and to get to there, doseiku are guided through a series of twists and turns that are impossible to replicate, and across terrain that climbs and falls at random intervals. Rai has a theory that the Miriseh walk everyone in circles for a while, just to be sure there's no chance of figuring out where they are. Etaro thinks it's more of a way to test our balance and sure-footedness. I'm certain it's both, and probably more besides; I can't imagine the Miriseh doing anything for only one reason.

By midday, while I'm resting with my squad eating some of the dried fruits, meat, and mushrooms we carried out into the desert with us, Yorri has likely reached the cavern. Maybe he's completed the ordeal or maybe he's still waiting in one of the small stone cells, expected to be silent.

Will he be among the first or not? I spent my long wait pacing the cell, working as hard as I could to guess the outcome of each trial from what I knew about the trainee and how long the ordeal took. I had to measure them in breaths, which wasn't the most accurate method, but I was right more often than not.

It was the waiting that almost broke me a year ago. The silence and the darkness of the cells made it too easy for fear to take over, fear of somehow failing even though I'd been in control of my magic for years, or fear of being the one case in a thousand that drops dead.

Miriseh, please don't let that be Yorri today.

"You're distracted." Etaro floats eir half-finished pouch of dried surnat fruit across the space between us. Ey always packs more than ey can eat; I never pack enough. "You're not worried about Yorri, are you? He's a kynacho. They'll barely test him. Everyone knows he'll be announced nyshin tonight."

On the rock across from us, Rai sketches outlines of the

class symbols on a boulder with a thin bit of charred scrub stick. "Khya is never not worried about Yorri," she says without looking up. "Even Tessen doesn't bother her when she's busy worrying about Yorri."

Remembering how he'd pushed me to watch Yorri train and the conversation we had in the weapon storeroom the next morning, I shake my head. "I don't think that's true anymore."

Rai looks up, and Etaro leans in, asking, "Really?"

Oh. I haven't told them what's been happening with Tessen recently, have I? They saw a bit of it when they came to collect me from Hishingu Hall, but I haven't told them the rest. There was Yorri to worry about and then the failure—and success—of the storm and then… I shake my head, my lips pursed to hide a smirk.

"Keeping secrets, Khya? I'm hurt." Pressing one hand against her chest, just above her full breasts, Rai frowns. "It's almost like you think we'll make sure the entire squad and half the zon knows Nyshin-ten Tessen has started following you around like a baby mykyn."

"You two gossips? That's exactly what you'll do." It's a lie, and we all know it. I grin when Rai rolls her eyes and goes back to sketching. "And it's not a secret, it just didn't seem important enough to talk about."

Etaro's eyes light up. "Something happened? Did Tessen—"

"Squad, up!" Nyshin-ma Tyrroh barks. We scramble to obey, stuffing our leftover food into belt pouches and thigh packs.

He and Nyshin-pa Daitsa were conferring in whispers higher on the slope, their gazes jumping between the plain to the west of us and the squad resting in the shade of the embankment. When he issues orders, it's to split us up, half going south following Nyshin-pa Daitsa—Tyrroh's second—and Nyshin-ten Ryzo, and the rest moving west with Tyrroh.

"We won't get close enough to check any of the wardstones at the border of the territory, but my desosa mages had better be on alert for the slightest hint of disturbance in the ambient energy. If the storm last week damaged the barrier ward, we need to know." Tyrroh is speaking to the entire squad, but when he mentions the desosa, his eyes are on me. It makes sense; I'm the only desosa mage in the squad who even has a chance of picking up the discordant energy of a damaged wardstone from this far away.

Before we split, Tyrroh signals something to Daitsa. The gesture is small, so slight I might not have noticed it if I hadn't already been watching him for further instructions. His hand moves in a circle with his fourth and fifth finger extended, the other three curled toward his palm. It's not a signal I know, but Daitsa nods sharply before she turns to prod us into motion.

"Did you see that?" I ask Etaro as we follow the nyshin-pa south.

Ey glances at me. "What?"

I look up to Daitsa, who is laughing at something Ryzo said, and shake my head.

It's probably from an extra set of signals Tyrroh uses with his second. I haven't noticed them before, but I'm usually moving to obey Tyrroh's orders after he gives them, not watching him for more. It doesn't matter. What matters is that there have been three early storms in the past moon cycle. What matters are the dozens of lives that have been lost when squads have been caught in the desert and unable to get to safety. What matters is making sure that those storms haven't done irreparable damage to the wards protecting our territory from the Denhitran and Tsimos clans.

We run for an hour, watching the rocks for signs of the animals we're hunting and feeling—at least on my part— for the power fluctuations of a broken wardstone.

I *try* to do that, anyway. Most of my mind is still with Yorri.

We make it back to Itagami with barely enough time to wash and change before the gate closes and the vigil ends. Whatever happened during the herynshi today, whatever illusion Kaigo Neeva cast, and whatever ordeal Yorri had to face, it's over.

There's only one likely outcome, but I can't forget the expression on Yorri's face when he spoke about Sanii. I can't forget his questions last night about lands that don't exist and his tendency to look for different solutions when he doesn't like the ones he's given. It's more than enough to send prickles of worry through my mind.

That worry eases as soon as the Miriseh appear on the western entrance to the square, because Yorri walks just behind Varan and Suzu.

It's official. He's nyshin.

I exhale a breath I've been holding since the gates closed and drop my chin to my chest. "Bellows, I'm glad that's over."

On my left, Rai snorts and shakes her head. Etaro is behind me, and ey whispers congratulations. At the end of our row, Nyshin-ma Tyrroh glances at me and winks. If even Tyrroh noticed, I've been less subtle about my Yorriinduced panic than I thought. Maybe that's why our squad is so close to the center walkway tonight, giving me a clear view of the procession as it passes through the square. Whatever the reason, I'm glad for it.

I catch Yorri's eye as he passes, my grin so wide it hurts. He smiles back, the expression maybe not as excited as it could be — as I wish it were — but definitely genuine.

The ceremony is the same as ever, but excitement buzzes through my blood like overactive desosa when the drummers beat out the first rhythms of the tokiansu. For the first time, Yorri is allowed to participate in the warrior's dance, and he's one of the few people I trust enough to dance with. Or, to dance *well* with, at least. Hopefully I can convince him to join me tonight. It's been too many moons since I've performed the complicated, deadly dance.

The first pairs pick the ceremonial weapons and jump into the circle. The gleaming, curved tudo long swords, the colorfully dyed, iron-bladed tessen fans, or the incredibly dangerous suraki.

With four-foot chains and a curved, double-bladed claw on the end, there aren't many pairs brave enough or skilled enough to dance with the suraki. I could do it, I think, as long as I had the right partner, but I don't know who that would be. There isn't anyone whose skill I have that much faith in, not even Yorri's. I'd dance with the tudo or the tessen, though, if Yorri is up to it.

When I spot him moving toward me in the crowd, I nudge people out of the way and run, flinging my arms around my brother's neck. For once, I don't hold back, not because of the crowd watching and definitely not for Yorri's sake. He's more than strong enough to catch me now.

"You did it! I am *so* proud of you, little brother." I step back, but grip his shoulders tight.

I see the others watching us, subtly monitoring the interaction to see if they need to step in to protect Yorri from the unwanted touch, but then he tilts my head down to plant a smiling kiss on my forehead.

The gesture—the trust in it and the contact—warms me in a way the desert never can.

As much as I wish this night could be one long celebration of his achievement, I know there's grief in this victory. At least for Yorri. "How are you?"

His smile turns resigned, and his eyes are so sad, but his voice is even and strong when he says, "I'm okay. Or I will be. You know me. I can adapt to anything if you give me enough time."

"And you've got plenty of time now." With the strength and speed of a kynacho, there isn't much that will be able to take him down. "But for tonight…" I raise my eyebrows and glance in the direction of the weapon racks.

He follows my gaze, his eyes crinkling at the corners as his smile becomes brighter and far more genuine, but when he turns his head back toward me he blinks and seems to focus over my shoulder.

"Congratulations, Yorri. I'm sure you made your sister proud." Tessen. Bellows. "Maybe now I won't find either of you standing on the ledge of the north wall so often."

The joke is dry, but it's enough to make Yorri smile. "Hoping for that will only end in disappointment. I like it up there too much." His eyes meet mine with questions: What do you want me to do? Stay? Leave? Kick him across the courtyard?

I lift one shoulder an inch, hopefully not enough for Tessen to see it as anything but an annoyed twitch, and Yorri returns his attention to the interloper. "But thank you, either way. It's good even if it's..." He looks down at his hands, flexing and clenching them, his smile turning wry. "It isn't what I expected."

"What did you expect?" I don't know the answer to that question. *How* do I not know that?

"I thought maybe I'd be an oraku like Kaigo Ono." It wouldn't have been surprising. The two lesser sensor mage classes—the single-sense-enhanced uniku, like the ahdo farseers on the wall, and the triple-sense-enhanced oraku, like Tyrroh and our blood-father Ono—are somewhat common. Yorri shakes his head, his gaze lingering for a moment on a group of yonin who pass by before returning to me. "Or maybe a zoikyo. Augmentation fit, since Khya's wards always seemed stronger when I was around."

"That's because you were always the one she wanted to protect the most," Tessen says. His tone is odd, off somehow, but without examining his expression I can't tell exactly how or what it might mean. I don't turn around, though. Not yet. Maybe he'll walk away if I don't. Probably not, but maybe.

"Khya." His voice dips lower as he steps into my peripheral vision, and if I didn't know better, I'd almost think his smile looked nervous. I try to ignore Yorri's smirk as he watches us both. "I did say everything would be fine, didn't I? But you probably still won't thank me for trying to tell you that weeks ago."

Yorri cocks his head, confusion on his face. I tense, looking into Tessen's gray eyes and raising an eyebrow. "I'm sorry, do you really think I owe you thanks for his skills?"

"No, that's not—" He closes his eyes, his lips moving minutely with words I can't hear. Exhaling, Tessen seems to force his shoulders to relax as he opens his eyes and steps closer. He glances at Yorri and then over my shoulder. All around us, the tokiansu circles inlaid into the courtyard are filling up, crowds gathering around each one as clashing metal rings through the air and the pace of the drums quicken. "I didn't mean it like that. All I wanted to say was that I'm glad it worked out. And to ask you to dance."

"No." I shake my head and step back. "Go ask someone you haven't spent half a decade stealing promotions from."

"I am. I'm asking you."

What? Did he hit his head today? "I'm getting the impression you remember the last few years very differently from how they actually happened."

Tessen steps closer until only inches separate us. "Please, Khya."

"No."

"Khya—"

Suddenly Yorri is in front of me, forcing space between us. Tessen stumbles backward, his hands reaching for the sword strapped to his back. It's instinct brought by the unexpected attack—I can see Tessen halt the reaction before his fingers close on the hilt of the blade—but my own instincts flare, instantly building a ward between them. Just in case.

"She said no, Tessen." The warning in my brother's voice sends a shiver down my spine.

"You're right." Tessen isn't smiling now. His lips thin and his eyes glint like iron. It only lasts a second before his expression relaxes, but his smile doesn't return. "Congratulations again, Nyshin-ten Yorri. It's well-deserved."

He turns and is lost in the crowd within seconds.

"We've always been so good at making friends," Yorri says once he's gone.

"We were once." Or I was before I had to spend all my time chasing Yorri, keeping him out of trouble when I could and getting into it with him when I couldn't. He went from picking the locks on the nursery's storage closet and reclaiming the puzzles our yonin guardians hid from us, to slipping away from the training classes to explore the maze of caves in the undercity. None of the other doseiku wanted to be caught up in his schemes, so early on I had to choose between Yorri and the rest of our yearmates.

It's been different the last year, since I became nyshin. Now I have the squad, especially Etaro and Rai. At first my friendship with both had been strained, habits from years of taking care of Yorri trying to surface in my interactions with them both. At least until Rai had snapped a reminder that they were both my elders by eight moons and if I told Etaro how to do something one more time, Rai would test which was faster—my wards or her fireballs.

The three of us have been friends ever since.

What was surprising, though I'm not even sure why anymore, was that they weren't the only bonds I formed.

Tyrroh seems to take a special interest sometimes, pushing me to accept more responsibilities and offering guidance when he can. There was the relationship with Ryzo and another with Kemi. Both had burned hot and bright for a while before settling into a comfortable camaraderie.

But none of that matters tonight. This is supposed to be Yorri's night to rejoice. Tomorrow, when he returns to his mage training, he'll be doing so with the full honors and rank of a nyshin. And the workload of one, too.

"I was going to ask if you wanted to dance tonight." I look toward the closest tokiansu circle, but my earlier excitement is mostly gone. Yorri, too, looks wearier than he did when he walked into the courtyard.

"Next time," he says.

"Come on, then." If we're not going to dance, I'd rather

not stay in the courtyard. It's far too loud and close to make conversation easy, and I feel like Yorri will probably want to talk tonight. At least for a while.

We walk toward the north road, but for once I don't head for the wall. Halfway across the courtyard, I turn toward Yorri.

He's gone.

I thought he was following, but I don't see— Oh. There. He's standing stone-still twenty feet behind me, and he's staring at something as intently as a teegra spotting prey. No, the expression is softer than that. It's full of longing and loss and…

Even as I follow his line of sight, I know I'll find Sanii at the end of it.

I hate myself for it, especially when the pain their separation has caused is so plainly written in the air between them, but I'm selfish enough to be glad that Yorri has the option to do *anything* he wants to. Whether he wants to one day join the kaigo council or he spends his life no higher in rank than a nyshin-ma, he can. If he wants to oversee the forges or design a new way to protect the rooftop gardens from the vicious desert winds, he can.

The only choice the yonin are given is whether they'd prefer to serve the city in the kitchens, the farms, the nursery, the forge, the mines… They have choices, but none of them are worth a lifetime.

This moment, though? Sanii and Yorri need this. It doesn't feel like a goodbye to me, but I hope for Yorri's sake that it is. Holding on to a bond this deep with a yonin will only cause both of them pain.

Yorri blinks, turning his head like he can no longer bear to look in eir eyes. Sanii, though, doesn't drop eir gaze. Instead, ey looks at me.

Ey is short, the top of eir head only coming up to the shoulder of the yonin next to em. Eir long face is dominated by large eyes and full lips, a combination of features that should make em look childlike, but somehow doesn't. There's too much determination in the set of eir strong jaw and too much strength in eir stance. Ey inclines eir head in my direction and then flicks eir eyes toward Yorri. A silent request to look after him?

Blood and rot. What exactly does ey think I've been doing all his life? I've always— Or... Okay, no. Ey may have a point. My most recent plan to help almost killed us both. Maybe I do need the reminder.

I nod and then break away from eir intense gaze, turning to Yorri. This time, when I move toward the street that will take me to my barracks, he follows.

As we leave, I search the faces of the people around us. I hope no one noticed that moment. Neither of them have done anything wrong, but it could cause problems. For Yorri *and* Sanii. They'd watch them both closely, and even though I know a sumai bond is impossible now, I don't expect Yorri to suddenly cut off all contact with Sanii. Yorri and I have worked so hard to get him here; I don't want him to get in trouble for something that —

Mirisehs Varan and Suzu are walking through the square, their path close enough to us they could have seen if they'd been looking in our direction. If they'd been paying attention—*please* let them not have been paying attention.

Their indigo hoods are lowered, baring their straight black hair. Varan's is long enough now that it covers the tops of his ears and, in the back, brushes the bottom of his neck, and his sharp jawline is accented by a short beard. Suzu's hair is long, far longer than almost anyone else's in the clan, but it's only obvious on nights like tonight when it flows in a single black sheet down to the middle of her back. Their skin, like all the Miriseh, is the same soft beige as the sand on the shore, several shades lighter than the citizens of the city they guard.

Out of everyone in the city, Varan and Suzu are the last people I want to be aware of Yorri in this way. If the Miriseh are aware of Yorri, I want it to be because he's kynacho or because he saved my life, not because he hasn't figured out yet how to sever an attachment to a yonin.

Out the corner of my eye, I watch them walk and hope for them to pass us by.

Varan's head turns and his eyes lock on mine.

My heart stops. My breath catches in my throat. The step I was in the middle of taking freezes in midair.

But then he smiles. Varan brushes his hand against Suzu's and directs her attention toward us. Suzu is frowning when she turns, but the expression blanks when she spots us, her full lips going slack. When her gaze lingers on Yorri's retreating back, she whispers something to Varan, who nods. Only when both of them look at me does Suzu smile, but the expression is odd on her face. I don't think I've seen her smile before. If they're smiling, though, they didn't see Yorri and Sanii. They didn't notice. Or they don't care.

I exhale, the breath heavier and shakier than it should be, and my pulse beats as though I just sprinted through the mountains. Tentatively, I smile back, bowing my head in deference to their attention. Only when they look away and move through the crowd do I jog to catch up with my brother.

For the first time since I left the doseiku dorm, my brother can visit my room. All doors and windows are warded, the magic held in place by chunks of quartz embedded in the stone. Miriseh Suzu created the wards centuries ago, and only citizens with a wardcharm keyed to the stones can pass through the doors—or windows— without getting shocked. Painfully.

The Miriseh and the kaigo that serve them can go wherever they like. As a nyshin, the only rooms I can't walk into are the third floors of the bikyo-ko where the kaigo and the Miriseh have their chambers. For the ahdo class, the restrictions are tighter, keeping them out of the nyshin barracks and the top two floors of the bikyo-ko. Doseiku and yonin have access to very few buildings.

Yorri follows me into the barracks, glancing up at the two crystals embedded in the corners of the frame and then down at his left wristcuff and his new wardcharm. He rubs his right thumb along the morning star token as we climb the stairs to my room on the third floor.

Tomorrow he'll move his few belongings into the student mage barracks. Once his teachers decide he's mastered his new skills, he'll be assigned to a squad and given his duties. It won't be long for him, not with how quickly he's always mastered our lessons on meditation and magical theory. If I had to bet, I'd guess it'll be less than a moon cycle before he's moving into a barracks with his squad. Maybe into *this* barracks.

It's unlikely, but not impossible.

"It's quiet here," he says when he walks into my room.

"It took a while to get used to." The doseiku dormitory is connected to the training yard, and the training yard is used day and night. We grew up with the sounds of bellowing officers and the clash of iron as constant background noise, but my squad is quartered half a mile away from the yard.

"I think being alone would be harder." He sits on the end of my sleep mat and leans back against the stone wall.

He's right. My room here is small, only six feet by eight feet, but it has stone hooks and shelves for clothes and armor and weapons, a padded mat for sleeping, and privacy. "That was the second-hardest thing to get used to."

From our infancy, we're raised with our yearmates, first in the nursery and later in the doseiku dorms. We progress through all of our training with the same group of children we were born with. It means we know our yearmates extremely well—sometimes too well—by the time we face our herynshi, but it also means that moments alone are rare.

Even after becoming a citizen, privacy isn't guaranteed. The yonin sleep in dorm-style caverns like the doseiku do. Lower-rank ahdo share quarters with two or three others from their squad. Growing up, we all joked that wanting to be placed nyshin was less about serving the clan and more about finally getting a room to ourselves and a moment of peace.

But now we have peace, and I have no idea what to say. Congratulating him on his new rank feels wrong after what I witnessed with Sanii, but I'm not going to pretend to be sorry he's here. Biting the inside of my bottom lip, I wait to see if there's something on *his* mind.

"I wanted to ask you, when you told me about the herynshi, why didn't you mention the stone?" Yorri asks.

"What stone? Almost the whole island is stone." I don't— Oh. At the end of the herynshi, after Miriseh Varan declared my class and Miriseh Suzu anointed my face and hands, Kaigo Neeva—Tessen's blood-mother—pressed a worn piece of glittering black stone to the center of my forehead. That has to be what Yorri means. "I forgot about it. It didn't mean anything compared to the rest."

Yorri blinks, lines appearing across his forehead. "You didn't feel it?"

"Feel what?"

"It felt like the earth shifted. I almost collapsed. If Neeva hadn't moved it, I…" He shudders, wincing and then rolling his shoulder as though he's trying to force himself to calm down. "It was awful. It was what I think it'd feel like to get trapped in Kujuko."

Kujuko? Every muscle in my body tenses so fast that I bite the tip of my tongue.

"It…it did? It felt like Kujuko?" Serve the clan with honor and skill, and no matter your class and rank, the Miriseh will grant you passage to Ryogo. If you're deemed unworthy or, worse, disloyal, death will leave you trapped in the depthless nothingness of Kujuko for eternity.

Yorri nods slowly. "I don't know how else to explain it. You really felt nothing?"

"Nothing but the stone. It was warm, but that was probably from Neeva's hand." I swallow, cringing slightly when my tongue throbs with the motion. "Are you sure it wasn't blood loss?" Injuries that severe aren't common during the herynshi, though, and Yorri hadn't mentioned that he'd been hurt. "Or maybe it was exhaustion?"

It's not unheard of. Warriors who have survived extreme battles nearly without a scratch have sometimes collapsed afterward for hours—sometimes a full day.

"That's what Neeva said." His tone conveys doubt.

"Then I'm sure that's right. She's seen a lot of people face the herynshi, remember. And you feel well now?" I crouch next to him and press my hand to his cheek, checking for extra warmth. He's overwarm, but that, and the way the desosa in the air around him seems drawn to him, seems to be his new normal.

Yorri smiles at my worry. "Yes, Khya. I feel fine."

"Well, good." I let my hand fall away and stand. "Maybe

all you need is a quiet night of sleep. You'll be too busy in the morning to even remember you felt poorly."

My brother gets to his feet, faintly amused smile still in place. "Wise advice as always, Nyshin-ten."

"It comes with my advanced age." A little more of my worry eases when he laughs softly, more of a heavy breath than anything, but enough for now. When he turns for the door, I catch his arm and pull him back. He comes easily. With one hand gripping the back of his neck and the other holding his shoulder, I press our foreheads together and look him in the eye.

"I *am* proud of you, little brother. I know there are things you lost, but I'm proud of what you've become." Pulling back, I glance up at the sky. "Maybe you'll be the one to figure out how to make the early storms work for us and invent a better water storage system."

"I'll see what I can do." Yorri smiles, only a tiny trace of sadness in the expression, and then he presses a kiss to my forehead. Neither of us says any more of a goodbye as my little brother leaves, heading back to the doseiku dormitory for the last time.

CHAPTER
SEVEN

've heard the Miriseh's speech before the herynshi celebration over a hundred times, once a moon ever since I was ten. It doesn't change much from one moon cycle to the next. The biggest difference is usually the names Mirisehs Varan and Suzu call out. Sometimes, though, they deliver crucial edicts or regulations as well. It's quicker than passing information through the ranks.

It's happening now. I hold my breath, waiting.

"In the five hundred years since we became guardians of this clan, we've never seen Shiara as angry as she's been the last two moons. To protect this city and its citizens, we pulled everyone we could back to the safety of Sagen sy Itagami." Miriseh Varan's deep voice booms through the square, echoing off the walls of the buildings surrounding the broad, open expanse. Even when he stops speaking, it's as though I can still feel his words reverberating through the courtyard.

Over the past moon, there have been five storms including the one that hit a few days ago while my squad was on the wall. After the first out-of-season storm, it took days before we stopped eyeing the sky. When thirty nyshin died during the fourth storm two weeks ago, after the bodies we recovered were laid out in the saishigi core, the Miriseh finally called a retreat, halving the number of squads sent out to guard the borders.

Death may be inevitable, but that doesn't mean any of us want to be swept off to Ryogo in a flash flood.

Varan places one hand over his heart. "Tonight we have to rescind that caution."

Oh, no. I exhale heavily. Beside me, Etaro tenses, and Rai looks back at us from her position a row ahead. The rest of the squad is shifting uneasily. Around us, whispers spread through the clan quicker than a breeze and just as quiet. I keep my eyes on the Miriseh and the carved walls of the bikyo-ko behind them.

"Two days ago, one of our border patrols found the remnants of a campfire high in the southeastern hills." Suzu's hairpin blades glint in the firelight; her long hair and the pins she uses to contain it are as much a symbol of her rank and status as her indigo hood or the sun-shaped wardcharm on her wristcuff. "Yesterday, a Denhitran raiding party was spotted by an oraku mage, but the distance was more than half a mile and the enemy escaped into the mountains. Today, two squads were ambushed. Only ten of the twenty-six nyshin made it to safety."

Blood and rot. The wardstones and the base camps in the desert have helped us keep all of our battles miles away from the city. The last full war was a century ago, and it was devastating enough that neither side has tried to launch an attack that big again. If they're risking crossing as far into our territory as the Kyiwa Mountains, though?

It could mean nothing, just a raiding party looking to

steal resources the same as always, and bellows I hope that's the case. There's little hope of victory if they attempt to lay siege to Itagami; the outer wall is ten feet thick and constantly guarded, and then, even if they somehow broke into the city, traps set to be sprung by the ishiji stone mages would crush them in minutes. The attempt would be a needless waste of life. For us and for them.

"We cannot let this trespass continue or the deaths remain unavenged." Varan steps closer to the edge of the dais. The angle of the firelight changes, picking out the thin strands of gray in his otherwise black hair and making his skin look almost white. "If they believe we've left our gates unguarded, they'll attempt to take what we built for you. We must show them that our recent caution is not weakness."

Suzu steps up next to him. "It's true there will be a risk if the storms continue, but it's one we must ask you to take for the safety of the clan."

Behind Varan and Suzu, the twelve members of the kaigo council and the eight additional Miriseh create a solid wall. Kaigo Anda and Kaigo Ono are there, nothing but determination on their faces. Their expressions are mirrored in the expression of every other council member.

I study them, trying to picture Yorri and me standing where our blood-parents are now. I have plenty of time to imagine it, because neither Varan nor Suzu speaks again for several long moments. They stand at the front of the dais, surveying the clan. There are ten thousand people in the courtyard, but as Varan's and Suzu's eyes sweep across the square, it feels like they're looking directly at *me*. From the way Rai is shifting in front of me, I wouldn't be shocked if she feels the same, like their eyes have somehow picked her out of the massive crowd.

The silence stretches long enough that we're not the only ones physically fighting off discomfort. Then, finally, Varan speaks.

"Because this is a more dangerous—life-threatening—task that we're asking you to complete, no one will be commanded to leave the city. If you wish to remain inside Itagami's walls, speak to your commanding officer. You will be given less dangerous responsibilities."

And you will be seen as a weakling who's left someone else to risk their life instead.

Varan doesn't say that, but I can't be the only one who understands the implications a request like that would carry. The only acceptable reason to turn down a responsibility assigned to a squad would be if your presence endangered other lives. Anyone doing it now, without that reason and knowing they're putting someone else's life in the line of a possible storm? Unthinkable. Someone willing to do that would never earn their place in Ryogo.

The Miriseh chant, "Serve the clan and you'll find your rewards in Ryogo."

"The safety of the clan comes before our lives. Urah!"

The drums start, each thud resonating off the stone walls and creating a rallying cry that carries high into the night.

"Am I the only one thinking that sounds a little too much like thunder to be enjoyable tonight?" Rai asks, watching our clan shift, the rigid, evenly spaced formation of the vigil giving way to the scattered groups and pleasant chaos of the celebration.

The drumbeats quicken, one pulse bleeding into another, and I shudder.

"At least we're *dry*." Etaro eyes the currently clear sky, and

I glance up, too, my eyes catching on the thousands of spots of light spread out across the sky. "I've missed being dry."

Rai shakes her head. "Don't get used to it. The actual storm season is less than four weeks out. We'll be drenched almost every day this time next moon."

They wander toward the tables of wine and food along the south side of the courtyard—I can smell the roasting mykyn meat from here—but I stay near the central tokiansu circles; I'm looking for Yorri.

He finds me before I spot him, slipping into place at my side. I hold back my greeting when my eyes meet his. Something that might be shock is widening his eyes.

There's a moment of silence, a breath, and then he quietly says, "They placed me with a squad. My first shift is in the morning."

"Under whose command?" I try, and fail, not to hope that I'll hear Tyrroh's name.

He clears his throat, but his voice still cracks when he says, "Kaigo Neeva."

"You're to serve directly under one of the kaigo?" Any disappointment I might've felt is crushed by a swell of pride. There are only twelve kaigo, and two of them are our blood-parents, Anda and Ono. "Bellows and blood. In that squad, you'll outrank me before half a year has gone!" I laugh and clap him on the shoulder. "We *have* to celebrate this. Do you feel like dancing tonight?"

He glances at the scattered tokiansu circles in use, but I'm not sure from his expression if he's leaning more toward a yes or a no. Then his eyes light up. "Willing to try the tessens?"

"Absolutely."

We jog toward the weapons racks set up on either side of the bikyo-ko dais, winding through the crowd to get there. Each of us chooses a tessen, a heavy fan made of viciously sharp iron blades and brightly dyed nyska paper. They're impractical in battle, but perfect for nights like this.

The trip back into the center of the square is slower; this time we're looking for an empty dance ring. It takes a couple minutes of searching before we find one.

I stand in the middle of the circle etched deep into the warm stone beneath our bare feet and face Yorri, six feet of empty space dividing us. Both of us raise our right arms, tessens held aloft, and let the thudding drumbeats fill our minds. Sixteen beats later, we begin.

Each weapon used for the tokiansu has its own personality, and each gives the dance a different feel. Holding tudo swords, the dance becomes something almost like a battle. The length and flexibility of the suraki feels more like performing visible magic. With the tessens, it's something else.

Dancing with tessens is like trying to become air.

Yorri and I move easily around each other, his new speed giving him more than enough time to adjust to each shift I make. We twirl and duck and spin, the tessens either wielded like daggers or locked open and tossed high into the air. We leap over each other to catch the falling spots of red and yellow before they hit the ground. The movements take us to the very edge of the circle surrounding us and back into the center, so close I can feel the heat radiating from Yorri and see the droplets of sweat beading on his tawny skin. Several times we switch fans, tossing them across the circle for the other one to catch and then spinning away with our prize, letting the way the fan catches on the currents of air guide the shapes our bodies take.

Unlike tokiansus with tudos or surakis, the tessen doesn't require a victor. The dance simply moves like the breeze until, also like the breeze, it fades. We dance, in constant motion and in wonderful synchronization until the dance comes to a natural end.

We end how we began, facing each other in the middle of the circle, but this time I'm nearly panting with the exertion of the performance and flushed with the joy of dancing with a well-matched partner. He's breathing quicker than normal but not as heavily as I am, and there's a broad smile on his face.

"We attracted a crowd." I nod toward the audience, and Yorri's grin grows wider. Then his jaw goes slack, something behind me catching his attention. I follow his gaze. Oh. Miriseh bless us.

Kaigo Anda and Kaigo Ono stand in the inner circle of the audience, their heads tilted toward each other but their eyes trained on us.

"Do you think they watched from the beginning?" I ask him quietly.

Ono whispers to Anda. When she nods, they approach.

Yorri audibly swallows. "I suppose we can ask, if you want."

Our blood-parents stop a few feet away from us. We cross our arms at the wrists, the tessens swung down to line up with our forearms so we can press our closed fists to our shoulders as we bow.

"No need for that tonight," Anda says with laughter in her voice. It doesn't matter how often I hear her speak; the high, soft tone of her voice is always surprising. She looks so much like me I expect to hear a lower, throatier tone. "In fact, we should be saluting you two."

"Don't get carried away," Ono chides. There's a smirk curving his lips. Yorri and I inherited Anda's pointed chin and close-set eyes, but the shape of our noses—broad at the base with a much narrower bridge—and the slope of our smiles come from Ono.

"When you both were young we thought you'd do great things, but I think you've managed to surprise us." Anda shakes her head, smilingly disbelieving. "A fykina and a kynacho—the impenetrable and the unstoppable."

"I told you we should have tried for a third." Ono gestures to us, but looks at Anda. "The three of them would be on their way to taking over the kaigo council by now."

Anda jabs Ono in the side. "And I told you that'd only happen if the hishingu figured out how to let *you* carry the child to term, so hush."

Laughing, Ono runs his hand over his sukhai's short, tightly curled hair before his expression becomes a little more serious. "You've both done very well. We're looking forward to seeing what you become."

"It should certainly be an interesting time," Anda says. Then, in full view of the clan, two kaigo who have the ear of the Miriseh bow to us.

"May your service to the clan earn you honors in Ryogo," Ono says.

When they straighten, there's a glimmer in Anda's eyes, as though she knows exactly the kind of stir they just caused and revels in the knowledge. I've seen that look in Yorri's eyes too often not to recognize it. Then, before Yorri and I have a chance to say a single thing, they're walking east toward the bikyo-ko where the kaigo are quartered.

Just like every other encounter with them, I'm left blinking in their wake. One day, maybe I'll feel capable of having a conversation with them instead of staring with hero worship in my eyes.

"I hate how my tongue stops working as soon as they

come within ten feet of me," Yorri grumbles.

"You and me both, little brother." I fan myself with the tessen, my eyes still tracking Anda and Ono's path. "Can you imagine if there *had* been three of us, though?"

"Horrifying." His voice is wry, and there's a smirk on his face when I look. "The training masters would all shudder at the very thought of it."

I snap the tessen shut and use it to smack his shoulder. "They wish they were lucky enough to get another one of us."

He laughs, grabbing my tessen when I try to hit him with it again, the motion so fast it's like the fan vanished from my hand only to reappear in his.

"Nice." I pat my brother on the back and grin at him, all the pride of his earlier announcement flooding back into me. "Come on. I don't think anything else that might happen tonight could be better than that. Let's get you moved into your new barracks. You've got to impress Kaigo Neeva in the morning."

"I still can't believe that." Yorri groans and tips his head back to the blue-black star-speckled sky and then rubs his hand over his face. Straightening, he rolls his shoulders and then looks down at the tessens in his hand. "It's too much too fast, Khya. I'm going to mess it up."

"You won't. Trust your training and follow orders instead of questioning every little thing. That's all you need to do."

Nodding slowly, Yorri turns toward the weapon racks so we can clean and put away our borrowed fans.

As we leave the courtyard, I pretend not to see the glance Yorri shoots at a group of yonin gathered by the northern edge of the courtyard.

I pretend I don't see Sanii there looking back at him, too.

CHAPTER EIGHT

We left Itagami the morning after the celebration, before the sun had cleared the mountains, and have been on the move ever since we checked in with the nyshin-co commander of the region's border fort.

The Denhitran incursions have gotten worse.

Nyshin-ma Tyrroh is an oraku, but even his enhanced vision, hearing, and smell can't pinpoint the path the Denhitrans took through the Kyiwa Mountains. We've been chasing old trails instead of new marks for two days. It's meant days searching the desert for the elusive enemy. Elusive to an absurd degree. From the reports we've heard the few times that another squad's path crossed ours, no one else has had much luck, either.

The Denhitrans have never been this hard to track before.

My eyes burn, dried out by wind and exhaustion. I've slept less than ten hours in the last four days and none of those hours were back-to-back. The sun beats down from a cloudless sky, blazingly hot even through the layers of cloth that are supposed to protect me.

When was the last time we stopped moving long enough to sit down? Hours ago? A day? I can't remember. It's been at least that long since I've had anything to eat that wasn't dried and salted beyond all recognition.

But there's work to do, so the rest of my squad and I push the exhaustion aside, chewing byka beans to stay awake until our jaws hurt, our hands shake, and our eyelids twitch.

We're protected from the sun, for the moment at least, by an outcropping of rock. The shade it casts is barely wide enough for half the squad to fit underneath, but it's worth the close squeeze to be out of the relentless light for a few minutes while Tyrroh and Nyshin-pa Daitsa scout ahead, leaving Nyshin-ten Ryzo in command of the squad.

That was almost three-quarters of an hour ago, though.

They've been gone long enough that Ryzo left, too, a few minutes ago. If none of them return in the next ten minutes, we're under orders to run straight to the border base five miles from here and send up a call for reinforcements.

"It's like they know where we're going to be before we do." Etaro's tone might sound like a whine if any of us had the energy left to whine. Even eir usual habit of hovering small stones above eir hand is halfhearted—the normally complex patterns that ey says help em think, simple and repetitive.

"Maybe they do." Rai is leaning against the wall of rock, her head tipped back and her eyes closed. "Maybe they found an akuringu mage."

"Blood and rot, I hope not," I mutter. Mages with the power to scry, to see across the island—or, if they're powerful, a short time into the future—are rare. They're rarer than fykina-level ward mages like me and basaku-level sensor mages like Tessen combined. "If they did, why wouldn't they use it to wipe out the squads searching for them?"

"I wouldn't." Etaro squints over the shoulders of the people standing in front of us, eir dancing stones pausing midflight and eir eyes on the direction Tyrroh and the others took. The direction Ryzo followed. "It'd put the enemy on guard too much."

"If they have an akuringu, they seem to be using the skill to evade us." Rai rubs her hands over her face. Her atakafu is pushed down under her chin, and both it and her usually sandstone-colored skin are coated with a thick layer of desert dust. "Which means they're either searching for a way to get their whole army through our border wards without detection or... I don't even know. Something worse."

"What could possibly be worse than that?" I ask.

Etaro shudders, eir narrow face pinched. "Not sure I want to find out."

Rocks scrape. We look left, those closest to the outer edge of the shade moving away from the rocks and silently drawing their weapons. Rai slips through the close-pressed bodies and rubs her hands together, her kasaiji magic creating sparks between her palms. I breathe in, drawing on the desosa around me to fuel my wards. Beside me, Etaro drops the pebbles and mentally raises three rocks the size of eir head, holding them in the air in front of em.

Tyrroh, Ryzo, and Daitsa appear over the rise.

We all exhale when we see them, lowering weapons and releasing pent-up power.

"Enemy incoming!" Tyrroh's warning blasts over us.

Swords come up and magic rises so quickly I feel the

ripples through the desosa surrounding the squad, their fear making it prick like thorns against my skin.

I glance at Etaro, wishing I could erase the echoes of our conversation from my head.

If they did, why wouldn't they use it to wipe out the squads searching for them?

Is that what's coming for us over the rise? I shudder.

Shoving to the front of the squad, I draw the desosa in like cloth draws water, shoring up my own magic with that energy. I wait for Tyrroh to pass me before I build my ward. If I'm fast enough, if I make it strong enough, I might be able to trap every single rot-ridden Denhitran in the pass and then—

Daitsa's shoulder slams into mine.

I'm not braced for it. She was running full speed. We fall.

The stone and hard-packed earth drive the air from my lungs. Bellows, that's going to bruise. I try to breathe. Sharp pain stings and then settles into a dull, constant ache. Blood and rot, I think the contusion goes as deep as my ribs.

"Bellows, Khya! I'm sorry." Daitsa is on her feet first. She grabs my wrist to haul me up. By the time we're standing and turning to face the Denhitrans running over the rise, it's too late for a ward to trap them.

They're here.

Daitsa blocks a blow meant for my stomach, but there's another aimed for her neck. Gritting my teeth against the pain in my side, I shove Daitsa out of the way of an enemy blade, thrusting a ward up between us and them.

At least ten Denhitrans have already clashed with my squad, and more are coming. A wall isn't an option. The most I can do now is use my wards to deflect as many blows as I can.

I stand in the center of the limited space, trying to watch and react to everything at once.

A dagger aimed toward Ryzo's back. Deflect it; not too much power or he won't—

No! Bellows. Enemy barreling toward Daitsa and me with lightning sparking in his palm. Ward wall to contain the magic. Break it when one of the squad is ready to—

Ryzo turns to slash at the throat of the enemy who almost stabbed him. They dodge the attack. I can do it, create a ward at ankle-height, just long enough to trip the enemy and—

A scream in a familiar voice. Rai. She throws fire at two Denhitrans coming over the rise. One of them absorbs the heat, prepares to throw it back. I can ward that. Protect her—

Stone meets the enemy's head before the fireball leaves the kasaiji mage's hands. Etaro's projectile found its target. The mage crumples; the soldier standing next to them runs. Coward.

I sneer at the dust they leave in their wake. How could anyone leave their squad and—

No. Wait. They're *all* running.

"Move!" Tyrroh bellows, leading the squad after the enemy.

We chase them through the mountains for hours, but no matter how hard we push or how fast we run, we never get within sight of them again. It's nearing nightfall and we're closing in on the Suesutu Pass far to the southwest of Itagami before Tyrroh calls a halt.

"They've probably found their way back to whatever Kujuko-cursed cave has been hiding them so well." Tyrroh's mouth and nose are covered by the atakafu, but I think that's disgust I see carved into the lines around his eyes.

"We're heading back to Itagami. We'll report to the border base's nyshin-co on the way, but I want us back inside the city before noon tomorrow."

Ryzo looks in the direction of the brief battle, confusion in his oval eyes. "Sir, shouldn't we collect the bodies first? At least one of them might still be alive, and we could—"

"No." Tyrroh shakes his head. "My priority is getting you all back alive. I wouldn't be surprised if the enemy has already circled back to collect their dead and wounded. It's what I would've done." He turns north. "Move out!"

The squad falls into two tight columns with practiced ease behind Nyshin-ma Tyrroh and Nyshin-pa Daitsa. I almost always bring up the rear, my wards ready in case of attack, but who runs by my side changes. Today it's Ryzo matching my steps as we run back to the border base. Rai and Etaro are directly in front of us.

I look behind us, thinking about the chase we're abandoning and the futile hunt of the last several days and how easily the Denhitrans turned and ran, when every other time I've faced them, they've fought down to the last soldier. It doesn't make sense.

"I think you were right," I say to Rai. "That wasn't a real fight, not from them. They're here for something else."

Ryzo looks at me, his attention locked to the side long enough that he trips over a dip in the path. He catches himself before he falls. Rai casts a look back over her shoulder before she rolls her eyes at me. "Tell me something I *haven't* figured out."

Not much later, we stop at a tiny spring-fed pool, something a brilliant ishiji mage created two generations ago, shaping the stone to capture water from all across the mountain during the rains and feed it into this drinking pool. There's shade, too. It should be a moment to breathe, to relax the overused muscles and bones, but Ryzo is standing stiffer than ever, holding himself with too much caution.

"Are you okay?" I check for injuries that might be causing him pain even though the idea of it is ridiculous. Ryzo is a hishingu. He'd have to be drained and near death to not be able to heal himself.

"Did you..." Ryzo presses his lips together, his square jaw clenched, and shakes his head.

"Did I what?" I ask when he doesn't continue.

Ryzo looks north, his broad shoulders tense. Lines and creases I usually see only when he's in the middle of a healing are deeply etched into the bronze skin around his eyes, all that's visible between his atakafu and his hood. Seeming to make up his mind, he leans closer to me and whispers so quietly it's barely louder than the wind. "I thought I saw the nyshin-ma *talking* to one of the Denhitrans."

"What? No!" I keep my voice just as quiet. Tyrroh is standing away from the group, looking out over the terrain to the north and speaking quietly to Daitsa. It's only about fifty feet—maybe seventy-five—so Tyrroh could easily hear us from this distance if he were concentrating on listening, but if we speak softly enough we might not catch his attention.

"Khya, I *saw* him standing within fifty yards of the enemy. No weapons drawn and no—" He shakes his head and hisses, "It wasn't right."

My heart is pounding, but not at the thought of Tyrroh hearing us. Tyrroh wouldn't betray the clan. Wouldn't and couldn't. He's the one who taught me what it meant to truly serve the city. He encouraged me to chase the promotions I want, but still challenges me to earn them. There is no conceivable way he would be a traitor to everything we both believe in.

But he's an oraku. His magic is in his senses, in the enhancement of his sight, smell, and hearing. There's no reason for him to be within sight of the enemy without drawing a weapon, because his magic wouldn't do anything to protect him against theirs.

If that's actually what Ryzo saw.

"How far away were you?"

He blinks. "I don't—less than a quarter mile."

"And how long did you see him before the situation changed?"

After a quick glance toward Tyrroh and Daitsa, he says, "Not long. A few seconds."

"So you could be wrong?" The Miriseh are fair and just, except when it comes to *this*. Shiara is dangerous. Our enemies are even more so. Even the breath of a rumor of treason can destroy someone's life. It can end it. It can bar them from ever entering Ryogo.

I refuse to believe that Tyrroh is capable of anything that even hints at treachery, no matter what Ryzo thinks he saw. The easier answer—and the only one I'll believe—is that Ryzo is wrong. "Are you sure? Because you know what will happen if you breathe a word of this to anyone."

He bites his lip, looks toward Tyrroh, and shakes his head. "If the mage was rikinhisu, they might've been holding him against his will. Or he might've been tricked by a rusosa illusion into thinking he was talking to another nyshin. Or… Bellows, Khya, I don't know."

"Exactly. There could be a hundred reasons for what you think you saw." Relief rattles through my exhale. "Especially because after that moment, he…"

"He broke away and ran back to the squad." Ryzo takes a long breath and lets it out slowly, smiling a little. "Maybe exhaustion is making me paranoid."

"It's possible." I keep a smile on my face, trying to pretend my heart isn't pounding far too hard and fast under my bruised ribs. "If I don't get a full meal before the end of the day tomorrow, I might forget what real food tastes like."

"Food, a long soak in the bathing pools, and an entire night of uninterrupted sleep." Ryzo sighs, his gaze turning distant and wistful. "Soon, hopefully."

"Soon," I agree. "Although, since I have your attention, any chance you can fix this?" I raise my arm, gesturing with my other hand to the site of the bruise.

Eyebrows furrowing, Ryzo gently places his hand over the site. To me, hishingu magic feels like water, cool and soothing as it sinks into my skin and begins to fix whatever is broken. He hisses through his teeth when he finds the injury, shaking his head at me and muttering about my tendency to collect bruises.

"I know," I tell him, smiling wryly. "But that's really only the other kind. The ones I used to get with you were a lot more fun."

He laughs, the sound muffled by his atakafu but the memories of the moons right after I joined the squad dancing in his eyes.

In a few moments, the bruise is healed enough that breathing no longer hurts. When I thank Ryzo, he squeezes my upper arm before he walks away.

My ribs may be better, but the thoughts he leaves me with are worse. Our conversation echoes in my head, and the repetition doesn't make the accusations any easier to hear. It doesn't matter. They're false, and Ryzo won't say anything because he isn't sure what he saw, and everything will be fine, and—

Rai and Etaro slide into place at my side, pulling me away from my dangerously spinning thoughts. Especially when Etaro asks, "What was Ryzo being so serious about?" Eir eyes follow Ryzo for a moment before returning to me. "Are you two starting something again? I thought he had a thing now with the guy and the ebet quartered in the Southeastern Zon, the nyshin-pa who— Bellows. What were their names?"

"It doesn't matter what their names are." I flick a pebble in eir direction. "And no, I'm not going to be sleeping with Ryzo again."

"You'd think someone who has no interest in lying with *anyone* would care less about everyone else's bed partners," Rai says to me, amusement and affection softening her round face.

"I was just asking!" There's a smirk in Etaro's eyes. "I take an interest in the lives of all of my friends."

Rai laughs. "Should I invite you to watch next time I bring someone back to the barracks?"

Etaro's eyes narrow and the bridge of eir nose wrinkles. "No. Definitely not. Hearing about it after is enough."

They fall into line and continue bickering about sex and who Rai should take to bed next, distracting themselves enough that I don't have to bother trying. Which is good, because I don't know what I would say if they asked about my conversation with Ryzo again.

When the squad leaves the shaded resting space and moves toward the border base, Ryzo is running next to me again. This time, he's silent. Which is good. Definitely good. I don't want to talk to anyone about anything right now.

I run the rest of the way home with my focus squarely

on the ground, inspecting each dip, crevice, and rise that I run over. I refuse to think about the Denhitrans' rot-ridden presence or their inexplicable cowardice. I refuse to wonder why we're turning back to the city instead of continuing the hunt—tired or not, we could have made it another day if we pushed ourselves.

I definitely don't think at all, even a little bit, about how, even among all the possible explanations for the position he'd seen Tyrroh in, Ryzo didn't offer a single one that simply said, "I was wrong, and I didn't see what I thought I did."

CHAPTER NINE

My dreams are full of water.

The squad is trapped under the roiling waves of the ocean, each person caught in a current that's threatening to carry them away. I'm hovering above them all, fighting to reach them but stuck. All I can do is ward them, send them bubbles of air that won't last long.

I'm cold, impossibly cold. My own breathing gets strained and tight, panicked. The farther the currents carry them from one another, from me, the harder it is to protect all of them. Rai is fighting toward the surface, but the waves tumble her over and over until it seems like she doesn't know which way is up anymore. Etaro's eyes are closed, eir body limp. Was the air for em too late?

I can't be too late. I *can't*.

Tyrroh shakes his head when I try to ward him. Though his eyes are wide and strained and precious bubbles of air stream from his lips, he points. The others, he seems to be saying. Save the others.

No, I try to scream. *I'm not leaving you behind. I'm not leaving anyone.*

He shakes his head again just as Rai's fight against the current weakens. She's running out of time. Tyrroh points at the others again, one more time before someone spears him, someone dressed in the darkly dyed cloth of the Denhitrans. He doesn't fight as the enemy pulls him away from us.

Rai stops moving. Etaro is gone.

Ryzo is watching me with fear and blame in his eyes.

This is your fault. You didn't listen. You didn't save us. You didn't—

A hand on my shoulder. Someone saying my name.

"Khya. Wake up, Khya."

The water drains away.

I sit up gasping. Something is wrong. My pulse is pounding, but my vision is a blur of light and dark.

Was I asleep? Yes. I was. I fell asleep in the barracks when we got back to the city in the late afternoon. There shouldn't be any danger here.

"Khya, it's…it's about Yorri." Is that Tessen? What is Tessen doing in my room? I blink at him, trying to focus.

Tessen is crouching next to my bedroll, he's not smiling for once, and he's filthy. His rich brown skin is three shades paler because he's absolutely covered in desert dust, and there are several scratches on his face and arms, some barely healed. He's even still carrying two zeeka blades strapped to his back. I know the look of someone just returning from a brutal border shift, but there's no reason for Tessen to come straight to me after one.

Worry begins to bite. "What about Yorri?"

"Yorri is—he…" Tessen shuts his eyes and rubs his hand over his face.

My stomach drops. "He *what*?"

If his squad finally found the Denhitrans we fought, or met up with a larger group, he might be hurt. He's a kynacho, though; he should've been too fast to have sustained any injury bad enough to keep him from coming to me himself.

I blink. If Yorri isn't here, and Tessen is looking at me like that...

"Khya," Tessen starts, his voice hoarse, almost raw. "Yorri died tonight. He died protecting Kaigo Neeva. It— they couldn't save him."

My stomach rolls when I force myself to stand. "That isn't funny."

"It isn't a— I wouldn't joke about—" He shakes his head, his eyes wide and more sincerely earnest than I've ever seen them. "I would never, Khya, you *must* know that."

I do. I do know that. But that means...

A chilling numbness starts in the center of my ribs and slowly spreads, seeping into every bone, muscle, and sinew. My legs tremble, and I brace myself against the wall.

Failure! some corner of my mind is shrieking at me. *You were supposed to protect him and you failed. He died not even a week into his service, and where were* you?

When I step away from the support of the stone, Tessen's hands hover as though ready to reach out and catch me. I don't need the help. "Where is he?"

Swallowing, Tessen glances out my window, toward the center of the city...and Hishingu Hall. "That's why I came for you. I was coming into the city when they carried him in and they...they're preparing him for saishigi, but I thought—I knew you'd want to say goodbye."

Saishigi. The last service any clan member can give, and the moment the Miriseh either anoint the body left behind to grant the soul passage to the afterlife in Ryogo, or punish them for their failure by tethering the soul between worlds, leaving them trapped in Kujuko.

That won't be Yorri's fate. If he gave his life to protect one of the kaigo, there's no chance the Miriseh will keep him from Ryogo.

"Thank you." I tell my head to nod, but I can't tell if it listens. "It was...kind of you to come." I might not have known otherwise, not until tomorrow when Yorri was already laid in the core and gone. Unless a special request is made, usually only sumai bondmates attend the final rites. They'll make an exception for a blood relative, though. They have to. They *have* to.

The completion of a single footstep has never taken this much concentration before. My whole mind zeroes in on the task, maintaining my balance and placing one foot and then the other on the cool stone of the floor. Down the stairs. Through the door. Turning toward—

No. Don't think about the destination, think about movement. Each bit of progress forward. One step and then another.

I know most of the city's twists and hidden alcoves by heart from the free days Yorri and I spent exploring it as children, but I've never been so grateful for that knowledge as I am now. It allows me to walk without thinking about exactly where I'm going or why.

Too soon, I find myself at Hishingu Hall, staring at a doorway I walked out of only two moons ago. I stop on the threshold, stalled in the doorway as though there's a ward barring the entrance. If I walk much farther, I'll see it. I'll see him. This will all be true.

"Come on, Khya." Tessen's hand rests on my elbow, the contact making me flinch. I didn't— He's still here? He is, and he's watching me closely, his eyes likely seeing far more than I want him to. Even more than his already-enhanced senses give him access to. "I'll take you to where they're waiting."

When he reaches out to touch my elbow again, I don't shake it off. The pressure of his fingers is light, guiding me through the torch-lit building, past the long, open halls and into one of the smaller saishigi chambers. There are people already inside—more than I expected. I don't recognize anyone except Kaigo Neeva.

She's standing at the head of the raised stone platform in the center of the room, her brown skin and short hair pale with the grime of the desert. Laid out on the platform in front of her is a body, one already almost completely covered by a saishigi shroud. Only the face remains exposed. I can't bring myself to look at it yet.

"Your brother saved my life." Neeva's rich voice is full of sympathy. "His place in Ryogo is assured."

Yes. He gave his life for the clan, but a place in Ryogo isn't the only reason I drove him to become nyshin. I wanted him here with me *now*.

Several bruised, battered, and bedraggled nyshin stand against the walls, watchful but keeping a respectful distance. Members of Neeva's team, maybe. Those who were there when—

I can't avoid it any longer.

Before I make myself look at his face, I press my fingers against his throat, hope and denial almost enough to trick me into thinking I feel a pulse flutter once under my fingertips.

Not even hope makes it happen twice.

My eyes lock on his face and a tremor runs through my body, almost strong enough to make my knees buckle.

Miriseh, no.

I never thought Tessen was lying—no one would be that cruel—but somehow I'd stupidly hoped that he was wrong, that maybe it hadn't been Yorri, only someone on Yorri's squad, and we would get here and Yorri would look at me with confusion in his eyes when I threw my arms around his neck and—

No. That's my brother on the platform, his body as still as the stone he's lying on.

How did he die?

I want to ask, but I can't make the words leave my tongue. There are no wounds on his head. Not a scratch or single bloodstain anywhere I can see. My fingers trail down over his cheek. His skin is still warm. If I didn't know better, if he weren't already half wrapped in the red-and-blue-dyed saishigi shroud, I'd swear he was sleeping.

His oval face is relaxed, slack and tranquil, but his skin is too pale. It's the kind of shade I saw on his face when he broke his arm or ended up with a dagger embedded in his thigh, when pain is so bad that it drains his skin of color.

But he isn't in pain anymore. Whatever he once suffered is over now.

I run my fingers over Yorri's untamable black hair. The strands are thick, with more than a little bit of a curl. He didn't like it too long, but he's been busy the last few moons. It got away from him, the wavy locks covering the top of his ears. Only a little shorter than mine.

Knowing I don't have much time left, I flatten my hand over my brother's heart and close my eyes.

Wait for me in Ryogo; your service here is done.

The prayer for the dead rises in my mind, the words clogging in my throat. I shouldn't have to say goodbye like this so soon.

Let go the trials of Shiara; your eternity has begun.

Even in my head, I can't get through the whole thing. Not at once. Not yet.

After I open my eyes and pull my hand away, the hishingu secures the last fold of the shroud over his face.

"As he was in life, so shall he be in death. The soul has left this world, but the body can still serve Sagen sy Itagami." Neeva's words are softly spoken as she draws the nyshin morning star on the cloth almost directly over Yorri's forehead with a stick of charcoal. "We send him into Ryogo with our thanks, and hope we will see him again when our time has come."

Two of Neeva's squad come forward to lift him from the stone platform. No! I almost push their hands away. I want to carry him like he carried me during the storm, but I can't. I don't trust myself to do it. I'm not as strong as he was. And I'm not sure I have the right.

I failed him.

Tessen steps closer, the movement drawing my eye. I look again when I notice the expression on his face. He's staring at my brother with his head cocked and a furrow between his thick eyebrows. When he sees me watching, the expression changes, concern and empathy overtaking everything else.

"Do you want to go with them, or would you rather return to your quarters?" he asks as they bear my brother out of the room.

I can't speak. I think that, if I tried, the words would be nothing but incomprehensible noise. Once I release that pain, I don't know how I'll get it to stop. All I can do to answer him is turn and follow Yorri out of the room.

Neeva leads the procession out of Hishingu Hall and across the wide street. The few people out in the predawn hours stop in their tracks, bowing deeply when we pass, hands crossed and fists to their shoulders, a sign of respect for the final sacrifice a citizen has made.

I keep my eyes on the back of the nyshin in front of me. If I don't, the burning in my eyes will turn into something I'm not ready to give in to yet. There's one last responsibility to see through for Yorri. Then I can allow myself to crack like overbaked pottery.

We enter the bikyo-ko through a door on the western wall that is only ever used for this. It leads into a wide hallway hung with four woven tapestries, each bearing the symbol of one of the ranks—yonin, ahdo, nyshin, kaigo. There are two doors, one unadorned and the other bearing an iron-and-brass sun emblem of the Miriseh.

When the Miriseh door opens, Anda is there, her face drawn. Ono is behind her, standing near the stone table in the center of the room.

Anda opens the door wide and steps back, allowing Neeva and the others to carry Yorri into the anointing chamber.

I don't meet her eyes as I pass.

Only the Miriseh are allowed to perform the final rite, and tonight Miriseh Suzu is the one who spreads oils, perfumes, and herbs over the saishigi shroud while murmuring softly. I can't hear what she's saying, and I don't try. No one is supposed to hear the prayers the Miriseh offer until it's their turn to lie on that table and listen.

But I can try to finish my own prayers for Yorri while I wait.

Wait beside the bluest lakes, in the fields of green and gold.

If I know that you are safely there, then I shall be consoled.

When the rite is complete, Suzu steps back and wipes

her hands clean. According to descriptions of the ceremony, the next step is to lift Yorri off the stone table and carry him to the saishigi core. Instead, Anda and Ono seem to be looking to Suzu with a question in their eyes. Whatever it is that they ask, Suzu nods.

Ono turns to me. "Would you mind if we said goodbye alone, Khya?"

I'm not sure whether to say yes or no. I don't want to leave him alone, not even for a moment, but how can I deny them? He wasn't only mine. Our blood-parents certainly have the right to ask for this.

They shouldn't need to ask at all.

It doesn't matter what I want to say, because words aren't possible. Their shape feels wrong on my tongue. I manage to drop my eyes, hoping they see it as acquiescence, but I can't make my feet move. Then Tessen's hand is on my elbow again, a solid connection to reality.

I should resent being led around like this, being touched again without permission, but I don't. I'm not sure I'd know how to make myself leave Yorri if Tessen weren't guiding me out of the room.

We step into the hall, and the door closes behind us. I'm glad for the barrier. Seeing our blood-parents' grief over a death that happened far too soon would send me spiraling into my own. I can't let go yet. Not until this is over.

Tessen's hand stays on my arm and his gaze on my face, but he doesn't say anything. That's good. I still don't think I'd be able to respond yet.

When the chamber's door opens again a few minutes later, Anda and Ono are the ones who bear Yorri back into the hallway. It's fitting, I guess. The ones who bore him into this world should be the ones who carry him out of it.

Tessen moves quickly then, almost jumping across the hall to open the door across from us for the procession to pass through. Miriseh Suzu takes her place at the head of the line this time, her indigo hood casting shadows across her face as she passes us. Anda and Ono follow close behind, Yorri's body carried between them on a bed of cloth and leather. Tessen gently nudges me into place after Ono, and everyone else falls in behind us.

Unlike most passages into the undercity, this is a gently declining slope instead of stairs. With oil lanterns only hanging every twenty feet, the lighting on the other side of the doorway is dim, but the top of the core is only a few feet below the surface of the upper city, so the lack of lighting doesn't matter. We don't have far to travel.

Except for the lanterns on the walls, there aren't any fires in the core. The heat is still somehow as bad as the desert at midday, relieved only by the two narrow shafts that ventilate the cavern. I don't know how the yonin spreading moss, mushrooms, and detritus over the top of the core—the thirty-foot circle in the center of the chamber—can stand the temperature. Waves of heat seem to rise from the core itself.

Focusing on the question of how they can stand it helps me forget, or at least ignore, *why* and *for whom* they're arranging that layer of earth.

Anda and Ono step closer to the core. I lean forward, my hand rising. They can't carry him out there. This *can't* be—

Tessen catches my wrist, his hold gentle but firm. Without saying anything—neither admonishments nor pointless platitudes—he restrains me.

Together we watch Anda and Ono walk to the spot the yonin have prepared.

After the ceremony is over, the yonin will cover Yorri with another layer of compost. Over the course of many moons, his body will return to the earth, time and nature breaking him down until the rich soil can be harvested several levels below our feet. It'll be used in the city's gardens and the nyska farms on the nearby mesas.

In this way he'll serve the clan one final time.

When we approach, the yonin look up, like they're checking to see if anything will be required of them. One—the youngest of the group—doesn't look away.

Why are they staring at me?

A second later they move toward another yonin, their steps tense and almost carefully slow, like they're trying not to attract attention. After brief whispered conversation, the one who stared walks to an archway that leads down to the undercity. Their even footsteps triple speed as soon as they're out of sight, each step echoing in the enclosed stairwell.

Tessen's eyes are following the yonin, too, but his attention returns to me as soon as they're out of sight. The empathy I see in his eyes, the sadness, it—

No. I look away, ignoring the way my throat clenches and my hands shake. What I see on Tessen's face makes this too real. I can't...I *can't*. Not yet.

Somehow, watching the ceremony is easier to handle.

Suzu leads Anda and Ono across the iron walkway stretching over the core. They kneel and then carefully place Yorri on the core.

"Nyshin-ten Yorri will be honored in Ryogo as we honor him here," Suzu intones. "He served the clan with dedication and distinction. We thank him for his loyalty and hope he will welcome his loved ones when the time for their end is at hand."

Suzu, Anda, and Ono take handfuls of the compost and sprinkle it over Yorri's enshrouded form. When they return to the stone ledge, Neeva and her second-in-command take their places, repeating the gesture. It's my turn, but I can't— My feet won't— How can this be…

Tessen touches my elbow, this time questioning. I nod without taking my eyes off Yorri, and then he nudges me toward the iron walkway and holds up the clay pot of compost so I can take a handful. This is my last chance to finish the prayer for the dead. I take it, even though the words tremble in my mind.

Wait beside the shimmering shore, I ask of you this boon.

Sprinkling the compost over his body, I try not to remember the shocked happiness on his face after his assignment to Kaigo Neeva's squad, or the way he'd laugh from his perch on the north wall when a storm blew in, or how he always trusted my advice even when he wasn't sure I was right.

Itagami needs my service now, but I will join you soon.

I know that's true, but it will be years—or decades—before that happens.

Failed, failed, you failed.

Tessen's hand on my hip leads me back to the solid stone ledge. It's over now. All we have left to do is wash our hands clean, a reminder to leave the past behind us, and then return to the upper city. Swallowing hard, I place myself last in the line. The memories are painful, but I can't wash Yorri away.

When Tessen's hand shifts to my elbow and his hold tightens, tugging me gently closer to him, I don't resist. Settling against his chest is easy and comfortable. Comforting. I turn my face into his shoulder and clutch him tightly, trying to remember how to breathe.

"I know how close you were, and I am so sorry, Khya," he says, curving around me and murmuring quietly in my ear. "But you'll see each other again."

I shake my head. "It shouldn't've happened. I was supposed to protect him and I wasn't there and—" My words lodge in my throat.

If my ear weren't pressed against his throat, I don't think I would have heard the pained noise he makes. "You did. For years. It was you who helped him earn his place in the clan."

My stomach flips. I push away from Tessen, stepping out of his reach quickly.

He's right. It was my help that forced him into the nyshin.

I helped him right into the saishigi core because I wasn't there to protect him anymore.

Footsteps on stone draw my attention to the archway. Is it the yonin returning? I grasp the distraction and focus on the door, waiting for their arrival.

All the pain of my brother's loss is reflected on Sanii's face as ey walks to the edge of the core. My stomach clenches, and the burn in my eyes that I've been fighting back and ignoring gets worse. I move closer to the large clay basin of water before eir eyes can meet mine. It's the single most cowardly thing I've ever done, but I don't think I can handle the accusations I'm sure I'd see in eir eyes: *he'd still be alive if he had been with me.*

I couldn't survive seeing it because I know it's true. It's true and it doesn't matter now.

Both of us have lost him.

CHAPTER TEN

Although the kaigo grant me two days of rest before I need to report for duty, I don't take them. The thought of staying inside Itagami—inside the too-close walls of my room—makes my hands shake. I need work. Distraction. I need something to focus on that isn't the memory of my brother's face being hidden behind a saishigi shroud.

"Are you sure?" Nyshin-ma Tyrroh frowns when I give him my decision. "I know you were close, Khya. It isn't weak to accept the time."

"I'm sure." More than sure. Itagami is too full of memories. I don't know if I'll ever be able to stand on the north wall without fighting the urge to leap from the embankment and join my brother in Ryogo.

Though hesitant, Nyshin-ma Tyrroh agrees. I'm back out with the squad the next day. Everyone but Etaro and Rai keeps their distance. I hate it. Each time someone drops their gaze from mine or refuses to argue me out of my stupider ideas is a harsh reminder of why they're being so overcautious. After two days of it, I'm ready to snap.

"I am going to *stab* Ryzo if he doesn't stop staring at me like I'm carrying a plague," I mutter to Etaro during one of our rests. The heat rises in visible waves from the landscape, making the desosa crackle lightly. There are gray-tinged clouds to the northeast—something to keep an eye on.

"They don't know what to say." Ey rests eir hand on my arm, eir sharp features somehow disarmingly sincere. "None of us have lost someone we were as close to as you were to Yorri."

"I half expected you two to declare sumai when he became nyshin," Rai says as she picks at something under one of her nails with the tip of her dagger. "Honestly, I was surprised when you didn't." She looks up then, contrition in her eyes. "Though maybe it's for the best."

If I'd ever considered bonding with anyone, it would've been Yorri. Siblings, friends, or ushimo—those who love deeply but never want sex—it doesn't matter. The desire to lie with someone has nothing to do with the sumai; the only thing that matters for the bond is trust, abiding love, and the desire to keep them close through this life and the next.

If it hurts this much to lose him without the soulbond, what would I be suffering with it?

My body tenses at the thought, like it's preparing for a physical blow. Now I understand why so few survive the loss of a bondmate. Pain worse than this would be unendurable.

"Even if I'd been considering it, we wouldn't have bonded." I tear a small piece of dried kamidi meat off the strip in my hand and press my short fingernail into the ridged surface. Should I tell them about Sanii? I guess it doesn't matter if they know now. The secret can't hurt anyone anymore. And Rai would start flicking sparks at me if she found out I was keeping more secrets. "He actually—well, before his herynshi he told me that—"

"Eyes out," Tyrroh bellows. We jump to our feet, eyes to the perimeter and waiting for orders. "Move west!"

Etaro reaches toward me, eir hand hovering above mine until I nod. Smiling, ey squeezes my hand gently before falling into line with the others.

I pour every ounce of myself into the work and accept every task Tyrroh throws at me. It mostly works, but it can't last forever. Not the Denhitrans we're supposed to be hunting through the mountains, not my energy, and not the dam I built to keep everything at bay.

I push myself harder than I ever have for four solid days until we return to the city. When I crawl onto my sleep mat, the only thing I have enough energy left for is to send up a silent prayer that I'm too exhausted to dream.

My face is wet. It's not what woke me up, but it's the first thing I notice when I open my eyes.

I could almost pretend I don't have a reason to cry if I hadn't woken up with the evidence on my face. Do I have the right to cry? I'm alive and Yorri is not, and I'm the one who started the chain of events that put him in harm's way.

Death comes for everyone on Shiara, but it shouldn't have come for my brother so soon.

I grit my teeth and wipe my face dry, quickly looking away from the small wet patch on my sleep mat, unwanted evidence of exactly how long I'd cried before I finally woke up.

At least I waited until I was alone.

Distraction. I need a distraction. Maybe if I head for the training yard one of the squads will let me run drills with them. I don't think they'd turn away a new fighter to spar against. Hopefully. I don't know what else I could possibly do that'd occupy enough of my mind. Since we just came back from a four-day desert mission, we're supposed to have the day off. Tyrroh will *order* me to rest if I go to him for work.

I shuck the loincloth and breast band I slept in, and stare at the spots of blood on the cloth. What? Did I injure myself or—

Oh. Right. Of course.

Muttering curses to myself, I toss my clothing in a pile to bring to the yonin in charge of laundry. With everything that has happened the last week, I lost track of the moon cycle and ignored the minor cramps. I should've been expecting my gensu. It's late, but that can happen. It was a week late in the cycle leading up to my herynshi last year. I clean myself and take a cloth pad from the stack on the shelf.

The process of tying the extra layer into my loincloth and getting dressed takes a few minutes, and it's something I'll have to deal with several times a day for the next few days. When I asked for a distraction, this wasn't what I meant.

Neither is seeing Tessen leaning against the wall across from my room. He straightens when I push my thick curtain aside and holds out a cloth-wrapped bundle.

"I brought you food." He's holding it with the tips of his fingers as far away from his body as he can reach, like he's expecting me to attack.

But I don't. Taking the food means I won't have to face the kitchens and the morning crowds. He smiles at me when I mumble thanks, and the expression grows brighter when I hum with pleasure at the first bite of what he brought me—a wide round of nyska bread stuffed with mykyn egg, teegra meat, greens, and spices. It's still warm, so he can't have been waiting long.

I almost avoid asking why he's here, but I remember how his silent but constant presence kept me functioning long enough to say goodbye to my little brother. I wouldn't have expected anyone—especially him—to do that. There had been dozens of moments when he could've left. No one would've blamed him for leaving, not even me, but he'd stayed.

Silently sighing, I meet his eyes. "Was there something you needed, Tessen?"

He blinks—because I called him by his name, or because I spoke at all? Whatever the reason, his surprise dissipates. "I came to see if there was anything *you* needed."

I keep walking down the hall. "Nothing you can do."

Not even the strongest hishingu has the power to pour life into an empty shell.

"I have the day to myself," he says. "I could run drills with you."

When I stop walking this time, he crosses to stand in front of me instead of making me turn to face him.

"Why would you want to do that?" I ask.

There's a flash of something, but whatever his instinctive reaction is, he smothers it fast. "You mean aside from the chance to practice with one of the sharpest sword masters in our year and one of the only people in the clan to master a suraki?"

My thoughts are mired in the morass of mourning, but the compliment is almost enough to make me smile. I worked hard for those skills, especially with the complex suraki. And if Tessen is with me, I won't have to waste time ingratiating myself to a nyshin-co just to be allowed to spar with their squad.

It's reason enough to agree.

"I don't want to talk," I warn him. "About anything."

"That's fine." His grin spreads across his face like the first glint of sunrise. "You know I can talk enough for both of us."

"That's what I'm afraid of." I brush past him, hoping he doesn't see the twitch of my lip that betrays my amusement.

Despite his claim, Tessen doesn't speak at all on the jog toward the northeastern yard or while we choose practice weapons and stake out a space for ourselves between the squads running training drills. We haven't sparred together like this since we were children and barely able to pick up the long, heavy tudo blades, let alone wield them.

"Ready?" he asks once we're facing each other with tudos raised.

I roll my eyes and lunge, bringing the tudo down in an arc that would've been a killing blow if he hadn't brought his sword up in time to block it.

Somehow, we immediately fall into a rhythm as natural as breathing. The conversation sticks to technique, and we teach each other disarming tricks they didn't show us until we joined our training squads. He seems to know when to stop for me to adjust my grip or change my stance. He notices when I'm so parched I can barely unglue my tongue from the roof of my mouth and steps back, flicking his eyes toward the small fountain bubbling with water fed from the caves underneath the city and not relenting until we've both rested. He doesn't protest when I need a longer break to run to the washroom attached to the training yard to deal with the necessary inconveniences of the gensu.

It's like we've been training together for years. It could be his skills as a basaku, but no level of enhanced sight, smell, touch, hearing, or taste should make it feel like he's reading my mind. Not even his ability to sense magic in the shifts of the desosa should help—I'm not using my wards today.

But then, there are legends of basaku so powerful that their six enhanced senses gave them a seventh sense, one that crossed into the realm of rusosa mages.

Neeva, Tessen's blood-mother, is a strong rusosa with the ability to delve into minds, to get a sense of their thoughts, to manipulate what they see or hear, to create hallucinations or pain. It's invasive. I hate to think he might've inherited some of Neeva's skills. The idea of Tessen hearing the impossible mess of thoughts in my head is uncomfortable.

Right now even I don't want to listen to them.

Luckily, that kind of power is only legend. No one can even confirm the identity of the fabled basaku who, once a long time ago, actually was that powerful; the name of the mage is different every time I hear the story, as is how long it's been since they lived.

And if Tessen is the one who finally proves that legend true, I don't want to know. I need the rot-ridden idiot right now.

In the late afternoon, Tessen lowers his blade, his breathing heavy and sweat dripping down his face. His tunic and shirt were discarded hours ago, and his pants are five shades darker than they were this morning, soaked in a mix of sweat, water, and dust. My shirts have been gone as long as his, only my breast band still in place. My pants, usually loose, are so soaked with sweat they're practically sealed to my skin.

"Are you ever going to eat again?" he finally asks around his deep breaths.

"It hasn't been that long." I think I might be wrong even as I say the words.

The disbelieving look on Tessen's face confirms it. "You haven't eaten since breakfast, Khya. I don't know how you're still standing." He shakes out the arm not gripping his blade and then tries to rub his opposite shoulder. Tries. Halfway there he gives up the attempt and shakes his head. "My arms feel like they're about to fall off, and my stomach has been screaming at me for an hour. Food, oh deadly one. *Food*. Even you need it sometimes."

Only as he speaks do I notice the grumbling roll of my stomach or the way my hands are trembling and my legs are starting to weaken.

It's irrational, but I hate it when my body betrays me like this. I don't want to stop.

Our teachers drill the need for hydration and sustenance into us before we're ever allowed to touch a weapon, but I want to push until I can sleep without a single dream. Then I want to wake up and repeat the process tomorrow.

Tessen hasn't complained once until now, though. He's pushed himself just as hard as I have without half the reason to bother, and I know from the determined gleam in his eyes that he won't leave the yard without me. The least I can do is make sure he doesn't pass out from hunger.

Grimacing, I gesture with my tudo toward the armory.

In each zon, the communal kitchen is directly next to the training yard and the nursery. The proximity makes it easier to serve the doseiku, but it also means we don't have to go far to find a meal.

We don't speak on the walk there or while we gather

what we want from the options the yonin cooked today. I fill my plate with fruit still chilled from the cave storerooms and add a lukewarm pile of cooked nyska grain mixed with dried surnat, spices, and small pieces of kamidi meat. Food might not have been on my mind ten minutes ago, but my mouth is watering looking at it now.

We came in earlier than those training are allowed their dinner break. There aren't many citizen squads here, either. The tables around us aren't anywhere near empty, but they're not as full as I'm used to seeing them. It gives us a chance to find some relative quiet away from the boisterous squads.

Even after I agreed to train with Tessen, I didn't think it'd last long. I'd guessed that either he'd get bored or I'd get so aggravated I'd try to stab him for real, but here we are. Almost all of the sunlight hours are gone and he's sitting across from me gratefully stuffing his mouth with steaming bites of teegra steak. I don't know how he can eat something that hot when we're both dripping sweat, but I don't question it. My cooler pile of food is much more appetizing.

I'm not sure if it's the quiet or the food that makes me think this peace between us might go on indefinitely. I've only eaten half of what was on my plate before he ruins everything.

"You're still blaming yourself for what happened, aren't you?"

Tessen's question cracks the dam I'd held around my thoughts all day. "Don't."

"I just— Khya, you've always blamed yourself for everything that happened to him, and you can't. He was a nyshin and he—"

"No." I slam my hand down on the table and stand,

anger flushing my cheeks. "I am *not* talking about this. Not ever. Don't mention him again, Nyshin-ten."

I leave my unfinished food behind and stalk from the room. More than one pair of eyes tracks my path out, but it's easy to ignore them.

My brain is screaming at me to get away. Away from the questions and the people who will try to convince me to forget him, to let go of the past as easily as they do, as easily as washing the dust of the desert off their hands.

Yorri isn't something I can wash off and forget. He isn't something I *want* to forget.

I just don't want remembering to hurt this much, either.

CHAPTER ELEVEN

Hands shaking and heart pounding, I run through the crowded main street, away from my barracks, and don't look back.

There is not a single doubt in my mind that Tessen is going to follow me; I don't make it easy for him. I stick to crowds where I'll be harder to spot and harder to track by scent. It won't be enough. I can't avoid my barracks forever—or even the rest of the night—and Tessen is smart enough to wait me out. He'll head there if he can't catch up to me.

When I reach the south wall, I slow down on the stairwell, walking instead of sprinting.

My mind doesn't slow at all.

It was stupid to snap at Tessen. He didn't say anything wrong, nothing that Etaro, Rai, and even Tyrroh haven't already said in one form or another. But I knew I couldn't handle it today, not after the way my squad has acted around me since Yorri died.

Coming out of the protected stairwell, I walk straight

to the outer ledge and press my clenched fists against the top of the wall.

I told Tessen at the beginning not to mention it at all. Why didn't he listen?

He spent years just watching as the rest of our yearmates ostracized Yorri for his curiosity, for the way his mind fixated on puzzles, and for his inability to stay out of trouble with the training masters. Tessen spent just as many years teasing me over my obvious desire to earn a place on the kaigo council while stealing every single promotion from me. He may not have said anything at dinner that deserved the way I left him there, but…

Bellows. I don't even know. I don't want to forget, but I can't let myself think about Yorri, either. Hearing his name will always be a blow I don't see coming.

This high, with no tunic, hood, or atakafu to offer protection from the arid wind, my sweat evaporates in seconds. My skin feels as dry as nyska paper, and my hands are starting to shake from more than just exertion and emotion.

I need water. And to clean the dust off my skin. And clean clothes.

I'll have to stop at my room to get a shirt before I go to the bathing pool. The yonin at the bathing pools won't give me a clean item unless I exchange it for a dirty one, and I left the shirt I was wearing in the kitchen. Tessen might drop it off later, but that does me no good now. And the longer I can put off the next meeting with Tessen the better. For both of us.

I walk the wall until I reach the stairs that will bring me back to the street level closest to my barracks. No one stops me or even acknowledges me beyond a nod in passing. There's no sign of Tessen, either, not on the streets or in front of my barracks, but he could be waiting upstairs. In fact, that'd be exactly the kind of thing he'd do. I take a deep breath and step inside.

"Nyshin-ten Khya?" The voice calls from the alley beside the building, but it doesn't sound like Tessen or anyone I know. I stop in the doorway. There's a silhouette in the shadows, shorter than most people I know well and with a squarer frame. Definitely not Tessen. Or Rai. Or...

Then they trot into the light of the setting sun. My breath catches in my throat.

Sanii.

The aggravation and confusion swirling in my head like a tornado since I left Tessen collapse into a fathomless well of guilt as ey stops a few feet away and inclines eir head stiffly. "Pardon my intrusion, Nyshin-ten, but may I speak to you? Privately."

No. I'm sorry, but I can't. I have to go sharpen a sword and then throw myself on it, because that'd be less painful than facing you.

Cowardice won the morning I faced em in the saishigi core. I refuse to give in to it twice.

"All right," I agree quietly. But I don't know where we could go. Eir wardcharm won't allow em inside my barracks. There's only one other place I've ever gone to be alone. Maybe it's fitting that the first time I consider going back there is because of someone so deeply connected to Yorri. Still, I have to swallow hard and force myself to ask, "Is the north wall private enough, Yonin-va Sanii?"

Eir eyes flick up to meet mine, the amount of white showing around eir dark irises giving away eir surprise. "No. I know a place, though, if you'd follow me?"

I gesture toward the street, but ey shakes eir head. Instead ey leads me into the alley beside the building.

"People will talk if they see you with me." The words are quiet, but the bitterness in eir tone is clear. "It'll be easier if we use the yonin passages."

"The what?"

Ey casts a quick glance over eir shoulder; the look in eir round eyes seems mocking. "There's so much of the city you've never seen, Nyshin-ten."

The words prove true sooner than I expect. My building isn't far from the northeastern wall and there, tucked beneath a staircase, is a door I've often passed and ignored. I've seen yonin approach it before, but it seemed like it was storage for gardening tools or something like that. Sanii leads me through the door and...okay. Definitely not storage.

When the door closes behind us and shuts out the last of the daylight, only a single flickering lamp lights the passage before us. The walls are rough-hewn and the stairs steep.

"You have to go mostly by feel," Sanii says just before ey begins to move comfortably down the poorly lit stairs. I follow close, unwilling to lose em in a section of the undercity I've never explored. Ey was worried what the ahdo and the nyshin would think if they saw eir with me above, but now I'm wondering what a yonin would do if they found me here.

We keep traveling down. Down.

When does this end? More importantly... "How many passages like this are there?"

"Many. I haven't had time to count them all, and I doubt anyone else has bothered trying. It's not like anyone cares where the yonin go as long as the work gets done." That thread of bitterness is stronger now. Maybe because we're away from most of the ears that might get Sanii in trouble if they heard em insulting eir own service to the city; as though they wouldn't feel the same way in eir place.

I stabilize myself on the wall when my already-overworked legs wobble on a narrow step. There are perhaps a third as many lamps in this stairwell as there are in any area except the saishigi core, and the deeper we go, the slicker the stones are, moisture gathering where cool cave air meets the heat of the desert. It's colder than the sections of the undercity I've spent time in before, cold enough that bumps rise across my overheated skin and I shiver more than once.

And still we keep moving down. "Where are we going? I thought you wanted to talk."

"I do." Ey pauses and looks up at me, most of eir face cast in shifting shadow. "But I need to show you something, too. You won't believe me otherwise."

"How can you possibly know that? You don't know me."

"I don't, but Yorri talked about you. Constantly." Ey shrugs and continues eir descent. "And because I wouldn't believe it if I were you. Not without proof."

Ey's silent then except for the soft pad of eir bare feet and the near-silent huff of eir breaths. I follow behind, just as quiet, as we traverse stairs, caves, and passages that I never knew existed. All of it reminds me of what the mesa must've been like before Varan and the other ishijis smoothed and civilized the stone. The ceilings are natural rough stone with the massive spears of rock hanging down, and the walls offer no smooth places to rest. Only the floors here are even, and that's likely from centuries of use more than anything else.

We pass other yonin on our way to wherever we're heading. They don't pay much attention to us, but I'm not wearing my tunic or any of my rank insignia outside of my wardcharm. I wonder what they'd think if they knew I'm nyshin. Maybe they wouldn't care.

"Yonin disappear sometimes, did you know that? Often enough that it's not uncommon." Sanii is only a step ahead of me and keeps glancing in my direction. "There are holes no one has ever found the bottom of, and there's a river a level below us that runs so hot it boils. If you fall in that, no one can save you, and they won't ever find your body."

I shudder. Dying from a fall down an endless dark hole or boiled alive in an underground river? Death may be inevitable, but Miriseh spare me ever having to face a death like that.

And it doesn't make sense. I thought that part of the purpose of keeping yonin in Itagami was to prevent their needless, untimely deaths.

"There are ten missing right now, and no one knows what happened to them. Taya and Resa have been missing for weeks," ey says as we cross through a long cavern that is used to grow row after row of mushrooms where the air smells like damp earth. "We thought there must have been a cave-in, but no one could find it. Because there wasn't one."

The way ey says it, the hint of scorn in the words... "You know what happened to them?"

"In part. That's what I want to show you."

Why? If it's too late to help them, why should it matter?

To keep from asking, I look up and try to place myself in relation to the upper city. Have we gone beyond the mesa, or are we still underneath Itagami? Unless my sense of direction is off, I think we're headed toward the center of the city.

The caves slope up, and then there are stairs, another

narrow, dim, winding staircase roughly hewn from the sandstone. It gets hotter with each step we take. If there were more noise reverberating down the stairwell, I'd think we were approaching one of the forges. Near the top, where it's gotten hotter than the desert at high noon, Sanii signals for me to stop. Ey continues up the stairs alone and peers around the corner before ey signs permission to approach.

"Promise that you'll listen to the rest of what I need to tell you, Khya." Sanii's expression is absolutely serious now. "You won't like where I've brought you, but you *need* to listen. For Yorri."

My pulse quickens. I hold my breath, trying to hide the sudden quaking of my nerves, but I won't turn away from em now. I'll face whatever Sanii has to show me because I owe em—I owe *Yorri*—that much and more.

I exhale and nod. Only then does Sanii step into the room. I follow em into—

Blood and rot. We're in the saishigi core.

Everything about the last and only other time I have stood in this room is burned into my memory. I know exactly where the iron plank, now leaning against one of the stone walls, had been set, and I know how far out over the core Anda and Ono walked to place my brother's body. I know there can't have been too many deaths between last week and now, so he's likely exactly where we left him, the top layer and one of the most recently laid in.

My throat clogs and my eyes fill so fast that there's no chance of holding back the tears.

"I'm sorry." I don't know if I'm talking to Yorri or Sanii, but the dead can't hear us speak, so I talk to the only person who might listen. "I'm so sorry. I just wanted him to have the chance to live. I didn't want him to…"

"To end up trapped underground for the rest of his days," Sanii finishes when I can't. "I know, Khya."

"If I hadn't pushed him, he might never have developed his magic or it might have taken years." I dig the heels of my hands into my eyes, the pressure hard and sharp. "He'd be alive and he—"

"Yorri is missing." Fingers wrap around my wrists and, with a surprising show of strength, Sanii drags my hands away from my face.

I pull away from the unfamiliar, unexpected touch. Yorri may have loved em, but I— Wait. "What?"

"He's *missing*, Khya."

Oh, no. I've heard about this before. Sometimes when a sukhai is lost, the living sumai partner can't acknowledge the loss. They refuse to believe their bondmate is gone. Yorri and Sanii may not have completed the bond, but they were on the cusp of one. Maybe that was enough to cause the same break with reality.

I clear my throat and meet eir eyes, trying to project a calm I don't feel.

"He's not missing, Sanii, he's gone." I shake my head and try to soften my voice. It's not much, but if I can do this for Yorri, maybe it'll help me as much as Sanii. Maybe I need to face his death as much as ey does. I look toward the spot in the core where Anda and Ono laid my brother, unable to meet eir eyes. "I saw them wrap his body."

"No. He's not where he should be."

When I force myself to face em, I expect to see pain, fury, or confusion, but ey looks resigned more than anything else. Sighing, ey carefully walks onto the core, leaving small footprints in the mixture of sand, moss, mushrooms, and finely cut scrub, stopping a foot away from where Yorri lies. "Come here, Khya."

I promised I'd listen, but I didn't think ey had lost eir mind when I made that promise. Despite it, I follow em onto the core.

"I needed to see him for myself to believe it," Sanii says when I crouch next to em. "It didn't feel— I mean, it happened so quickly. I just... I needed to see him and say goodbye."

Ey grips a tiny corner of fabric poking out from the earth and pulls. I tense, trying to prepare for signs of decay marring my brother's face.

But that isn't my brother.

"This is Taya." Sanii brushes the shroud clean, showing me the smudged nyshin morning star sketched there. "Yonin-po Taya, who everyone assumed fell to his death more than a moon ago, is wrapped in a shroud that's marked nyshin and should belong to Yorri."

This is not Yorri. This is where he was laid in, this is definitely where I watched them place his body to rest, but that is not my brother. Taya is older by a decade or more, and his skin is several shades darker, and he is *not my brother*.

"I thought I'd gotten the wrong spot, so I kept looking. Then I found Resa. She'd been marked nyshin, too. One could be a mistake, but two?" Sanii shakes eir head, covers Taya's face, and begins to push the dirt back into place. "I found two more that had gone 'missing' recently before I had to get out of here. I think I'd find more if I dug deep enough."

"But where— *Why?* Yorri is..." He isn't here. But he was in Hishingu Hall, laid out on the table. Unmoving. Not breathing. I touched him, so I know he was real, and I—

And there had been that moment, that single fluttering beat of a possible pulse under his skin. I'd dismissed it as delusion, but what if—

No. If I let myself believe it, if I even let myself think it, and it turned out to be wrong, I don't think I could survive the loss.

But...what if I *did* feel a pulse?

Where is Yorri? Who could have possibly moved him? Why would they want to if he wasn't alive? Where is my brother? How did Taya and Resa die? If Yorri is dead, what possible purpose would they have for his body? What the bellows is happening here?

Where is my brother?

My hands shake. Breathing hurts, each lungful of air stinging. The questions tangle so completely that when I open my mouth no sound emerges at all.

Nodding once, Sanii leads me toward the stairs. We go down faster than we climbed, and when we reach the lower level, we don't turn the way we came. Instead, ey heads east.

Maybe this is a trick. Convincing me he's still alive would be the cruelest thing anyone could do.

But would Yorri love someone that malicious? I don't think he would. There was too much mercy in his soul for that.

Sanii finally stops in a small alcove through an archway so short we have to nearly drop to our knees to enter. It's dark with only flickers of light from the lamps in the main passage filtering in.

We haven't passed a single other soul for a few minutes, but ey still whispers when ey says, "I think something happened with Yorri that the Miriseh and the kaigo do *not* want anyone to know about."

"That doesn't even— So, what? The councils, the *Miriseh*—who have protected us for centuries—moved Yorri's body for...for what? Why?" Even if something had happened, if Yorri did something he shouldn't have or learned a secret no one but the councils should know, that wouldn't give them any reason to move his body.

"I don't know, but whatever they did to him, I think it's why Taya and Resa and the others went missing." Ey runs eir fingers through eir short hair, leaving it standing in spikes. "Maybe they used the threat of the Denhitrans to fake Yorri's death so that no one would question his disappearance."

"But why would they need him to disappear?" Right now, thinking is like trying to walk through one of the desert washes during a flash flood. "And how would they fake something like that?"

"Taya and Resa and the others." Eir whisper is as fervent as eir expression. "After the first Denhitran attack, we went days without another sighting. And when your squad found them, they basically ran."

"How do you know—"

Ey waves a dismissive hand. "I overheard it. People don't pay attention to the yonin, especially not in the undercity."

"Oh." The bitterness that keeps slithering through eir words makes even more sense now. I wouldn't take well to being ignored.

"Half a day later—less, maybe—the same Denhitrans supposedly ambushed Neeva's squad. Twenty miles away. Twenty mountain miles." Skepticism is etched deep on eir oval face. "Unless every one of them could run as fast as Yorri, that trek should've taken them a day and a half or more. Khya, it doesn't make sense."

"There could have been more than one raiding group." The words sound unsure even to me, because I don't know what happened. Was it that far between where I met the

Denhitrans and where Yorri died? I never asked.

Why didn't I ask where my brother died?

Ey shakes eir head. "I think someone forced Taya and the others to pose as Denhitrans, attack Neeva's squad, and..." Ey digs the heels of eir hands into eir eyes and growls. "I don't know, all right? I don't know what happened out there, but I know they faked his death. Because now he's gone, and I can't *find* him! But I know he's—"

Ey gasps for air, a long, shuddering breath that ends in a sob. We're so close I can feel em shaking with the force of it, feel the emotional strain making the desosa ripple around em, but I don't... What do I do? Touch is the only thing that might shock me out of a moment like this if the roles were reversed, but ey isn't watching me. I can't ask for permission.

The sobs are getting worse.

Hoping ey'll forgive me, I slowly rest my hand on eir shoulder.

It's several minutes before ey takes a breath that doesn't send shudders through em, and it's another minute before ey rests eir hand over mine on eir shoulder and straightens.

Forgiven, then, I guess.

"I know you don't believe me, but he's alive. I *know* he's alive, and I want to know what happened to him, Khya." Ey sounds drained and lost. It's like hearing my own voice the night Tessen told me Yorri was gone. "I wanted to say goodbye, but he wasn't there, and I never believed he was dead to begin with, and I want to know *why* they took him away."

Me, too. I want to know. Believing, though? I don't know if I can. Putting my faith in this and being wrong could easily be the blow that sends me to Ryogo.

"He might be dead, Sanii." I have to say it. For both of us. Yes, something strange is happening—disappearances, yonin given last rites in nyshin shrouds, missing bodies; I can't deny that—but that doesn't mean he's still alive somewhere.

"He's not. I know he's not." Ey shakes eir head quickly. "If he was dead, why move him? There's no *reason* for it."

And that is the question I can't answer. Why move a corpse? No reason unless there was something on the body you needed or...or the body wasn't a corpse after all. But there's something else it seems like Sanii hasn't considered.

"If we look into this and anyone finds out, the Miriseh will kill us for disloyalty."

It is the strictest law of the clan, to have faith that the Miriseh act in our best interest. And they do. They're fair, but their rule is absolute. To question them, to go against their orders and their decisions, is asking for death. A public death. A demonstration.

I've spent the last twelve years—ever since I was old enough to know what I wanted—working to rise through the ranks of the doseiku and then the nyshin once I was placed there. Nothing I have ever been able to imagine would be enough to make me throw that dream aside.

"He would've died for me," Sanii says, eir voice soft and full of longing. "How can I do any less for him?"

And he almost did die saving me. There's no chance I can repay that, or the lifetime of devoted affection that came before it, by leaving Sanii to risk everything alone. I take a long, deep breath, expanding my lungs until I feel my ribs protest the motion. "If the Miriseh figure out what we're doing, they'll bar both of us from ever entering Ryogo. If you're wrong and Yorri is dead, we'll never see him again."

"I'm not wrong, Khya. He's alive."

"What about after? Even if you are right— Say we find him and then…I don't even know. Something. Are you willing to risk an eternity in Kujuko for a few more years on Shiara with Yorri?" Am *I* willing to?

"Yes." There is zero hesitation in Sanii's answer.

Can it be that simple for em? Maybe it is.

I hadn't thought there would be anything that could make surrendering my place in the afterlife worth it, but for Yorri… My brother has always been the exception to my rules, and the only person I'd break the clan's rules for. If he needs my help now, am I going to turn away just to hold on to the chance of becoming kaigo one day? Or to avoid the curse of Kujuko?

I feel like there's something ey's not telling me, but even so, there are too many unanswered questions after what ey showed me. Digging beyond what the surface layer of the saishigi core proved would mean risking everything— my future place in the clan, my life, and everything that comes after—and there's a chance, despite Sanii's hope, that he really is dead.

But it doesn't matter. I need to know for sure.

"All right. Tell me what I need to do."

Sanii leads me back to familiar passages before ey heads to eir shift in the mushroom farms and I can trudge to my rooms. The need to *do something* burns in my chest, but we can't start tonight. I still need to wash the day off my skin. The tremor in my muscles from running drills has gotten worse, though. Climbing to my room on the third floor of the barracks to get a clean tunic and then trudging back to the undercity to bathe sounds like more than I can handle. Maybe—

I stop short, staring down the hall toward my room.

Why am I surprised? I shouldn't be. Of course Tessen is leaning against the wall across from my room, almost precisely where he waited for me this morning, with dirt still caked over his bare chest and two tunics hanging from his hand. One is the shirt I left in the kitchen.

"I was getting worried." He says it quietly, like he's trying not to wake up the people sleeping in the other rooms on the floor. "Where were you?"

"Avoiding you." It's the safest answer, and it carries at least a small grain of truth. I had been avoiding him, but only for the first ten minutes of the last... I don't even know how long I've been gone. It's full night now, so longer than an hour.

His gray eyes scan my body, lingering on my feet. "Were you walking in the gardens?"

I look down, noticing small grains of dirt from the core stuck to the tops of my toes. Only the gardens, the mushroom farms beneath the city, and the core have dirt like this. It's a battle I almost lose to keep from wiggling them. Maybe I do need to bathe tonight.

"Yes." He'll probably think it odd I went to the roofs, but it'd be far stranger for me to claim a desire to sit among the dank mushroom caves. And no one ever goes to the core except to attend saishigi rites.

The muscles in his face shift, then he closes his eyes and exhales heavily, a weary sound far too old for someone who's only seventeen. "I wish you didn't distrust me so completely, Khya."

Is he joking? "You've earned that distrust, Nyshin-ten."

He laughs, a soft breathy sound more pained than amused, and opens his eyes. "I really haven't." After he rubs his hand over his face, he looks at me; his eyes seem sad. "There's proof I'm nowhere near as awful as you think I am, but you wouldn't believe me if I told you. You never have."

The words are so close to what Sanii said before ey took me to the saishigi core that I bite back my instinctive retort and actually think for a moment.

His persistence has never made sense. Everyone else in our year group gave up on me and moved on long ago, but never Tessen. He made it a point to "check in" even after we were placed on different squads.

Less than a moon after I joined Tyrroh's squad and met Rai and Etaro, Tessen approached us in the training yard. He'd only stayed for a few minutes—five at most. That brief meeting had been enough for Rai to look at me with arched eyebrows and say, "Well, that was interesting. You've been holding out on us, Khya."

I still don't know what Rai saw to make her ask that. She won't tell me.

"Then why do you keep trying?" I finally ask.

"Because I see you." He steps closer, not crowding me but close enough I feel his presence in the desosa around me, like his energy electrifies my skin and somehow makes it more sensitive even to the air. "I remember how you used to correct the younger doseiku while we were training. And I saw you help Yorri make one of his puzzles once— you were so obviously bored, but you stayed there for hours helping him shape the pieces. I've heard how Etaro and Rai talk about you. They adore you, did you know that? And she isn't an easy woman to impress, but you were always Ahdo-mas Sotra's favorite."

I don't breathe as Tessen reaches out to brush the tips of his fingers along the line of my jaw, an almost sad smile on his lips. "I see you, Khya. I've always seen you. And except for your tendency to pretend that you hate me most days, I like what I see."

Then Tessen leans in and, when I don't move away, presses a light kiss to my cheek.

Shock holds me still. Long enough for him to drape my shirt over my forearm and walk away, leaving me standing there staring at the spot where he'd stood and finally remembering to exhale.

What just happened? What did that even mean?

Why can I still feel the exact spot his lips met my cheek?

I can't think about it, not tonight. Probably not ever. The weight of too many questions and too few answers is already so heavy I feel like I'm about to be flattened against the stone floor.

Habit alone carries me to the bathing pools so I can clean the evidence from the core off my feet. It's habit that conveys me to my room, too, and habit that forces me to lie down on my mat.

But it's the unanswered questions—both Sanii's and Tessen's—that keep me awake most of the night.

CHAPTER TWELVE

The wind howls and lightning cracks through the sky, illuminating the city with a heartbeat of pure white brilliance. Another storm, the sixth to hit us too early.

"Where are we going today?" I ask Sanii. The rain and the wind and the tornado threatening in the distance have kept anyone sane indoors. There's no one in the streets to see Sanii leading me across the city and through a door in the southern wall, one that leads us to a stairwell almost identical to the one ey showed me last time.

Ey shakes eir head and keeps leading me through the yonin tunnels. I only recognize some of the passages and caverns from our last trip four days ago. Wherever we're going, it's not, thank the Miriseh, the saishigi core. I don't think I can handle a repeat of that.

After ten minutes of walking a circuitous path that avoids the center of the undercity, ey turns into a small side passage we have to duck to enter. I stop just inside the entrance and peer up into the absolute blackness.

My pulse rate jumps, and my hand closes around a protrusion of stone. The passage might continue for miles or end five feet in front of us. I can't see deep enough to be sure.

Is this what Kujuko will look like? Will it feel like being trapped in the still, inky blackness of the undercity, alone and lost for eternity? Will I—

No. Stop. I have to think about something else.

Swallowing hard, I ask, "Do you have a lantern? I don't trust my footing blind."

"Not a lantern exactly."

"So what exactly do you— Bellows and blood!" I jump away, my back pressed against the rock wall behind me and my hand falling to my weapon.

Sanii has started to glow. No, the air *around* eir is glowing. It's a soft white light that ripples like heat waves from the desert. It's gorgeous. It's also impossible.

"How... What?" I reach out carefully and brush my finger against the air surrounding em, testing for a tangible difference. There's a buzz to the desosa around em—the buzz of magic in someone who isn't supposed to have any.

"I discovered it after my herynshi." Sanii holds out eir hand, offering me a closer look. "There was a small cave-in and I was trapped alone for...hours. It was so dark, I..." A shudder runs through em, one I feel in the tips of eir fingers as I examine the light. "Then this."

"Why didn't you tell someone? They would have moved you up to ahdo."

Ey snorts. "You don't think I tried? They didn't believe me, and I couldn't do it again."

"But you can do it now."

Sanii pulls eir hand out of my grip. "By the time I mastered it enough to turn it on and off when I wanted, Yorri was…" Eir lips thin. "There wasn't a reason to tell anyone."

"And now?" Ey has a power I've never even heard of. No one else can produce light without also creating heat and fire.

"Now I can use it to find places like this." Ey proceeds down the passage without another word. The roof is so low I'm almost bent in half; Sanii simply curves eir shoulders and ducks eir head.

"You never answered my question," I say a few minutes later.

"Which one?"

"Where are we going?"

"I wanted to show you this last time, but it was too far." Sanii huffs when a rock under eir foot slips. The glow gets brighter, a single pulse of stronger power brightening the light before it settles back into the steady illumination. "We couldn't have made it here in the time we had."

"There are more secrets?"

"More than you can imagine," Sanii says. "No one knows the undercity better than the yonin, but they never look for the things no one tells them to find. I've barely begun searching, and I've seen things I think even the Miriseh have forgotten."

"Do they ever come down here?" My foot almost slips on a loose rock, but I brace myself on the wall and continue moving forward. "Beyond the bathing caves, anyway."

"Rarely." Ey peers at the left wall before taking the right fork of the tunnel. When I reach the same spot, I notice the glint of an iron button stuck into a crack in the stone, a perfect marker for a hidden path. "The Miriseh and the kaigo leave the undercity to the yonin."

Ey stops talking when the narrow path begins to climb.

We have to drop to all fours to keep our balance the incline is so steep, and no ishiji has smoothed the way. There haven't been enough feet pressing oils and sweat into the rocks to flatten out their edges, either. In a way it makes it easier—the divots in the rock give us places to grip and pull ourselves up to the next handhold.

"How did you even find this?"

"I've been searching the outlying tunnels for anything that might lead to Yorri, and this one opened up after one of the tunnels in the mine below us collapsed."

I look over my shoulder. The drop is steep. If we lost our grip or the rocks shifted under our hands, it'd be a long slide down. Protrusions extend at just the right angle for someone to crack their head if they fell, too. If someone were unconscious, this drop could kill them. Eventually, though, it brings us to the level surface of what looks like an antechamber with three shadowy archways leading off. Sanii doesn't lead me to those; ey heads toward a stretch of blank wall.

"Have you ever seen these?" Sanii points at a section of the wall. From a distance it looked like the stone was covered with natural crags and divots, but it's all too even, straight, and deep for it to be a natural occurrence.

"No, I've never seen it." The lines and curves must have meaning, but I can't even begin to guess what that meaning might be. "What is it?"

Ey heaves a frustrated sigh and props eir hands on eir hips. "I was hoping you'd be able to tell me. I thought they might be the marks the nyshin mapmakers and supply masters use."

"There are similarities, but I've never seen these formations before. If they're nyshin marks, they're not something they teach the –ten ranks." I run my fingertips along the carved-out marks, tracing them over and over to memorize them. I want to recognize this if I ever see it again. "What's beyond here?"

"That's what I wanted to show you. I think it might be part of the original city." Ey walks toward one of the arches, but gestures to the other two. "Those dead-end in empty rooms, but this one." Ey glances at me, light that has nothing to do with eir magic glimmering in eir eyes. "This one might take you a while to explore."

"Lucky we have time, then."

"At least until the storm breaks up," Sanii agrees. "No one should miss us before that."

Well, Tessen might notice I'm gone. In the days since Sanii took me to the saishigi core, it's like he's been following me. The kitchens, the bathing pools, the training yard for extra practice—suddenly Tessen is everywhere, but he hasn't once tried to speak to me. I don't know what to make of it, especially since it feels less like he's suspicious and watching me and more as though he's worried and watching out *for* me.

It's…strange. It's not something anyone else has ever tried to do, not even Yorri.

I take a breath—the air here smells like water and metal and stillness—and walk into the dark mouth of the left passage. When Sanii steps in behind me, the light ey casts shows smooth walls like the ones in Itagami. It's narrow enough that I could reach out and touch both walls with my fingertips, but not so close that Sanii and I can't walk side by side.

The room at the end of the short hallway is empty. The walls are not.

"Ryogo." I breathe the word into the silence of the cave. It *has* to be Ryogo. The colors are faded, but the pictures are clear. I lean closer, straining to see it all. Mountains and plains and sprawling gardens, all of it in shades of green. Buildings in dark brown and white dot the landscape, their shape and style nothing like the rectangular forms of the barracks of Itagami. These have multiple levels and roofs that come to a sharp point.

My lungs and my eyes burn.

I'll never know if this is what it looks like.

"Khya, look." Sanii's voice calls across the cave to a section of the wall untouched by color but carved with hundreds of tiny markings.

One near the upper right edge catches my eye, and I raise my hand to trace the lines with my fingertips. "This one looks like the one we saw outside."

"Which doesn't help us unless we can figure out what it means." Sanii nearly growls the words.

"This is so old I doubt that anyone but the Miriseh knows where it came from. If I wanted to hide something, though, this might be a good place to put it. Maybe someone discovered part of the old city and is using it to…" I trace the next marking and then the next, trying to commit as many of them as I can to memory. And trying to use them to chase out the thoughts of what exactly they might be using these hidden caverns to do. "Yorri might be here somewhere."

Sanii doesn't respond, but ey doesn't need to. Everything ey's doing is because ey thinks it might lead us to my brother. I pull my hand away from the marks on the wall, wishing I had a lump of clay to etch or a stick of charcoal and some nyska paper. Anything to duplicate the marks. There are more farther down the wall, etched into a rusted iron-and-stone door. It's open partway, which is good. The lock has disintegrated, and the hinges look shaky. I wouldn't want to risk moving it. The gap is narrow enough that we have to squeeze through sideways.

Like the previous chamber, this one is covered with murals. Some depict Ryogo—the wide rivers and the plentiful green match the stories' descriptions too well for it to be anywhere else—but one wall is different. On this one, a group stands in formation, each off the shoulder of the previous. They must be at least twenty feet tall from floor to roof, and all of them are wearing oddly cut and brightly colored clothing with wide sleeves that seem like they would get tangled in everything.

The detail to each face makes them look so real it's easy to believe they're about to blink, breathe, and step into the room with us. The detail also makes them impossible not to recognize.

The Miriseh.

If this section of caves truly is part of the original city, it makes sense that there would be a portrait of the Miriseh. Their arrival five hundred years ago heralded the change of our entire society. They gave us a city that would protect us from the dangers of Shiara and the other clans. They showed us how to gather enough food and resources to not just survive but thrive here. They taught those of us who could how to harness the desosa and make our magic a thousand times stronger. Of course the original citizens would have honored their ten leaders like this.

Except there aren't ten people on the wall. There are twelve.

"If this is a painting of the Miriseh, and the Miriseh cannot die..." Sanii looks up at the two faces we've never seen before. "What happened to the other two?"

CHAPTER
THIRTEEN

I leave the barracks early to give myself time alone before my shift, so it's barely sunrise when I reach the top of the western wall. The only people here are the guards about to finish their shift, and they don't bother me when I leverage myself up to sit cross-legged on the outer ledge.

There's no water west of us, only rock and sand and scrub. Nothing down there will cushion my fall if I ever have to take this leap. If I threw myself over the side, I doubt even my wards could save me.

Will it come to this eventually? The choice between taking my own life or knowing my death will be a lesson for the rest of the clan? I'm doomed to Kujuko either way, so what does it matter?

I suppose making this choice, leaning over the edge of the wall and not coming back, will depend on what else Sanii and I find. How deep do the secrets buried under Itagami go? The Miriseh are hiding something. That much is certain. What's unclear is how that something connects to Yorri and the missing yonin. I need to know what ties it all together. I need to know why my brother lost his life to keep that secret buried.

There's no way I'll be able to live the rest of my life pretending to be a faithful citizen if Varan, Suzu, and the rest of the Miriseh are responsible. The thought of constantly wondering which of my clansmen are working to hide the councils' secrets is exhausting enough to give me a headache. More likely than not, I'd be serving years or decades more only to end up in Kujuko anyway.

It's almost time for the shift change. Rai will be here soon looking for me, and I'll have to force a semblance of a smile and pretend everything is fine.

Exhaling, I stand and lean farther over the edge.

"That's a messy way to go."

I turn so fast I almost lose balance.

Tessen is standing several feet away, his wary eyes watching me closely. What is he doing here? I don't ask, a little afraid of the answer. Instead, I leap backward off the ledge and look away, watching the horizon instead of him. "You should stay away from me, Nyshin-ten."

"And you shouldn't be thinking about throwing yourself over the city wall."

I whip back to face him. "I wasn't."

Tessen glances at the wall, his face tense. "You were."

"You can't know that." Really, how could he know that? And it wasn't as though I was considering doing it *now*.

"Actually, with you, I can."

What does that even mean? I can't handle any more secrets or enigmas. "Don't you have work to be doing? Go away, Nyshin-ten."

"Hear me out, Khya." He takes one step closer, his hands held away from his weapons. "That's all I'm asking."

"You should leave before Rai shows up." Where *is* she?

Rai's never late. "Some of us do have work to do."

Tessen's lips twitch, but he doesn't smile. "She wanted to let me tell you I'm your new partner. She's serving with Etaro now."

"*What?*" My jaw clenches.

"The transfer happened fast. And I think Rai thought she was playing matchmaker." He clears his throat, looking nervous, but his eyes don't drop away from mine. "I don't know if that makes you more angry or less, but—"

"You were serving under a nyshin-lu." I'll figure out what to say to Rai later. Tessen is the problem standing in front of me now. "Why the bellows would they transfer you into *this* squad? What'd you do? Insult one of the Miriseh?"

The nyshin-lu were only one rank below the kaigo. As much as I admire Tyrroh, he's only a nyshin-ma; there are two ranks in between him and Tessen's apparently former commanding officer.

Tessen shrugs, his face impassive. "I requested the transfer, and the councils didn't think it was too much to ask."

"You *put* yourself here?" I can't believe this. The idiot! He had everything I wanted. He's never appreciated it, but now he's literally giving it away? I step closer; he moves back, just enough to stay out of reach.

"I've been trying to catch you for days, but you wouldn't let me talk to you." He runs one hand over his close-cut hair, brow furrowed. "This was the only way I could think of."

My heart pounds. What could he possibly have to say to me that warrants this? "There's nothing you can say that I want to hear."

"Maybe not, but you need to listen."

"Why?"

He pauses then, his eyes jumping from my face to the

horizon where the Kyiwa Mountains glow fire-red in the early morning sunlight. His shoulders pull back and he faces me again, determination in his eyes.

"I tried to find you yesterday, during the storm." Tessen's expression is intense, his gray eyes gleaming with dark determination. It's something I've only ever seen in flashes on his normally smiling face, and it makes my pulse jump, the beat erratic.

This is how he looked when he teased me about pushing myself so hard to earn a place among the kaigo. It's the expression I saw when they awarded him the kaigo-sei position and, earlier than that, when they put him in charge of our training squad. What could he possibly have taken from me now?

"I might know where to find what you're looking for."

My focus narrows to Tessen's face, my body stilling and even my heartbeat seeming to stutter to a stop. "What exactly do you think I'm looking for?"

With a step, he moves inside my guard, closer than I let almost anyone get outside of training exercises and sex. Yorri had been one of the few exceptions—Rai and Etaro some of the only others—but standing so close to Tessen isn't anything like that. This is an extra layer of heat and a pulsing awareness of the scant inches between us, as though the desosa filling that space is somehow electrified.

Then his voice drops until it's barely a breath on the wind. "You're looking for Yorri."

His words knock all the air out of my chest.

"How did—?" The question—the *confirmation*—is out of my mouth before I can bite it back. My hands shake. His eyes light with triumph.

Blood and rot! Is this why he transferred here? Maybe the councils found out I'm looking for Yorri and they sent

Tessen to discover the truth. I don't know what Sanii or I did that gave us away, but that has to be why Tessen is watching me, his thumbs hooked around his teegra-skin belt. He's taking everything in and giving me nothing.

"Even if that *was* true, why would you help me look?" If the Miriseh and the kaigo are already willing to kill to protect their secrets, I don't think they'll care about adding one more nyshin-ten to that list. Not even if that nyshin-ten is the strongest fykina mage they've seen in generations. Being a kynacho hadn't saved Yorri.

I draw my anto and use our bodies to hide its glint as I press the tip just above his hip. Tessen grunts but doesn't move.

"Is this a trick?" My hands aren't shaking now. "I *will* kill you before anyone else can reach us."

"*Think*, Khya." Frustration makes his voice hoarser. "If I meant to turn you in, would I come here to tell you?"

"Maybe." It's the more logical choice, but not the only one. "Or maybe you're under orders to find out what I know."

"I already know what you know, because I followed you and Sanii into the saishigi core." Tessen sighs. We're standing so close that his words are below a whisper and his breath is stronger than the breeze against my cheek. "You haven't learned anything new since that night. You would've done something by now if you had."

Oh. His pointed questions about where I'd been walking that evening, and his disappointment when I let him think I'd been in the rooftop gardens—it makes sense now. He knew, but he wanted me to tell him more.

"After I heard what Sanii told you, I asked Neeva about the night Yorri died."

My heart skips a beat. "What did she tell you?"

"Hardly anything at first." He doesn't look at the blade pressed to his side, but his body shifts, angling half of his body away while bringing the other half closer to me. I don't follow him, letting the pressure of the blade ease. "But I told her knowing the story would help you move past his death."

"And then?" I pull the anto away completely, dropping my hand to my side.

"Tonight. After shift?" He leans closer, brushing his cheek against mine before looking away, focusing on something behind me.

Bellows. The wall. We're exposed. How did I forget where we were? There are probably more than a dozen uniku mages stationed with the ahdo guard tonight. Sight is a more common single-sense enhancement than hearing, but it'd be deadly stupid to risk the chance of someone overhearing us. I'd suspect myself of having a case of brain-rot if I didn't know better.

And I don't even want to think about what it looks like we're doing standing this close in the open. Rumor will have us in bed together before we're even off the wall. Better they see that than what's actually happening, though.

"Why?" We're still close enough that I can feel the way the desosa ripples and flows around his body. We're close enough that our words are more breathed than spoken, but I know he can hear me. I keep my stance relaxed, but my anto finds its way back to that soft spot right above his hip. "Looking for these answers will break every rule that matters, Nyshin-ten. This marks us as traitors. Life without honor. Death without a chance of passing into Ryogo. Tell me why you're willing to risk everything you've worked so hard to steal from me just to save someone I don't think you ever liked."

Tessen swallows and shakes his head. "The why doesn't matter."

"No. Tell me." I press the blade in, feeling the finely honed edge bite into his flesh. "Why now? Why this? Why would you betray the clan and everything we've ever known?"

He never flinches, and he never looks away. "Why would you?"

"You know why."

Tessen smiles. "And you wouldn't believe my reasons even if I told you."

"Try me."

He stares into my eyes and seems to be considering something. Or searching for something. Whatever he's looking for, he must find it, because he takes a deep breath. "Because if Yorri is alive, then it means the Miriseh are lying to the clan, taking the lives of the people they're supposed to be protecting. Because if they've lied about this, they've probably lied about more. Because there's more going on here, and I want to know what it is."

Is it true? Is it enough? It wouldn't be enough for me if our places were reversed. I don't know if I can trust him, but I think that if I don't keep him beside me, there's a chance he'll be behind me. Maybe it's better to keep him close.

I step back and sheathe my anto. "Why did you even follow us?"

"You know me." Tessen's smile grows, like he knows he's won this argument. "I've always been too curious for my own good."

That is definitely true, because now his curiosity is leading him straight to Kujuko with me.

CHAPTER FOURTEEN

I manage to make it through the shift on the wall without punching Tessen or even getting into another argument with him. Part of me wants to grab him by the tunic and drag him into the undercity as soon as we're free, but we have responsibilities that people expect us to complete. It'd be noticed if we disappear now. Luckily, with the two of us working together, it shouldn't take long to finish everything his former nyshin-lu expected him to take care of before sundown.

Despite the questions and buzz of anxiety in the back of my mind, I play nice long enough to help him pack his things, clearing his old room for whoever is replacing him on his squad. Our truce almost ends when I see Etaro and Rai in our hallway, all of Etaro's belongings piled in their arms.

"Oh! Umm..." Etaro shoots a panicked look at Rai, who rolls her eyes.

"Ey's moving next door to me, and Tessen now has the room across from you, Khya." She kicks Etaro's calf, nudging em toward the stairs. "Congratulations. You can thank me later. Have fun, and please try not to keep the rest of us awake when we're trying to sleep."

They leave quickly, Rai's large eyes twinkling with mischief and Etaro still looking like a doseiku caught doing something they'd been specifically told not to.

"I'm going to permanently ward you both in your rooms one day!" I call after her. She and Etaro grin over their shoulders at me. I turn to Tessen, glaring over the pack I'm carrying. "Did you have anything to do with that?"

"No, so I owe them both favors at some point for thinking of it." He seems pleased as he looks down the hall to where, apparently, his new room is awaiting.

"I'm going to regret not pushing you over the wall today, aren't I?" I mutter as we walk together toward our—our?—rooms.

"Given my luck with you, possibly. But I'm hoping not." We drop his packs in his room, but then he follows me into mine. "You never know what the future might bring, oh deadly one."

I roll my eyes and pick up the hunk of molding clay I took from the storeroom. If Tessen is going to join our little hunt, he needs to see everything we have seen, and if we're going back to the mural cave, I want to copy those markings.

Tessen looks at the lump in my hand oddly—obviously confused—but doesn't ask. In fact, he's completely silent as we grab something to eat and go down to the bathing pools. It's a change I could easily get used to.

Yesterday, Sanii introduced me to Reeka, a yonin who works at the bathing pools. Reeka and Taya had been lovers, a step away from requesting a sumai bond, and his disappearance had wounded her deeply. Reeka didn't know what we were doing, but she was willing to help Sanii because ey'd found Taya's body and given her the chance to grieve.

I spot Reeka as soon as Tessen and I enter the pools, and I nod when she briefly meets my eye. Tessen notices, looking at me with questions in his eyes as he pulls off his tunic, questions he thankfully doesn't ask.

We quickly divest ourselves of our clothes and wade into the warm, shallow pool. There's a scar on his shoulder blade that looks new—it's faint, almost unnoticeable if I weren't looking for it, but there's still the halo of bruising from the healing of a deep wound.

I freeze midstep for a second, mind spinning. Why had I paid so much attention to where his scars were that I noticed a new one? I bathe with Etaro and Rai more often than I have with Tessen, at least for the past year, but I don't think I know the placement of their scars this well.

I know Yorri's scars like that, though.

Knew.

Know?

Growling under my breath, I clear my mind as much as I can. There's enough that I have to deal with today. Adding more isn't worth it.

Finding an empty spot, I wash the dust and the sweat off my skin and watch the others. An ebet I recognize from the training yard floats by, and two doseiku are splashing each other in the far corner, well away from the possible ire of adults. Do they know? Does anyone in this room know about the missing yonin, the Miriseh's secrets, the forgotten caverns, Yorri...

The room is crowded, and I have never felt so alone. Not once in my life have I felt this separate from the clan. The questions in my head, and the quest I know I have to finish, have already changed me somehow. Can they see it? Something like this feels like it has to be marked on my skin and visible in my eyes.

But no one seems to notice or care. No one but Tessen is watching me.

Pushing away the useless cycle of worries, I meet his eyes and nod toward the exit. The yonin attendant quickly scans our bodies before searching their shelves for something close to our sizes.

Dry and dressed, we head through the caves as though returning to our barracks. Only after we're away from the crowds do I slip into the shadowy side tunnels even the yonin rarely use. Tessen's extra-sensitive basaku senses are useful here, catching the sounds of someone approaching far sooner than I could have. Everything moves smoothly, far more smoothly than I expected, until we reach the small alcove where Sanii is waiting.

Eir eyes widen when ey sees Tessen. "You!"

"Me," Tessen says. I can't read the expression on his face.

Sanii's fury, though, is obvious. And it's directed at me. "What are you *thinking*?"

"He came to me." I feel Tessen move to stand behind me like an honor guard. Why does he always have to stand so close? There's at least an inch of space between us, but I can *feel* him in a way that makes my skin seem sunburned— warm and prickly to the point of painful. "He says he has an idea of where to search for what we're looking for, and I want to hear what he has to say before I decide what to do with him. I thought it might be a good idea to show him the murals."

Distrust and resentment color eir expression. "Are you sure about this?"

"As sure as I can be. It's not worth the effort trying to

make him leave." I sigh and run my hand through my damp hair. "I've been trying to run him off for years. Nothing has worked."

"That may not be the best recommendation." Tessen's breath is warm across my neck and the curve of my ear.

"No." I clamp down on the shiver that threatens to run through me, but I can't stop the bumps from rising on my skin. If I moved away, I know he wouldn't follow, but I stay exactly where I am. "But it's true."

"It's not," he insists. Somehow he moves closer without actually touching me. "Today was the first time I've ever stayed when you actually asked me to leave."

I almost throw back an automatic denial. Our encounters over the last few years have been all sharp edges and veiled insults, but… Oh. Blood and rot, he's right. Most of it has been aimed from me to *him*. Each time, as soon as I said no, or honestly asked him to go away, he did. The realization is…unsettling.

Forcing an annoyed huff, I cross my arms. "He's a nuisance, Sanii, but he knows I'll gut him if he betrays us."

It's not as though I have a place in Ryogo anymore, anyway.

Sanii seems unsure, but ey nods and turns in the direction of the mural caves. As we walk, I smile. Tessen hasn't seen Sanii's glow yet.

"What has you so amused?" he asks.

"I'm thinking about what your face is going to look like in a minute."

Ahead of us, Sanii chuckles. Tessen's face pinches, nervousness appearing in the lines around his eyes. "Is it that bad? Where are we going?"

"You'll see," Sanii singsongs.

I was right to hope. Moments later, when we're well-hidden from anyone who might be wandering down here, Sanii lights the small space brighter than a ring of oil lamps could.

The shocked gasp he emits and the way his eyes grow large and round like oversize buttons—it's the funniest thing I've seen in moons. It's even better when he straightens, a calm mask falling over his face, and tries to pretend that none of it happened.

Sanii and I glance at each other and laugh. We're still laughing when we duck down and begin the long climb to the mural caves.

Tessen stands in the middle of the cave painted with the dark mountains and lush greenery of Ryogo, awe on his face. "Do you think it really looks like this?"

"It's how the Miriseh have always described it." Doesn't matter anymore if it's true. I'll never see it, and now neither will he. I pinch the trailing edge of his tunic and tug him toward the opposite wall. "What about the marks? Do you recognize any?"

He shakes his head slowly. His eyes move across each line of marks, starting at the top right edge and ending at the bottom left corner. "Some of them almost look like signs the kaigo use, but there are too many strokes. Nothing I've seen with them is this complicated."

It's something, but not what I was hoping for.

"This isn't what we wanted to show you." I pull on his tunic again and then let go, walking away from the wall.

Sanii walks toward the rusted door and we follow, Tessen walking half-turned so he can keep studying the Ryogo murals and the indecipherable marks. He's almost too broadly muscled to squeeze sideways through the partly open door, but he manages. And comes to a stumbling halt when he sees the mural that makes it feel as though the Miriseh are towering above us.

"Oh." His eyes jump from face to face quickly.

I point to the two I hadn't known, a woman with long hair more brown than black and a bald man who looks older than most of the others, lines around his eyes and gray streaks in his beard. "Do you recognize them?"

Tessen shakes his head as he moves closer to the wall.

"Why is he here?" Sanii points accusingly at Tessen, who is running the pads of his fingers along the painted wall. "You said he knew something!"

"I said that *he said* he knew something," I clarify, watching Tessen's inspection.

Tessen pulls his hand off the wall and clears his throat. "Do I get to speak or should I let you two keep talking for me?" When the only response he gets from Sanii is a dark glare, he says, "I told Khya that I might know where Yorri is."

Eir face lights up, the glow surrounding em getting brighter. "How? Where?" Wariness clouds eir expression. "And how did you even know we were looking for Yorri?"

There's a strange amount of guilt in Tessen's eyes. "Because I followed you the night you took Khya into the core."

"Blood and rot, you need to learn how to mind your own business," Sanii mutters. Ey looks away, though, color flushing eir cheeks. "Do you just go around following *everyone*?"

The look on eir face is strange, somewhere between embarrassment and fear. What did Tessen find out by following Sanii where he shouldn't have? And how long ago was that?

Whatever happened between them in the past doesn't matter. I'm still waiting for an answer to what he knows *now*.

"Can we please focus?" They both shut their mouths, the snap of their teeth clicking together audible in the quiet cave. Shaking my head, I face Tessen. "You've spent time with the kaigo." I flick the kaigo-sei pendent hanging in the center of his chest. "Have you ever heard anything that mentions twelve members of the Miriseh?"

"No, definitely not." He looks up at the strangers' faces.

"Come back to the other room." I step toward the door leading back to the Ryogan murals. I should have asked about the hints he dropped about Yorri already, but... What if what he has to tell me isn't anything that will help us get him back? "I want to copy those marks before we leave, and you owe us information."

"Not a good idea, Khya," Sanii grumbles. And not for the first time. "What if someone who knows what the marks are sees you with it?" Despite the protests, ey follows me to the Ryogan murals and stands to best light a large portion of the wall. Tessen walks out right behind em.

"If I make it small enough, I can keep it with me. No one will find it." I hope. "And the only people who could possibly know anything about this place are the Miriseh. Maybe some of the kaigo council."

I trace the first mark in the row with my fingertip several times. Once I understand how the swooping curve of the top line connects to the lines and smaller dashes below it, I carve it into the clay with a shard of rock.

"So, what do you know?" Sanii demands of Tessen after a few moments of silence. "Why should we trust that you won't turn us over to the kaigo?"

"It's been longer than most people think since the clan

has had a basaku," Tessen says.

"Fifty years," I say under my breath, glancing at him out the corner of my eye.

He rolls his eyes, but there's a small smile on his lips when he looks at me. "Okay, well, people who *weren't* in my doseiku training class tend to forget."

That is absolutely the truth. Our training masters gushed about that for weeks, as though it was somehow something *they* had done that made Tessen such a strong sensor mage. It caused quite a stir the moons of our herynshis. A basaku and a fykina joining the nyshin in the same year. The Miriseh had seemed positively childlike in their excitement.

"The rest of the clan doesn't really understand what a basaku can sense. They tend to forget how much I can hear when I'm concentrating. They're not always cautious, especially when they don't know I'm nearby."

He's silent for long enough that I glance over, wondering what stopped his tongue.

Weight shifting and eyes distant, he looks like he's choosing his words with exceptional caution. "Two days after your visit to the core, I heard Miriseh Suzu tell Kaigo Neeva that the magic in this generation was stronger than anything she'd seen before. I wanted to hear more, so I followed them."

"Looking for another secret to hold over someone's head?" Sanii spits the words at him, the bitterness I've heard in em before coming back in full force.

"Yes, that's exactly why. Because I like collecting secrets I then threaten people with." Tessen squeezes his eyes shut and presses two fingers to the space between his brows. "Why am I trying to help you two?"

Sanii tenses and looks down. I hold my breath, waiting

to see which one of them will explode first and readying my wards just in case, though I doubt it'll come to that.

The moment stretches longer and tenser.

As soon as Sanii's shoulders drop, the tension in the room drains away.

Clearing eir throat, ey murmurs, "I apologize. Please continue."

Tessen looks at em, his head tilted, but then he nods. "Apology accepted."

Good. Now we can move on. "Why did you follow them?"

"Because I knew neither of you would listen to me unless I brought you something you didn't already know. And you definitely wouldn't let me tag along to help," he says. "As soon as I left you that night after the saishigi core, I went looking for a way to find Yorri."

It sounds ridiculously paranoid of us when he says it like that, but what we're doing is treason. Of course we wouldn't let just anyone *tag along*. This search will cost us our lives if the wrong person finds out. It will probably cost us Ryogo even if no one ever does; this betrayal of the clan stained our souls the moment we made this choice.

"What did you hear?" I'd love it if he could get to the point.

Resignation in his eyes, he says, "Suzu asked when Neeva had last been to Imaku."

"*Imaku?*" Sanii's glowing hands clench.

My heart misses a beat. "No one can get to Imaku."

Although groups of yonin manage the fishing nets strung between the rocks near the shore, learning to swim is rare—the ocean is too dangerous and the bathing pools are too shallow. Those who do learn know there's an enormous difference between the slow river that feeds the bathing pools and the ocean's raging, unpredictable currents. A decade ago, a nyshin-ten tried to swim the half mile between Shiara and Imaku. He drowned less than ten yards from Shiara, and his body washed up onto the shore more than a mile and a half down the island.

"Yes, I know." Tessen looks at me, this time with a hint of hesitation. "That's why I think Yorri's there."

I try to speak, but my mouth has gone dry. Only a rasping breath escapes.

"I heard Suzu ask about restraints and…" He swallows. "She told Neeva that underestimating a kynacho would be a disaster they can't risk when they're this close."

Restraints. No one would bother restraining the dead.

He's alive.

Yorri isn't the only kynacho in the clan, but none of the others are missing. So that means Sanii was right.

But…restraints. They have my brother tied down somewhere, trapped and… How did they trap him? *Why* did they?

"Close to what?" Sanii asks. "Why did they take him?"

"*That* they didn't say," Tessen admits. His fingers trace the shape of the anto on his belt and he shifts his weight. "But it makes sense that they're keeping Yorri on Imaku rather than somewhere in the city. Even a place like this would be too risky. Someone could find it."

"How do they *get* there?" Sanii's eyes are wide and eir glow has gotten brighter.

"I—" Tessen tries.

Sanii talks over him. "I've been looking for anything that heads away from the city, but there aren't any tunnels that head north very far."

"I—"

"Do they use magic?" Sanii asks. "Maybe there's a way

a rikinhisu mage can lift someone from rock to rock if they—"

"I don't know! For all I know, they strap themselves to a couple of mykyn birds and *fly*." Tessen's voice echoes off the stone walls. Sanii's mouth shuts with an audible snap, and ey steps back, away from both of us, eir light dimming. Sighing, Tessen tries again. Quieter, but no less insistent. "I don't know how they get there. They didn't say anything that hinted at how, only where."

I refocus on the markings. If I don't, I might scream. Or get us all caught by rushing through the undercity to search for a possibly nonexistent tunnel to Imaku. Behind me, Sanii and Tessen are silent. The air feels charged with something...uncomfortable.

"We'll find him." I don't look up from my work, but I feel their attention shift to me. Copying the markings helps keep my voice calm—a lot more level than I feel. "We've eliminated a lot of starting points thanks to Sanii, and now we know what direction we need to travel."

I have time to duplicate three more marks before Tessen clears his throat. "I'll keep an ear out. See what else I can learn."

"And I'll keep crawling through the caves looking for something that leads north." There's only a little resentment in Sanii's voice. It gets stronger when ey asks, "What will *you* be doing, Khya?"

Well, that's probably the easiest question ey could have asked. "After you two figure out where we're going, I'll be the one keeping us all from getting killed before we get there."

Neither of them says much after that.

●●●

When we crawl back to the undercity hours later, Sanii seems to have reverted to eir usual prickly self, and Tessen has receded into strained silence.

"You can find your way back from here, right?" Sanii asks, eying Tessen with barely less wariness than the first time we stood here.

I nod. "I know how to get back."

Sanii tilts eir head toward Tessen. "Keep an eye on him. He looks one question away from cracking."

With one more annoyed glance at Tessen, Sanii ducks under the low wall and disappears.

"Something tells me ey doesn't like me much," Tessen mutters once ey's gone.

"You did invite yourself into this without eir permission." I duck under the low opening and step into the wider passage. It takes a moment for Tessen to join me.

"You don't trust me, either." He says it like a statement instead of a question this time.

"No. I'm not sure I do yet." Facing him, I try to read his expression in the flickering light of the two distant lamps, but there are too many shadows moving across his face. "We're giving up everything, Tessen. In this life and the next. Sanii and I have a reason for that. You don't."

He stares into my eyes for a moment, then looks away.

"You have realized that if we find him and free him, we can't stay in Itagami, right?" I need to know he's thought about this. "Everything you spent the last twelve years striving for will be gone." Everything he worked so hard to make sure I didn't have. "We'll end up begging the Denhitrans or the Tsimosi for help or hiding in the desert until Shiara kills us. When we die, whether that's in one moon or twenty years, we'll be trapped in Kujuko for however long eternity lasts. Is that really something you're willing to suffer?"

His voice is strong and certain when he says, "Yes."

Tessen shifts and the glow from the lantern mounted to the wall falls across his eyes, giving their silver-gray color a fiery glimmer that makes my breath catch. Under his steady gaze I have to fight to suppress a nervous twitch, but I know Tessen can hear how fast my heart is pounding.

I pretend it's not true, if only to make myself feel better. "All right. I guess it's a good thing that you went and transferred yourself to my squad."

"That *had* been part of my plan, I admit." The right corner of his lips curves up just enough to bring out the smile lines on that side of his face. It makes him far more attractive than I want to admit. And far more attractive than I wish I noticed. "I figured I'd still call it a good idea as long as you didn't gut me before I could convince you to let me help."

"Don't worry. I still might." I smile, feeling like we're back to familiar, solid ground.

We haven't made it halfway toward our barracks when Tessen's hand closes around my wrist. He pulls me to a stop seconds before I would have crashed straight into Ryzo's chest.

"Khya?" Ryzo looks at me, then Tessen, and then the tunnel, suspicion in his eyes. "What are you doing out here?"

My mind is blank. Blood and rot, why didn't we think of an explanation before now?

"We were just taking a walk." Tessen's face is innocently bland, but there's something in his tone that implies more than a walk. "Looking for somewhere quiet."

"Hmm. Aren't you the one who just transferred into our squad?" Ryzo asks as he examines Tessen.

Tessen nods. "It's good to meet you, Nyshin-ten Ryzo."

The smile Ryzo gives Tessen is brief and forced before he turns to me and asks, "Have you seen Tyrroh?"

"What? No, not since he checked on us after noon." I look down the passage, back the way we came. "Why would you be looking for Tyrroh down here?"

"I thought I saw him coming this way. You didn't pass him?" Tessen and I shake our heads and Ryzo grunts, running his hand over his close-cut hair. He drops his arm and smiles at us. "Carry on, then. We'll be in the desert the next few days, so you better get all your fun in now."

When he winks at us before he walks away, I almost groan and drop my face into my hands. This is great. By tomorrow everyone in the squad is going to think Tessen is my new lover. Actually, they probably think that based on his transfer alone. This will just make it worse.

"Well, at least we won't have to come up with a hundred different excuses to keep slipping off together," Tessen says a few seconds later.

And he's right. It'll be easier if we let people make assumptions and fill in the blanks. The fewer lies we tell, the harder it will be for anyone to catch us in one.

But I wish it hadn't been *this* assumption.

CHAPTER
FIFTEEN

lthough Tessen, Sanii, and I spent as much time as we could risk creating a map of Itagami—the upper city and the undercity—we couldn't figure out any way to get to Imaku without being seen from Itagami. Swimming under the waves would have been a possibility for the Miriseh, but the kaigo would probably die in the attempt. The sole option that made sense was a tunnel, only we couldn't spot any new places to look for those, either.

With the possible exception of the herynshi cavern.

Sanii suggested it. It fit in some ways—mostly because it's hidden and hard to get to—but I didn't believe we'd find the entrance there. Even if we could get to the cavern itself. The Miriseh rarely leave the city. The herynshi once-a-moon cycle is one of the only exceptions. Someone in the clan would've noticed additional comings and goings. The actions of the Miriseh are *always* noted.

Two days later, I still can't decide which answer is more likely, and I have no idea how I'm going to talk Sanii out of wasting time looking for the location of the herynshi cavern. Right now, though, in the middle of our squad's trek into the desert to hunt for the Denhitrans, I have more pressing concerns.

After two days in the desert, my clothes are stuck to my skin. Dust and dirt has found its way into every pore and crevice. It's too hot sitting here in the baking sun, and it'll be too cold tonight. And I am tired of dried everything—meat, mushrooms, and fruits.

But, of course, it can always get worse.

"You know, when I told you to keep it quiet with Tessen, I didn't mean you had to go find some hidden cave or wherever it is you two have been disappearing to." Rai smirks, entirely unconcerned by my ire when I glare at her. "I mean, you're more my preference than he is, but that doesn't mean I can't see the appeal. No need to be ashamed. Sex is perfectly natural. Everyone does it."

"Almost everyone," Etaro corrects, cheeks flushing darker. Ey once told me that ey couldn't see the appeal of rolling around naked with someone. When most of eir yearmates started experimenting, ey declared emself ushimo. "But she's right. *I* wouldn't want to do anything with him, but you two are perfect."

I shrug, not looking in the direction I know Tessen walked to get a better look at the open plain on the other side of the escarpment we're using for cover. Maybe they'll let it drop.

"No one else can keep up with you quite like he can. Not even us," Rai persists. "You need someone willing to fight dirty against you every once in a while."

"Why would I ever want *that*?" That sounds awful. This entire conversation is awful, but I shouldn't protest. Letting people make up their own stories makes my life easier.

I didn't think it would bother me, and it doesn't with

the rest of the squad. Rai and Etaro are different. I don't like lying to them, but protesting would only make them more certain they were right. Or, if they did believe nothing was happening between Tessen and me, they'd start wondering what we actually have been spending our time doing or try to "help me along." I'm not sure which one would be worse.

"It's not 'fighting dirty.'" Etaro's lips purse. "It's more like Tessen challenges you. I don't think you could put up with someone who didn't challenge you. Not for long."

"Always the diplomatic one." Rai rubs Etaro's head and ey bats her hand away, a fond smile on eir face. "Ey's right, though. Tessen doesn't get angry at every single barb you throw, but doesn't let you get away with it when you go too far."

"Are you saying everyone else does?" How often do I go too far?

Etaro's nose wrinkles as ey looks away. Rai laughs. "I can't speak for everyone. Your sharp edges don't bother me, though, and Etaro is too nice to say anything."

Frowning, I shift backward on the rock and pull my hood over the top of my head. We unwrapped our atakafu and pushed back our hoods to eat, but now I want the privacy the layers provide.

"You've always claimed to hate Tessen, yet you've spent more time with him than you have with us this past week." Rai leans closer, her round eyes bright with curiosity. "Do—"

"Nyshin-ma!" Tessen's voice rings out over the group. "Enemy southwest. More than a mile away and moving northwest."

The squad is on their feet in seconds, atakafus re-wrapped and food stashed in belt pouches and thigh packs.

Nyshin-ma Tyrroh climbs to the top of the escarpment and peers into the distance with Tessen, though even with his enhanced sight, I doubt he's seeing what Tessen can spy at this distance.

It's been more than two weeks since our brief battle with the Denhitrans—more than two weeks since they supposedly killed my brother—and they've escaped our squads every time they've been spotted, somehow slipping past watchers and warriors alike.

Whispers have spread through the nyshin squads, the possibility of an akuringu too real to deny. Because they shouldn't be able to hide themselves from *all* of the clan's oraku mages. They especially shouldn't be able to hide from Tessen. An oraku might miss a weaker scent trail or miss seeing someone a mile out or misinterpret the faint sound carried in echoes through the mountains, but the strength of a basaku's senses are supposed to be able to catch that. All of it.

It makes me think…

Even if the rumors of an akuringu strong enough to scry the location of every single Itagamin squad aren't true, what Ryzo saw weeks ago might be. I don't want to admit it, but betrayal from the inside, someone misdirecting our squad and keeping us far from the trail of the enemy, fits even better than a mythically powerful akuringu.

"An ambush. We'll attempt to cut them off at the Suesutu Pass," Tyrroh announces. He casts a quick eye over the squad. "You'll lead half of the squad to the southern edge and press forward," he tells the recently promoted Nyshin-pa Ryzo. Very recently promoted—Tyrroh made the announcement less than an hour before the squad left the city two days ago. "We'll close them between us. Do not let them get past you."

"Urah, Nyshin-ma," Ryzo says.

I watch Tyrroh's hands as he issues specific commands to Daitsa and Ryzo, waiting to see if he uses that signal again, the one I thought I saw him use weeks ago. His quick gestures are all familiar as the nyshin-ma separates his sixteen nyshin-ten into two groups.

Rai and Etaro and six others follow Tyrroh and Daitsa. The rest of the squad, including Tessen and me, are placed under Ryzo's command. I pretend I don't see the knowing smirk Rai sends me when Tessen jumps from the top of the escarpment and moves to stand off my left shoulder.

We run swiftly through the rocky landscape, watching carefully for signs of previous passage. Nothing catches my eye, but it's easy to cross this terrain without leaving anything but a scent behind—and Tessen is the only one of us capable of picking *that* up.

Suesutu Pass is dangerous and narrow, a meeting of two larger mountains that is so difficult to cross that it barely warrants being called a pass at all. The way through is steep and filled with pitfalls and sharp drops. Hopefully these invaders won't know the dangers.

Trapped in the space between my atakafu and my skin, my breath feels almost hotter than the desert air. My blood burns under my skin, the thrill of the chase pushing me faster. Tessen stays as close as the path allows as we follow Ryzo into the mountains.

When we approach the south end of the pass, Ryzo signals for Tessen to scout ahead. Tessen moves toward a solid wall of rock, and I watch as he climbs, his tunic flaring out behind him in a sharp gust of air, until he's precariously perched on a narrow ledge about fifteen feet off the ground. He leans toward the pass once he's stable, then freezes.

None of us move. I don't think I'm the only one holding their breath. No one wants to be the one who distracts Tessen from whatever he's listening for on the wind.

It takes a few moments, then his hand moves, signaling—movement; coming south; fast; soon.

All eyes shift to Ryzo. In a series of swift, sharp motions, he orders us to spread out and seek cover in the rocks. Eyes sharp, weapons drawn, magic ready.

Before I move into position, Tessen catches my eye. *Caution*, he signs. *Safe*.

Wards, I remind him. *You caution*.

Though all I can see of his face is his eyes—and at this distance in the bright sunlight, I can't even see those well—I think he's smiling.

The last time we scouted this pass, I found a side path that wound away from the main. Less a path and more of a crevice, since I have to climb sideways after the first foot. For someone looking to hide in the mountains to protect themselves from an enemy, it's perfect. And a shortcut to where I want to go.

It takes a few minutes to scramble over the rocks and across the high outcropping that separates one side of the mountain from the other. Soon, I crouch behind a boulder in one of the few places this path widens. It's a dangerous choice—it gives me more room to maneuver, but it gives the enemy the same benefit.

Shade from the boulder protects me from the scorching heat of the sun, but the rock also deprives me of the breeze. Heat settles over my body like an extra layer of clothing.

I keep my breathing even and deep. I focus on what I can see and hear of the passage, and I remain motionless. Ready.

Clashes of iron and distant shouts echo over the rocks,

distortion making the source seem both near and far. I tense and draw my zeeka, adjusting my grip on the leather-wrapped hilt.

Instinct screams at me to go to my squad's aid. I remain hidden and still. No one would thank me for disobeying orders and allowing the enemy to escape.

A rock clatters down the mouth of the passage.

Someone's coming.

Their breathing is labored. They're moving fast and making a lot of noise; something metal—armor or weapons, maybe—keeps scraping against the sides of the ravine.

My fingers twitch and resettle on my blade. I bring up my wards, pulling the magic tight against my skin, invisible armor to protect me from magic or metal.

A dark-skinned, mostly bald, uncovered head appears at the top of the pass. They're looking over their shoulder, watching for whoever is following as they clamber noisily down the path. Shorter than me. Stocky and well-muscled. Dark skin littered with scars of battles fought and survived—must not think them an easy target. Long ahkiyu bow strapped to their back and a sword in their hand. It's almost as short as my zeeka, but with a wider blade.

As soon as the Denhitran scout is within range, I spring. My shadow on the rocks gives them warning. They bellow and bring their blade up to block mine.

I grin. Good. I'd hate for this to be easy.

Using the advantage of higher ground, I push forward. Our swords clash, the echoes turning our duel into a cacophony of sound. I strike faster. Their responses are too slow. My opponent falters. I swing my blade under theirs and slash across their forearm.

Crying out in pain, my foe falls. Their sword clatters to the rocks.

I place one foot over the hilt of their blade; the other I place on their chest. The tip of my sword I bring to rest over the largest of the veins in the neck. One move and even the strongest of hishingu will barely have time to save them.

"Tessen!" The rest of the squad is a quarter of a mile away. I hope he'll hear me over the battle in the distance. "Send someone to help me carry this useless bloodbag in."

"No, please," the Denhitran gasps, clutching their arm to their chest and straining to ease their head away from my sword. "We've done nothing. Let me go!"

I snort, not moving the tip of my blade from their throat and keeping watch for anyone who might be approaching.

"Please, we only— The storms!"

The storms? I look down at them. "What about the storms?"

"We just wanted to know—"

Something slams into my side.

I'm lifted into the air. I pull in energy from the desosa and throw it into my wards, shoving the power outward hard and fast.

The magical hold breaks.

Before I crash to the ground, the force is back. It shoves me against a rock so hard I'm left blinking to clear my vision, even with the protection of my wards.

I can protect myself against almost any kind of magic, but I'm facing a rikinhisu mage with the mental power and control to effortlessly hold me twenty feet off the ground. Chances are good that this mage can outlast me. Fantastic.

Whoever they are is standing in front of the setting sun. They're a slim silhouette, a shadow of a person who, thanks to the blinding rays, almost looks as though they're glowing like Sanii does.

"We're not here to harm you, little fykina." The voice sounds like it might come from a woman. It's soft and soothing and nothing like the unbreakable hold she has on me. "You may not believe this, but we are not your enemies."

Not our enemies? The people who poach our animals, attack our soldiers, and raid our border bases aren't enemies? I want to spit in her lying face, but she's too far away. And she'd likely kill me for it.

She strides into the shadow and I finally see her. Her skin is pale compared to the other's deep brown, and she's lean height where the rest of that clan is stocky muscle. This rikinhisu doesn't resemble any Denhitran I've seen or heard described. No, she'd fit better inside the walls of Itagami. But the half-moon eyes, the long, brown-black hair, the sharp squareness of her jaw is offset by the curve of her cheeks...

Standing before me is one of the missing Miriseh.

I open my mouth to pour out all of my questions—to lay everything I want to know at the feet of this impossible woman—but the only sound that escapes is a choked gasp.

"They're coming," someone hisses.

She looks over her shoulder at the Denhitran I'd nearly captured. "Yes, I know. I think we've learned all we can." Her brown eyes return to me, and there's a smile on her face I do not like. It is far too knowing. "If you get the chance, little fykina, pass along a message to your Miriseh. Tell them that Tsua sends her regards."

With that she leaves, but the pressure against my chest and my throat remain until Tsua and the Denhitran are well out of sight.

"Khya!" Tessen vaults over a boulder, his eyes wide and panicked.

He reaches out to touch me. The pressure releases, dropping me to the ground. He tries to catch me, but the impact drives us both to our knees. I gasp for air, my head spinning as oxygen rushes into my blood.

"Did—did you see? Her! It was her." My words are broken and I know he can't make sense of it. *I* can barely make sense of it. "The painting— The missing woman. It was her."

Half of the squad arrives, swords drawn and magic ready, just as realization sinks into Tessen's face. I watch it appear, and then I watch him push it away.

"Are you hurt?" He runs his hand over my shoulder and then presses it into my lower back. "Can you stand?"

"I'm fine." Speaking without stammering isn't easy, but I manage. It's enough to soothe the worry on Etaro's face, but Tessen doesn't buy it. Then again, Etaro can't hear the too-fast beat of my pulse the way that Tessen can.

His lips press tight, but he helps me off the ground and surreptitiously leaves his hand on my arm, stabilizing me when I might've tilted off balance.

"What happened?" Nyshin-ma Tyrroh's dark eyes search me. "Report, Nyshin-ten."

I take a breath and draw strength from Tessen. When I explain, I'm talking to Tessen more than I am to Tyrroh, but I keep my eyes on our commanding officer. The details have no relevance for Tyrroh; they're meant for Tessen instead.

"She had a message, she said," I tell Tyrroh when I finish. "For the Miriseh."

A flash of fear crosses Nyshin-ma Tyrroh's face before he looks away, eyeing the position of the sun. It's beginning to sink behind the mountains, its vibrant red light seeping across the horizon like a bloodstain. "Even if we have to travel through the night, we have to get back to Itagami. The Miriseh have to know what's happened here."

He calls out an order and everyone falls into formation.

What did happen here? I'm not sure I know.

The first one said they were here because of the storms. Tsua said they weren't our enemy. I don't believe her, not without knowing why her face is painted in old Itagami. She said they were here to learn something, though. And Sanii and I suspected that the Miriseh used their presence to fake Yorri's death. Maybe whatever Tsua and the others are here to learn is connected to what happened to Yorri, whatever he saw or discovered that was enough to trap him on Imaku.

It might be a trick, a new way of searching for a weakness before they launch a war. I suppose I'll have to see how the Miriseh respond to Tsua's message. There have to be layers to those simple words, because nothing that's happened in the last several moons has been simple.

Over a thousand died in the last Denhitran war. If another one is coming, how many might we lose this time?

My eyes track Tessen as we run back to the city.

Maybe who we'll lose if a new war starts is the more dangerous question.

CHAPTER SIXTEEN

Nyshin-ma Tyrroh and I walk at the head of the squad through Itagami's wide gates. We're filthy, covered in dust and sweat from the overnight trip through the desert, but at least we made it safely. Behind us, the others surround the three Denhitrans they managed to capture, but we haven't been able to pull anything useful out of them so far.

Our prisoners gather more than a little interest from everyone we pass, their dark, woven clothing clearly marking them as Denhitrans. More than one hand rests on the hilt of a sword or readies its magic, ready to fight as soon as it's necessary. I glance back at the prisoners. All of them stand tall, their eyes locked straight ahead. They're captured but not defeated.

We lead them up the three stairs to the dais, across the wide, empty platform, and through the broad front door of the bikyo-ko. Inside, Kaigo Ono waits, his stance relaxed but his eyes avidly watching the transfer of the Denhitran prisoners to two nyshin-ri and their seconds.

Once the prisoners have been handed over, he signals for Nyshin-ma Tyrroh to approach. Then Tyrroh signals for me to follow him. Ono's thick, straight eyebrows rise; he seems more intrigued than upset.

"Report, Nyshin-ma," he orders when we stop in front of him.

Tyrroh crosses his wrists and bows. "In addition to the prisoners, Nyshin-ten Khya has a message from someone who escaped. It's for the Miriseh."

Ono's dark eyes narrow and tension tightens his shoulders. "Miriseh Varan should be in the upper chambers."

Tessen is standing close behind me—I know he is; he's barely left my side since yesterday. The specific way he affects the desosa, the way that energy seems to boost my own, is becoming familiar and almost soothing. Which is stupid; I shouldn't trust him yet, no matter how many levels he's beginning to appeal to me on. I shouldn't, but somehow I'm starting to.

When I glance at him over my shoulder, I have to guess at his expression. It's somewhere in between "be careful" and "I'll be waiting here when you get back." Either way, I nod and take a breath, trying to prepare. Even though I'm not sure what I'm about to face.

Tyrroh and I follow Ono up the central staircase. Its carved stone steps are steep and broad, wide enough for ten to walk abreast. At the second level the stairs split, the new paths curving outward and upward to bring us to a different half of the third floor. The north side of the building holds the quarters and meeting halls for the kaigo, but the south side is reserved for the Miriseh. I've only heard stories about this level, and I'll likely never be here again, so I look at everything. Or try to.

The smooth stone walls are covered with bright murals,

the colors glaringly vibrant compared with the ones in the forgotten cave Sanii found. They don't end, one blending smoothly into the others down the hall, only the doors on either side breaking up the story. Because it is a story—the arrival of the Miriseh and the creation of Sagen sy Itagami.

Is there some clue in these paintings that might explain why there are two Miriseh no one knows about? Is there a clue hidden somewhere in the image of Varan carving Itagami out of the mesa that will tell me why they've trapped my brother on Imaku?

If the answer is in the murals, we walk past them too fast for me to find it.

At the end of the hall, a wide iron door. Ono stops in front of it and uses the circular disk stamped with the Miriseh's sun emblem affixed to the door to knock.

"Enter," a deep voice calls from inside, the words muffled by metal and stone.

Ono pushes down on the handle and the door swings inward.

The room is four times larger than any nyshin room I've been in, with a long table dominating the center of the space. Battle-scarred weapons hang on the walls and murals cover the rest of the space, all of them depicting Ryogo instead of the Miriseh's personal accomplishments, and there is a plush niora-skin mattress on the floor.

Varan is bent over the table studying papers and clay tablets scattered across the surface, but he looks up when we enter. His hair hangs long enough over his forehead that he's looking at us through the fringe of black strands. The steady stare of his downturned eyes falls on Tyrroh and me for only a moment before it turns to Ono. "Explain."

"Nyshin-ma Tyrroh's squad captured three Denhitran

raiders yesterday." Ono stands opposite Varan, his back to us. "Nyshin-ten Khya also has a message. For the Miriseh."

Unblinking, Varan stares at Ono. After a moment Varan tilts his head toward his right side. Ono nods and rounds the table, standing at rest a few feet off Varan's shoulder. Ono's skin is a rich brown, and the contrast next to the pale beige of Varan's skin is stark.

Miriseh Varan's brown eyes are intense, unwavering, and almost enough to make me feel like I'm trying to match wits with a rusosa. But he's ishiji. He may be able to reshape every stone in this room, but he can't dig into my mind.

Bellows, I'm glad Neeva isn't here. I don't know if my wards would be enough to keep her out.

"What did you see, Nyshin-ten?" Varan's feet are planted hip-width apart, and it looks like his hands are linked behind his back. "Take me through it from the beginning."

"Isagysu, Miriseh Varan." The formal greeting and the deep bow I give him are only ever used for the Miriseh. I'm glad for the formality now, because it gives me a chance to cast my eye over some of the markings on the maps he was studying. None of the ones I see match the marks I copied from the mural wall. Straightening, I mimic his posture and try to find words that won't give away the fact that I didn't just talk to Tsua, I recognized her.

Everything is fine until I mention Tsua by name.

Varan's nose twitches, nostrils flaring and lines appearing on the bridge before the expression vanishes. I swallow and finish telling the story. On the other side of the table, Varan and Ono are unnaturally still. They share a long, weighted look before they return their attention to me.

This time, it's Ono who speaks. "Think very carefully, Khya. Was there anything else?" He steps closer, his steady gaze almost as unnerving as Varan's had been. "We need you to tell us everything you heard. Remember it as exactly as possible."

"Only Tsua?" I ask.

Varan shakes his head. "Anyone who spoke to you."

I could keep it from them and they'd never know...but maybe I shouldn't. If I mention what the other Denhitran said, the one Tsua helped escape, maybe their reactions will tell me something.

"The only thing the other one mentioned was the storms." I furrow my brow, forcing confusion onto my face. Bellows, I hope it doesn't look as fake as it feels. Any confusion I do feel about their purpose is being burned away by the fear running under my skin like chilled water from the deepest well in the undercity. "It didn't make much sense, but he said something about looking for the storms? Or looking for something about them."

Varan's expression doesn't change, but he shifts his weight forward. My blood-father blinks rapidly, his narrow eyes thinning to slits. His gaze darts toward Varan before wrenching away.

"Was that all they said about the storms?"

"Yes, Miriseh Varan. He barely had time to say that much before Tsua arrived."

Varan's face remains unreadable, but Ono? Several muscles in his face twitch as though he is trying to suppress an expression he didn't want us to see, and his eyes shift toward Varan again.

Maybe Ono is as afraid of the storms as the rest of the city and is looking for assurance from our leader that they'll stop. Maybe he hopes Varan knows why the Denhitrans are coming onto *our* territory looking for answers about the storms. Maybe Ono already knows those answers and is rotten at hiding his reactions. Maybe none of that is true and all I have is more questions and no answers.

"You've done well, Nyshin-ten. I think your next promotion might be sooner than any of us expected," Varan says after a long moment of silence.

I bite my tongue and lower my eyes, hoping he reads it as respect and gratitude.

All my life I've wanted the attention of the Miriseh. Now all I want is to get away.

When I risk looking up, Varan's gaze has shifted to the door. "You're dismissed."

"Isagysu, Miriseh Varan. Thank you, Kaigo Ono." I bow and turn to leave.

I want to run, to bolt out of the room and down the stairs and out of the building, but I keep my pace even and carefully open the heavy iron door. Stepping into the hall, I close it and stand with my palm pressed against the cool metal and my head tilted toward the room. I can't hear anything from inside. Tessen could, but he's two floors away. I don't know if even his hearing is that good.

Gritting my teeth, I follow the path I walked with Tyrroh and Ono in reverse, looking for Tessen as soon as I reach the first floor. I thought he'd be nearby, but I don't see him. Maybe I misread the glance I caught from him before I went with Ono?

For the past three moon cycles I've wished him gone. Now, just when I actually want to talk to him, when I've finally begun to count on him working with me, he's gone.

Ridiculous. A week ago I wouldn't have noticed whether he was around or not, because it wouldn't have mattered. It doesn't matter now. It shouldn't matter.

But Etaro and Rai were right, a little. He challenges me.

He helps me, and doesn't make me ask him for it. And, rot take it, during our squad's two days in the desert, I spent more time than I want to add up wondering what his lips taste like.

And now he goes and disappears on me?

I leave the bikyo-ko and head for the barracks, but I hesitate when I pass a stairwell that would take me down to the undercity. Maybe I should try to find Sanii. But no. Ey is working. Pulling em away would raise questions at the least. More likely, it'd get em into trouble that we don't need.

I walk back to the barracks alone, head up to my room alone, and, alone, I sit on my sleep mat, trying not to think. Not about Yorri restrained on a rock in the ocean, not about Sanii laboring beneath the city at a task ey despises, not about Tessen's sudden disappearance when—for once—I actually hoped to talk to him, and definitely not about encountering an impossibly familiar face in the middle of the desert.

I also try not to think about how, without knowing why they took my brother, I have no idea how much time we have left before it's too late. Before we're recovering a corpse instead of performing a rescue.

CHAPTER SEVENTEEN

wo hours after my meeting with Varan and Ono, Tessen walks into my room and says, "I know."

Pulse stumbling, I silently mouth, "Yorri?"

As soon as he nods, I'm on my feet. Suddenly Tessen's disappearance isn't as frustrating as it seemed a few minutes ago.

We're down the stairs and about to leave the barracks when Rai calls my name and asks, "Where are you two going now?"

My mind goes blank except for curses.

Should I tell her? Maybe I could...

"We don't have to explain that to you, do we?" Tessen glances back at Rai, nothing but amusement on his face. Almost nothing. I don't think I would have noticed the tension tightening the cords of his neck if I hadn't spent so much time with him lately.

The corner of Rai's wide mouth quirks up, but her eyes still narrow. "You'd prefer a random cave to a comfortable room with a padded sleep mat or two?"

No. I can't tell her. Considering it at all is wishful thinking at its worst.

Rai worships the Miriseh with all the untempered ardor of a doseiku. She's never going to believe they're capable of...whatever it is that's happened to my brother. Even if she did believe it, I'm not going to ask her to condemn herself to Kujuko because of me. She deserves the honor of Ryogo.

"Not everyone likes to make a spectacle of their affairs, Rai. Knowing the whole barracks is listening in isn't exactly a pleasant thought." Which is half a lie. Which Rai knows.

My heart is beating too fast. The longer this goes on, the more likely it gets that someone else will come see what's happening. And ask where we're going. And maybe decide it'd be a good idea to follow us.

"You didn't mind making a spectacle of yourself with Ryzo," she says. "Or Kemi. You *loved* making a spectacle with her."

"And now I've changed my mind." I grip the front of Tessen's tunic and drag him out of the building. "We'll be back later."

"Much later!" Tessen calls over his shoulder.

Grinding my teeth, I tug on his tunic, hauling him off balance and smiling when he stumbles a step. He's grinning back at me, though, unbothered by...anything, apparently.

"Was that necessary?" I flick my gaze back to where Rai is watching us from the doorway and then quickly away.

"Did I say anything that wasn't absolutely true?" he asks as we turn the corner.

"Don't play that game with me. You know full well what you implied, Nyshin-ten."

Tessen opens his mouth, but then he takes an audible

sniff and stops. Another breath, sharp and deep. He looks up at the roof of the closest building with confusion in his eyes.

"What is it?" I don't see anything worth stopping for. Especially not *now*.

"The gardens smell…wrong. Like it gets late in the storm season when everything starts to rot. Right before that sweet dampness gets so strong you can't smell anything else."

"Maybe *you* can't smell anything else." The walls protecting the garden from winds prevent me from seeing the plants. Sighing, I look at Tessen. "What does it mean?"

"I don't know, but it's not a good scent. It's far too early." He swallows, and I watch the muscles in his throat contract, then he lowers his chin. His gray eyes glimmer with worry. "Normally, we get another moon to get the gardens and the farms ready for the rain and the growing season, but if the rot is starting already…"

He doesn't have to finish. In a normal year, Shiara produces only enough for us to survive, and that's with the irrigation system we've run through the rooftop gardens and the farms on the closest mesas. Rain only comes three moons of the year, and the undercity's pools are fed by that water collecting in the mountains and traveling through underground rivers to the city. The rest of the year we're left to the nearly cloudless sky, the parched desert, and oceans of water that take more resources than we have to spare to make drinkable.

Scarcity is always a problem near the last third of the storm season. If rot is setting in now, then what we once thought of as scarcity may look like plenty soon. The food stores won't carry us through more than a moon once the gardens and the desert plants die.

Tessen looks up again, worry becoming clearer on his

face. "We should tell someone."

"Do you really think the yonin in charge of the gardens don't know?"

He meets my eyes, skepticism on his face. "Can you smell it? Because I barely can. If there is a single yonin capable of picking up this scent, they need to be reevaluated and moved out of the yonin entirely."

I want to say no, that drawing attention to ourselves right now—any kind of attention—is a bad thing, but... *The safety of the clan comes before our lives.* No matter what the Miriseh and the kaigo have done, the clan isn't responsible for it. That's a law of the city: the actions of one cannot, and should not, be paid for by the suffering of many.

I nod once. "We'll report it to Tyrroh tonight."

Tessen hesitates, casting one more look up at the gardens he can smell but that even he cannot possibly see. "Yes. He'll know who to tell."

I wouldn't call the shift in Tessen's expression relief, but it's close. Whatever it is, it's enough that when I begin to move toward the stairs down into the undercity again, he follows without complaint.

t's hard to tell how long we've been waiting for Sanii. Twenty minutes? A full hour? Time passes oddly in the undercity. However long it takes for our message to reach em and for em to arrive, it's a lot longer than I want it to be.

And when Sanii does arrive, ey looks furious. "You may not remember this, but my life isn't *like* yours. I can't always escape my duties just because you snap your fingers and—" Ey skids to a stop, eir round eyes growing wide when ey sees us. "What happened? What is it?"

"Here?" I look to Tessen, waiting for him to check our surroundings.

He tilts his head, then signals, *No. Up.*

So up we go. Guided by Sanii's glow and our own growing familiarity with the passage, the trip is swift and silent, only our breathing ringing back at us from the rocks.

As soon as we're on level ground and safely surrounded by the comforting haven of the Ryogan murals, Sanii's impatience returns. "What happened? What did you find?"

Ey is looking at me, but I look at Tessen. I'm waiting for the same information ey is.

"Tell em what happened in the desert first," Tessen says. "The rest will make more sense if we start from the beginning."

I blink, surprised. I've told the story several times already—to Tyrroh out in the desert, the squad as we returned, to Varan and Ono when we got back to Itagami. I forgot ey didn't know.

"*Someone* tell me *something*!" Sanii demands, full lips pursed and hands on eir hips.

And glowing brighter than ever.

I take a breath and tell the story again, including all of the details I hadn't told the squad or Tyrroh. Or Varan and Ono.

"You met her?" Sanii looks over eir shoulder at the door leading into the portrait room.

"Alive and well and living with the Denhitrans."

"Whatever caused the rift between the two who left and the rest of the Miriseh must have been bad," Tessen murmurs, his gaze cast in the same direction as Sanii's.

"The *two* that left? I only saw Tsua."

Tessen turns back to me. "You really think that the eleven others are going to still be alive but somehow the twelfth isn't?"

"Maybe. It's possible his death caused the rift in the first place." I shake my head, running my hand over my hair, still slightly damp from the bathing pools. "We can't assume anything one way or the other. Maybe he's alive and with Tsua. Maybe he's somewhere in the city and we simply haven't ever met him. Maybe he's dead. Until we know, we can't do more than guess, and guessing won't get us anywhere."

Tessen considers this for a moment and then nods. "Especially given where and how we discovered Tsua's existence, you're likely right."

"I know. Now tell us what you found before I have to beat it out of you."

The smile Tessen gives me has an edge that's both wicked and soft, almost inviting. It heats my blood faster than Rai boils water. It makes me want to taste far more than his lips when he says, "I think I'd like to see you try."

The way he looks at me heightens the urge to stride across the room, pin him to the wall, and see just how far he'll let me push him.

But not now. Not here. Possibly not ever.

Attraction is instinct, but action is a choice.

I repeat that lesson in my head, one we're all taught to take to heart as soon as our bodies begin to change, but right now it doesn't make it any easier to turn away from Tessen.

Sanii groans. "Would you two tease each other into bed later? When I'm not around to see it, preferably."

Tessen's smile gets a little warmer, the look in his eyes a little more inviting, and then he focuses on Sanii. It takes me a second to shift my focus as well, my mind too ready to linger on the line of his throat, the challenge in his eyes, and the strength in his stance.

Pay attention, Khya.

Right. Yes. Yorri.

Smile fading, Tessen explains. "I knew what Khya was going to tell the council, so I followed and found a room on the second floor below Varan's chambers."

"The floors must be more than a foot of stone." Sanii looks at him, curiosity and a little bit of awe in eir face. "Can you really hear through that?"

"Yes. Especially when I climb on top of a table and press my ear against the ceiling."

I almost laugh picturing him contorting himself into position, but why he was doing it—and the fact that he was willing to do it at all—eliminates most of the humor. Erasing that, though, only leaves me with an uncomfortably deep well of gratitude.

"After you left, they spoke to Tyrroh for a few more minutes, checking to be sure your information was correct and banning him from talking about it with anyone else."

"Did he tell them that the squad knows?" It slipped my mind when I was in the room.

"Yes and they issued orders of silence to be passed on." Tessen leans back against the wall, propping his foot up next to his knee. "First priority, Varan said."

Sanii tucks strands of eir short hair behind eir ear. "Did he say why silence was so important?"

Tessen shakes his head. "But he did say he wanted to speak to the clan soon."

"How soon? The storm season is supposed to start in a couple of days."

"Storm season started weeks ago," Sanii mutters.

"Which might be what they need to talk about." Tessen closes his eyes. "I think the gardens are already beginning to rot."

"Someone thought they saw a lykis bug yesterday." Sanii's comment is quiet, but the words ring loud through the cave.

Tessen's foot drops back to the floor and his eyes open. "Are they sure?"

"No," Sanii admits. "But if they were right, then…"

Then rot might be the least of our problems. The hordes of bugs born every decade or so consume everything that stays still long enough. One of the tasks of the scouting teams is to destroy egg nests to lessen the next swarm; nothing we can do is ever enough. The last appearance was only eight years ago, but an excess of water could be enough to force the buried eggs to hatch early.

The appetite of the lykis, plus the incipient rot…

It's far too easy to picture Rai, Etaro, Tyrroh, and Ryzo swatting away clouds of the green-brown insects while desperately searching for whatever scraps of food the animals have left behind. An entire city starving. But no. "None of that is our fault or our concern. We have our mission. Abandoning the search for Yorri won't change what'll happen to Itagami."

Both of them look at me, but neither says a word.

"If anyone wants out of this plan, now's the time. Once we go much further, there won't be any chance to turn back." Punishment for betraying the Miriseh is swift, bloody, and lasting. "Either of you feel like walking away?"

"Don't be a fool." Sanii crosses eir arms, eir chin raised. "I was the one who brought *you* into this."

I hadn't thought ey would back away, not even at the threat of death, but seeing eir resolution still so strong calms me a little. Then I turn to Tessen. "And you?"

"It's a bit late to be second-guessing everything now."

He stands firm, neither his weight nor his gaze shifting. "I'm in until the end, Khya."

"Good." I take a long, slow breath and release it just as evenly. "So what else did you hear?"

He clears his throat. "After Tyrroh left, Varan and Ono talked about the announcement—not what they were planning to say, just that it has to happen sooner than they'd planned."

I shift my weight and clench my teeth. The desire to urge him on is practically an itch under my skin, but I shove it back and wait.

"Varan warned Ono to be cautious using the Imaku tunnel because even in their own domain there would be those paying close attention to their movements."

Their own domain. "Oh."

It makes sense. I wish it didn't, but it makes so much sense.

The entire city is their domain, but one place in particular belongs almost exclusively to the Miriseh and the kaigo. There's one building in the city where no one would ever think their presence was odd. Most nyshin wouldn't even pay attention to it.

"I don't understand." Sanii leans in, eir weight shifting almost entirely onto the balls of eir feet. "We were already leaning toward it being a tunnel. Where is it?"

"Sometimes the best place to hide something is somewhere everyone has become so accustomed to seeing it that they ignore it. And the way he said 'our own domain'..." Tessen's gaze flicks between the two of us, the gray of his eyes looking like pale silver in the light of Sanii's glow. "I think the entrance to the tunnel is below the bikyo-ko."

No other building in the city is so consistently busy. No

other building in the city is better fortified. Also, no other building in the city houses every single one of the most powerful warrior mages in the clan and ten immortals.

"That..." I rub my hand over my face. "That won't be easy to get to."

"I know."

"Are you certain it's there?" I ask. If we're going to take that big a risk, we have to be as sure as we can be.

Tessen winces. "I can't be certain, no. But we've eliminated a lot of the other logical possibilities. Add that to what they said... Plus, instinct tells me it's probably right."

"That is a lot for us to risk on instinct." Sanii looks stunned. I can't blame em.

"Possibly, but he's not wrong. It makes sense." I expect the look of surprise from Tessen, but I get one from Sanii, too. "Citizens come and go at all hours, so no one pays much attention. Plus, the Miriseh and the kaigo have rooms there. No one would think it odd for one of them to walk into the bikyo-ko and not be seen for hours."

"It's also the largest building in the city." Sanii says this as though it's both confirmation of the theory and an argument against searching. Which it is. "The nyshin-co and nyshin-lu who work there may not pay much attention to the presence or absence of the councils, but they will notice two nyshin-ten and a yonin somewhere they shouldn't be."

"We've already seen a good portion of the ground floor," Tessen says. "It can't possibly be in either of the map rooms off the main entrance."

"Exactly. Far too many people cross through there each day. Even at night it's not empty." I close my eyes and try to picture the different rooms on the first floor. "Could it be hidden in the weapons store?"

"Doubtful." Tessen sighs, and I open my eyes. "You know the entrance won't be somewhere that easily accessible."

"I know." If the entrance were somewhere the nyshin were regularly allowed access, someone would've found the door. "We have to be sure. They could be counting on everyone being so used to their surroundings that they don't notice what's right in front of them."

"What you don't see can kill you," Sanii murmurs, repeating the lessons bellowed at us by every training master we ever had.

"That's just it, though." Tessen tilts his head back. "They train us to be observant. Wary. Overcautious." He drops his chin and looks at us. "Do you really believe they'd place it in plain sight like that?"

Sanii shakes eir head. "They're already taking a chance by placing it within the bikyo-ko at all."

"So, what? We should look somewhere else?" I try to keep the frustration out of my tone, but I can hear it when my voice bounces back at me off the cavern walls. I clear my throat and try again. "There's no other place to begin. Nothing Sanii has found under the city leads anywhere useful. Not even anywhere else like this." I wave my hand toward the mural-covered walls.

"Of course I'm not saying we shouldn't look there." Tessen pinches the bridge of his nose. "Bellows, Khya, I'm the one who suggested it in the first place!"

"Well, then what?"

"I just…" His hand drops away and he huffs out a heavy breath. "I don't want any of us to start thinking this is going to be easy."

"*Easy?*" The word hits like a dull spear thudding into my chest. "Nothing about this has been easy. *Nothing*. This"—I throw my arm out, including Sanii, Tessen, and the cave itself in the gesture—"*all* of this started with my brother dying. *Dying*. What about any of this makes you believe I'd delude myself into thinking it would be *easy*?"

Tessen's lips almost disappear, he presses them so tightly together, but I don't wait for him or Sanii to regroup enough to respond.

I stalk away from the light cast by Sanii's glow, feeling my way back to the passage. The darkness, so complete I can't see my hand before it strikes my nose, focuses my attention on every movement. By the time I reach the edges of the undercity, I no longer feel like needlessly spilling the blood of the first person I see.

Which is a good thing, since the first person I see is Tyrroh.

We approach the intersection of two tunnels from opposite ends. He doesn't stumble or stop when he sees me, but his pace does slow and his gaze shifts from my face to the tunnel behind me. "Khya. This is an odd place for a walk."

I could say the same to him. The only place this tunnel leads is the nyska farm mesa. Questioning my commanding officer, though, is…generally frowned on. Even if Ryzo did see Tyrroh talking to the Denhitrans. Even if I've also now found him wandering tunnels he has no reason to walk.

But, blood and rot, I don't have an excuse ready to give him. I left my excuse in the mural caves with Sanii. Clearing my throat, I glance back the way I came. Tessen comes around the corner, adjusting his belt as though he just got redressed and had done it in a hurry.

"I thought you were going to wait for me," he grumbles as he steps up behind me and loosely wraps his arm around my back until his hand comes to rest on my upper arm. The touch—and the fact that I don't shake it off—says more than words possibly could. He inclines his head to Tyrroh. "Hello, Nyshin-ma."

"Tessen." Tyrroh looks between the two of us and then up the tunnel again, but I can't read the expression on his face. "I've been meaning to ask you, Khya. How are you doing?"

I can't stop my eyes from narrowing and my nose from wrinkling. "I'm...fine?"

Tyrroh's expression mirrors mine. "You are dealing with it better than I expected, especially after how you threw yourself into your work the first week."

Oh. I tense, and Tessen's hand tightens on my arm. I haven't been mourning, not in the way that I was. Everything changed when I found a reason to hope and a goal to work toward. I stopped pouring every ounce of myself into my duties, instead focusing it into finding Yorri, and it was Tessen instead of my squad who bore the brunt of my anger. But no one else knows that. To them, it must look like I went back to my usual self within a week of Yorri's "death."

"I've been distracting her as much as I can, since throwing herself into danger won't make anything better," Tessen says with a shrug. "It's taken a while to convince her of that."

Tyrroh's gaze shifts to the tunnel one more time, but the confusion on his face fades as he nods. "I can't say I wasn't worried about watching that happen. I'm glad you found each other." He smiles then, fully focusing on us for the first time. "You should try to get some *actual* rest while you can. I have a feeling the next three moons are going to be an ordeal."

Inclining his head, Tyrroh turns the corner and strides toward the main cavern of the undercity. Tessen doesn't release my arm until Tyrroh is out of sight.

"You know I didn't mean it like that," Tessen says quietly. "Of course none of this is easy, I just... Sometimes it's easy to lose sight of the journey because we're focused on the goal, and we can't do that here."

I know that, but I don't want to dig up that conversation again, even though he seems to be on the verge of apologizing. If he does, I'll have to, too.

Close? Hear? I sign the questions and then gesture in the direction Tyrroh walked. Tessen tilts his head, checking automatically. Only when he signals that we're clear do I say, "Did I tell you that Ryzo thought he saw Tyrroh talking to the Denhitrans?"

Tessen sucks in a sharp breath. "When?"

I tell him about the first encounter our squad had with the enemy, before Tessen shoved himself onto the team. I tell him about the hand signal I spotted Tyrroh using with Daitsa and how odd it was that Tyrroh's enhanced senses could so rarely pick up a fresh trail even when we knew the enemy had recently been in the area. Into the space between us I spill all the suspicions that had been slowly pooling in the back of my mind since Ryzo told me what he thought he'd seen.

A part of me is hoping Tessen will tell me I've let myself get paranoid, that I'm seeing conspiracies where there's only coincidence. Instead, he exhales heavily, his gaze locked on the empty tunnel Tyrroh had left behind, and asks, "Do you think he knows where Yorri is?"

"I don't know," I admit. "But if he *is* working with the Denhitrans, he might know about Tsua and the other Miriseh, the one we haven't seen yet. There's also a chance he's helping the Denhitrans look for whatever they were risking their lives to find. Which means he'll be on alert and far more likely to notice anything out of the ordinary with us. Which will make it interesting to see how he reacts when we tell him about the rot later." The shock of seeing him here had temporarily driven that particular threat out of my mind.

"Oh, fun." Tessen rubs his hand over his hair as we follow the passage our nyshin-ma took. "Another complication was the last thing we needed."

Complications, however, are all we get.

It rains for two solid days, sheets of water pouring from the sky nonstop from before sunup on the first day until well past midnight on the second day. The storm lacks the bite and bluster of the preseason storms, but there's so much rain that the entire plain surrounding Itagami floods.

Late on the second day, I stand in a sheltered alcove on the outer wall and watch the landscape turn from desert to lake. Only the rocks jutting out of the water—both on land and in the sea—distinguish Shiara from the roiling ocean that envelops her. No one can leave the city in this, so that means every public space is full to overflowing.

I stay away from it all, impatience giving my temper an edge I don't want to test on the unwary. Even Tessen gives me space as the city drowns in water it, for once, doesn't need or want.

When it stops on the third day and some normal duties resume, Tessen and I search what we can of the bikyo-ko. For the three days after the rains stop, we search.

We find nothing.

CHAPTER
EIGHTEEN

The day of the next herynshi, our squad is assigned to the wall. I despise being trapped here for eight hours, but today it's useful. This assignment on the day of a herynshi means Tessen and I will be able to put the next phase of our search plan into motion sooner than we hoped.

Of course, we have to survive the shift on the wall first.

"If you don't stop pacing, you're going to draw attention," Tessen says.

I keep pacing. "People would pay more attention if I stopped. It's not exactly a secret that I hate being stuck here."

"True. You never have been known for temperance."

"Why should I be?" I turn to make another pass of the ten-foot wall. "I'd rather be doing something useful than standing here watching the desert grow."

The true beginning of the storm season has brought the cloud cover and steady rain that, most years, feeds and fuels our city for moons. Usually we don't see the desert bloom fully until the end of the rainy season when the sun comes back, but something in the world has broken this year and the seasons are running out of order. The plain is no longer a stretch of red, brown, and beige; it's a thousand shades of green.

Looking at that green only unsettles me, so I pace. I don't know who's more relieved when our shift ends—me, Tessen, or the ahdo guards watching us go.

Most days I'd go to my room or meet the squad at the training yard. Today Tessen and I head straight for the undercity. In our other trips through the undercity and to the bikyo-ko, we kept to areas where our presence could be justified. Today we won't have that luxury.

Today we're searching the saishigi chamber. The last room I know for certain my brother was in.

Below the city, we walk through the caves with purpose. My mouth is moving, but I'm not fully aware of what I'm saying—something about Etaro and the time ey almost tumbled over the wall watching the flight of a mykyn bird. It's harmless if anyone overhears it.

I stop talking once we reach the yonin tunnels. I try not to even breathe loudly when we approach the stairwell that will bring us to the top of the saishigi core. Sanii said it'd be empty, but Tessen inches forward, listening at the bottom of the stairwell. He presses his hands against the stone and closes his eyes. The expression on his face is so intent that I know, even without understanding how, that he's experiencing the world in a way I never will.

When Tessen smiles, the curve to his lips is the same one I saw last week in the mural caves. I've seen that smile more than once since then, and each time I have a harder time not acting on the invitation there.

The way the left side of his mouth lifts higher than the right is a challenge and a plea at the same time. I want to answer both.

My obsession with that smile has gotten so bad it's started invading my dreams. Twice in the past week I've woken up gasping, my heart pounding, my body tingling, and my mind filled with sharp, clear memories of tasting that crooked smile, biting those lips, and everything that came after that. With Tessen sleeping across the hall, I'd been left to hope he wrote my shortness of breath off as the aftereffects of a night terror.

"Coming?" Tessen asks quietly, lifting an eyebrow. His smile becomes more temptingly crooked.

"Are you going to get out of the way, or do you expect me to walk through you?" I manage to shoot back.

His iron eyes crinkle with suppressed laughter, but he does turn and begin to climb the stairs. The core is as empty as Sanii promised it'd be, but ey had no way of guessing what we might find beyond the door leading to the bikyo-ko.

Tessen eyes the thick door in front of us with wary determination. "Are we sure about this?"

"It's either this or finding a way to sneak in through the street-side door." The door we used the night Yorri died is the only other entrance we could find. "Unless you've developed some serious skills as an ishiji? Because it's that door or breaking through a wall."

"Fine. Hush and let me listen." He gently places his palms against the metal-and-stone door and leans in. Eyes closed and lips pursed, Tessen remains in that position for a minute. Two. Three. He takes a deep breath and pushes away. "As far as I can tell, it's empty. No movement and no magic. That I can sense."

The qualifier makes me hesitate. "Is there magic you *can't* sense?"

He nods slowly. "I never would've noticed Sanii's magic

if ey hadn't shown it to me. There might be more I can't see."

Despite the potential dangers and obstacles, there's only one choice. "Let's go."

We open the door as quietly as possible and step into the hall. My memory of this place has been made fuzzy by the daze of grief I'd sunk into, but it's familiar—the four sigil tapestries and the Miriseh sun on the door opposite the core. Tessen listens there, lowers his hand to the lever handle, and then pushes down to release the latch so we can step into the room.

There are no paintings or tapestries on the walls of the anointment chamber, only a stone table and several rows of stone shelves built into the east wall. I saw that all before, so my eyes almost skip over it now. What I didn't notice last time is the door in the south wall.

It could be storage. I tell myself that, but it's no good. Hope rises, radiating warmth like Sanii radiates light. I catch Tessen's eye and he nods, easing past me to listen at the metal door.

"I don't hear or sense anything," Tessen murmurs a minute later.

My growing hope gets stronger when I try to open the door. It's locked.

Tessen sighs. "Of course, it won't matter if we can't open the door."

"Not an issue." I nudge him out of the way and then kneel, reaching into the pack strapped to my thigh. Yorri's insistence that I learn how to do this no longer seems like a waste of time. It takes me a minute to remember the correct arrangement for the tools Yorri had fashioned out of iron scraps, but then the lock clicks.

"Bellows and blood, Khya. How do you even know how to do that?"

There aren't many locked doors in the city—ward-stones work just as well and mean we don't have to waste time with keys—so I can understand his surprise. The nursery is one of the few buildings without any wardstones. It's only children and yonin, most of them ebets. Since they can't physically bear or sire children, many ebet yonin request the nursery in order to contribute to the strength of the next generation.

They guarded us well and taught us everything they'd learned when they were young, and they also did their best to keep us away from dangerous playthings by locking them away each night. For Yorri, those locks presented a puzzle that had to be solved. It's lucky for both of us that he taught me to solve it, too.

I can't form the words to explain any of that to Tessen. Slipping the tools back into my pack, I stand and say, "Yorri taught me."

When I press down on the lever handle, the door swings open silently. These doors are too heavy to ever be silent, but somehow this one is.

I don't know what I thought would be here—a small landing and a staircase, maybe, since we're too high up in the mesa for the tunnel to start directly from this point. No way did I expect a close copy of the saishigi chamber. There are three stone tables instead of the one in the other room, and the shelves I search are full to overflowing of anointment jars and folded shrouds, but otherwise it's the same.

Thud. Click.

I glance back. Tessen stands near the closed door, his gaze moving carefully across the room, seeing more than I ever will. "If they traded the bodies while we were nearby that night, this is probably where they did it."

"How did you miss that?" I can't not ask. Tessen is the

strongest sense mage in the clan. How could he have stood by while they replaced Yorri with someone else? He didn't hear anything that made him suspect a switch? Didn't detect a different person's scent when they carried my "brother" under his nose?

"The dead feel nothing and hear less." Tessen's eyes bore into mine. "I was more worried about you than Yorri, Khya. I thought he was beyond anything I could possibly do for him."

It only takes a few seconds before the weight of eyes that see too much—and have always seen too much of me, even before Tessen became a basaku—is more than I can bear. I turn away, searching the shelves one more time.

Unless there's a key hidden at the bottom of a jar of oil stored here, this room holds nothing new for us.

I cross to the opposite wall and then take out Yorri's lock picks again.

"Wait." Tessen hurries behind me and leans in, checking the other side before giving me the motion to go ahead.

This lock takes longer to open; the mechanisms are more complex. Not impenetrable, though. It unlocks with a *click*. When I press the handle to open the door, darkness greets us.

Tessen huffs. "I suppose it was too much to hope that they'd keep their secret tunnel lit."

"Look at it this way, next time we walk this route, we're bringing our own light."

Snorting with laughter he tries to stifle, Tessen places his hand on my shoulder to stay within reach in the darkness.

Or maybe that's not why.

He pulls me back, placing himself in front of me and picking up my hand, dropping it onto his shoulder and pressing down. "You can't see."

"And you can?"

"Yes."

"You're joking. It's blacker than the desert at midnight in here."

He moves forward, and I follow. "It's more like I see with my ears."

"Like an obaitto?" Those flying rats are nearly blind, but when they're in motion they squeak constantly. Like a rusty hinge. As far as anyone has been able to tell, they use the noise to keep from flying themselves straight into a cave wall.

"Yes," Tessen admits. "Now let me focus unless you want to fall down the stairs."

"There are stairs?"

"See?" Tessen's shoulder drops a foot lower than it was a second ago. My hand stays where it was, now holding nothing but air. "Stairs."

Quickly, I lower my hand until it hits Tessen's shoulder. Then, gripping his tunic tightly, I descend behind him. Silently. I don't feel like visiting Ryzo for a healing because I distracted Tessen at the wrong moment.

I trail the fingers of my other hand along a wall for balance. The stone is cool and, I suppose because Varan himself uses this passage, completely smooth. The temperature keeps dropping, this tunnel noticeably cooler than most of the undercity, and I think we head farther north each time we hit a flat stretch.

One hundred eighty-three stairs later, Tessen whispers, "Landing. Don't move."

It's hard to keep from following when he steps away. It's even harder not to jump and draw my zeeka when something cracks.

Light flares. I flinch and look away, but the flash lingers

behind my eyelids—Tessen leaning away from a torch, his eyes closed and his hands outstretched to ensure the oiled head of the torch caught the spark from his flint.

Cautiously I open my eyes, keeping them squinted.

"I may not be able to pick locks, but I do try to be useful every once in a while." Tessen watches the torch for a second, like he's checking to be sure the flame has truly caught before lifting it free of the holder mounted to the wall.

"Do you always carry flint with you?"

"Do you always carry lock picks?" He smirks. "I've spent an awful lot of time in dark caves recently, so I thought that fire might become useful at some point. Looks like I was right. Again."

That light enters his eyes, the one getting harder not to answer every time I see it. I avoid looking at him, but even turned away, I feel him watching me with the same sort of focused attention he gave the doors of the saishigi chamber. It's unsettling. And invigorating.

Mostly, though, it makes me wonder how much he sees that I never wanted to show him.

Then he sighs. "You still don't trust me, Khya?"

Do I? I don't know. He slid into my life so quickly and with such ease that I've barely had a chance to consider that question.

I *want* him. I'm beginning to like him, too—his skills, his intelligence, his determination, his humor. Trust, though... I haven't given that to very many people, and rarely completely. I trust Yorri. I mostly trust Nyshin-ma Tyrroh—though maybe not as much anymore. I trust Sanii to follow through on our plan. Etaro and Rai I trust to save my life, to watch my back, and to tell me when I've become more of an annoyance than a help to the squad. Tessen...

Apparently my hesitation is answer enough. "Sooner or later, if this plan is going to work, you're going to have to trust me."

"Trust has to be earned." I begin to descend again.

Tessen keeps pace. "What the bellows do you think I've been trying to do for the past seven years?"

"Before the night we thought Yorri died?" I shrug and continue down the stairs, hoping the exertion will excuse the unsteady too-quick beat of my heart as nerves I shouldn't feel assault me. "Mock the fact I wanted to be part of the kaigo, and snatch away opportunities that you never appreciated? Watch everyone else ostracize my brother instead of helping me? I don't know."

"You don't know Yorri as well as you think you do," he mutters, expression tense.

"Of course I know him. Definitely better than you do."

"He kept secrets from everyone, Khya. Even you."

"He did not!" But he did, didn't he? I didn't know about Sanii until he lost em. And I'd wondered before what other parts of my brother's life I hadn't been privy to. And Tessen thinks *he* knows? I skip the next step and spin to face him, placing my hands on the walls to block his path. "Why should I believe you?"

Whatever he sees in my eyes makes him rub his free hand over his face. Dropping it to his side, he nods down the stairs. "Go. We have time, but it's not unlimited. It'd be a bad idea for us to miss the beginning of the vigil."

"Giving up?" I cross my arms over my chest. "Not going to tell me some tale?"

"No." His face is blank.

I frown. "Why not?"

"Because you won't listen." Brushing past me, he continues the descent.

"What's that supposed to mean?" I hurry to catch up with him.

"Exactly what I said." He stops and faces me.

"Then you don't know what you're talking about, Nyshin-ten." I continue past him down the stairs. Tessen's footsteps pick up almost instantly.

"Sometimes I wonder if you even remember my name," he huffs.

As though I could forget it.

He was an ally back when we were children, or at least something close to one. He was also the doseiku I measured myself against and worked to keep up with.

But then he came into his magic first, laughing when I asked how he'd done it.

And he earned the first leadership position they awarded in our training class, mocking me when he heard me telling Yorri that I should've gotten it.

And he became kaigo-sei, but only ever looked annoyed whenever the responsibilities of the position demanded his time.

And, and, *and*.

"Khya, *stop!*"

I skid when I try to halt, bouncing down one more step and holding my breath when the desosa sharpens, the sting more painful than the precursor to a lightning strike. Tessen grips my waist and yanks me tight against him.

"There's a ward," he says, his lips brushing my ear. "I almost didn't feel it in time."

I exhale, willing myself to stop trembling. "I noticed."

Locked doors inside hidden rooms, and now a ward with more power than a lightning strike? Yorri. This has got to be the tunnel to Imaku. What other secret could they possibly put this much effort into guarding?

The solidity and warmth of Tessen's body pressed against my back is more comforting than I ever thought it could be. No one has ever held me like this, not even Ryzo or Kemi. I'd never let them. Now I lean into the embrace, too shaken by what I almost walked into to resist. I don't fight when he pulls me up another step and turns me to face him.

Torchlight casts strange shadows on his face, making his expression unreadable. "How did you notice it?"

"It's strong enough to affect the desosa. It feels…" The crackling energy pulses again; it bites and stings. I flinch, shuddering as I bring up my wards to protect us. "It's the same as the air before a lightning strike."

He somehow manages to look impressed, fond, and exasperated at the same time. "I really wish you'd stop playing with lightning, Khya."

"I don't do it on purpose," I grumble, pushing away from him and forcing myself to face the invisible barrier.

I've never felt a ward before. Strong ones, like the border ward, create a ripple in the desosa that I can detect at a distance, but I'm not actually feeling the ward itself. Out there, I'm aware only of the impact that invisible barrier has on the energy surrounding it. That's not what's happening here. Now, with Suzu's ward, the barrier itself is what's buzzing and stinging against my skin, and it feels like this one will do a lot more than simply bar the passage.

They keep telling me I'm the strongest fykina mage the clan has seen in generations. What if I can match Miriseh Suzu? Or if I'm stronger than her? Her wards are powerful, but she's only a sykina—able to ward against magic, but not metal.

Slowly extending my hand, I grit my teeth against the sharp sting of the barrier. Even through my wards I can feel it, and it gets worse with every inch I move forward.

"What are you doing?" Tessen tries to pull me back.

"Testing a theory." I yank myself out of his grip. "If this doesn't work, get ready to run."

"Bellows. You're really going to get me killed one day, aren't you?"

"No, I won't. You're proving yourself useful, Nyshinten." The sting gets stronger. I pull desosa through my body, funneling it into my wards, and push through Suzu's barrier.

It pushes back.

Tessen replies. I hear his tone, but not his words. He's probably repeating what we learned in every lesson on magic: pouring too much of yourself into your magic will kill you.

Stopping isn't an option. I have to know if I can do this.

Yorri is on the other end of this tunnel.

Buzzing fills my head, the sound so loud it drowns out my thoughts. A faint light appears. The pushback from the ward gets stronger, and the noise gets louder.

I funnel the desosa through my mind until it feels like liquid fire running under my skin. The harder I push, the more energy I have to pour into my wards.

The light gets brighter, streaks shooting in every direction. My eyes are closing. My limbs are heavy. I can't tell if the deafening buzz is only inside my head or if we're about to have all ten of the Miriseh running in to investigate.

And then the scales tip.

My hand passes through the wall as easily as it would air.

I fall, half my body crossing the barrier.

Just as I catch myself on the wall, Tessen grabs my arm. The buzz in my head is deafening, but the lightning-like sting has almost vanished.

My muscles are quivering, and my mind is fogged.

"Bellows and blood, Khya." Tessen drags me upright and gently lowers me to the stone steps. "What happened?"

Lifting my hand, I cover his mouth. Or try to. I miss the first time and scratch his cheek, but I catch his lips before he can protest. His eyes are wide and his breath comes in sharp, shallow pants for a moment. I wait, listening.

There's nothing louder than our breathing.

I smile and let my hand drop. "I can get through the ward."

His eyes narrow. "Really? Because it looked more like you were trying to get yourself cooked by the ward."

"I wasn't." Giddy relief nearly makes me laugh. We found it. There's no other reason for a tunnel to be hidden, locked, *and* warded. Yorri is down there somewhere. Soon—once I can walk on my own again—we'll be able to free him from Imaku.

I lean against the wall, my eyes closing. I'm tired, so very tired. My mind and my body feel like they're weighted with sacks of sand, every movement and thought sluggish. He asked a question, and I wanted to answer, but... Oh. "No guards. Passing through the ward doesn't alert the Miriseh."

"Is *that* what you were trying to do?" Tessen exhales; I feel the breath rattle in his chest. "I saw it, and I'm still not sure what happened."

"I can do it." I used to be able to stand without leaning on the wall. My body doesn't seem to remember how. "But I don't think I can bring all three of us through."

I expect him to pelt me with questions, but Tessen is silent. I can't open my eyes yet; all I have is the warmth coming off his skin, assuring me he's still with me.

"Come on, Khya." His words are soft, but the hand he slips around my waist is softer. I lean into it, using his heat to chase away my chills while I try to draw in the desosa surrounding us to replace what I used.

He practically lifts me off the wall, settling most of my weight on him instead of the stone to guide me up the stairs. The grip he has on me somehow balances between comforting and secure. Or maybe it's comforting because it's secure. Either way, I don't even pretend to fight his hold, trusting him to guide us out of here.

I've never drained myself like this before. I didn't know I could. It takes all of my focus to put one foot in front of the other. It's as though penetrating Suzu's ward didn't just draw the desosa I funneled through my body from the world around me but some of my life force, too. If I close my eyes again, I might fall asleep walking. If I'd pushed myself much further, I might not have made it through alive.

How am I ever going to get three of us through in one piece?

I need something else, some sort of reinforcement for my own power so I don't have to work so hard. Something that'll ensure Tessen's and Sanii's safety if I falter. Something that will ensure they'll be able to finish the mission and free Yorri. Even if I'm not there to see it happen.

CHAPTER NINETEEN

We reverse the trip in silence, stopping at the doors only long enough to ensure no one is waiting on the other side. Exhaustion nips at my heels and plagues my mind, but the desosa seems to be sinking into my skin, slowly filling up the well I'd emptied. By the time we reach the saishigi core, I manage to walk on my own.

I can't possibly survive protecting three people through that barrier, but I can't see any other solution. It's as unsolvable as some of Yorri's puzzles.

But those were never actually unsolvable, were they? Yorri knew the answer even if he hadn't been the one to create the puzzle in the first place. If he were here, he'd probably see the answer in an instant. He'd say something like, "Bellows, Khya, stop overthinking it. All you need is something that can store the desosa and a way to—"

Oh. I almost stop walking. Something to *store* desosa.

Ahead is a familiar tunnel entrance, one that leads past one particular locked cave. Did the idea come from seeing that tunnel or trying to think about what Yorri would suggest? It doesn't matter. I don't know if it'll work, but it can't possibly make things worse.

I step out of the circle of Tessen's arm and head up the tunnel.

"Khya? Where are you going now?"

"You should probably go. It'll be bad if we're both late."

"It'll be *better* if we're both late. What are you doing?"

"Something that could get us in a lot of trouble," I whisper. "There's no good explanation if I get caught. You should go."

"Stop trying to get rid of me." Tessen looks defiant.

I shake my head. "Your determination to get into trouble with me is odd."

In the bikyo-ko is a room where the cut and polished pieces of quartz, each one designed to serve a specific magical purpose, are stored. They're mostly used as wardstones in Itagami and on the border. That room is locked and warded, and the crystals inside are counted weekly.

I'm not bothering with that.

I head for the undercity storeroom where the raw crystal mined by the yonin is kept, waiting for an ishiji to work on it. They're neither counted nor sorted. And this cave is only locked, not warded. That's a good thing, because I don't think I could handle forcing my way through a second ward.

Most of the clan is probably in the courtyard already, so the undercity is far emptier than usual. It doesn't take long for us to reach the cave. It takes longer than it should to will my hands to grip the lock picks with the strength and precision the heavy iron mechanisms demand.

With a *click*, the lock disengages, and I open the door.

The crystals aren't arranged in any sort of order, so it takes a second to find a stone the right size. I hold up a piece of quartz that would fit comfortably in the center of my palm. "Look for ones this size or smaller. We need as many as we can carry out without drawing attention."

"You don't think one of the oraku is going to notice these?" He's arguing, but he's doing it as he picks up a crystal about the right size. "We don't have time to drop these off at the barracks. I'm not sure we *should* drop them off at the barracks."

"I know. And no, I don't think they'll notice." I put three stones into my belt pouch and six into my thigh pack. "You're the strongest sensor in the clan. Did you know this was here?"

"No, but I wasn't looking for it."

"No one else will be, either."

Tessen's eyes narrow. "You're willing to bet our lives on that?"

"Yes." I collect five more small crystals. "We'll be in the middle of a vigil formation on a night when there are rumors of an important announcement. No one will give us a second glance."

"Let's hope you're right," Tessen murmurs.

Ignoring him, I gather more stones. When I can't possibly fit another in my pouch or pack, I stuff flatter crystals in my breast band and the lower half of my pants where they're tightly wrapped to my calves. This plan might not work, but if it does I need plenty of stones to work with. A second theft would be a truly stupid risk.

The stones carry a natural concentration of desosa, and the energy pulses against my skin like an extra heartbeat. It's subtle without the shaping of an ishiji or the implanted focus of a sykina's wards, but undeniably there. I draw strength from it—not enough to recover the rest of the energy I'm missing, but enough to continue moving under my own power.

"I can't carry more without looking like I've started growing mushrooms on my skin," Tessen says.

I look him over critically, but if I didn't already know he had crystals stashed inside his clothes, I don't think I'd spot them. I grab one more crystal from the shelf, and then slip it into the side of my breast band. "Let's go, then."

Each step toward the upper city shifts muscles, which shifts limbs, which shifts the stones stuck inside my clothing. It's like I have to relearn how to walk. Should one drop to the ground, it won't take an oraku to spot it. If any nyshin suspects we've stolen unworked wardstones, they'll yank us before the Miriseh.

We walk quickly but carefully through the caves, crossing the undercity to come up through the staircase inside the Northeastern Zon's training yard.

The sunlight strikes my skin like fire.

My eyes water. My vision blurs into a flood of orange light. My skin feels like it's burning.

Nearly biting through my lip to keep myself from screaming, I stumble.

Tessen catches me. "What is it? What's wrong?"

"Nothing. It's nothing." I make myself say the words as soon as I remember how to move my tongue.

Of all possible sources of desosa, I've always drawn the most from sunlight. Now, my body is nearly overloading trying to soak up the energy. I close my eyes and try not to fight it, pushing the pain away until it begins to fade. Slowly, I open my eyes.

My vision is spotted with orange circles, but clearer. And my skin doesn't feel like it's about to boil off my bones.

Apparently draining myself is dangerous. More than I realized and in ways that our mage training never hinted at. Good to know. Better to find out now than when it really matters. Like when we're running for our lives.

My breath catches in my throat. I think that's the first time Tessen has been automatically included in that "we."

"It doesn't look like nothing." His hands shift from my arm to my face as he stares into my eyes. "You're pale and shaking."

"I'm fine." I step out of his hold, shaky but able to stay standing. "Let's go."

Tessen huffs, his jaw tense, but we don't have the time to deal with his exasperation now.

We aren't the last to arrive, but we're far from the first. As I walk into the courtyard, I search the faces of the yonin in formation along the edges of the courtyard until I find Sanii. Ey looks near desperate for news. All I can give em is the smallest of nods before I look away and step into place with the squad, squeezing between Rai and Etaro in the formation.

The pulsing beat of the drums calls the stragglers into the city center, and a few minutes later the vigil begins.

This time is supposed to be used for meditation, to center ourselves and, for those of us who can, tap into the desosa radiated by the clan to create a magical bond. In other moon cycles, I've done that. Today I'm still struggling to regain stability after facing Suzu's ward, I'm still planning our next, and last, trip through the saishigi chamber, and I'm still mentally staring down that dark tunnel wondering how much farther we'll have to travel before I finally see Yorri.

The Miriseh's procession returns from the herynshi, and the introduction of the new citizens progresses as usual. Once the formalities are complete, Varan and Suzu exchange a look.

A shudder runs through me, and I barely restrain the urge to check the crystals or look at Tessen. They can't have found out what we've done already. Suzu's ward was still active when we left, and I can't imagine anyone would notice fifty or so smaller crystals missing from a room of hundreds.

Varan turns the full attention of his dark eyes onto the clan. "The Miriseh want to put to rest the concerns and the exaggerations we've heard the past few days."

Everyone else seems tenser. My shoulders sag with relief. This isn't about us.

A murmur as soft as a breeze blows through the clan, but it dies when Suzu's throaty bellow rings out over the crowd. "The storms have struck early and often, drowning Shiara during what's usually the height of the dry season."

This time I let myself look toward Tessen. He's worrying his bottom lip with his teeth, his gaze fixed on the Miriseh. If this is starting with the storms, maybe they listened when we reported the rot to Tyrroh. But if they found something worth announcing to the clan, the news can't be good.

"If the season lasts no longer than usual, we may be fine," Varan says. "If, however, the season lasts for three more full moons, the survival of the clan is in jeopardy."

Tessen had caught it before anyone else. How long would it have taken the Miriseh to notice the rot?

"A basaku sensed incipient rot in the gardens of the city and reported it before anyone who worked in those gardens noticed the impending disaster, and if the gardens die, the island won't grow enough to sustain us through the next dry season," Suzu says, throwing her arm out with one finger pointed toward the gardens on the closest roof. *A basaku*, she says. As though there's more than one. "If the storms worsen, and the food supply both in the city's farms and in the desert dies, our ability to make it to the next dry season will be in question."

"The storms aren't a foe we can fight, but we can plan." Varan steps closer to the edge of the dais, his hands linked behind his back. "We can ration and dry and store, take what Shiara gives us now and plan to better use what it provides once the rains end."

"The basaku and the fykina who reported this may have saved the clan, for we now have time to find a solution." Suzu moves even with Varan, and I cringe. Why did she have to mention who brought this news in? "Continue to work with dedication, and you will survive, though it may be the hardest season our people have seen."

"Know this," Varan shouts. "The Miriseh won't rest until we find a way to ensure that Itagami will not perish."

"We'll save this clan, even if we must create a bridge to the gates of Ryogo itself!" Suzu throws her hands into the air. I shiver as the desosa surrounding the clan shifts from something practically intangible—even for me—to something as real as the tunic wrapped around my body. The energy vibrates so quickly the hairs on the back of my neck rise.

"Are you strong enough, Sagen sy Itagami?" Varan demands.

"Urah!" the clan answers, fists pumping into the air.

The drummers change beats, switching from the stolid heartbeat of the vigil and introducing the frenzy of the celebration. I turn to Tessen, ready to drag him into the undercity. Etaro grabs my arm first.

"You knew." Eir narrow eyes are flung wide as they can go. "What should we do?"

"Why the bellows do you expect Khya to know?" Rai smacks Etaro's shoulder before I can come up with an answer. "She's not Miriseh."

"No, but she knew!" Etaro's voice gets louder to carry over the drums, the conversations of the crowd, and the first clashes of the tokiansu. "She and Tessen—they knew about the rot before *anyone*."

Those words fall into a moment of near-silence. Every head in the vicinity turns, and all hope I had for leaving without notice vanishes. A ripple of whispered excitement spreads. Even more people are now staring at us like we know the Miriseh's plan.

"Do you think they can do it?"

I glare at Etaro. "Do I think who can do what?"

"The Miriseh!" Ey says it like it should've been obvious. "Do you think they can create a bridge to Ryogo?"

Rai smacks Etaro again before I have the chance. "A bridge to Ryogo? Are you sun-mad?"

Somehow Etaro's eyes get wider. "But they said—"

"They weren't being literal, Etaro." The two of them devolve into their own argument.

Is that it? Can I leave?

I step away from Etaro and Rai, and someone from the circle of watchers breaks from the crowd and approaches, worry and curiosity shining in their eyes.

No, I guess I can't.

"You knew before the Miriseh?" They don't ask quietly and their voice carries. The watchers press closer, all of them leaning in to catch my answer.

"How should I know what the Miriseh know?" I ask.

"But you did know before it was announced tonight?" A man I don't recognize is the voice of the crowd now. "You and Tessen? He's the only basaku in the clan and you're the only fykina on his squad."

It was my squad first, I almost say. Blessedly, I manage to hold my tongue.

Our names, citizen titles, and mage levels spread like a ripple through water.

I dreamed of this once, of being recognized and honored by the clan. I dreamed of walking through the streets and watching citizens stop and salute. Of course it'd happen now that anonymity was what I needed.

"All I told our nyshin-ma was that the gardens smelled too sweet." Tessen throws his voice out over the crowd, claiming their attention. "That's all we reported."

"You *smelled* the gardens?" the man asks. "From where?"

"The street," Tessen replies.

More whispers. More watchers. More attention.

It's not like I truly wish we hadn't reported the rot, but bellows. If he hadn't insisted on reporting something the Miriseh had likely already known about, we'd already be out of the courtyard and no one would be wondering where we went.

Tessen meets my eyes briefly before his hand closes around my wrist. I can't read his face; he turns toward the crowd too quickly. "If we learn anything else, we'll report it to the Miriseh. Now excuse us, please. We have somewhere very important to be."

It must be something they see on his face that sends amused chuckles through the crowd, because there's nothing funny in his words. They're disconcertingly true, in fact.

That truth is why I let him lead me toward the Northeastern Zon. Surprise is why I don't draw a blade on him when he pulls me so tight against his chest that, around the sharp edges of the hidden crystals, I feel each sloping curve of muscle.

Habit has me pulling back, fighting his grip.

Then Tessen's lips are against my cheek, and he's breathing words into my ear. "Relax, Khya, or we'll never get out of here."

Oh. Yes. Every thought I've been pushing away for days rushes back. Here's a chance, possibly my only chance, to see if my imagination got it right.

I slide one hand up to grip the back of his head and run the other up his back, holding tight to his tunic. Tessen's breath catches. His body tenses. When I smile and brush the tip of my nose against his as I draw my nails across his scalp hard, he shudders and closes his eyes, leaning against my body so heavily that it feels like he's gone boneless.

"If anyone is going to believe it—this—*us*," I whisper in his ear, "then it's not going to be you they see giving orders, Tessen."

His breath dances over my cheek in staccato bursts, his hand on my lower back grips the fabric of my tunic until it's pulled tight across my chest, and his other hand lifts to hesitantly—oh so hesitantly—rest on my shoulder.

Ignoring the heavy, too-quick thumps of my heart, I pull him into a kiss. Lips—dry and cracked, but warm—brush against mine, hesitant until I run the tip of my tongue across his bottom lip, softening skin broken by the dry desert air.

His body melts down to meet mine, sinking the scant inches between our heights and willingly shifting with each subtle change of my grip.

The crystals hidden under our clothing hurt, their sharp edges digging in where there should only be the press of cloth, but in this moment that only makes me kiss him deeper.

The bite only reminds me exactly how much Tessen is risking to help Yorri. To help *me*.

I feel his whimper more than I hear it. Can almost taste it. The groan he releases next, the one that rumbles through him when I bite his bottom lip, that one I hear.

His grip on me tightens, trying to change the angle and the pace of the kiss.

I release him, stepping away quickly enough that he sways on his feet.

When Tessen's eyes flutter open, it looks like he's waking from a dream. I smirk when his gaze meets mine, then I walk out of the courtyard.

This time, no one tries to stop me, but dozens of them watch me go.

Noise from the celebration fades into the background as I get away from the courtyard, but it's enough that I don't hear Tessen's approach until his hand closes around my wrist. I let him turn me around without trying to break his arm for the privilege.

For a moment, we stare at each other in the firelight of the lamps affixed to the buildings.

"What was that?"

I can't pretend indifference and expect Tessen to believe it, so I don't. I lift my fingers to the edge of his jaw and draw them lightly up the side of his face. "You started it."

"I was trying to make sure you didn't cut my hand off." He swallows, the movement visible in the muscles of his throat. "I didn't expect...that."

I shrug and let my hand drop. "All right. I'll keep that in mind next time."

"There's going to be a next time?" His voice is as dry as the desert.

"I suppose not." I move backward toward the training yard and the stairs. "Don't we have somewhere important to be?"

The look on his face is somewhere between lost and intrigued, and he seems to follow me without consciously thinking about the movements. He closes the distance quickly, his mouth opening to speak. I cover his parted lips with my finger.

"Shhh." I step close enough to feel the heat radiating off his body. I want to press closer, but I don't. Not again. Not tonight. "It can wait, can't it?"

Tessen's nostrils flare, and he sucks in a breath as his pulse starts visibly jumping in his neck, but he shuts his mouth and nods.

"Good." I trace the curve of his upper lip, my fingertip barely skimming his skin, and then pat his cheek. The sharpness jolts him out of his daze.

His eyes narrow. I smile and turn to jog into the training yard.

With most of the clan at the celebration, our progress through the undercity is quick and unobserved. Still, when we reach the passage to the mural caves, Sanii is pacing and pulling at eir short hair. When ey sees us, ey practically growls. "What took you so long?"

"Leaving without attracting attention— It was— It became…an issue."

I smile when Tessen stumbles over the explanation, and I shrug when Sanii turns eir glare on me. "Blame Etaro's bad timing. We're here now and—"

"And you found it?" Sanii surges forward, eir hands gripping my upper arms. I tense under eir touch; ey doesn't seem to notice. "Did you find him?"

"If the tunnel on the other side of the saishigi chamber doesn't lead to Imaku, then the tunnel entrance isn't anywhere we can get to from inside the city walls." Tessen's words are soft, and so is the hand he places on Sanii's shoulder, gently encouraging em to loosen eir grip on me.

I've spent so much time with Tessen recently that I'm starting to *want* unexpected contact instead of just accepting it. Sanii and I aren't there yet. It's a relief when ey lets me go.

We fill Sanii in, Tessen and I talking with and over each other as though we've been giving mission reports together for years. Throughout the story, we carefully pull out all the crystals stowed within our packs and clothes, lining them up along one wall. Soon, Sanii is biting eir lip, hope and disappointment at war in eir face. Disappointment will win if I don't find a way to get all of us through the ward alive.

"When do we go?" Sanii asks. "Tomorrow I'm supposed to be down in the farms, and they'll notice if I don't show up to a shift, but—"

"We don't try again until the next herynshi. At the earliest." Tessen sounds like he's already bracing for a fight.

"That's not for another moon cycle! We can't afford to wait that long." Sanii can't seem to stay still. Pacing, picking at the hem of eir tunic, pulling eir short, curled dark hair.

"Can we risk *not* waiting?" Tessen asks. "Khya has to figure out how to get us through the ward first. And the herynshi is the one day when every one of the Miriseh and kaigo are required elsewhere. We might not even be able to go in one cycle. We might have to wait two. You both know that, don't you?"

I clench my fists so hard that my short nails bite into the skin of my palm. I know how to find Yorri, and I want him off that charcoal-black island *now*. But there's a voice in my mind whispering reason. A voice that bears a scarily strong resemblance to Tessen's.

Waiting one cycle will be pushing my patience, our luck, and maybe the limits of whatever time Yorri has left, but that doesn't mean Tessen isn't right.

"The day of the next herynshi," I say, unable to completely hide my reluctance. "But not longer than that."

"Khya, you don't know yet—"

"Then I'll figure it out!" I scream the words so loud they rush back at me off all four walls of the cave.

Sanii jumps. Tessen flinches. I close my eyes.

For a few seconds my steady, too-loud breathing is the loudest sound in the room. The hardest part isn't keeping my voice level when I speak again, it's breaking the silence at all.

"I have a plan, and I think it'll work. I just need some time. One moon cycle should be enough."

I hope.

"The crystals?" Tessen asks quietly.

Meeting his eyes for a second, I nod, but then I turn back to Sanii. "And Tessen is right. The day of a herynshi is the best chance we have of getting him off Imaku. Trying to get someone who's supposed to be dead through the undercity on a normal day would be next to impossible, and it's not like we'll survive a swim. We don't even know for sure if Yorri will be *able* to swim when we find him."

Throwing ourselves into the merciless ocean would be asking for death to claim us, but it's one of only two possible escape routes from Imaku.

Sanii crosses eir arms. "He's alive. He'll be fine once we get him off that Kujuko-cursed black rock."

I sigh and rub the back of my neck. "Sanii, we shouldn't…"

The words won't come. I can't make myself tell em to be realistic. That Yorri might not be alive when we find him. *If* we find him.

I expect Tessen to argue the point for me, repeating his pleas for pragmatism and realistic expectations, but after only a quick glance at Sanii, he nods.

He believes em? I stare at him, trying to figure out what he's thinking. The clenched jaw and squared shoulders—determination. Nothing else about his expression or his stance is decipherable. Despite his reminder about realistic timelines, it seems like he's holding on to the possibly delusional hope that Yorri will still be alive when we find him.

I'm not sure if that kind of optimism makes me want to hug him and say thank you, or shake him and tell him to wake up. I don't do either, but grateful relief at his steady belief warms my chest.

"So, one moon cycle," I say. Only in my head do I add *unless absolutely necessary*.

It takes a few seconds before Sanii agrees. "The next herynshi."

One moon cycle from now, we'll betray our clan for the chance to save my brother's life.

I think about my shattered dreams of one day leading Itagami with Yorri and ten other kaigo, and I picture the paintings in the mural cave, the images of a place I'll never see for myself now.

I've got one moon to make peace with all of that, because there's no turning back now.

CHAPTER TWENTY

Every day for a week, it rains.

The water falls in solid, drenching sheets that soak through to my skin as soon as I step outside. It's so inescapable that most of the clan wears as little as possible. Drying skin is easier and quicker than cloth. Breast bands and loincloths are more common than pants and tunics in the upper city. Only in the undercity—cooler than usual without the baking heat of the sun—do people dress in desert layers.

Worse than the constant wet is how the rain drives everyone into the undercity. Sneaking away from the clan is harder than ever, but the lie we let people believe—and more or less confirmed at the last celebration—serves us well. When people notice Tessen and me wandering off on our own, they smile and wish us a good time.

We're not the only people taking advantage of the lighter workload; we're just the only ones not doing what they think we're doing.

"Why is everyone so obsessed with us having sex?" I ask

while all three of us are climbing to the mural caves.

I expect sarcasm or innuendo from Tessen, but it's Sanii who speaks. "They're more than obsessed. There's already speculation on how powerful your children would be if the Miriseh gave you permission to have them."

"Really?" Tessen sounds more intrigued than he should be. "What do they say?"

"Mostly they're debating how impossible it'd be for someone to be capable of both your abilities." Sanii grunts and heaves emself over the ledge. "The whole thing is ridiculous."

"The gossips always go into overdrive once the rains start," I say as I haul myself up.

As I follow em into the cave, I wonder if children is ever something Yorri and Sanii talked about. It would've been impossible for them even with the blessing of the Miriseh, but that doesn't mean they didn't wish otherwise.

"We'll be giving the clan something else to talk about soon enough," Tessen mutters, pulling himself into the cave and then brushing the rock dust off his clothes.

Sanii walks into the Ryogo cave. Once there, ey sits cross-legged in the middle of the cave, eir light shining bright but eir face drawn and tired. "Do you honestly think the Miriseh will tell them the truth if we succeed?"

Sighing, Tessen sits against the wall. "No. But they'll be quick to make us examples if we're caught."

While they talk, I gather the crystals I left here the night we found the tunnel. There was nowhere to hide them in the barracks since the squad, especially Etaro and Rai, had a habit of barging into my room, a habit that's gotten more common since Tessen joined the team. Leaving them here was safer, but it means getting far fewer chances to work with them or find a way to test my theory.

This is the first chance we've had to return in three days.

Sitting near Sanii to use eir light, I arrange the stones by size and clarity. Then I stare at the forty-eight crystals, trying to figure out where to start. It takes a few minutes of silence before Tessen asks, "What exactly are you planning?"

Sanii runs eir glowing hand over the rows of stones. The crystals glitter in the light.

"I can't get three of us through the tunnel's ward." I don't take my eyes off the stones. "If I can't do it myself, we need another plan."

"And that involves stolen wardstones?" Sanii eyes the regimented rows with obvious skepticism.

"She's going to try to give us our own wards," Tessen says.

"That doesn't make this any better." Sanii shakes eir head. "If anyone catches us with these…"

"I know. That's why I left them here." My gaze snags on a small cluster with one flat side and several sharp protrusions. If I wrapped a leather thong around the base of it, that might sit perfectly against the center of someone's forehead.

As I pick up the cluster, Tessen says, "If she can activate the crystals the way the upper-rank sykina do, she might be able to bring us through without draining herself dangerously low."

Without moving my head, I glance at Tessen. I hadn't explained my idea yet, not really, but he knows. Somehow. I'm a little surprised at how *not* surprised I am by that.

Sanii looks between me and the crystal cupped in the palm of my hand. "How do you know how to create a wardstone?"

"It's the final test of control for a ward mage—fykina or

sykina." Most of my focus is on the crystal and the ambient energy drifting around us, so my explanation comes out barely above a murmur. "You have to create a wardstone and attune it to a wardcharm."

I lift my hand until the stone is level with my eyes, focusing on the center of the crystal and the desosa vibrating against my hand. The desosa responds, gathering around the stone like thousands of tiny invisible soldiers awaiting orders. If this ward was going to be strong enough to break through the barrier, I had to wait until enough of that tremulous vibrational power gathered in and around the crystal. I let the power build...and build...waiting for—

"Is that what you're doing now?" Sanii's question shatters my concentration. The gathering energy dissipates into nothing. "Making a token stone?"

I clench my hand around the crystal and stuff my temper down, knowing the flare of it is irrationally strong. Somehow I answer evenly. "Don't interrupt, please. I need to concentrate or this won't work."

"Unless you can sense the desosa, it doesn't look like anything, but..." Tessen looks almost awed. "Trust me. She was creating a very powerful wardstone."

Warmth fills my chest. The desosa around my body reacts, tickling my skin as it changes vibration and pulls closer to me. Why do I like that look on his face this much?

Getting back to where I was before Sanii's interruption is easier than I expect. The desosa surges and swirls around my hand, gathering quickly.

I remember the feel of the saishigi ward—and more specifically how my wards felt at their maximum power— and pour an equal amount of energy into the crystal.

The quartz flares bright, white washing out my vision completely. When it recedes, spots of color remain. The crystal glows with a soft white light. It's not like Sanii's light—not nearly as bright—but it's pure and strong.

"Well…all right then." Sanii swallows and laughs softly, the sound almost helpless. "I honestly never thought I'd see someone do that."

"Could you see it?" Tessen asks before I can.

Sanii tilts eir head—not a yes or a no. "Only at the end. When it flashed."

I tune them out, watching the light inside the cluster instead. Whoever creates a ward can automatically pass through it, but I can't help wondering what this would feel like. Would Tessen feel the same pain from this that I felt from Suzu's ward?

A hand enters my field of vision.

"No!" I try to warn Tessen. He reaches to scoop the crystal off my palm. "Sto—"

"Blood and rot, Khya!" Tessen hisses, dropping the crystal and shaking out his hand. "Of all the rot-ridden, Kujuko-cursed…" His words devolve into a growl as he runs his hands over his short hair; the strands are all rising from his head like the spines of a kicta plant. Every few seconds he shudders like he can't shake a strange sensation running across his skin.

I grin and focus on the stone. It glows brighter and the color shifts, the pale white light now tinged with red as the stone attunes itself to a new energy. The adjustment only takes a moment. I hold the crystal out, challenging him with a smirk. "Care to try again?"

Taking a deep breath, Tessen reaches forward. "Is it safe?"

"Coward," I taunt.

He flinches when his fingers are a hairbreadth above the crystal. Exhaling and gritting his teeth, he grabs the stone.

Nothing happens. Which is exactly what should happen now.

"How did you do that?" Tessen stares at me with that same respect-filled awe. "*What* did you do?"

The relief that it seems to have worked—so far—makes me smile. "I didn't create that to recognize tokens, I taught it to recognize people."

"I didn't know they could do that." Sanii peers at the crystal. From a safe distance.

"It's too much work to rekey the wardstones every time someone's rank and permissions change," I explain as Tessen turns the wardstone over in his hands. "We don't have enough ward mages for that kind of constant adjustment. The tokens are easier."

Since I was careful to use only the energy I siphoned from the desosa, I'm not as drained. But I'm not untouched, either. I take a deep breath and hold it, letting my chin dip toward my chest as I exhale.

Then I pick up another crystal.

It's harder this time. The desosa is there, but it's like the channels in my mind are clogged. Or maybe like they've multiplied, and each one now carries less energy. Either way, I manage to create a second stone. The process only takes slightly longer than the first time.

I don't know how many more I can make tonight. Maybe it's good we're waiting a full moon cycle. It might take me that long to turn all of these into wardstones.

Taking another deep breath, I place my hands around the crystal, cupping it between my palms, and look at Sanii. "Put your hands over mine."

"What?" Ey looks at the crystal and then at me. "Why?"

"Because it's the only way I can make the wards work for you."

"Tessen didn't need to touch it," ey protests.

Bellows. I really wish ey hadn't mentioned that. Tessen's increasingly familiar smug smile blooms on his face.

"I've known him my entire life, and he's taken to stalking me the past moon cycle." I'm pretty sure I'd recognize his energy blindfolded.

The only other person I could ever identify that way was Yorri.

Refusing to think about what that means, I stare at Sanii and wait. Finally, ey places eir hands on top of mine. Everyone affects the desosa around them, even people who don't have magic. The effect is stronger, more noticeable and distinct, if the person is a mage, though.

Lucky for me, Sanii is one if eir ability to glow is any indication.

Feeling for eir desosa, I pass a thread of it into the wardstone. In my mind, the crystal glows bright and strong, but the color is only softly tinted with pale yellow. It's not a shade I expected from what I've seen of em, but it makes sense in someone my brother would've considered bonding with.

I exhale and pull my cupped hands out from under Sanii's. Ey blinks at me. "It felt like you were tickling my hands with a feather."

"As long as it worked." I toss it across the short space dividing us. Ey catches it against eir chest and doesn't jump like it shocked em. "I'm just glad it didn't hurt."

"Will these be enough?" Tessen runs his thumb along the planes of the crystal, but his eyes are on me. "I saw what that ward did to you. Will these…"

His hand closes around the cluster. I focus on that motion, and on trying to figure out what he's thinking, to help myself ignore the way my head is spinning. "Will they what? Work?"

"Yes. Will they work?"

"Not alone." I pick up another crystal, bringing it close to my chest. "We need more."

"I still don't understand." Sanii's attention jumps between the wardstone in eir palm and me. "How will these get us through the protection on the tunnel?"

"Think of it like the wards that guard the barracks and the border. They're anchored by the crystals, yeah? And they're tuned to protect a certain area." I flatten my hand and lift the crystal up. "If I can tune enough of these to your energy and you wear several of them scattered across your body, then they should—they *might*—create a ward that'll protect you."

"Should?" Sanii asks, looking up sharply.

Tessen, though, is looking at the row of crystals in front of me. "How many of them will you need to make?"

"All of them." And I'll only be able to do a few more tonight.

It's harder to find the desosa the third time. It's still there—the ambient energy of the world is always there—but it's like my skin and my mind are going numb. The desosa is harder to feel and harder to direct. I manage, pushing power into the center of the crystal.

When I finish, my hand drops, my arm as weak as if I'd been running drills with a weighted tudo for hours. My breathing is shallow, close to panting. Spots of light dance at the corners of my eyes. Even seated, I sway, so off balance I nearly fall. I might've fallen if Tessen hadn't caught me and held me upright. I can't see him, but I know it's him and not Sanii.

I really would know his energy blindfolded.

"No more, Khya." His arms wrap tight around my waist. "That's enough. I can't carry you through that tunnel, so you have to rest."

"'M fine." My words are as slurred as they were the night I had too much ahuri wine.

Tessen was there that night, too, drunker than I was and grinning like a fool.

The memory makes me laugh, a helpless laughter I can't stop. I turn my head, hiding my face against my own shoulder, and Tessen's cheek rests on my head. Which makes me laugh more. This breathless, woozy feeling really is like being drunk. Or closer to that than to the terrifying drain I felt after testing Suzu's wards.

I should sit up, push away from Tessen and lie down on the cool stone floor, but *should* doesn't help me find the will, the energy, or the desire to follow through. Tessen's warmth seeps into my cool skin, his heartbeat is steady and soothing, and the vibration of his energy has become nearly as familiar to me as my brother's was—almost as familiar as my own.

I stay.

I must fall asleep, or at least out of awareness, because the murmured conversation Tessen and Sanii are having makes no sense. It seems to jump, starting and stopping in fits. Either that or I'm fading in and out of consciousness and missing bits. I can't tell. I also can't tell how long this floaty feeling lasts; I'm only peripherally aware of the conversation, the room, and the fingers running softly over my short hair—loose now that Yorri isn't around to braid it for me.

Eventually the drunken numbness begins to fade.

I become aware of the desosa first, the way the energy is concentrated around me, seeping into my skin like the first rays of sunlight after a cold desert night. Bit by bit, my mind and my body realign.

When I'm strong enough, I push out of Tessen's hold.

He releases me, and I look up at him, hoping he can see my gratitude so I don't have to speak it. From the way his lips quirk and the way his fingers trail a slow, lingering line down my arm, I think he understands.

"Are you all right?" Sanii is sitting cross-legged across from us and eir elbows are resting on eir knees as ey leans forward. "You looked sickly pale, Khya."

"Do I still?"

"No," Sanii says at the same time Tessen says, "A little."

Tessen shrugs when I look at him. "It isn't obvious, but you're still not the right color."

"I'm fine."

"That's what you said before," Tessen reminds me.

"Tried to say," Sanii corrects.

"I *am* fine." My insistence gets a resigned sigh from Tessen and outright skepticism from Sanii. I hold out my hands, twitching my fingers at them. "Give me the crystals."

Neither argues. They place the crystals I created in the palm of my hand and I pick up the third crystal. They're warm against my palm, but somehow cool, too, like the physical surface of the stones is separate from the energy within and my body is processing both. They don't feel the same, either. Each one has a slightly different vibration and a hint of color—the deep scarlet for Tessen, the pale yellow for Sanii, and the rich blue of my own wardstone.

I'm the only one in the room who can tell the difference, and that could be dangerous for them. I juggle the stones for a moment and then toss one at Tessen. He catches it even as he flinches away from it. It's his, so nothing happens.

Smiling at the relief on his face, I hold out my hands, Sanii's crystal centered on my left palm and my own on my right. "Just in case something happens to me, I need you to—"

"Nothing is going to happen to you." Tessen says it instantly and adamantly, but the way his fist closes around his crystal and the visible tremor that runs through his body gives away his fear.

I raise my eyebrows. "We're betraying the clan, Tessen. The likelihood of something happening to me—to any of us—isn't exactly low." He opens his mouth; I cut him off. "In case something does happen, you need to be able to tell which ones are keyed to you or Sanii and which ones aren't."

I raise my hands an inch and wait.

Though he still looks ready to argue, Tessen holds one of his hands over mine. The pugnacious expression on his face is slowly overtaken by concentration and curiosity.

"Which one is which?" I ask.

His hand moves several times, shifting from the crystal in my right hand to the one in my left. After a few minutes he halts over the wardstone in my right hand and his fingertips brush mine, sending a small jolt of warmth up my arm. "This one is yours."

"Yes. It is." I pull my hands back and set the crystals down in the rows with the others. "Good. Now you just have to remember it."

"Don't worry." He eyes the two stones with a healthy amount of wariness in his eyes. "I don't think it's a lesson I'll forget anytime soon."

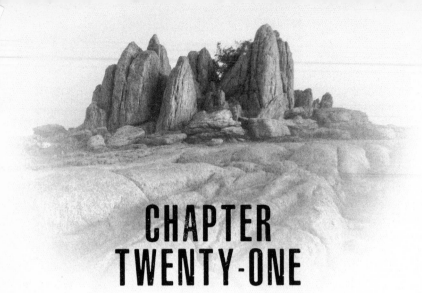

CHAPTER
TWENTY-ONE

We leave the mural caves as soon as I convince Tessen I can climb down the passage without losing my grip on the rock. Sanii leaves us as soon as we're close to the main system of caves.

There's a full quarter of the day left, but because of the rains, we have nothing to do.

"I don't like being bored," I mutter as we walk through one of the main tunnels.

"You never have." Tessen's smiling when he says it, so I don't do more than flick the center of his forehead. He bats my hand away, still smiling. "The patsu games start today."

"I know." And we should go today because Tessen rarely misses a match. My absence from the first day of the qualifying games might not be noteworthy, but his would be. "How angry was your squad to see their best goal guard transferred to another team?"

"Furious," he says with a wry smile. "But at least I didn't make the switch in the middle of the tournament." He casts a glance at me, the look in his eyes serious enough that I pay special attention when he says, "I think it starts at the end of the season's first moon cycle."

My smile grows. "Which should fall near the next herynshi, shouldn't it?"

"I think it will."

It's perfect. There will be something to distract almost every citizen in Itagami. I clear my throat and try to keep my face from expressing the sheer relief of the realization. "That'll be a busy day for the clan. How fortunate."

"Fortunate indeed." Tessen tilts his head toward the enormous open cave used for patsu games. "Should we watch the matches and see how the teams will fare this year?"

It's better than sitting in my room with nothing but my thoughts. It's much better than climbing to the north wall and having to face Yorri's prison rising from the impassable ocean, so close and yet impossibly far away. "Of course we're going. It's you, isn't it? When have you ever missed a match?"

Tessen's smile seems genuinely happy. I know he likes these game days, but does it really take that little to please him?

As we walk, he watches me more than the path. He doesn't need to look ahead of us to avoid people and pitfalls, something he proves when he steps neatly out of the way of a group of sweat-covered ahdo carrying long patsu sticks and animatedly rehashing the game they'd won. I narrow my eyes at the little flourish of a hop Tessen does to move to my other side. He winks, apparently unconcerned.

The sound of the crowd cheering reaches us first, followed quickly by the clang of metal. I learned to play young—and I can play well enough to serve as a substitute for our squad's team—but I never fell in love with the game the way Tessen and most of the clan has. Even Etaro and Rai are mad about this game.

Tessen pulls me to the side hard, hissing a wordless warning. I duck and move with him, bringing up my wards fast enough to deflect the hollow iron patsu ball that would've struck me in the side of the head. He's grinning when I peer up at him, the patsu ball clutched tight in his hand. A quick glance around proves that his little display wasn't missed. That's good, I guess. The memorable entrance means people will remember seeing us here if anyone asks later.

Laughing apologies are thrown our way from the team on the nearest playing field. Tessen waves them off and pitches the ball back to the players.

This cavern sits in the center of the undercity, not directly underneath the bikyo-ko, but close enough. It's the only space in the undercity large enough for the entire clan to gather, so we use it for vigils, celebrations, and the patsu tournament during the rainy season.

Two rows of broad columns divide the room, solidly and visibly creating separate arenas. Wide stairs line the southern and northern walls, creating multilevel viewing platforms and seating for those who want to keep an eye on more than one of the patsu games. The western and eastern sides contain alcoves for storage—mostly patsu equipment, food, and iron casks of ahuri wine. In front of those alcoves, long stone tables are filled with food and metal cups of wine, all of it refilled constantly by the yonin working here today.

On playing fields marked by borders and lines deeply etched in the stone, there are three patsu games happening simultaneously, and each of them is in a different third.

The hollow, fist-sized iron balls fly between team members, caught in the woven net at the end of the patsu pole. The goal is to pass the ball through one of eight hoops mounted on poles of various heights and scattered across the playing field. Each hoop is color-coded for one of the teams, and players try to steal control of the ball by slashing and fighting with the six-inch blade at the opposite end of the stick, aiming for wounds just deep enough for a momentary dip of the net and a chance to change the course of the game. Wounds deeper than a scratch are penalized, automatically giving a point to the opposing team.

From the sidelines, watchers laugh with each other while either taunting or cheering the players, eating and drinking the specially spiced mykyn meat or fish wrapped in nyska bread that is always prepared for game days.

The merriment is the same as it's been since I was ten, when I was first allowed to attend the tournament. It's the same, yet I've changed so much that it feels different.

None of them know about Yorri or the missing Miriseh, but they do know about the garden rot and the dangerous storms. How can they eat and drink past their fill after that announcement? Maybe I'm the only one who sees every bite we eat now as a day of starvation next year. It doesn't work exactly like that—the food we have now will go bad far before the food we would've grown could have been harvested—but their apparent lack of concern irks me.

"Look." Tessen nudges me toward the west wall. Above the storage alcoves is the area reserved for the kaigo and the Miriseh, a ledge ten feet above the main floor. Today, Anda, Neeva, and Suzu sit there, their eyes on the fields and their heads tilted together, mouths moving with words I can't hear. But maybe Tessen can?

I look at him, that question in my eyes.

"Some," he murmurs. "There's too much other noise in here. I need to be closer to single out their conversation, but that might draw attention."

Below the ledge is an arched entrance to one of the storage alcoves, and the space below it looks mostly empty.

Ignoring the rational voice whispering warnings in my head, I grab Tessen's hand and haul him south. In the alcove, I spin him around and shove him against the wall with enough force that he eyes me warily when I place my hand flat against the wall on either side of his head. I lean in to run the tip of my nose along the curve of his cheek and keep my words well below a whisper. "If this isn't close enough, then you're out of luck."

Tessen shivers when my breath touches his skin, but he seems to refocus quickly, closing his eyes and tilting his head. For anyone watching from the main cavern, it likely seems as though he's baring the long expanse of his throat—which I'm more than willing to take advantage of—but the look of concentration on his face and the angle of his head tell me that he's listening. Intently.

"Was that Khya and Tessen?" I can hear Neeva, but how? I don't have Tessen's senses. Then I glance up. I can see the bottoms of their feet swinging in midair from the top of the archway. They're closer than I thought.

"That is one bond I would be more than happy to endorse," Suzu says. There must be something about the shape of the platform above us that amplifies their voices, because while I can't hear them perfectly—the noise from the crowd and the distortion of the stone changes the tone and muffles the edges of their words—I can definitely hear enough.

"My son has certainly outpaced my expectations." The distortion isn't enough to mask the pride in Neeva's voice. Tessen tenses.

"Really? Khya was perfectly in line with ours," Anda replies, something that's either laughter or smugness in her voice.

"And your other?" Neeva's question and her tone seem

needle-sharp.

A pause, brief but loaded with something. "He did outpace our expectations."

"More than," Suzu agrees. "It's a pity. The three of them would've made a formidable team."

Anda laughs. "Blood and rot. Kynacho, fykina, and basaku? The day I have to face a combination like that in battle is the day I see Ryogo."

The sound of them laughing grates on my ears. I tighten my grip on Tessen's shoulders to keep myself from bursting out of the shadows. Tessen wraps one arm around my waist and holds tight. Too tight for me to break away easily.

"Is everything ready for tomorrow?" Neeva asks.

"Unless something has changed since yesterday," Suzu says. "We'd talked about not even beginning the project until now, when the storm season was already underway, but maybe it's better that we didn't."

"It is better, I think, because the effects are clearer this way," Neeva says. "It'll continue to be as long as it works."

"And if it doesn't?" Suzu's question is calmly spoken, but I still shiver, like my mind is picking up a threat my ears didn't hear.

"Then you'll try again," Neeva says. "If the Miriseh have waited this long, what's another season?"

"Nothing. But losing the work we've accomplished here would be a catastrophe that costs us a lot longer than a single season."

There's more hope than confidence in Anda's voice when she says, "Hopefully, it won't come to that."

"Izujo is almost ready." Neeva seems to have all the assurance Suzu and Anda don't share. "Ey's been managing the effects better since the first attempts."

Izujo is an uncommon name; I only remember one—

an ebet a couple years older than me who grew up in the Northwestern Zon. Ey was placed nyshin, I think, but I don't remember anything else.

"We'll see tomorrow." Suzu's voice sounds distant, like she's moving away. I look behind me and only see two pairs of feet dangling in the entrance of the alcove.

"Do you honestly think it'll work?" Anda asks.

Whatever Neeva says is lost in a raucous cheer from the crowd—something loud enough that it could only mean the end of a game or an incredibly spectacular play. Tessen must hear it. He tenses, his body tight as a bowstring.

"Drag me out of here and look happy about it." Tessen's lips move against my ear, but the words are so quiet I have to strain to hear them. But hear them I do.

Fine. But if we're going to pass thousands of eyes, this has to look convincing.

I slam my lips against Tessen's. He gasps, and I trace the shape his mouth makes with my tongue. The kiss-plump lips and slight daze to his eyes when I pull away look real. Because they are. I pull him out of the alcove, moving fast enough that he stumbles keeping up with me.

We get well wishes as we pass through the cavern. I grin at them, hoping no one notices how forced the expression is. Etaro and Rai are standing with the rest of our squad's patsu team watching a match. I head away from them, just to be safe. Once we're out of sight, I head toward the mural cave passage.

As soon as we're hidden inside the dim entrance to the tunnel, I ask, "What did she say?"

His wrist flexes in my grip, but he doesn't pull away. "Neeva said she did believe it would work, but if it didn't..." He swallows, his eyes darting from my face, to our hands, to the floor. "She said that if Izujo fails it won't be starvation that kills us. The storms will drown us first."

"The *storms*?" I rock back onto my heels. My hand closes tighter around Tessen's wrist, like it's the only thing keeping me standing. I shudder at the thought of water flooding the streets of Sagen sy Itagami. It would take a storm more immense than anything we've ever seen, but that doesn't mean it's hard to imagine the undercity and the bowl created by the city's walls filling with water.

"I don't understand how it's possible, but they sounded like whatever project Izujo is working on somehow affects the storms. I think that might be what Tsua was looking for."

"How could one person have anything to do with the storms?"

"We don't know it's only one person." With the hand I'm not restricting, Tessen gently rubs my upper arm. "Izujo is just the only one they named."

"They were talking like eir role was all that mattered," I remind him.

Tessen closes his eyes, his shoulders and head dropping. "I know."

"What should we do?" We told Tyrroh and the kaigo about the rot. Who do we report *this* to?

"Neeva asked if everything was ready for tomorrow. I guess we wait and see if there's a storm in the morning."

I lean into Tessen's touch when his hand on my arm tightens. "And if there is?"

Even knowing that the Miriseh trapped Yorri on a lifeless rock in the ocean, I don't want to believe they're responsible for the storms that have killed more than a hundred.

He looks at me, the deadly light I so rarely see in his eyes kindling. "Then we feel no guilt at all for betraying them."

Using my grip on his wrist, Tessen pulls me closer, bringing our linked arms between our chests and wrapping his free arm around my shoulders. "Maybe we're wrong. Maybe it doesn't mean what we think it does. There might not be a storm."

I hope he's right, but I think that what they said was exactly what they meant.

Tessen was wrong to hope.

The storm lasts two days.

Winds destroy three entire gardens and damage so many more.

Twenty-six people die.

Four ahdo are blown off the wall; they die broken and bleeding on the streets of the city. Twelve yonin drown in a mine shaft. Ten nyshin hunting with their squads perish outside the city walls—six from a flash flood, two from lightning, one from a fall, and the last from a head injury the hishingu couldn't heal.

I run from all of it, hiding in the mural caves. Being out there, watching the storm tear Itagami apart, makes the temptation to scream the Mirisehs' betrayal too strong.

I spend two days making wardstones until I pass out. When I wake up, Sanii and Tessen are with me. My head is resting on Tessen's thigh and ten completed wardstones are lined up in front of me.

Ten of them. It's not enough.

CHAPTER
TWENTY-TWO

This season began with storms, and with storms it will continue.

From the west wall, I peer over the waist-high ledge into Itagami; it looks nearly abandoned. There have been three vicious storms and twenty days of rain in the moon cycle since the last herynshi, and it's driven most of the citizens into the undercity. Missions outside the city have been all but eliminated. Wall shifts are doubled right now, though guards have started tying themselves to the stone after the four ahdo died. People aren't willing to brave the streets, not even to prepare for the celebration this evening.

The one Tessen, Sanii, and I won't be attending.

Rai and Etaro are going to be so mad at me when they realize I'm gone.

It's taken weeks of cautious hoarding to gather and hide everything we need to survive in the desert long enough to head toward Denhitra. To look for Tsua and the twelfth Miriseh. Five lashes in the courtyard—the punishment for taking more than you need—is bearable, but getting caught would've brought too much of the wrong kind of attention. Which, right now, is any kind of attention.

Grinding my teeth, I turn and walk to the outer wall, staying under the ward keeping the deluge of rain off my head and Tessen's. I never bother when I'm in the desert— it's harder to manage when I'm running, and there are usually more important things to worry about—but it's simple when I'm stuck in one place like this. Plus, it gives me something to focus on other than the countdown to the moment this Kujuko-cursed shift is over. At least with my wards up, Tessen and I won't look like we went for a swim.

My hands clench and flex. I just want to be *done*. What does this shift matter? Not even a teegra out of its mind with hunger would be stupid enough to go out in rains like this.

I turn to make another pass. Tessen's eyes follow me.

"Stop it." I smack Tessen's arm as I pass.

He sighs. "I'm not doing anything."

"You're staring."

Another sigh, but he looks out over the drowning desert. Lightning flashes, cracking through the sky and casting a burst of blue-white light across Tessen's eyes. The light turns the purple-black clouds a silver-gray, and it makes his eyes gleam almost white.

"I know you're impatient to get down to the tournament, but our shift isn't over yet," Tessen says. "Pacing isn't going to make the time go any faster, Khya."

"It's keeping me from doing something drastic."

"What's that?"

"Something that'll make you stop talking." Like kissing him.

From the curve of Tessen's smirk, I think he knows what I didn't say.

"You're more than welcome to try." He leans against the wall looking so self-satisfied that I want to smack him again. Instead, I yank my wards back.

Tessen gasps as the cool rain hits him, shoulders rising and head ducking low. There's nowhere to hide; the heavy drops instantly soak through his tunic and into the shirt underneath.

He glares at me from under his sodden hood. "Childish, Khya. Extremely childish."

Maybe, but it does make me feel better. I shrug, smirking and extending the wards again. There's an hour left in first shift, so he should be partially dry by the time we leave.

My chest clenches and my stomach sinks. By the time we leave, exiling ourselves before the Miriseh have the chance to do it for us.

At the inner wall I stop and watch Tessen. He's looking down, muttering and wringing water out of his clothes. The longer I watch him, the more questions buzz in my head.

Are you sure you want to go through with this? Will you regret it tomorrow? Next week? In a year? If we go to Denhitra and Tsua turns us away, will you hate me? What if we end up living in the desert, scrounging for food and hiding from storms? If I kissed you again, would you mind?

All I can make myself ask is, "Is this worth it for you?"

"What? Biting my tongue so you'll keep me dry during shifts like this?" His expression changes when he looks up at me, the annoyance melting. The motion of his hands never falters, but his voice is deadly serious. "Yes. It's worth it."

"How can you be sure?" My question is so quiet that anyone else wouldn't have heard it.

Tessen is not anyone else. "The same way you are."

But I'm doing it for someone I love. I bite the words back before they trip off my tongue. I'm afraid of very few things. Tessen's response to that is one of them. One day I might ask, maybe, after we've escaped and survived and adapted, but not now.

He straightens and crosses the wall, cautiously lifting his hand toward my face, but not touching. "One day, you won't be so wary of me."

"I'm not wary." I don't think that Tessen would ever hurt me. On purpose. Probably. However, to think and to know are two incredibly different beasts.

"It's almost time." Tessen's thumb brushes my cheek. "Are you ready?"

"No." My stomach clenches. All my impatience is washed away by a deluge of fear.

So many things could go wrong. We could be caught before we get to the saishigi chamber. The wardstones I made could fail. Imaku might not be unguarded. We might not be able to bring Yorri back through the tunnels. Even if we escape Imaku with Yorri alive and well, what do we have to look forward to?

To live solely to continue living is not much of a life... but at least it *is* life.

Neither Tessen nor I speak for the final half an hour of the shift, staying silent even as we head to the kitchens. We've slowly gathered dried meat and fruits, spare weapons, and changes of clothing over the past moon, all of it done carefully because it would be stupid for food, of all things, to be what ruins our plans. That's why everything is hidden in the passage to the mural caves. All that's left now is to collect it and leave.

I look at the long stone tables and the groups gathered around them. The smell of the spiced meat cooked over open flame is in the air, and so is the physical and intangible warmth of the kitchens, the knowledge that I can count on every person here to save my life…all of this will be gone after today.

Laughter bubbles up from the southwest corner of the room, and more than a few heads turn to see why, indulgent smiles on their faces. When I look, I wish I hadn't. My chest clenches.

Rai. Etaro. Daitsa. Ryzo. Tyrroh. Everyone from the squad's patsu team is here, all of them laughing at Ryzo, who's standing up and waving his arms, reenacting something that happened in whatever story he's telling. He was always good at that, throwing himself into the retelling and playing up all the parts.

I'll miss that. I'll miss Rai's sense of humor, too, and Etaro's unfailing compassion. Despite my doubts about Tyrroh, I'll even miss him and Daitsa—his solid leadership and her quiet calm. I'll miss everything about the squad that has become my family the past year and a half.

I'll miss them all, but I have to let them go.

I couldn't even let myself find a subtle way to say goodbye, because I didn't—and I don't—think I could've done it without giving away too much.

Tessen catches my eye, concern and a question on his face. I recognize it because it's the same question I've already asked. *Are you sure? Is this what you want? The time to back out is now, because we'll have to continue if we take even one more step forward.*

"Are you finished?" I nod at his mostly empty plate and try to ignore the tightness in my throat.

"Nearly." With the last of his bread, he scoops up the grain mixed with bits of kamidi meat and pops it into his mouth. His eyes close as he chews. The look on his face is intense, like he's trying to memorize the taste. I've done the same every meal we've had this past week.

Standing, Tessen casts one last look around the kitchens before his eyes land on me.

This time, we take as much dried food as we can carry. It doesn't matter if someone sees us do it. We won't be there if they go looking for us later.

Thankfully, with everything happening today, the saishigi core and all the tunnels leading up to it are empty. After we meet Sanii in the yonin tunnels, we're able to move quickly. There're a few hours before we'll be missed, when the vigil begins and we don't take our places. After that, it'll take another few hours before anyone has the time to look for us and realizes that we're gone instead of simply late or distracted.

Tessen leads us across the core, listening at each door, and soon we're descending the hidden stairwell with Sanii's light guiding us down.

As we move deeper, getting closer to Suzu's ward, I clear my throat. "We can't count on getting as much time as we should have."

The stairwell and the tunnel may be empty now, but there's no guarantee at all it'll stay that way. Though we've always assumed the kaigo and the Miriseh who accompany the doseiku to the herynshi cavern stay there through the entire trial, we don't know that for sure.

"She says this like she thinks we don't know," Sanii mutters.

"It's easy to lose track down here, though," Tessen says. "Better to have the reminder now than when it's almost too late."

Sanii exhales heavily and nods, but eir hand rises to eir hair, pulling lightly on the short strands. It's the only sign of exactly how anxious ey is.

Since I know what to expect, I feel the ward several steps above its actual placement. The usual faint glow of the wardstone anchors are hidden by the sandstone walls they're embedded in. I couldn't have before, but this time I could probably point to exactly where the crystals are placed. The effect these stones have on the desosa feels so similar to power from the wardstones I created. Did creating so many of my own give me a stronger awareness of these stones? Maybe.

I stop and reach into my thigh pack.

"Stand still," I tell Tessen. He does.

I find his wardstones and secure them to his body, each tied with a leather thong: one on each ankle, one on each wrist, one in the center of his waist, one tied over his forehead. I do the same for Sanii. The stones' glow casts strange shadows on their faces but isn't enough to reach the walls.

The placement should encase their bodies with a ward, and although we tested my theory as best we could, none of us have offensive magic, and my wards won't protect anyone from themselves. I can't be entirely sure it'll work.

Sanii and Tessen are risking their lives on a theory. *My* theory.

I don't know what to do with that kind of faith. The only person who has ever had that unquestioning trust in me is Yorri.

Swallowing, I tie wardstones to my own limbs and face the ward.

"I'll go first. In case these don't work." I try to focus on my current strength and not the drained feeling this ward left me with last time.

"It'll work," Tessen says. "You don't know how to fail."

I wish I had the same confidence.

Breathing deep, I step into the ward.

Buzzing fills my head. The lightning-like energy is still there, but it's at a distance.

The wardstone on my forehead glows so bright I have to close my eyes. It burns through my eyelids, searing my vision with spots of color.

I shake. My pulse races. I'm coming apart at the joints, being torn into pieces.

And then I finish the step.

I stumble, falling three steps and landing on my knees.

"Khya?" Tessen hisses. "Khya, talk to me!"

"Hush." I suck in air like I've been without it for minutes. Underneath the painful wheezing, excitement bubbles in my chest, warming my body against the chill of the stairwell. It *worked*. It worked and I'm through the ward and Yorri is closer now than he's been in moons.

I turn my head, looking down the remaining stairs. The urge to keep going, to rush ahead of Tessen and Sanii and find my brother, is so strong I shift my weight forward before I can stop the motion.

On the other side of the ward, Tessen releases a wordless protest.

Impossible boy. He knows me too well.

Smothering my excitement—and trying not to let hope overrule all of my reason—I turn my face toward them. "What happened? What did you see?"

"When you stepped into it, there was a bright flash," Sanii whispers. "Then you fell."

Still shaking, I push to my feet and climb two of the stairs I stumbled down moments ago. "How long did it last?"

"The light?" Sanii looks at Tessen and then shakes eir head. "A second or two."

"It felt like longer. A lot longer." I stare at them through the invisible barrier. "No matter how it fights you or how it feels, you have to keep pushing forward. The stones will work, but it'll be bad. Probably be the worst, strangest thing you've ever felt."

"Oh, this should be fun." Tessen takes a deep breath and steps into the barrier.

He convulses, pain twisting his face. Blindingly bright light flashes from Suzu's barrier and Tessen's wardstones. The light vanishes. He falls forward.

I catch his arm.

We fall sideways. My back slams against the wall and Tessen lands flush against my chest so that I'm pinned in place by his body.

The impact forces the air out of my lungs. It takes a second before I get enough back to ask, "Are you all right?"

Eyes closed tight, Tessen shudders. "If I never have to do that again it'll be too soon."

He opens his eyes, and it seems like it takes a second for his vision to clear.

For the first time, the desire to kiss him isn't driven by anger or lust. For the first time—or the first time I let myself admit it, maybe—having him close is pure comfort, and the urge to slide my arms around his neck and bring his lips down to mine is solely about reassuring myself, and possibly him, that we're both okay.

Then he takes a shaky breath and leans closer. I freeze, waiting. He dips his head until the stone in the center of his forehead touches mine. "I told you that you couldn't fail."

Taking another breath, he places his hands on the wall on either side of my head and pushes away. And, yes. Distractions aren't a good thing right now. We're so close to finding Yorri. So close I can almost taste the ocean air on my tongue. *That's* what matters.

Once he steadies himself, Tessen turns toward Sanii and beckons em forward. "It'll be a strange kind of pain, but it'll work."

Sanii squares eir shoulders and walks into the ward.

The sizzling flash passes faster, but when Sanii breaks through, ey is gasping and trembling worse than either of us. Tessen squeezes eir shoulder and helps em regain eir balance. Ey sags against Tessen, eir head resting on his chest, and I hesitantly run my hand over eir hair.

Shuddering, ey mutters, "Never again. Never, ever again."

"Neither of us is going to try to change your mind," Tessen promises. I nod quickly. Definitely not. I sincerely hope I never have to face a ward like that again.

Now that they're both with me here, the drive to *go* is even stronger. But so is the fear of what we might find at the end of the tunnel. I trace the edges of the wardstone bound to my wrist and try not to shift impatiently while Sanii regains control of eir body. Thankfully, less than a minute passes before Sanii straightens and walks down the next step.

The staircase continues for another twenty steps, around one last curve, before we reach a split. My heart jumps, fear momentarily overriding hope. The division of the passage is clean, each direction unnaturally straight, smooth, and even. There isn't a single hint which way we should go. There's not a hint *I* can see, but...

I catch Tessen's eye and, using hand signals, ask, "Which way? Hear? Smell?"

He listens and sniffs the air, breathing deep and slow. Then he points to the left-hand tunnel before signaling, "Clear. That way. Ocean."

Oh, bellows. We're under the ocean, aren't we? Or, if

we're not yet, we will be soon. I hadn't thought about the fact that, if it's going to take us to Imaku, the tunnel has to travel under the waves. The heavy, unforgiving, tumultuous waves. I glance up at the very solid-looking ceiling and hope that today isn't the day the first crack in that stone appears.

We move quickly because the only way to go is straight ahead. After the initial split, no tunnels veer off from this one. We pass one cavern set up like the second saishigi chamber—several stone tables in the center of the room and shelves carved into one wall.

My chest clenches. Was Yorri here?

We look, but nothing in the room tells me anything about its purpose, or why they'd bring anyone here. Nothing on the shelves seems of any use at all. Oils, different stones, and pieces of silver metal that I don't think are iron. I grunt and stash several pieces of the silver metal in my pack, frustration rising like a heat wave in my chest. I want to chuck one of the clay jars at the wall. I don't do it, but I want to.

Not far past the small cavern, the tunnel begins to slope upward. Now even my nose can detect the brine in the air.

Another hundred yards or so after that, the rock changes.

It's not a fade or gradual shift; the line is straight, sharp, and stark. The familiar reds, browns, beiges, and grays of the sandstone and limestone of Shiara become charcoal black.

The black rock of Imaku.

We stop and I eye the darker, sharply sloped tunnel ahead with something that runs deeper than wariness. This is the first time I've ever seen the island's rock up close.

"Tessen, does this look like the stone they tested us with

during the herynshi to you?" I touch it with the tip of my finger, braced for a reaction that doesn't happen. "Do you think this is where that stone came from?"

"It has the same kind of glitter." Hesitantly, Tessen touches the rock, too. He's right. The sparkle of the stone shifts with the movement of Sanii's light. "It feels similar."

My heartbeat stutters. If Imaku is made of that stone... "We need to get him out of here. Yorri said the moment they touched that stone to his skin felt like being trapped in Kujuko."

Sanii makes a pained noise. Tessen's fingers brush the inside of my right wrist, the touch gentle and somehow full of concern.

I move faster than before—almost sprinting across Imaku's border and up the slope. I won't leave my brother in nothingness any longer than I have to. It's already taken too long to find him.

The higher we climb, the more I notice a noise that had been relegated to the background. It sounds like wind, and there's the *whoosh-crash* of waves striking rocks, repetitive and hypnotic. We're getting closer to Imaku—to *Yorri*—but...

Ahead is a solid wall. No. It can't be a dead end. I can hear the ocean. There's light that isn't from Sanii. It *can't* lead us to nothing!

Moving faster, I come up on the wall and— Yes! There. The passage curves.

Every instinct in me wants to rush around that bend and see if this search has been in vain. Tessen's hand closes around mine, holding me back. He places himself in front of us, and he searches the cavern beyond us without sight, ensuring it's as empty as the tunnel was.

Tessen's stillness lasts far longer than it has any other time he's done this kind of a check. This time, when he faces us, frustration lines his face. "It's harder to be sure here—the waves are too loud and the wind doesn't help—but I don't think there's anyone moving in there."

Anyone *moving*. Which might mean he senses someone who isn't moving.

Unmoving, but not necessarily dead.

"Do you think they can spot us from Shiara if we leave the tunnel?" Sanii shifts eir weight forward as though the only thing holding em back from bursting out of the tunnel is eir hand pressed against the wall.

"No." Tessen shakes his head, most of his attention still seeming to be on whatever is beyond the tunnel's curve. "There'd be rumors and stories about the sightings if the tunnel exit weren't hidden."

"Well then, let's *go*." I push past him and into the cavern.

Three walls of the oblong room are bare; one has rows of shelves packed with boxes in different sizes and other odd items. The roof of the room is high—at least twenty feet above our heads—and the only light is coming from Sanii's glow and two passages on either end of the room that must lead out to the ocean. Those ends of the cavern are wet, coated with spray from waves and rain, but the water doesn't touch anything else.

I take all of it in and then dismiss it for what's in the center of the room.

"Bellows and blood," Tessen breathes behind me.

Rows upon rows of stone tables. It's like the long row of beds in Hishingu Hall, but these are black rock and nothing else. No mattresses or mats. Three rows of fifteen tables, and most of them are occupied.

It's not just Yorri.

Whatever purpose the Miriseh have, it's affected so many more people than I thought. How many times have people "died" or gone "missing" and ended up here? Thirty-eight more, at least.

Thirty-eight times, squads and partners and friends have grieved someone who wasn't gone. Thirty-eight times, the Miriseh have broken our trust. My heartbeat feels too slow, but I feel each thud through my whole body. What *is* this? Are they...

They can't be dead, can they? The only use corpses have is to become food for the gardens and farms. This doesn't make sense.

It takes more willpower than I want to admit to move to the closest table, to press my fingers against the throat of the body and wait for a pulse. Nothing. I do it harder, the pads of my fingers digging into a stranger's neck. Still nothing. But I felt nothing when I said goodbye to Yorri, too, and Sanii insists he's alive. So I wait.

There.

"They're alive!" Bellows. My hands shake. Alive. Barely, but alive. The beats of their heart are impossibly slow. I count, pacing them against my own... Less than half the beats.

By the time I pull my hand back, Sanii is already halfway through the first row, eir head moving back and forth quickly as ey searches the faces of those trapped here. I move to the last row and do the same. I don't recognize anyone. How long have these people been here? They look young—none of them can be older than twenty—but who are they?

If touching the rock of Imaku is enough to drop them into unconsciousness, will simply carrying them past the black rock in the tunnel be enough to wake them up? I hope so, because even carrying this many people that far one by one will be time-consuming and exhausting. There is no possible way the three of us could carry more than one farther than that.

But can we really leave them behind?

"Yorri!" Sanii cries out. I run to the third row. There, laid out like the others in a simple tunic and pants, is my brother.

Yorri. Even after the proof of the stranger's pulse, I need to feel life under his skin. It doesn't seem as though his heart is beating. He doesn't look like he's breathing, but there's a touch of tension on his face, tightness around his eyes and across his forehead that reminds me of what his face looks like just before a nightmare. I press a shaking hand just below his ribs, feeling for the expansion of his lungs. The movement is shallow, and so slow I can't see it, but he's breathing.

I close my burning eyes, but tears gather at the corners to trail down my cheeks anyway.

Sanii was right. He's alive.

We need to get him off this island as fast as possible, especially if we're going to have to repeat the trip thirty-eight more times in the next couple of hours. There's no time to lose. We need to be gone.

"Do you think it's safe to move him?" Sanii asks. I open my eyes and watch em trace the line of Yorri's jaw, relief and worry so mixed on eir face that ey looks pained.

"Maybe, but I don't like the look of these." I gesture to his wrists.

Red cords are wrapped around his wrists and ankles. They don't bind him to anything, but they're too bright, and everyone trapped here is wearing them. I reach for the cord around my brother's wrist, but I can't make myself touch it. The energy around it feels wrong.

Sanii doesn't hesitate. Ey grips the cord around his right wrist and tugs.

The light of eir wardstones flares.

Sanii cries out—maybe in shock, possibly in pain—and stumbles back. One hand presses to eir chest, the other to eir head, and eir breath comes in near-panicked gasps.

Tessen rushes to eir side. I stay with Yorri.

I hold my hand over the cord on his left wrist—not touching, just feeling the desosa that moves between my hand and Yorri's body. It's frenetic, the vibrational pattern faster and stronger than any magic I've ever felt before. Stronger even than Suzu's ward.

Drawing my anto, taking a breath, and ignoring Tessen's hissed admonition, I try to break the cord.

Iron touches leather. Blackness engulfs my vision.

My mind pulls away from my body.

I see myself from above, watch my hand go lax, dropping the dagger to the table. I watch my legs buckle. I watch Tessen nearly miss catching me before I hit the black stone floor.

Then there's nothing.

CHAPTER TWENTY-THREE

I settle into my body one sense at a time.

First touch, the awareness of the cold under me and warmth above. My body is buzzing like I ate too many byka beans.

Hearing next, but slowly. Words in a voice I recognize—Tessen?— but I can't make sense of what he's saying. The roar in my head, like ocean waves are crashing inside my skull, nearly drowns him out. Lips brush against my cheek just before the waves in my head retreat.

"Wake up, Khya, please." Tessen is leaning over me, and it was his body heat that I'd felt before. "Come back, come back, *please* come back."

Smell—brine and sweat and leather.

Sight—the black stone overhead, dimly lit by the gray light coming through the short hallway at the end of the cavern, and Tessen's face inches from mine.

Then memory surges back and finally, *finally*, I can move.

Yorri! I sit up, gasping for air.

How long has it been? Not more than minutes. Any

longer and Tessen's energy would feel more frantic. And if anything had happened to Yorri, Sanii would be in pieces instead of watching me with deep furrows across eir forehead.

Groaning, I put a hand to my aching head and wait for the world to stop moving.

"Are you all right?" Sanii asks. Ey's kneeling in front of me, eir wide eyes full of worry. And frustration.

"I'll be fine." My voice comes out hoarse and harsh. "How long?"

"Minutes," Sanii says.

"A quarter of an hour," Tessen corrects.

Time enough before we're missed at the vigil, but it was still too long. "Help me up."

I pretend not to notice Sanii's hesitation or how ey looks at Tessen, almost for permission. Before I can snap at them to hurry up, Tessen places my arm over his shoulders, lifting me to my feet.

Yorri hasn't moved. Not even an eyelash, as far as I can tell.

The first moment I touched the cord with my dagger, I felt like I was somehow outside myself, watching everything. Is Yorri watching us, aware of the world but unable to interact with it? I shudder. The nothingness that came after would be more merciful.

"I don't think I can break through the cords." I keep my eyes on Yorri, but I know in my mind that it's Sanii I'm talking to. "Whatever this magic is, I don't know how to ward against it." Trying to learn how will take time and energy I probably don't have, and there's no guarantee I'll ever figure out how to get those Kujuko-cursed things off him.

"We can't leave him like this!" Sanii's eyes overflow with tears. Agony etched in the lines of eir face, ey runs toward the shelves lining the wall, pulling down a box and rummaging through the contents. "There must be something!"

I move to follow, but Tessen's grip on my waist stops me.

"Can you walk?" he asks.

"Yes." Maybe. When he releases me, slowly, my shaky legs hold.

Sanii has searched and discarded two boxes when I reach the wall. I pick up a smaller, tightly sealed box and lift the top. Inside are pieces of something like nyska paper. It's not, though. It feels different. Thicker. Softer too, like thin, overworn leather. Hundreds of marks like the ones in the mural caves cover the papers.

"Tessen." I hold a sheet out to him.

His eyes widen. "Should we take it?"

"Yes. Take anything with these marks." Anything they're keeping on this island, well beyond the reach and sight of anyone from the city, has to be important. If we can get it to Tsua, maybe offering her what we stole from the Miriseh will be enough of a trade: information for safety. Maybe she'll even be able to understand the marks. Maybe we can figure out how to come back and free the rest of the people trapped here, because unless they really will wake up away from Imaku, there's no way for us to take them with us now.

"How are we going to carry them?" Tessen looks from the page he picked up to the narrow passage that seems to lead to the ocean.

"We'll think of something." The tunnel that split off at the bottom of the stairs might release us somewhere useful. Even if we have to escape into the ocean, knowing the marks will be devoured by the ocean's chilly maw is enough. They took my brother from me; even stealing everything we can carry won't balance the scales. All I can hope is that losing this will make it harder—hopefully impossible—for them to trap anyone else here.

Tessen gathers the pages and rolls them tightly, tying them with a loose piece of leather—brown, not red—and then holds the thick roll to me. "If it's in the pack with your wardstones, that might be enough to protect them."

I fit as many as possible into the thigh pack. In our other bags we place pieces of Imaku's black rock, several full iron flasks of something that smells like gasuren sugar and kamidi venom, and anything else that catches our attention and is small enough to carry.

The longer we search, the more frustration burns in my chest. None of it gives us any idea of how to remove the red cords. There are no ointments, wardstones, or anything else that seems like it might work to free the thirty-nine people. My stomach churns. Rot take it, I hope they wake up in the tunnel. If they do, we might be able to save at least a few of them, but we have to escape soon. We've already been here too long.

The first step toward Yorri is hard, the weight of everything that might still go wrong physically pressing me down, but the second is easier. Tessen is close behind me, his soft footsteps nearly lost under the sound of the waves.

Sanii reaches Yorri first. "Can we carry him without being knocked unconscious?"

Tessen backtracks, moving to the shelves and taking down a folded swath of cloth. "I don't know if it'll be enough, but we can wrap his wrists and ankles with this."

"It's worth a try." And adding the six wardstones I made for him—all of them worn in the same places as ours—might protect us from the cords as much as they'll protect him from harm.

As Tessen jogs toward the table, he unfolds the cloth.

With his help I cut strips several inches wide, passing each one to Sanii. Ey carefully wraps one wrist, starting at his hand and moving up to the middle of his forearm while avoiding contact with the red cord. Once the end has been secured and a wardstone tied over it, ey grits eir teeth and touches Yorri's wrist.

Hissing, Sanii yanks eir hand back and shakes it out, but then ey smiles. "It's not as bad. I think we should be fine."

Sanii and Tessen wrap the other limbs. I follow behind them, tying a wardstone over each. The crystals glow brighter as soon as they're in place. Maybe they're already working, creating a shield between us and the magic of those cords.

Since Tessen needs to focus on keeping watch, Sanii and I shoulder Yorri's limp weight. We carry him between us and follow Tessen toward the tunnel. The weight we added to our packs and the dragging of Yorri's feet against the stone make our movements slower and noisier. Noise might draw attention. Slowness might get us killed. I push my fears aside as much as I can and keep moving.

Tessen stops, his body tense and his head cocked to the right. Trouble is ahead; I know it even before he spins to face us, stepping so close that our bodies are pressed together from thigh to shoulder.

He speaks so soft and low I don't even feel his breath stir against my ear. The words send shivers across my skin. "Someone's coming."

"Fight," I whisper back, trying to move forward.

"No." He uses his weight to push me back a step. "Three—Neeva, Anda, and Varan."

My pulse thrums faster. Neeva could cast illusions that make us believe we're fighting twenty. Anda could make our own weapons fight against us. Only if we slit their throats before they knew we were there would we have a chance. And Varan...

Varan could collapse the tunnel, letting the ocean drown us, and nothing we could do would stop him. Tyrroh once told us he saw a misfired arrow strike Varan in the heart, and by the next day the wound had completely healed. No blow we're capable of landing would be worse than that.

"Go, Khya." He nudges us back another step. Back to Imaku. "*Go!*"

We run.

"Why are they here?" Sanii hisses. "I thought they would be gone all day!"

"Anda said something about a test." Tessen keeps glancing over his shoulder, his expression tight and fear in the wideness of his eyes.

Using the others' wardstones as anchors, I reinforce their protections. Only when we're back in the cavern of Imaku where the waves bury our whispers do I ask, "Can we hide?"

"Do you really think they won't notice one of their captives missing?" Tessen looks pointedly at Yorri. "They'll search this rotten rock until it's a pile of rubble." He shakes his head, rubbing his hand over his face. "Can you give us air under the waves?"

"Not for long." I adjust my hold on Yorri. "And it doesn't help us against the current. Those waves will push us right back to shore."

"Do we have any other choice?" Sanii's attention is on the entrance to the tunnel, not the escape to the water. "I am not leaving him here for them to do—to do *whatever* this is!"

"Of *course* we're not leav—"

"Hush!" Tessen's eyes close, defeat casting a shadow over his expression. "They know someone's here."

"How?"

"A piece of the paper." He straightens and looks away from the tunnel, turning instead toward the archway that leads to the ocean. "It must have fallen in the tunnel."

Rot take them! The only escape now is the water, though the waves might be just as dangerous as facing Varan in the tunnel. At least the waves won't actively try to kill us.

Sanii and I follow Tessen, with Yorri dragging between us.

I refuse to look at a single table we pass. They'll all plague my mind enough. If they have faces, it'll be worse.

Any chance we might have had to rescue them is gone.

Now more than ever, I'm thankful for Suzu's ward on the tunnel. Without it I never would have made the wardstones, and protecting us now would be impossible.

It takes a moment to find the twenty-four active stones, the six worn by each of us, glowing in my awareness. They're already tuned to the people wearing them, so what I have to do now is change what they protect from.

It's like molding clay, creating the shape and purpose I need the wards to take. They'd been intended originally to keep us safe from magic and metal, but now I strengthen the barrier, thickening it until it's as solid as the one I used during our shift earlier today to keep Tessen and me dry. This ward has to give us air underwater.

"Khya!" Sanii hisses.

I almost walk into a stone wall.

Blinking, I come back to the world. My hands are shaking. Reshaping the stones' purpose drained me more than I expected. More than I can afford with the danger coming after us.

The path to the water is steep and treacherous. The clouds dump near-solid sheets of rain on us, making the stones slick, but none of those drops hit us. Like earlier today, the water hits my ward and rolls off, following the line of the invisible shield. It worked. I almost laugh. The wards will give us air—at least for a few minutes—and we're almost to the edge of Imaku. Almost to the dubious safety of the ocean.

I stumble twice. Sanii loses eir footing three times. Tessen keeps close behind us, and I hear him curse more than once.

Looking out over the water, I almost laugh. It's ridiculous. How do we expect to survive swimming a mile or more in these choppy waves? We can't— "What is that?"

There's something out there, like an enormous oblong bowl, and it's floating on top of the water.

"It doesn't matter! We need to jump!" Tessen shouts behind us.

We're still ten feet above the waterline, but there's a rock that juts away from the shore. I run toward that ledge, the safest place I can spot to jump into the ocean from, and use Sanii's hold on Yorri to drag em along. A wave slams into the rocks below. The droplets strike my ward, stopping in midair. We run, leaping as far from the island as we can.

Pain shoots up my arm, like it's being torn from its socket. I lose my hold on Yorri.

Water surrounds me, chilly even through the ward. It holds, though; I breathe air, not water.

Yorri. Where is Yorri? I must have lost him when we hit the waves.

I try to reach for him; my left arm won't answer.

The current slams against my wards, spinning me around and shoving me deeper. Bubbles and foam cloud the water, but I see Sanii to my left, eir face frantic. Yorri should be between us.

He's not there.

Tessen plunges through the waves above me. When the water clears enough for me to see him, he's holding his right arm tight against his chest, his face pained.

I suck my ward closer until my hands and feet are outside the protections. Finding up isn't easy, but finally I spot gray clouds and roiling crests of the waves. I push through the water, fighting each shift of direction, and breach the surface.

Heart pounding in my ears almost loud enough to drown out the ocean's crash, I search for Yorri. He has to be here. We had him. I had him literally in my arms! Where is— *No!*

Yorri's head hangs limp and his body extends out over the water, like time somehow stopped just before he dove into the waves. His arms are pulled behind him and his feet haven't left the black rock, like whatever magic is in those cords won't allow him to leave Imaku.

I try to swim closer, but fighting the force of the current is as futile as fighting a storm.

Neeva and Anda have almost reached Yorri, their arms outstretched.

Desperate, I throw my magic like a dagger, aiming for the wardstones around my brother's wrists and ankles. I pour everything into those wards.

A moment, the space of a breath, a blink, or a heart-beat—that's all he needs. With his weight tipped over the ledge like that, the smallest span of time should be enough to release him into the water, for the current to catch him and carry him away.

Yorri's wardstones glow brighter than Sanii. Anda and Neeva throw their hands up to shield their eyes. I squint into the light as the waves pull me farther away. Chills creep up my arms and legs. The light-headed wash of nothingness threatens to engulf me.

A hand clamps around my left wrist.

My body jerks. My concentration breaks. My wards weaken, letting water seep through.

No!

It's less than a moment, but it's enough for Yorri's ward to dim and for Anda to yank Yorri back from the ledge, away from safety.

My ward drops.

I'm pulled out of the current's flow, rising slowly—painfully—out of the water.

The hand around my wrist tightens and pulls harder. Pain, white-hot like a smoldering length of iron and so strong it's nearly blinding.

It isn't as painful as watching Anda drag my brother back onto Imaku.

My chest is cracking. No. *No.*

An arm locks around my chest like a restraint and pulls, hauling me out of the water and onto—into?—something that floats on the waves and yet somehow not in them. The massive floating bowl I spotted from the island? I struggle weakly against the hold, trying to get back into the water. Trying to get back to Yorri.

"*Kyushi, monoka.*" The stranger lays me down. An unfamiliar face with an unfamiliar voice speaking unfamiliar words with an unfamiliar accent. I try to roll back to the water; my body feels too heavy to move. "*Ya wa*—ah!" A sharp thud against something hollow. The stranger leans away. "*Nen. Shen ya*—"

The words cut off with a shout, and then there are too many noises to follow. Clangs and curses and shouts bleed into each other until one element of the cacophony is indistinguishable from the next. The surface I'm lying on moves, and the motion sends my head spinning. My stomach rolls almost as much as the waves beneath me. Somehow beneath me.

Out of the ocean and into the rain and Yorri isn't here.

My eyes burn, and the ache in my chest almost drowns out the sharp, thudding pain in my shoulder. It drowns out the world, pushing everything back to a safer distance. Where it won't hurt me as much.

Tessen leans over me, his mouth shaping my name. I think I hear Sanii's voice, too, screaming for Yorri. Then Tessen looks away to stare wide-eyed at something. Another threat? I should look, get up and try to protect us from whatever is scaring him so much, but...I can't. And I'm not sure I want to.

It feels like we're skimming the waves on the back of a mykyn, rising and falling with each new crest. The sky is a solid mass of dark gray clouds spitting water down on us, and they don't hint at the passage of time or distance. Only Tessen's worried face gives the landscape depth. Only the movement of his lips as he speaks words whose meaning is lost on me proves time hasn't stopped.

I wish it had.

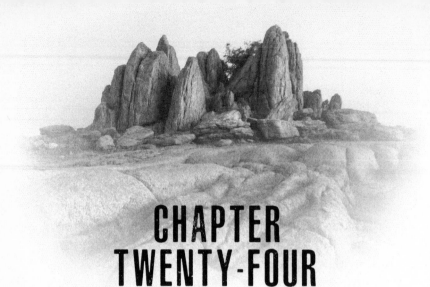

CHAPTER TWENTY-FOUR

"**W**ho are you? What is this thing?" Tessen is standing over me, his zeeka pointed at someone.

I lift my head—it hurts and seems like it weighs more than a cart of iron ore—and see a stranger, someone who looks like the Miriseh but isn't a face I recognize from the mural wall. His black hair, worn long enough to fall straight to his shoulders, is sodden from the rain and hanging limp around his face. He's holding his hands out, palms up, hands empty, and head dipped as though he's afraid to look Tessen in the eyes.

"*Shen ya! Shen ya! Waheiwa, yuji-in.*" I don't recognize the voice or the words. "*Waheiwa. Ta deshoh ketasu. Ta ketasu. Waheiwa, yuji-in.*"

"I don't know what you're saying." Tessen's blade is still pointed at the stranger, but his tone and what I can see of his face seem more frustrated and confused than hostile and scared now. "Who are you?"

"*Kaisubeh ketasu tai,*" the man mutters, seemingly to

himself. Then he looks at us and speaks very slowly. "Ahh, I am Osshi. I am...friend? Help you?"

"Well, *friend*, I guess we'll see if that's true soon." Tessen lowers his weapon and turns his head facing in the direction—I think—of the shore. "I hope you can fight, Osshi. I think we're about to find trouble."

Trouble? No. No more. I want to curl on my side, body tucked tight into a ball, and just let whatever is coming take me. But if I die, I'll never get a second chance to save Yorri. And I *can't* leave Tessen to face whatever is coming alone, not after everything he's given up for me. I can't fail Sanii any more than I already have.

Oh, no. Sanii. Where is Sanii?

I gather my strength, and with the arm that doesn't feel one bad jolt away from being torn off my body, I push myself to sit up. It's like my mind has split, half of me locked in the far back corner of my head where no one will hear me screaming, and the rest left to calmly focus on the world.

There. Sanii is curled up into a tiny ball at the front of this long, narrow floating platform.

As the brief flare of panic fades, the world goes distant again. Even the rain striking my face and the wind rushing in my ears as we fly through the waves seems like it's happening to someone else. No matter. At least I can think.

The material under my hands is strange, hard like stone yet it can't be. It's almost like wood, but there's too much of it. Making something this size out of wood would clear half the scrubs in Itagami's territory, if it was possible to do at all. Whatever it is, it's light enough that, even though four people can sit in it with room to spare, it can still float on top of the water. We're not in danger of drowning thanks to this...thing, so that can't be the trouble Tessen spotted.

I scan the shoreline and the water, but there's nothing that raises even a hint of alarm. "What's coming?"

Tessen looks at me, worry in his eyes. My voice sounded wrong, too hollow and dead even to my ears, but Tessen only says, "Something is pulling us east along the shore. It has to be a rikinhisu mage, but I've never heard of one who can move objects this large at such a long distance." He turns to the shoreline, his eyes focusing on something distant enough that I can't see it. "I think we're about to meet Tsua again."

"Tsua!" Osshi exclaims. "*Ohwa temasu za Bobasu*!"

When we both look at him with nothing but confusion, the excitement fades from his expression.

"Ahh, apology I be making." His face scrunches, frustration clear. "It is not being easy to be thinking in the old tongue like this, yes? Only to be reading now. Speaking is rare and you do not be speaking it the same as me, yes? But Tsua. This is a name I be knowing! It is of the—the *Bobasu*. The ones who were exiled, yes?"

"I'm only half sure I understood a portion of that," Tessen says.

"Then you know more than me." I turn away from Osshi, a stranger who looks too much like the Miriseh. My eyes fall on Sanii, and my chest clenches. My hands shake.

I look toward the shore before guilt and pain rise up and choke me.

I never thought I'd see Shiara from the ocean. Even with the recent explosion of greenery, it looks stark and forbidding from here, a seemingly unending strip of red, brown, and gray rock. There's so little sign from here that anyone calls Shiara home.

"How much longer do you think we have?" I ask.

"A minute at most. We're not running parallel to the

shore anymore. I think Tsua is drawing us in."

If it is Tsua at all.

Seconds later, even I can see that Tessen is right. We're aimed more toward the shore, our path cutting between the piles of rock rising out of the water, and there's a shadow on the cliff face ahead that's darker than the ones surrounding it.

"Is that a cave entrance?" I point to the shadow.

Tessen nods slowly. "I can't hear much over the waves and the rain, but I'm pretty sure that's where we're headed. And that"—he points to a ledge high above the cave's entrance—"is where Tsua's been guiding us in from."

It had been hard in the open water to see how fast we were moving, but the cliff goes from something on the horizon to a wall looming a hundred or more feet over our heads in minutes. By the time my eyes find the ledge Tessen is pointing at, we're almost underneath it.

I look back when the floating thing slows and passes through the narrow, nearly hidden entrance to the cave. There are too many rocks between us and Imaku. I can't see it. I don't know how far we've come.

"It's about a mile back," Tessen says quietly. The cave is dim and dark, and it seems to be empty.

"Only a mile?" It took long enough, and we were moving fast enough, that it felt like the distance should be more.

Tessen opens his mouth to answer, but then his attention focuses to his left. There in the shadows of the cave is someone who *isn't* Tsua.

"You're safe here," the stranger says, his accent hinting at the rolling tongue of the Denhitrans. "For a while, at least. Varan and the others will come looking soon. They'll break this whole cliff apart and send it into the sea if they have to, but we're safe enough for now."

The floating thing is moving slower now, and then it bumps against the rock ledge surrounding the water. Closer, I can see the newest stranger better. Not much older than us, he looks like he could be Osshi's blood-brother. He looks like he could be Miriseh.

I thought there were only two missing, Tsua and whoever the twelfth face in the mural was. But these two…

"Who are you?" Tessen jumps out of the floating thing, his hand clenched around the hilt of his zeeka. It stays pointed at the ground for now.

"I'm Zonna."

"You're Denhitran," I say.

He lifts one shoulder. "In a sense."

Tessen clears his throat, his grip on the zeeka tightening and the tip of the sword rising. "Are you Miriseh?"

"Only by blood." Zonna is smiling pleasantly, as though he can't see Tessen's blade. But if he's Miriseh, a blade wouldn't matter, would it? He nods toward the floating thing. "Leave the boat, but take everything else you can carry. It's safer in the next cavern."

Zonna turns around, presenting his back without any visible concern that Tessen might shove the zeeka through his spine. And also seeming absolutely certain that we'll follow him.

"Why should we trust you?" I don't want to lead Tessen and Sanii into some kind of trap.

He stops and turns halfway, looking back at us with his eyebrows mildly arched. "Because Tsua and I just saved your life."

"He has a point," Tessen whispers to me, lowering his weapon. He looks at Sanii, who hasn't moved from the front of the floating thing. A boat, Zonna called it.

I close my eyes and breathe, but only for a moment. Tessen and Osshi help Sanii out of the boat, and the four of us follow Zonna through a break in the cave wall, into a small cave where a fire is burning. It seems more for light than heat. A hole about three feet wide and three feet off the ground is carved into one of the walls, and it's through this that Tsua appears, dropping into the cave and landing with a small puff of dust.

"I didn't expect to see you again, little fykina." Tsua stops two feet away, her face unreadable. "I especially didn't expect to see you leaping off Imaku."

"You would have seen us sooner or later, even if you hadn't pulled us away from—" My throat closes around the rest of that sentence. I shake my head, the motion making me dizzy. Grief crackles in my chest, and my whole body aches. Pushing all of it aside, I breathe and try to focus. "We were going to head toward Denhitra looking for you."

"Were you? That's a story I haven't heard in years." There's a secretive smile on Tsua's lips as her words sink in. This is a story she's heard before? I can't think of anything else to say yet, so for a moment we watch each other in silence. Then she asks, "Do you trust me?"

"Not really." I'd hoped that, when we found Denhitra, Tsua wouldn't kill us before hearing our story, but I don't trust her.

"Then you know I don't trust you either yet. But we do want to help."

In looks, Zonna is younger by at least a decade—there's no gray in his brown-black hair and his skin is smooth of all the creases and wrinkles that age usually brings—but they have the same thin-bridged noses, high cheekbones, and square, determined set to their jaws. General similarities may make Zonna and Osshi look like blood-brothers, but there's absolutely no denying the relationship between Tsua and Zonna.

She nods toward Zonna. "He'll heal your injuries if you don't try to fight him."

Healings mean allowing touch and someone else's magic to sink under my skin. I've never enjoyed it even when the hishingu was a trusted clan member. Now? With a stranger who has been and might remain an enemy?

"And if I do fight?"

No flicker or twitch of Tsua's expression reveals her thoughts. "Then you'll be in pain."

"Let him help," Tessen whispers in my ear, almost pleading.

I don't want to, but it'd be stupid to refuse when I need to be able to protect myself—and Tessen and Sanii—if Tsua changes her mind about helping. So I relent.

Still smiling, Zonna steps closer and places one hand on my left shoulder and one on my right hip. Tessen steps in behind me, his hands on my back like he's trying to brace me. Or be close enough to defend me if anything goes wrong.

Closing his eyes, Zonna takes a breath.

For those who can feel the way the desosa shifts, each hishingu mage is recognizable. Zonna's magic is quiet and cool. Instead of attacking the points of pain, he coaxes. He wears down the pain in my shoulder—and a lesser pain in my back I hadn't noticed until my shoulder stopped throbbing—like water wears down rocks.

A moment, and both my pain and Zonna's magic are gone. I'm still sapped and fatigued, drained low by all the magic I shoved into the wardstones on Imaku, but now my body doesn't have to pour energy into healing. I thought those aches would take weeks to fade.

"Better?" The corner of Tsua's mouth curves up.

I breathe deep, relief from the pain making me light-headed. "Thank you."

"You're welcome, youngling."

I blink at the epithet. Zonna gives me a bright grin as he steps back. How much older is he, really? He doesn't look more than five years older than me.

"If you were on Imaku, I already know a large part of your story," Tsua says, looking over the three of us before she turns her attention to Osshi. "But you, I can only guess at."

"He said his name was Osshi, I think," Tessen supplies. "I had a hard time following what he was saying."

"Osshi, yes." He smiles and presses his palms together at the center of his chest, his fingers pointing toward Tsua and his head bowed. "Osshi Shagakusa, I am."

"Oh, Kaisubeh bless you, Osshi-tan." Tsua's eyes light up, widening enough that they catch the firelight and make it look as though they're glowing. Osshi, too, looks delighted by whatever rank or title Tsua added to his name. "If it were at all safe to stay here, I would have so many questions for you. It'll have to wait until we're farther inland."

"Moving we will be doing?" Osshi asks. "I must be speaking with my boat now if we are to be away from the shore for long."

Zonna purses his lips. "How? If your friends saw what happened and went looking for you, they've probably already been captured."

"No, no! When I was seeing these ones leaping from the Kaijuko—the black island, I was getting a message to them to be waiting and to be hiding." He looks down, opening one of the pouches on his belt and lifting something out of it. It's perfectly round, perfectly clear, and no bigger than the palm of his hand.

Tsua makes a delighted noise and stretches out her hand. Osshi hesitates only a moment before placing the object on her palm. As soon as it's in her hand, she lifts it up to the firelight. "I never thought I'd see a *garakyu* so clear. What is the range?"

"No more than five miles it is reaching," Osshi seems torn between excitement over the sphere and disappointment that it can't do more.

"Maybe save the spell theory discussion for later," Zonna says with a smile.

"Hmm. Yes, you're right." She gives the sphere an almost longing look before handing it back to Osshi. "Get your message out quickly. I wouldn't be surprised if Varan sends half of Itagami after us."

Osshi nods and raises the sphere to his lips, murmuring incomprehensible words to it and making it glow. If that ball can somehow send messages over a distance of miles, it's impressive. And not a kind of magic I've ever seen before. I'm not even sure what it's made of. Not crystal, definitely. It's too clear for that.

I may be healed, but a lack of pain doesn't fix the fact that I've used up almost every ounce of magic I possess. Energy can't be healed. Healing usually drains it more. But I can either stay here, rest, and probably die, or push through the exhaustion to follow Tsua.

"You might have to catch me if I fall," I tell Tessen as Tsua and Zonna gather their few things.

"You know I will." Worry tightens his lips and his eyes, but he has to know we can't wait for the hours of sleep it'll take for me to feel close to normal again. Getting away from Itagami is more important. Besides, if I exhaust myself enough, sleep will be dreamless.

Sanii hasn't said a word since Imaku, has barely moved except to get from the boat to this cavern. When I kneel next to where ey is sitting, though, ey looks up, eir large eyes glassy and bleak. It looks like one sharp strike would shatter em into thousands of pieces.

"Can you walk, Sanii?" I force myself to ask.

Ey blinks slowly and then exhales, eir chin dropping to eir chest. There's defeat and absolute blank despair in every line of eir body. The bitter anger that seemed to fuel em before has disappeared; it doesn't look like there's anything left to keep em going now that it's gone.

This is the loss I've seen when someone's bondmate dies. This is the kind of grief that eats away at purpose. This is the pain that I'm trying so hard to ignore.

Tessen's hand rubs gentle circles between my shoulders. I think he's trying to offer comfort, but the touch only makes me feel worse. It was my failure that left Yorri in the hands of the Miriseh. It was my weakness that left Sanii lost and broken. My weakness that left me struggling not to curl up next to em and wait for it all to end.

But Tsua is edging toward the mouth of the cave and Zonna and Osshi are moving to stand with her. I failed, but at least now we know that Yorri is alive. We know where he is and what kind of magic is keeping him trapped there. If we stay here we really will have failed, because I have absolutely no doubt that the Miriseh have ordered us to be killed on sight. We'll never have a second chance to save him if we're dead.

"We need to leave, Sanii." I try to say it gently, but my voice is too hoarse and my mind too numb. There's little chance I'll be able to haul em up without losing balance, so I look to Tessen for help when ey doesn't move. He nods and leans down to help em to eir feet.

Once Sanii is standing, I grip eir face between my hands, leaning forward a little to look down into eir eyes. "If we're alive, we can try again. It's only once we're dead that his chances are gone, okay?"

Sanii blinks, a little of the determination I'm used to seeing coming back into eir eyes. After a long, slow breath, ey nods. I run my hand over eir hair to grip the back of eir neck, and then I release em and move my hand to Tessen's shoulder.

I hate the weakness in my body right now, the way my legs are trembling, but I can't make it stop. If it weren't raining, I'd be able to regain some energy from the sunlight. Since that's not an option, I'll have to lean on Tessen if I want to make it far without collapsing. One of Tessen's hands slides on top of mine while the other fixes the knot keeping his damp atakafu over his face.

The only thing left to do is follow one of the missing Miriseh into the desert.

CHAPTER TWENTY-FIVE

t was late afternoon when we left the shore, and we've been walking southeast for hours since then, crossing into and through the Kyiwa Mountains. Darkness has fallen, making the path three times as treacherous as usual, but Tsua's and Zonna's lanterns give us enough light to at least keep from killing ourselves.

"Light?" I'd signed to Sanii once the gray twilight settled. Ey had shaken eir head, casting a nervous glance at the strangers. I'd let the suggestion drop then. Tsua and Zonna saved our lives today—and they're still saving them now—but Sanii's magic is unlike anything I've seen on Shiara, and we don't know how these strangers might react to what ey can do. Better to hold that back until it becomes necessary. Or at least until we can predict how they'll respond.

I'd suspected the Denhitrans had set up a protected camp in these mountains—there's no other way they could've avoided the storms and the patrols. Now it seems like I'll see for myself. As long as I don't fall asleep on my feet and tumble off a cliff before we get there.

The rain is still falling, but not as hard as it had been before. Walking, however, is much harder than it was. I lean on Tessen more with every step, my legs heavy and almost numb. If we don't reach our destination soon, someone is going to have to carry me the rest of the way. I think I need sleep more than I need air.

We're walking along a narrow ledge, the mountain on our right and a sheer drop into darkness on our left. I haven't spent much time in this particular section of the range, but I have been here before. And I'm pretty sure Tsua is leading us to a dead end.

"Do you think she knows where she's going?" I murmur to Tessen. I should probably be more worried about it than I am; I'm too tired to care much.

"She isn't hesitating at all. I think she does." But Tessen sounds confused, like he knows we're headed toward a dead end, too.

Soon, the path takes a sharp right, and there's nowhere to go. Unless we plan on either climbing the too-smooth face of the mountain or somehow crossing the hundred or more feet of empty space between us and the opposite mountain.

"Stay here." Tsua pushes off the ground hard, sprinting toward nothing.

"Stop!" Reflex and sheer, stupid exhaustion has me reaching out as though anything I can do will bring her back from the impossible —

Or maybe not so impossible.

"Show-off." Zonna's smile is fondly exasperated.

Tsua flies across the gap like there's a cord around her waist yanking her toward the opposite mountain, the lantern in her hand leaving a glowing trail in the night. She isn't ever in danger, not for a second, of falling.

"That is terrifyingly impressive." I don't think that even the most powerful rikinhisu mage in Itagami would dare a jump that distance.

"She *has* had time to practice," Tessen says wryly.

True. I can't imagine what I might be able to do with my wards if I'd had centuries to learn how to control them. "I hope she's not planning on us being able to do that."

"She has something else in mind for us, don't worry." Zonna shakes his head and gestures at the gap. "I can't do that either."

Tsua glances at what looks like a pile of stones to her right, only barely visible in the light from her lantern. With a sharp gesture, they rise into the air, shooting across the gap like arrows.

Tessen sucks in a sharp breath and pulls me out of the line of fire.

It isn't necessary.

Ten feet away from our ledge, the wide stones, all of them with one side almost perfectly flat, slow. Tsua's gestures turn the stones so their flat side is facing the sky. The first one places itself less than a foot from the ledge, and the rest line up behind it. Dozens of rocks of various sizes hanging in midair, each of them reflecting what little moonlight manages to seep through the clouds overhead, and my legs are trembling worse than ever.

I look at the bridge of floating stones, then at Tessen. He holds out his hand. I grip it hard, letting him lead me onto the first stone.

Though the rock does shift under my weight, the motion isn't enough to unbalance me. It feels more like walking on the springy earth of the saishigi core or the sections of moss in the deeper parts of the undercity. That similarity makes it a little easier to take another step. And then another. It makes it easier, too, that the bottom of this ravine is so far below us that I can't see it in the limited light.

I focus every bit of remaining energy I have on not falling. Not letting my legs buckle like they're threatening to do.

"This is the worst idea I've ever seen," Tessen mutters.

"This is nothing." Zonna's grin is a little mad. "You should see the bridges in Denhitra."

Tessen grips my hand tighter. I feel the shudder that runs through him. "I don't even want to imagine them."

I keep my eyes focused on the path, trying to look neither through the spaces between the stones nor at our destination. One foot in front of the other. Don't look, don't speak, don't fall, and, most important, don't drag Tessen down with me.

Our progress is slow, giving me time to adapt to the slight give of the stones. Stepping onto ground that doesn't shift under my feet nearly throws me off balance.

Tessen tightens his hold on my hand and drags me across the wide ledge, bringing us both up against the side of the mountain. "I wouldn't mind never doing that again."

The sound of a body hitting stone chases away the words I'd been about to speak.

"*Osensu so Kaisubeh byseh tai ka aihitsu so kannofu riburji.*" Osshi is flat on his stomach, his arms outstretched like he's trying to hug the mountain.

Sanii and Zonna follow close behind, and then Tessen clears his throat.

"We're going to have to stop soon if we've got a lot farther to go tonight." *Because otherwise I'm going to have to carry Khya,* Tessen doesn't say.

"No." Tsua smiles and walks around the mountainside. "Not far now."

I try to follow. My leg nearly folds. Tessen's hand tightens on mine to the point of pain. He swings to my other side and wraps his other arm around my waist. Our clasped hands press just under my ribs and he nudges my arm until I drape it over his shoulders. His arms are caging me in, but I don't feel trapped.

"We're almost there," he whispers. "I can hear something over the ridge. Just a little longer, Khya."

I nod once and walk with him. It feels like my feet are dragging, like each step only brings me a few inches forward. Tessen stays with me, silent and steady as we round the mountain and approach a portion of the path that slopes sharply upward, the angle almost extreme enough that we'll have to climb. I don't want to. I don't think I can.

"*Dria'ampha, alarahy,*" Tsua calls in the rolling tongue of the Denhitrans. Telling someone it's safe, I think. "*Izireo anama fantramapha iziha tsyama. Lianaova ny Chio.*"

"*Tsi, Tsua,*" a gravelly voice responds. Chio, I assume, since what I'd understood of her request asked the people on the ledge to find him. "*Ina tyho.*"

My breath locks in my throat when a lantern on the top of the slope lights.

The twelfth Miriseh.

Despite a bald head where Varan's hair falls past his ears and wrinkles around his eyes where Varan has none, there's something about the way this man moves and the expression on his face that gives him an impossibly strong resemblance to the leader of the Miriseh. I hadn't seen it when he and Varan were both faces on a wall.

Tsua practically flies up the path, coming to rest next to him and placing her palm against his chest. She leans in to kiss him before she turns to stand at his side, his arm circling her waist. They present a unified front, seeming even to *breathe* in tandem. I eye them both warily.

I'm not sure what to say, so I clench my teeth and stay silent.

My hands refuse to grip the divots in the stone with anything close to enough force, so Tessen and Tsua have to help me up the path. Mostly Tsua, her magic levitating me to the ledge where they're waiting.

It takes only a few minutes for Tessen, Sanii, Osshi, and Zonna to scramble up behind us. Zonna moves to stand next to Tsua, but the others arrange themselves next to me.

"This is Chio," Tsua says, glancing at her partner. "You've met our son, Zonna. There are others here, some Denhitran or Tsimos, but they're not your enemies. We expect you to treat them with the same respect you'd treat your clan with."

There's a silence then that feels like a breath, as though everyone pauses for air at the same moment. She wants us to treat them with the same respect we treated the clan we just betrayed and abandoned?

Chio breaks the silence. "Do you swear to a truce?"

They ask as though we have any other attractive choice. It almost makes me laugh, but I manage to swallow it down. A good thing, because I don't think I'll be able to stop if I start. "We'd deserve death if we harmed the people who saved us."

"Especially when those people might be willing to answer questions we never dared ask Varan." Tessen's hand presses into the space between my shoulders. It's a welcome reminder that he's with me. He's been one of the only solid things in my life the last several moon cycles. The only person who hasn't changed, even if my perception of him has.

"We can't promise answers without knowing the questions," Chio says. "But we promise to tell you what we know about the Miriseh."

"Then we promise to do no more than defend ourselves." I refuse to concede any more autonomy than that to people I have only a short list of reasons to trust.

"We'd expect nothing less," Tsua says.

Chio tilts his head to the south, gesturing for us to follow. Luckily, the final destination isn't far.

There's a narrow crack in the ravine wall, barely visible unless you know to look for it and so cramped that we have to divest ourselves of all of our packs before we can follow Chio and Tsua through the passage. It widens abruptly.

Gray-tinted light pouring in from the various small holes in the roof of the cave illuminates the people already inside. More of them than I expected, and a dozen of them dressed in the darker cloth of Denhitra and Tsimo. Our one-time enemies are easy to ignore, though, because with them are faces I never thought I would see again.

Standing in the center of the group are Tyrroh, Daitsa, Rai, and Etaro. More than half of our squad is arrayed behind them.

I've never seen Rai so mad. The sparks that normally stay contained to her hands are spreading up her arms. I'm nearly certain that if she thought she could get through my wards, she'd be raining those sparks on my head.

I probably deserve it.

Rai opens her mouth, but Tessen talks first.

"If you have to yell at her, you can do it tomorrow. When she's no longer sleep-deprived and nearly delirious." His tone is as commanding as a kaigo's. Rai blinks. "Whatever you think you've lost because she kept secrets,

I promise you it's nothing compared to what she has. You can save whatever you have to say for tomorrow."

Rai's jaw clenches—and so do her sparking hands—but she doesn't stop Tessen when he half carries me past her to the far end of the cave.

"I'll keep watch," he says as he gently lowers me to the rocks. "Rest as long as you can, because we're going to need you in the morning."

No one should need me, I want to say. *I couldn't save Yorri, and I probably can't save them, either.*

My tongue won't form the words, but I fall asleep with them ringing in my head.

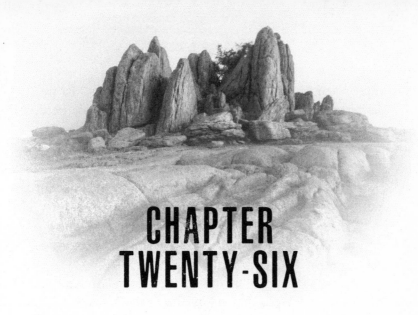

CHAPTER
TWENTY-SIX

Consciousness returns in insignificant pieces, like grains of sand; I don't notice how much I've gathered until my mind is overflowing with it and I open my eyes.

The walls of this cave are the striated, multihued limestone and sandstone of the Kyiwa Mountains. A group is gathered near a small cooking fire in the center of the cave, their backs to me. By their clothing, I can identify their clan. The Denhitrans and the Tsimosi I expected to see, but there are several more, and they're wearing the hooded tunics of Itagami, their heads tilted together, deep in whispered conversation.

Am I still dreaming? Rai and the squad can't be here...

Sanii sits against the far wall, knees pulled in tight to eir chest and face hidden in the crook of eir arm. Osshi is sitting a few feet away, eyeing em with wary concern even as he carries on a conversation with Tsua and Chio.

Leaning against the wall nearby is Zonna. The healer, the thirteenth Miriseh, and Tsua's blood-son. Another of

Varan's and Suzu's lies laid bare. They always told us that the burden of serving as gatekeepers to Ryogo was never being able to contribute their bloodlines to the clan. That they physically couldn't.

I shift and suddenly Tessen's face is hovering over mine. He smiles gently when our eyes meet. "Morning. Feeling better?"

"Oh, look," someone says before I can answer. "The girl who thinks she can take the Miriseh on with an army of *three* is finally awake."

"Rai?" It's impossible, but that's Rai's voice. And it's Rai whose face appears over Tessen's shoulder. I have no idea what my expression looks like. It's enough to make her snort with a suppressed laugh.

"You look surprised to see me. You never liked surprises, did you? Or asking for blood-rotten *help* when you need it, you absolute imbecile."

"Enough, Rai." Tessen's expression goes hard and his voice is sharp. "Not now."

"Oh, shut up." She brushes him off with a sharp wave of her hand. "You're no better than she is! And you said I could yell at her in the morning. It's morning."

Etaro is there, then, a hand on Rai's shoulder and more than a few emotions flashing across eir face. Ey takes a short, but deep breath, and eir eyes narrow, determination overtaking everything else in eir face. I've never seen em look more serious.

But I shouldn't be looking at em at all! "How are you here? *Why* are you here?"

"They came with me." Tyrroh stops behind Etaro and Rai, his arms crossed but something close to relief in his eyes. "It's good to see you in one piece, Khya."

"I…" The questions I want to ask tangle on my tongue,

the words all mashing into one confused noise. "You really were working with the Denhitrans?"

"Food first, I think," Tsua says from the fireside. "Khya still has some strength to regain, and Tyrroh isn't the only one with a story to tell."

Though everyone moves with somewhat grudging expressions on their faces, they all follow Tsua's instructions. I guess a lifetime of training to obey the Miriseh is hard to ignore. She isn't wrong about the food, though.

They let me eat in peace for a few minutes, and I devour everything they put on my plate. Mykyn eggs cooked with spices and greens, a thick piece of fish, and several pieces of bread. It's good food. It's *real* food, not the usual desert rations. They really must have been holed up here for a while.

When my chewing begins to slow at last, Tessen starts the conversation.

But not in the way I expect.

"Who did you lose, Nyshin-ma?"

Tessen's question makes Tyrroh close his eyes, a blink that lasts too long. There's pain there, but it's an old pain. Something he's learned to live with and, most of the time, hide.

"A boy named Hykin," Tyrroh says. "Not my blood-brother or a lover, but he was my closest friend. He was only a few moons younger than me, and he disappeared the night of his herynshi. Varan and Suzu claimed Denhitrans ambushed the group when they were returning to the city. Hykin was the only one who didn't come back. Someone claimed they saw him fall, but everyone else said the Denhitrans carried him off."

"We hadn't," Tsua says. "Which we explained when

Tyrroh and several others found us on their rescue mission."

"After Tsua and Chio explained, the others refused to return to Itagami." Tyrroh rubs his hand over his bald head. "I volunteered to be their eyes inside the city when I could."

That was why Ryzo saw him talking to Tsua. I half expect Etaro, Rai, or one of our squad to interrupt with a question, but Rai is glaring at me, Etaro is concentrating on the pebbles ey's dancing in the air above eir palm, and the five others are watching the fire and the pot of something cooking over it. Daitsa, at least, gives me a smile that is almost encouraging. The Denhitrans and the Tsimosi are watching me with wary caution; thankfully, it's no different than the guardedness in their eyes when they look at anyone else from my squad.

It seems like they've heard this part before. Which makes sense. Tyrroh would have had to tell them to convince them to leave the city with him.

Clearing my throat, I avoid Rai's eyes and ask, "How did you explain your absence to the Miriseh?"

"I told them the truth, mostly." Tyrroh's smile is bitterly wry. "I'd been trying to rescue a clan member, and I was the only one who made it back to the city after the attempt. They punished me for acting without orders, but not harshly considering how devoted to the safety of the clan I seemed."

"That was the first time they'd tried to pin a kidnapping on us," Chio says. "They didn't try again."

"They started faking deaths instead." Tsua huffs, her nose wrinkled in disgust.

"You're lucky there wasn't a rusosa as strong as Neeva in the kaigo then," Tessen says to Tyrroh. "They would've shown you whatever it took to convince you he was dead."

Speaking of convincing... I look between Tyrroh and

the squad. "How did he convince you all to come with him?"

Daitsa looks chagrined, her half-moon eyes sympathetic. Etaro's eyes flick up to meet mine, but ey looks down at eir pebbles again too quickly for me to read eir face. One of the others opens his mouth to speak, but then grimaces and shakes his head. The rest sit in stony silence.

Except Rai.

"He told us the truth." Rai has no problem glaring at me, her eyes gleaming with anger, hurt, and worry, and sparks of fire running across her palms. "That the reason you'd been gone so much and acting so strange and not mourning your brother like you did those first few days was because Yorri hadn't actually died. He said you and Tessen needed help trying to save him or you'd probably get yourselves killed." The sparks around her hands flare brighter. "Which is what it looks like almost happened."

"We would have helped if you'd come to us, Khya." Etaro isn't looking at me, but eir voice is strong and steady and eir hand is clenched tight around the small stones. "You didn't even like Tessen and you asked him for help. You should've come to us."

"I didn't go to Tessen!" I cry, smacking Tessen lightly. "He followed me and forced himself into this mess. What Sanii and I did was treason, and we were ready to die for it—to spend eternity in Kujuko for betraying the clan, if it came to that—but I was *not* going to ask anyone else to die with us."

Etaro looks up. "The safety of the clan—"

"No." I shake my head, ignoring the interest on the faces of several of the strangers in our audience. "No. This isn't that. This is the exact opposite of what they've trained into us since we were doseiku. This is me putting Yorri's life above what the Miriseh and the kaigo had decided."

Rai opens her mouth.

I cut her off. "And if I had come to you with a wild story about missing yonin given nyshin saishigi rites, a *feeling* that my brother wasn't dead, and two Miriseh that Varan and Suzu never told us about, would you have believed me? Or would you have claimed Yorri's death had driven me over a mental cliff?"

When the words finally stop rushing out of my mouth, my heavy breathing and the crackle of the fire are the only sounds.

Then Tsua cocks her head. "How *did* you know I was like your Miriseh?"

I take a slow breath and close my eyes, glad to grasp the subject change. "We found a cave that had been hidden until a different section of the undercity collapsed. It had murals painted on the walls. In one room was a landscape that could only be Ryogo and—"

"You know of Ryogo, too?" Osshi scrambles to his feet, his face bright. He rushes toward us, and I'm struck by the similarities between him and the Miriseh. His skin is close to the same shade of warm beige as theirs, noticeably lighter than almost everyone else on Shiara, and his hair has the same brown-black sheen. "I hear the words she said, and they are sounding like Ryogo. Of course the Bobasu were knowing of the land when we spoke last night, but I was not being sure others would. But you know of the land, yes? I hear the words in the correct way?"

"Later, Osshi-tan. Please. It will be too much for them all at once." Tsua talks to him, but her eyes never leave my face. "What else was there, Khya?"

"There was another cave with a portrait of the Miriseh,

ten we recognized and two we'd never seen. One of them was you, Tsua." I look at Chio. "You were the last one missing from the portrait."

Chio and Tsua look at each other, communicating something in the twitch of an eyebrow and a flicker of the eyes.

"You found the *osukiga* portrait?" Chio asks.

"Sanii did." I want to ask about the term, but that can wait. My eyes drift to em. Ey looked up at the sound of eir name, but eir eyes are so blank I'm not sure ey's actually hearing anything. Tsua knows the Miriseh, so maybe she knows about Imaku and the cords and what we have to do to save Yorri. "They told us that my brother, Yorri, died fighting your clan—that he died saving Neeva's life. I *saw* them enshroud him, but Sanii... Ey didn't get a chance to say goodbye before the laying in. When ey went to unearth him..."

"It wasn't him that you found." Tyrroh's words are full of sorrow.

"No, it wasn't. Ey found the cave after discovering the truth about Yorri." I glance at Sanii in the corner of the room where ey is watching the conversation as though it's a game of patsu ey has no stake in. As though neither the words nor the outcome matters to em. "Ey was trying to find Yorri, but ey found the—what did you call it?"

"*Osukiga*." Tsua repeats the word, but doesn't offer its meaning. "How many people are there now on Imaku?"

"Thirty-nine," Tessen says.

Tsua hisses through her teeth, her expression pinched. "So many?" She looks at Chio, pain in her eyes. "*Zen'ni di izika nytsi*, Chio."

"No." Chio shakes his head, turning toward Tsua. His hand grips her shoulder. Around us, the other Denhitrans watch the exchange with sympathy in their eyes. "This is not our fault. If we'd stayed, Varan would've trapped us on that black rock eventually. You know we never could've weathered the heat of Varan's vengeance."

"Vengeance on *who*?" Did everyone from their land live for centuries? "And what does vengeance have to do with my brother and everyone else on Imaku?"

"More than we have time to explain in detail," Tsua says. She raises one hand when I try to protest. "But we can give you the beginning."

"We know what Varan and Suzu have taught the clan to believe, but very little of that is true, Khya." Chio rubs a hand over his bald head. "We came from Ryogo, but we're not its gatekeepers. None of us have seen that land for centuries."

"Ryogo!" Osshi is nearly vibrating. "That is where I is from! Ryogo!"

"You came back from the *dead*?" Is that why he looks so much like the Miriseh?

"Dead?" Osshi's bouncing stops.

"Khya, Ryogo isn't the land of the dead," Tsua says quietly. Gently. Like a hishingu delivering news of a death.

I open my mouth to protest, but what can I possibly argue? If the Miriseh who taught us the stories of Ryogo have already been proved liars, and the people who saved my life are telling us that Ryogo as I know it is a lie…

I almost laugh. It catches in my throat for a second, but the relief is too strong. Covering my mouth and closing my eyes, I give in to it.

It isn't real?

If Ryogo isn't real, then the Miriseh can't be the gatekeepers for it. If it's not their decision who passes on to a paradise afterlife, then they can't banish anyone to

Kujuko, either. If where our souls go when death finally claims us isn't in their hands, then...

Then I'm free. I might be free of the fate I thought I'd damned myself to—damned *everyone* who walked away from Itagami to.

Tessen has to start explaining why this is humorous at all to Tsua and Chio.

But if Ryogo isn't the afterlife I've always imagined, if it's instead a land that the Miriseh and Osshi came from centuries ago, that means Yorri was right. When we stood on the wall and he asked if I ever thought there might be something else. *He* had. He'd seen that, despite everything the Miriseh told us about the world.

And if Ryogo is a real place, another land that the Miriseh possibly *can* build a bridge to, how much more is there beyond that?

I'm still laughing; my chest aches and my eyes burn, giddy tears gathering in my eyes and trailing down my cheeks.

Bellows and blood, how can the world be so much bigger than we thought if Yorri isn't here to see any of it?

CHAPTER
TWENTY-SEVEN

"**W**hat *is* true?" Rai's words are sharp, like darts aimed across the cave.

"Ryogo is real." Tsua's eyes go distant. "It's green and beautiful in ways that are hard to describe to someone who's only seen Shiara, but it's *not* the afterlife." She exhales and refocuses on me. "The twelve of us were cast out from Ryogo, and Varan is desperately trying to get back there."

"It's insanity." Chio sighs. "But I learned centuries ago not to underestimate Varan, even when his goal is supposedly impossible. Nothing I've ever done or said has changed his mind about trying to go back. Even though it's been so long that no one who banished us is still living."

"He'll be destroying the lives of people who probably only know of us from legend." Tsua places her hand on her husband's knee. "We've been gone so long that we're a story to frighten children. The people who'll be punished when Varan finally crosses the ocean had no part in the original crime."

Ryogo isn't real, but it is? Varan and the others aren't

gatekeepers, but exiles. There are centuries of secrets between one end of the story and the other.

I need them to start at the beginning. "I don't understand."

"I thought..." Etaro bites eir lip. The rest of the squad is angry or lost, silent or conversing in hushed whispers. The Denhitrans and the Tsimosi are having their own whispered conversations, but it seems like sympathy is overtaking the suspicion they'd been watching us with before. "I thought this was about Yorri and Imaku?"

That's what this was about for me, but my portion of this story doesn't come until the tail end. I turn to Chio. "Why were you exiled?"

Tsua and Chio look at each other. She nods, and he begins to talk.

"Varan is my younger brother. He always had a strong talent for magic—especially when he worked with stones—but it wasn't enough for him. He studied obsessively, always looking for more power." Chio grinds his teeth, the muscles in his jaw jumping. "He eventually decided he had to learn directly from the Kaisubeh."

"The what?" Tessen and I ask at the same time. I feel more lost now than when the training masters taught us Denhitran language back when I was a doseiku.

"The Kaisubeh are the ocean and the wind and the power that makes day and night," Tsua says. "They are the creators of the world and the sky and everything that happens between the two. They are everywhere and have the power to unmake the world as we know it."

Rai shakes her head, disbelief in her wide eyes. "Not even the Miriseh have that kind of power."

"They know not of the Kaisubeh?" Osshi doesn't stay silent long enough for Chio or Tsua to answer. "What you were saying in the night before made it be seeming that the Bobasu were trying to be making themselves into the Kaisubeh."

"Don't think the idea didn't cross his mind." Chio nearly laughs, but the grimace on his face when he swallows the sound erases any trace of humor. "It's lucky for all of us that as much as he tried, Varan couldn't actually make himself a god."

"And you're making the mistake of thinking any of the Kaisubeh are human," Tsua says to Rai. "You must think of them as the air or the waves. They are infinite and permanent in a way even someone who has lived hundreds of years can't comprehend. Long before I was born, they existed, and they'll continue to do so for eons after I finally find death."

"And Varan wanted to become like them?" I ask. This conversation is like being back in the ocean, each new revelation another wave that sends me tumbling.

"He was obsessed with it." Chio rubs his palm over his face and then drops his hand back to his knee. "And by the time he started trying to *become* them, I'd learned to be wary of his obsessions."

"He never came close to talking to the gods." Tsua continues rubbing circles on Chio's back, but now her attention is more on us than him. "But he said his failure proved they didn't exist anymore—maybe that they never have. That's when he decided to make himself immortal."

Chio shakes his head, his lips pulled tight. "He was only twenty-three then, but he already feared age and death enough to spend the next two decades finding a way to cheat both. Even once he did that, it wasn't enough. He thought that what he'd discovered gave him some right to rule, so he started a war."

"And he almost won," Tsua said. "His own pride lost him

his victory. He was outsmarted and then exiled along with every single follower he'd gathered—immortal and human."

Chio looks up at the roof of the sandstone cave. "We've been here ever since."

I take a breath and force myself to ask. "What does he want *now*? Why did he take Yorri and everyone else on that island?"

"He wants the same thing he wanted five hundred years ago: to invade Ryogo and eviscerate anyone who opposed him. He wants the Chonochi family to pay for how he thought they'd wronged him." Tsua doesn't look at Chio, but she shifts closer to him slightly, her shoulder brushing his. "He wants to place himself on the emperor's throne and rule forever."

"There is being no emperor, though." Osshi shakes his head, his small mouth pursed. "Ryogo is having its last royal ruler more than two hundred years past. It is a council chosen by the people of the territories now, though the ruling they do is done from Jushoyen city and palace of the old Chonochi family."

"I'm convinced the Kaisubeh are laughing at him," Chio says. "Varan was fixated on taking over the Jushoyen palace—the house where the leaders lived."

Because apparently the city he built with his own power for his own people in a land he could truly call his isn't enough of a prize. My stomach turns at the realization. It feels like we've been putting our faith in someone who thought nothing of us.

"So, wait. You're saying that the Miriseh were once all, what?" Rai looks like I felt when they told us Ryogo is a lie. "Like *us*?"

"Once, yes." Chio shifts his weight like someone resettling a burden. "He experimented for years in secret, testing the potions he formulated on animals. I might've been able to stop him if I'd known, but I had my own life." He closes his eyes, but his shoulders stay straight and strong. "If I'd sacrificed my goals to end his…"

"It might've changed everything," Tsua agrees. Her words have the rhythm of something spoken often. "But it also might've changed nothing."

Chio glances at her, but then grimaces and continues. "The truth is I never believed he'd find what he was looking for. It seemed impossible. I was wrong, but I only found out after he tested it on me. I was violently ill for days—fever and delirium and so much pain—but when I came out of it, I was different." He takes a long breath. "A week later I was attacked walking home. Someone drove a knife into my heart. It should have killed me.

"As soon as I saw the look on Varan's face when I walked into his house alive, I should have killed him." Chio rubs his jaw. "I'm still half certain he hoped it would kill me."

Though I might do more for people like Yorri, Tessen, Sanii, Rai, and Etaro, give up more of myself to make sure they were safe, I'd still put my life on the line for anyone in my clan. I thought that was the point of having a clan.

"Chio tried one last time to convince Varan that his plan would unravel unimaginably fast." Tsua sighs and the corner of Chio's lips curls up, the expression more than a little self-mocking. "Varan didn't listen."

"Did you honestly think he would?" Curiosity makes me ask.

"No. And when I hadn't been paying attention, Varan had gathered an ardent following. As soon as he told them his potion was ready, they all swore fealty into eternity if he offered them the same chance he'd given me." Chio snorts. "As though he'd given me a choice."

"It didn't work on everyone who took it." Tsua rubs the palms of her hands against the leather of her leggings. "He and fourteen of his most dedicated acolytes voluntarily consumed his rhetoric and his potions. Of that group, two weren't affected. Three died screaming. We didn't know about that until after..." Tsua glances at Chio.

Chio takes her hand, squeezing so tight that his knuckles pale, going nearly white. "Convincing Varan to give us the potion wasn't easy, but he owed me that much for dragging me into this."

"He knew he had to do what Chio asked or he risked creating an enemy out of someone as indestructible as he was." Tsua is still holding on to his hand.

Before this year, I don't think I would have been able to imagine that kind of manipulation or that much hatred. I'd never even hated the Denhitrans and the Tsimosi who were supposedly our mortal enemies.

In the past few moons, Varan has taught me about manipulation, and I hate him for it.

"Because Varan has always thought too highly of himself, he called us all Miriseh." The wrinkles at the corners of Chio's eyes deepen and his nostrils flare, his eyes flashing with annoyance. "Endless. Something that stretches on forever. I've always hated that word."

"After the first fifty years on Shiara, I started calling us the Andofume—the trapped. The chained. The undying."

"And you were exiled for starting a war?" Tessen asks. It doesn't make sense. War is constant. It's survival. Fighting for food, resources, shelter—it's the only way we can live on this island.

"War isn't a way of life in Ryogo, not like it is here," Chio says. "If we explained, you still wouldn't understand.

Not because you couldn't, but because our world is so fundamentally different from yours."

Yours, he says. And is, not was. *Is* different.

Is he separating himself from Itagami or the entire island? If this place doesn't feel like home even after centuries, how much of his soul must be entrenched in Ryogo?

Osshi, who has been biting his lip hard, his eyes jumping from face to face as he tracks the conversation, nods emphatically. "Different in many ways from the little I am seeing."

Tsua tilts her head, acknowledging what Osshi said. "What's important is that we were cast out, all twelve of us and anyone connected to us. I think it was either accident or the intervention of the Kaisubeh themselves that led to the student mage who discovered the properties of the black rock from the island you call Imaku."

"You had rock from Imaku?" Etaro is leaning forward, eir expression somewhere between horror and wonder. "How did you get it?"

"During the war, a fishing vessel saw a light in the sky and sailed toward it." Chio settles into a cross-legged pose, his hands on his knees and his gaze roaming his audience. "They almost capsized in the wave that followed, but they were far enough away from the impact to survive. Imaku had fallen from the sky in a blaze of fire. They were sure it was either a gift from the Kaisubeh or a warning from them, so the sailors filled their ship with pieces of the rock and brought it back to Ryogo."

"After the student's discovery, Emperor Chonochi ordered weapons and cages made of the rocks." Tsua shudders, and Chio frowns, putting his hand on her knee. "They captured us and shipped us all to Imaku. Or they tried to."

Chio's gaze seems to lock on something only he can see. "A storm pulled the boat off course before they could land on Kaijuko—the island you call Imaku. We escaped when the ship crashed on Shiara, but most of the boat's crew perished in the crash. As did many of the others forced into exile with us. The boat itself was unsalvageable."

Imaku was supposed to be Varan's prison, so he turned it into one for others? "None of this explains why they took my brother."

"First you had to understand Varan's story before what happened to Yorri, and *why* it happened, would make any sense." Chio tilts his head toward Zonna, and then he sighs. "One thing Varan hadn't expected was that the immortality he created by potion would be passed down—without any predictable pattern—to our descendants."

Their descendants. "Yorri is a descendent of the Miriseh?"

"Yes," Chio says, smiling at me. "And if he's your blood-brother, it means that you are, too."

Oh. That… I don't know how to even think about that.

"After Chio and I left Itagami with Zonna—he was only a child at the time—that's when they began neutralizing those they discovered were born with the Andofume trait." Tsua holds her hand out to Zonna. He gets up, crossing the cave to sit on her other side.

"I think they realized that anyone born on Shiara wouldn't share Varan's driving need to get back to Ryogo." Chio looks at his family, concern lining his face. "They might be loyal to him beyond anything else, but they might not. If they chose to fight for Shiara, the odds of that battle would be far too even. Varan obviously wasn't willing to take that chance."

Zonna nods. "The Itagamins who fled the city told us how Varan used the herynshi to test every single member of the clan with a rock from Imaku."

I rub my palms along my thighs, nodding. "Yorri compared it to falling into Kujuko."

Sanii and Tyrroh close their eyes. The rest of the squad mutters curses. Tsua shudders, and even Chio barely hides his wince. He's the one who recovers first. "I wish I could tell you that he was exaggerating, but we've both felt that darkness. It's not something you forget."

"That's why we've never been able to help the ones on Imaku." Tsua looks at Zonna and then me, her face tight. "We can't touch the rock without falling into the same sleep."

Which means that none of the Miriseh can personally imprison their descendants on Imaku.

"That's why the kaigo know, isn't it?" It explained why the Miriseh would trust a constantly changing circle of people with their deepest secret and, in a sense, a way to neutralize their seemingly vast power. They *had* to. Varan and Suzu didn't have a choice.

"Yes. And why the one time we did try to rescue them from Imaku, we had to send others. They barely escaped." Chio looks grim. "By the time they tried again, Varan and Suzu had found a way to recreate a *niadagu* spell—the red cords that kept your brother on the island."

The cords!

"You know about the cords?" Sanii asks.

"Do you know how to break them? I can't get him off that island until we break the cords, but when I tried, I—" I cut myself off, shuddering at the memory.

"You got trapped in the same sleep as Yorri," Tsua says. "It's an effect of the cords, but not their main purpose. If they're using the spell I think they are."

"*Nia—niadagu?*" Tessen stumbles over the new word.

"It binds a soul to a place or a promise or whatever the

mage creating the cord wants," Chio says. "If Yorri and the others are wearing those cords, they won't be able to leave Imaku."

"And because I have no idea what sort of binding they used, I can't tell you how to break the cord without potentially hurting yourself." Tsua shakes her head, her lips pressed thin. "If Yorri and the others weren't just as immortal as Varan, breaking the cords could kill them. That's not a major concern here, but without the spoken binding spell or the notes they made to make sure they could re-create the cords, we can't guarantee the binding would break. Even if it did, we can't promise it won't be excruciating for you and the ones trapped there."

Yorri can't die.

I close my eyes, holding on to that. My brother cannot be killed. I may have failed to free him from Imaku, but he *will* be alive when we try again.

"Notes? Oh!" Tessen dives for our packs as I open my eyes, pulling them closer and almost frantically pulling out everything we stole from Imaku. "Do you know what any of this is? Will this help?"

The noise Tsua makes is wordless, but full of surprise and excitement. She takes the papers and eagerly unrolls them, and Chio leans over her shoulder, mouth hanging open and his eyes roaming the pages.

Osshi leans forward, his finger tracing the edge of one of the papers. Eyes alight, he says, "This is *omikia*. My father would be being happy to the most to be seeing this still written."

"How did you know to take this, Khya?" Tsua flattens her hand against the paper, holding it to the stone floor. "With this… I might be able to get you a way to cut the cords, but how did you know to take it off the island with you?"

"We'd seen the marks in the room with the"—what had she called it?—"the *osukiga* portrait, and so we guessed they were important to Varan and Suzu. When we found these on Imaku, we thought that you might be able to decipher the marks if we found you in Denhitra."

I clear my throat and glance at Tessen. He picks up what I didn't say. "We also thought you might be less likely to kill us if we brought you something potentially useful."

"Only emperors and gods can fail to distrust those who arrive with gifts," Chio says. Smiling softly, Tsua bends and spreads the papers out as though she's trying to take them all in at once. Osshi kneels next to her, and they begin a whispered conversation. What little I can hear of it makes no sense at all. Spell theory and properties of oils and words in what can only be Ryogan.

"How did you know we were on Imaku?" After the day I encountered Tsua in the mountains, everyone in the city thought the Denhitrans had retreated completely. For them to be so close to Itagami without any of the scouts spotting them, and for their hiding place to put them in line of sight of Imaku the day we jumped from the rocks…it seems more than impossible.

"You're not the first to discover someone they love trapped on Imaku." Chio looks at Tyrroh, who nods.

"I signaled them from the nyska farm when I couldn't find you yesterday," Tyrroh says.

"And we're there often. We have been ever since we discovered what was happening on Imaku, so we could keep watch for people fleeing the city as best we could," Tsua says.

Chio clears his throat. "Not everyone who's learned what you have made it away from Itagami alive—many of them were caught and killed as traitors for whatever crime Varan accused them of. And almost no one has ever made it to Imaku. We protected the ones who wanted sanctuary and, for anyone who was willing, asked them to keep watch inside the city."

"Neeva and Anda saw us escape." Tessen shifts uneasily. "What will the Miriseh do?"

"Varan hasn't ever pursued someone beyond the borders of Itagami's land," Tsua says, drawing each word out a little longer than necessary. "However, no one else escaped by boat."

"What *is* a boat?" Rai's voice is so unexpected that I'm not the only one who jumps.

"We are doing the talking about my boat now?" The words burst out of Osshi, louder than he intends I guess by the way he winces. "It is worrying to me that the Miriseh will be trying to capture my boat and will be hurting my crew. To be leaving soon would be a good plan. It will be a danger to Ryogo if the Bobasu are finding the ship and sailing it to my home."

"The craft that carried Khya, Tessen, and Sanii away from Imaku is a boat," Chio says, answering Rai's question. "What Osshi has waiting to take him home to Ryogo is a ship. It's much larger, like a building that floats on the water and can carry people across the ocean." He frowns and shakes his head. "It's hard to imagine until you see one for yourself, especially after growing up here."

I try to picture a ship, but even taking the memory of the boat and making it bigger doesn't seem right.

What had the boat been made of? Rock sinks straight to the bottom of the bathing pools. I don't think iron would fare much better. Cloth or leather don't make sense, but what else is there? If something like Osshi's boat could be made from the wood in the island's scrubs, Varan would have done it. Probably centuries ago.

"We can use the boat to get back to Imaku, right?" Sanii is looking between Osshi and me with hope in eir eyes, hope I want to share but don't dare grasp too tightly.

But I can't let go of it completely, either. Looking away from eir ardent eyes, I nod. "I'm certainly going to try."

"If we can figure out how they adapted the *niadagu* spell and teach them how to break it…" Another glance that speaks in silence passes between Tsua and Chio.

Zonna sighs. "Yes, but that will give them another chance at the ship. If Varan captures it, he'll head for Ryogo and steal a whole fleet. His plans will go from impending to inevitable."

The storms. The announcement of the rot. The conversation about Izujo. It's like trying to put together one of Yorri's puzzles while wearing a blindfold. I don't know where the pieces connect. I can barely tell which pieces I'm holding.

I look at Tessen to find him already looking at me.

Do you think we should tell them everything now? I ask with the tilt of my head.

He must understand because his hand covers mine where it rests on my leg and he presses down lightly before he takes a breath and begins to tell our story. He fills in the larger pieces around the little snippets of information we've mentioned already, laying the tale out piece by piece, like the bridge Tsua built. Each step seems inescapable looking back on it from where we sit now.

Through it all, his hand doesn't move, and I don't pull mine away.

By the time we finish, everyone is staring at us, wide-eyed but intent.

When Tsua exhales, the breath is shaky. "Has the time finally come to end this?"

"I think so." Wrinkles and lines appear across Chio's brow. "If Osshi's ship is still in range of the *garakyu*, we might be able to figure out a way to get to where it's anchored."

Garakyu? Oh, the little clear message sphere Osshi had.

"We're out of range of his ship now, but if we take Osshi closer to the shore, we might be able to signal them to sail around...to the bay in Nasera inlet, maybe?"

"What would we be leaving Shiara to face?" Tsua bites her lip, her large eyes narrow with worry and their attention focused on the Denhitrans and the Tsimosi. "If whatever Varan is doing has altered the storm patterns enough, it won't just endanger Itagami. Denhitra and Tsimo will have to be ready for an impossible season if this continues to worsen, and for whatever Varan will throw their way."

Altered the storm patterns? Tessen, Sanii, and I had already guessed that the Miriseh were responsible for the intense and far too early start to the rainy season, so why had none of us thought about what those storms would do to the weather cycle of Shiara? I look up even though I can't see anything but the stone ceiling of the cave. Probably we didn't think about the storms' impact on the weather because none of us had any blood-rotten idea what that effect might be. I don't, at least.

"We'll have the chance to come back and help them once we warn Ryogo." Chio says it, but he doesn't seem certain.

"We will keep them within their own territory until you return," one of the Denhitrans promises.

"Varan will do everything in his power to make sure we can never land on Shiara again once we leave," Zonna says, a heavy sadness in his eyes.

The Denhitran nods, their expression determined now. "We'll warn Denhitra and Tsimo before we leave, tell them to prepare as best they can. They've already done all they can for the rains and floods, but they won't be ready for Varan."

"He knows he has to make his move now, so he'll raid the entire island for resources and food and whatever else he can steal from them," Chio says. "He'll conscript their warriors if he can, too."

"It won't be easy for us to head southwest from here," Tyrroh says. "Itagami will have the border wards up as strong as they can make them."

"Khya's wardstones can get us through that." Tessen pulls out one of his stones, holding up the glowing crystal. "This is how we were able to get through the ward protecting the Imaku tunnel."

Tyrroh reaches to touch the stone, but Tessen moves it away. Shaking his head, Tessen wryly explains, "You don't want to touch them before they've been keyed to you. Trust me."

Pulling his hand back, Tyrroh casts an impressed glance at me before he nods. "All right. If we help you get through the wards, you'll get a message to Denhitra and Tsimo?"

Chio nods. "And we can show you where there's a passage through the northern end of the mountains. It'll save two days of the journey to Nasera."

"The sooner we leave the island the better," Tsua says.

Leaving the island. Even though they've told us it's possible, even staring at Osshi who so obviously doesn't come from here, it's hard to believe there's anything else to this world. But maybe that's enough proof to hold on to hope.

If the ocean isn't as endless as it seems, maybe the Miriseh aren't, either.

"If we can use those to pass through Itagami's border wards, I can lead a group there and be back in three days." Tyrroh looks over the squad, or the ten of them that followed him out of the city, and I know orders are coming soon.

"We can't leave before we go back to Imaku." I don't care if Tsua, Chio, and Zonna are immortal or not. Yorri is still on that island. "You said those papers might tell you how to break the cords. I need that answer, because I won't—I *can't*—leave Shiara without taking him with me."

Nearby, Sanii nods with me, nothing but grim resolution on eir face.

"Fair enough, fykina," Tsua says, nodding. "Will you, Sanii, and Tessen stay near the coast with us while Tyrroh and the others pass the message to Denhitra?"

I nod and open my mouth, but Tessen talks first.

"No. I'll go with them." Tessen's jaw is set and he doesn't even blink when Tyrroh eyes him incredulously. "With respect, Tyrroh, you should stay with Khya and Osshi. My senses are better than anyone in the clan. If I go, we'll have a much better chance of evading the patrols."

Blood and rot, he's serious? He'd be walking right back into the reach of everyone with orders to kill us! I open my mouth, ready to volunteer for that mission.

"Good. Tessen will travel with Zonna, Daitsa, and me to lead our messengers," Tyrroh says. "Khya, you'll lead the rest of the squad to the coast with Osshi."

"Wouldn't it be better if I went to help with the border wards?" My heart pounds faster. I don't look at Tessen. Maybe with this many people in such a small space, he won't notice the jump in my pulse. Then his hand brushes mine.

Tyrroh shakes his head, sympathy shining in his eyes. "The border wards are stable and there are a lot of less-closely-watched spaces we can try to sneak through. But since Neeva and Anda saw the boat that carried you away from Imaku, Varan will have his strongest farseers near the coast to search for the ship it came from and stop us. If Itagami find them, they'll need someone strong enough to deflect whatever Varan can throw their way."

And that can only be me. It makes sense. I *hate* that it makes sense.

Tension tightens all the knots in my shoulders and coils in my stomach, hard and angry and violently strong. I don't want Tessen to go. The only other person I care about vanished—was *stolen*—when I wasn't watching him. The idea of the same thing happening to Tessen now? Especially so soon after...after Imaku?

I barely repress the shiver that runs down my spine, arms, and legs. No. I don't want it to happen. I can't handle it happening. Not to both of them.

But no one asks my opinion, and I can't seem to open my mouth to protest as plans are made and strategies worked out. By the time I've found the words, it's done. They'll leave in the morning, and I won't be going with them.

CHAPTER
TWENTY-EIGHT

While Sanii, Tyrroh, Rai, Etaro, and the others are preparing dinner and portioning rations for the trips, the Denhitrans and the Tsimos are sketching maps on the floor of the cave and plotting their route. Against the opposite wall, Chio, Tsua, Zonna, and Osshi are poring over everything we stole from Imaku. They're looking at the marks like they mean something and examining the flasks. When I offered help—to either group—it was kindly but firmly brushed off. I'd done enough, they said. I needed to rest to regain my strength for whatever would come in the next few days.

But inactivity leaves too much space in my head for thoughts. Of Yorri. Of Ryogo. Of Tessen. The cave feels like it's closing in. If I don't leave, I might snap at the next person who talks to me. It'll probably be Tessen, and he doesn't deserve that. He hasn't done anything wrong.

With a quick word to Tyrroh so that no one worries about my absence, I sidle through the narrow opening and out into the cool desert night. The clouds haven't cleared completely, but they're hanging low on the horizon, leaving the sky over the mountain bright with stars. The lights of Ryogo, according to the stories. I wonder, as I walk southwest along the path, what they actually are.

I don't go far—that would be stupidly risky—but the night is so empty and quiet that it feels like I'm the only one for miles. Until Tessen appears.

"You're upset with me."

"Of course not." I can't make myself meet his eyes when I say it, which is stupid. I don't want to care this much. I don't want to care at all. Somehow, though, Tessen has dug his way into my life, into my mind, and onto the incredibly short list of people for whom I'd betray everything I once held dear.

Tessen exhales heavily and slides his fingers through mine. His hand is warm and calloused, the skin rough from weapons drills and climbing through the Kyiwa Mountains. Every mark on his skin is a sign of exactly how competent he is, and that competence is as much a comfort as the touch itself and the soothing, familiar vibration of his desosa against my mind.

He pulls, leading me farther away from the cave.

"Tessen, you're being ridiculous. I'm not upset with you." I *shouldn't* be upset with him. I shouldn't and therefore I refuse to admit I am. It doesn't matter how much time we've spent at each other's sides the past six weeks—we're nothing to each other. Or…not nothing, precisely, but we're not anything that can lay claim. We're nothing that gives me the power or the privilege of asking him to stay.

He turns us around and for a second it seems as though he's going to press me back against the mountain. He doesn't. Instead, he backs himself up until he's the one leaning against the wall, and I'm standing over his legs, almost caging him in. One of his arms circles my waist until his hand presses flat against my lower back.

It would be so easy to keep him here, for me to trap him between my weight and the wall until I'm ready to release him. Something about knowing that, about seeing and feeling him here—*safe*—makes it easier to breathe. And somehow he knows I need this.

I rest my forehead against his temple, place one hand over the pulse point on his throat, and tighten my grip on his other hand.

For a long time—several minutes at least, but maybe closer to half an hour—we don't move. Before now, before this place and this moment, I hadn't ever let myself sink into stillness like this. Not with Tessen, certainly, but not with anyone else, either.

My time with Yorri was about teaching him to protect himself or teaching him to read the other doseiku so that he knew when to stand up and fight and when to back away. My sexual encounters have all been about release and relief, scratching an itch that no amount of sparring could reach. My time alone was usually spent training, learning, or sleeping, perfecting everything about myself to one day earn the respect and the fear my blood-parents had attained.

I've never allowed myself to have this. I've never let myself trust anyone enough to dare let my guard down enough to have this. No one else has pushed past my walls persistently enough to *earn* this.

Now he's leaving, and he might not come back. No matter how careful he is, he's not like Tsua and Varan. He's not a Miriseh. A Bobasu. An Andofume. Whatever the word in whatever language it's described, he's not immortal.

I lift my head to look at him, letting my eyes trail along the slope of his jaw and the curve of his full bottom lip. In the moonlight of this unexpectedly half-clear night, his skin loses several shades of color, shifting away from its usual red-brown and closer to the color of the sandstone around us. I study each of his features individually—thick, straight eyebrows; oval face; low cheekbones that soften his cheeks—but I avoid looking him in the eye.

He's been chasing me for moons, and I think I'm ready to be caught, but what if the hunt was what he was after? I don't think he'll just walk away—not after everything he's given up already—but the fear that I won't see what I'm hoping for in his eyes keeps my gaze elsewhere for a long time. Too long.

Our breaths have been in sync since he settled against the wall, something I don't even notice until his pattern changes. One deeper breath. As though he's about to speak.

I don't let him.

Shifting my hand on his throat to the back of his head, I tilt his head toward mine and kiss him, moving quickly from a light brush of our lips to bringing his plush bottom lip between my teeth and lightly biting as I draw my nails across his scalp.

His breath stutters. He exhales a single sharp gust, one hand gripping my tunic to pull me closer while his other releases its hold on my fingers to cup my cheek.

Warm, gentle, calloused fingers trace the lines of my face, their motions smooth and soft and a sharp contrast to my weight pressing him into the rock and the nips of my teeth against his lips, his jaw, his neck.

I grip him so tight that my fingers will likely leave impressions behind.

The thought only makes me hold him harder.

I want him to carry the memory away on his skin, the reminder of everything left unfinished and a promise of more as long as he comes back to me to claim it.

His finger trails fiery lines down the side of my neck, but it's the fear that he won't come back that makes my pulse race faster. Realizing that I don't have the right to ask him not to go—and that I'm not sure I could make myself ask even if I did—sends knife-sharp prickles down my spine.

I break away, pressing my palms into the wall on either side of his head and, for a second, letting myself sink into his gray eyes. They're glazed, the pupils blown wide, but he's focused on me so completely that I almost believe he wouldn't notice if someone else approached, even with his basaku senses.

"Two days, Tessen. If you don't meet us at the inlet in two days, I will never forgive you." I can't quite smile, but I do trail my hand across his cheek, putting all the gentleness the kiss didn't contain into the touch.

I walk away before he can speak, and keep a distance the rest of the night. I can almost trick myself into thinking the separation was my idea if I'm the one doing the leaving.

It doesn't happen until the next morning, just as the earliest rays of dawn shift the sky from the impenetrable darkness of night to the murky gray-gold light of morning, but as our group splits in opposite directions, I can't completely tamp down the fear that this is the last time I'll see him.

If the Miriseh have bolstered Itagami's border wards or reinforced the patrols, they could be falling into an inescapable trap. For all his skill and cunning, Tessen is only a single warrior. He can't defeat an army.

But it needs to be done. Because Tsua is working on a way to save Yorri, and with the eventual help of Ryogo, we might have a chance of stopping Varan. Because Tessen knows we need this chance to exist, this hope to grow, if we are going to keep moving forward.

Still, as he and Zonna disappear into the mountains with the others, all I can think is, *Come back alive, you madman. I'm not done with you yet.*

CHAPTER
TWENTY-NINE

he night is dark and gray, not enough starlight to even separate the ocean's horizon from the sky. Somewhere out there is a ship that will take me to Imaku, and then on to a land I thought I'd see only when I died. After a full day of traveling, Tessen should be past the border wards. A day of running west along the coast, our path almost parallel to the one Tessen would have taken, and now I'm sitting with Tsua, Osshi, Sanii, Etaro, Rai, and three others from our squad.

Osshi got a message to his ship, telling them to meet us forty miles west in the Nasera inlet, and now we're supposed to be resting before we continue toward the rendezvous point.

But I doubt that will happen for a while. My mind is racing even if my body is exhausted, and with everything that's happened in the past two days, I can't imagine I'm the only one who won't find it easy to sleep.

We're hiding in a cave fifty feet above the ocean. It's dug into the cliff and the waves batter the rocks so hard the spray reaches us even here. Dangerous in that way, but safer in a lot of others. No one can see the mouth of this cave from Shiara, and the noise of the ocean will hide our presence from everyone except Tessen, and I'm not even sure he'd be able to hear us.

Across the fire, Tsua is going over more of the Imaku papers and Osshi is sitting with one of the flasks we stole, running his thumb over the etchings in the metal. With the overload of history and information I've gotten from Tsua and Chio, I never did ask Osshi what *his* story was.

"What brought you here, Osshi?" I ask. He looks up, and so do most of the others. "Why were you alone so close to Imaku?"

"Imaku is the black rock island, yes? The Kaijuko?" When I nod, Osshi continues. "That is why I be coming here, to be looking for the Imaku and the Bobasu. In Ryogo, this story is being long ago, so long that it is a tale few be believing as truth, yes? But I is making a study of such things, and permission I be earning to be looking for Kaijuko—for Imaku. Looking for something to be proving that the Bobasu are being real. And that, if they are being real, the Kaijuko is being still their prison."

He looks at Tsua and Chio and shakes his head. "I am finding half of that to be true—the Bobasu are being very real. For the rest, I will be bringing warnings of the danger that the Bobasu be threatening soon, and I must be hoping that the Jindaini and the council of territories will be listening to me."

Might they *not* listen? I don't understand how they could possibly deny it when we're bringing three of their fabled Bobasu to Ryogo with us.

Osshi settles back against the wall when I don't ask him anything else, staring at the flask. Near him, Tsua has put away the papers and instead is sharpening her dagger. Several of the squad have moved off to the back of the cave where the sleep mats have been unrolled. Sanii, Rai, and Etaro are the only ones still sitting near me at the fire. Rai and Etaro look exhausted, but Etaro is playing with pebbles again, making them move in complex patterns.

"I'll take first watch if you want to get some rest," I tell Rai and Etaro.

"Why didn't you tell us?" The question bursts out of Rai. Etaro freezes and the small stones drop to eir palm.

How many times is she going to make me have this conversation before she believes it?

Looking at the hurt, the resentment, the *anger* in Rai's eyes, I wish I could tell her that I debated for hours over whether or not to tell them, that I almost did it more times than I could count...but I can't.

"If I had come to you then, pulled you aside out in the desert maybe, and told you I was sure Yorri was still alive, would you have believed me?"

"Yes."

"No, you wouldn't have." Etaro says it before I can, a surprising amount of resolution in eir voice and eir eyes. Ey meets Rai stare for stare when she turns her wrath on em. "You said it once after Khya seemed to snap out of that black mood—maybe a week after Yorri died. You said, 'I think losing her brother may have cracked her mind.'"

Both of my eyebrows rise as Etaro speaks. When ey's done, I slowly switch my focus to Rai. "It's understandable, but that's why I couldn't take the risk. We made this choice knowing we'd have to beg protection from one of the other clans or spend our lives trying to survive in the desert. Why would I ask you to leave Itagami for that? Why would I have asked you to give up *eternity* for it?"

Though we know now it's not what would happen, that's not what I believed a moon ago.

"I would have asked you." Etaro's voice is tense and honest. "If it had been me in your place, I would've trusted you not to turn me over to the councils even if you didn't want to help."

"And you couldn't even give us the choice, Khya." Rai gets up and stalks to the other side of the cave, sparks running across her palms and up her arms, and Etaro follows. Sanii doesn't say anything, but ey places a hand on my shoulder and squeezes gently.

"Give them some time, Khya." The look Tsua gives me is full of empathy. "You were able to adapt in pieces, but their whole world has changed in just a couple days."

"I don't…" I clench my teeth to keep in a sigh. "I'll try, but waiting hasn't ever been something I'm good at." Or forgiveness, though I've gotten a lot of practice in both recently. "Do you know how we can break the cords yet?"

Sanii leans closer at that.

"Potentially," Chio says. "There was enough in the notes to hint at what the spoken key might be, partially because I know how my brother thinks. Thank the Kaisubeh that Varan and Suzu used the same knowledge base we're familiar with to create the spell."

"But without seeing it for ourselves, all we can do is give you our best guess," Tsua admits. "We think it will work. There isn't any way we can promise that, though."

"No one can." It would be dangerous to believe it even if they did.

So they teach me new words—*ureeku-sy rii'ifu*—and spend an hour explaining how to feel for a particular shift in the desosa, the lock for my spoken key. All the while, they remind me that this is a guess. They can't be sure. But

I know that, and I know that even if they're wrong, it won't kill Yorri. I can't say the same is true for me, but that's a risk I'll take.

But despite caution and tempered hope, I test the words a thousand times on my tongue and repeat them a thousand times more in my head. I put everything I can into making sure it *does* work, because I can't keep myself from hoping that they're right.

Because if they're right, I might actually be able to save Yorri this time.

CHAPTER THIRTY

We leave the cliff cave well before dawn and travel hard all day. Everyone is carrying one of the wardstones I made—the rest went with Tessen—and the squad's oraku guides us around the Itagamin patrols. A single stone, even one keyed to them, isn't enough to protect them from everything, but wearing it at the center of their chest might help deflect the worst injuries if we come across an Itagamin patrol.

We make good time, and we're as safe and hidden as we can be. An hour before sunset, we're only a few miles away from Nasera inlet.

But now, less than a mile to the southeast, several squads—almost an entire company—are approaching fast.

Itagami has found us.

I don't need to tell them what I saw. From the way everyone is watching me descend, they already know what I've seen.

"Are you with me?" I ask them.

Sanii blinks once, but then the determination I was so

used to seeing on eir face comes back. It glows like fire in eir eyes and across every line of eir body, strength now radiating from a face that has only seemed lost for the last several days.

Rai, Etaro, and my squad nod, looking resigned.

I'm not happy about the prospect of fighting against people I've known my entire life either, but we don't have much choice here. Escape is my first choice, but if they catch up with us, they mean to capture or kill us. If we aren't willing to fight back—to kill if necessary—we may as well lay down our weapons now and surrender.

They array themselves behind me, a silent proclamation of trust. The relief almost makes me smile.

We run for an hour. Sweat drips into my eyes and the packs I'm carrying weigh down every step. It doesn't matter. If we're not close to the inlet before the fighting starts, we won't make it there before Varan's forces. We probably won't make it there alive.

Tsua shouts orders back to us, her voice carrying on the wind. "The tunnel that will take us down to the shore in Nasera isn't far."

Then an eerily familiar shiver runs through the desosa. I could be wrong, and I hope I am wrong, but when I look northwest, there's the proof that I'm not. Purple-gray clouds are rolling in fast, ripped apart by lightning. Thunder shakes the mountain. The ground trembles; cracks appear under my feet. Sanii slaps eir hand against the wall to stay on eir feet.

"I don't like the sound of that," Etaro mutters.

"We need to get through the tunnel before it gets worse." Not even my most powerful wards can withstand the weight of an entire mountain.

The clouds rolling in are charcoal-dark, blocking out

almost all of the light. It's far enough away that we should be able to stay in front of it. A good thing, because this looks like the worst storm we've seen this year.

Rai looks up as lightning streaks across the sky. Thunder booms, a deep rumble that shakes the rocks.

"That was louder," Etaro says.

The storm is getting closer. And so is everyone chasing us.

Tsua ducks into a shadow and seems to disappear. Only when I get closer do I see the depth of the darkness.

"There's no signal." Tsua is running her hand along the wall, searching for something. "Zonna isn't here yet. He would've left a marker for us."

"Then we need to make sure Varan doesn't reach the inlet before us," Chio says.

"We can't just stand here and wait," Rai says, eyeing the southeastern sky. "They'll be on us in minutes."

Chio opens his mouth, but pauses. Head cocked, he listens for a second, and then he smiles. "We won't have to wait for long."

Tessen, Zonna, Tyrroh, and Daitsa come sprinting over the rise, weapons drawn and fear shining in their eyes. The anxiety that had been sitting, mostly ignored, in the pit of my stomach disappears at the sight of him. He made it.

"Run!" Tessen screams as soon as he's close enough to be heard. "They're coming!"

None of us hesitate. Rai takes the front with Chio, her hands burning bright to light our way. The squad's other kasaiji runs in the middle, making sure the rest of the group can see where we're going.

The tunnel continues for at least a mile and then releases us a hundred feet or so up a steep embankment. Tsua and Chio lead us down, sure-footed and quick despite the howling wind and the blinding rain. I slide on the dangerously muddy rocks, and the wind almost blows me off balance more than once, but I keep my feet. Tessen and I watch out for the others, catching Rai when she almost falls on a particularly steep section.

Near the shoreline the ground levels, and Tessen moves to walk beside me, his hand on my arm. His grip tightens. "Bellows and blood."

On my other side, Etaro stops short. "What is *that*?"

Swaying with the force of waves strong enough to crest and crash is a massive…ship?

It's very much like they described it—a building somehow floating on the water. It's mostly brown with black stripes along the side and designs of red painted on one end. Four tall poles jut into the sky from the top level holding massive red… It's cloth, I think, but I don't understand why they'd waste it by hanging it in the sky like that.

Getting closer doesn't make the ship any more comprehensible, but it's the chance of safety, for now, and a goal we have a chance of reaching. As long as we have a way to get to it.

Osshi *must* have a plan. He can't expect us to swim.

Fifty feet from the water, I see them.

There are four boats, and they look like the one that carried us away from Imaku, only bigger. Two people wait in each. They stand when they see us coming.

Osshi runs to the front of the group, beckoning us to follow. "Come! Be getting in quick. We must be away from this place."

Tessen and I leap into the first boat with Sanii, Etaro, and Rai. Once we're in, Osshi and his companion push poles into our hands that remind me of patsu sticks without the blades. Through exaggerated examples and shouted words I don't understand, they teach us what to do.

The citizens of Itagami are well-trained to follow orders. We fall into a synchronized pattern easily, using the flat ends of the poles to guide our small boat through the choppy, cresting waves. We're all facing the shore instead of the direction we're moving, but Osshi is perched at the edge of the boat to shout directions, his hands gripping the low sides of the boat to keep him from toppling over into the storm-tossed waves.

Sooner than I expect, we thump against something solid. I look up. There's a rope hanging off the side of the ship, the end only a few feet above our heads.

I look to Osshi and shout, "Should we go up?"

"Yes, but the—"

"Go!" I order Sanii and the others. "Get up there and help the others."

Rai grips the rope hanging over the side of the ship and begins to climb, Etaro close behind her. Both of them rise quickly despite the unpredictable motion of the ship.

"Kaisubeh bless it. The crew were going to be dropping a ladder," Osshi says, staring up at Sanii disappearing over the side of his ship with awe in his wide eyes. Then several more ropes drop over the side, and Osshi blinks. "Take this and tie it in a knot on the front ring. Do as he does."

He sends me off with a sharp gesture to the opposite end of the boat before grabbing Tessen's shoulder and shoving a rope into his hands.

Osshi's companion does the same with me, saying, "*Suku za yona-ike onyo!*"

I don't understand the words, but his meaning is clear enough when he points to a metal ring bolted to the edge of the boat and demonstrates a knot in a series of efficient motions. It's one I know well.

Nodding, I move to the ring, my tired fingers slipping only once as I lock the rope through the ring.

"Up!" Osshi orders, pointing to a ladder of rope and panels of something wood-like. I shake my head and move to the rope the others used. It'll be quicker. There can't be much time left before the Miriseh reach the shore.

When Tessen and I land on the top level of the ship, I move to help Osshi's companions pull the rest of the people and boats out of the water.

"*Nen!*" one of the strangers shouts, nudging me back to the center of the deck. "*Doido!*"

Another shakes his head when I approach again, his hands held out as though to tell me to stay where I am. "*Ware temasu ina ware ri keya, monoka.*"

The message is clear: we don't need your help.

It seems like he's right. The men work smoothly, each well-practiced at their tasks. When Osshi climbs over the railing, I expect him to take charge. Instead, he stands next to a man with hair the color of iron who's been shouting orders. I'd thought this was Osshi's ship, but that man seems to be in command. The others jump into motion every time he barks out a new order.

As they climb over the railing of the ship, the rest of my squad joins me in the center of the wide platform to stay out of the way. Someone presses close behind me, one of their hands resting on my hip. Tessen.

"Is this real?" he asks me.

Next to us, Chio smiles and gestures to the ship. "It's hard to believe even when you see it, isn't it?"

"It's more impossible than any dream I've ever had." It feels as impossible as a dream, too.

"I think it'll only get stranger when this beast starts moving," Chio says as he walks toward Osshi and the iron-haired commander.

I lean back against Tessen's chest and place my hand over his on my hip. Exhaustion is settling into my bones, an almost-solid weight pressing me into the surface of the ship. Leaning on Tessen is nearly the only thing keeping me standing, and I think he knows that; he shifts to make sure I'm braced against the center of his chest.

"I'm glad you're okay. If you'd gotten yourself killed playing hero while I was gone, I don't think I'd ever have forgiven you, Khya." Tessen's lips brush against my neck under my ear.

"Ryogo is a lie, remember?" I utterly fail to keep the bitterness of that particular betrayal out of my voice. "I wouldn't have ever known you were angry."

"You would've known." Another brush of his lips against my rain-slick skin. "I'd find you and make sure you knew."

The boats that carried us from the shore are secured and out of the way, two hanging off the side of the ship and two strapped down to the top level, so the frenetic movements of Osshi's companions shift.

On a raised platform at the front of the ship, several people grip thick pole-like extensions from a central circle and push it, visibly straining with the effort. The circular support column underneath the extensions is attached to a thick chain, one that slowly wraps around the column as they push. Others gather around the four poles stretching toward the sky, yanking on ropes to change the position of the massive, oddly shaped red panels of cloth.

What possible use could these things have? The poles we used to push the boats through the water made sense, but this… I don't understand this at all.

Tessen tenses, his hand gripping hard. "They're almost here."

I see nothing, but I trust Tessen's senses. Rising to my toes, I try to spot Osshi in the chaos. "Osshi!" I bellow when I find him, trying to be heard over the wind and the shouts of the men working. "Faster!"

He nods, passing the message to the iron-haired man. Another set of incomprehensible orders travels over the ship.

The wind gusts, making the reinforced red panels snap. We begin to move. In less than a minute, we're a hundred feet farther from the shore. By the time Neeva and her squad are at the shore, we're beyond their reach.

I expected to face the unknown if we managed to rescue Yorri, but this...this is beyond anything I could have known to imagine. But Yorri *had* dreamed of this, hadn't he?

"Do you ever wonder if there's something else?" he'd asked before his trial. It was so obviously something he'd thought about. Possibly something he and Sanii had talked about, though I don't dare ask em yet. Not until we sail to Imaku and get him back.

I'd never wondered, not once. Now I'm standing on a ship and heading toward a second chance to save Yorri.

Possibly my last chance.

CHAPTER
THIRTY-ONE

Osshi introduces me to Taikan-yi Kazu, the iron-haired commander, as soon as the ship is safely out to sea. The first thing Osshi translates from Kazu is a warning: "We don't have enough food and water for so many people. Not enough to last until Ryogo."

It takes a lot of planning, and an argument about whether risking capture or starvation was the stupider move, but eventually it's decided. Sanii and Tyrroh will lead a small group into Itagami, using an entrance Tyrroh found and yonin passages in the undercity, and carry out food and water. Not a lot, but enough, hopefully, to see us back to Ryogo without dying.

We're lowering one of the boats into a cove as close as we can get to the city. Before climbing down to the water, Sanii stops in front of me, eir gaze serious and focused. "Promise me you'll do everything you possibly can to get him off that island."

"You know I will." If this doesn't work, there's no telling what will happen to him. Tsua's assurances that Yorri cannot die did shockingly little to assuage my fears once I had the chance to think about what that meant.

There's so much pain a determined mind and a relentless hand could inflict on someone denied the escape of death.

Once Sanii and Tyrroh's group is safely away, Kazu's men turn the ship toward Imaku.

Tessen and I watch the black rock from a distance, trying to figure out what dangers are waiting there. What dangers I'm leading Rai, Etaro, and the others into. They're only daring this because I asked for their help.

If anything goes wrong—and so much could—it'll be my fault. If anyone gets hurt, it'll be because I put them in the way of harm.

The plan is for the ship to wait well out of range of any of Itagami's rikinhisu mages, but for four boats to carry eight people to Imaku. Eight people who aren't under Taikan-yi Kazu's command. Neither Kazu nor Osshi had liked that part much.

"Are you being sure you are not wanting someone who knows the boats to be going with you?" Osshi asks when we approach.

"We can't afford to lose the space," I say. "And I refuse to endanger their lives, especially when all of them look at our swords like they've never seen them before."

Osshi grimaces and translates what I said for Kazu, whose scowl grows deeper before he nods with what looks like grudging acceptance. I don't dare hope that we can save all thirty-nine people. Maybe, though, we'll fill the seats on all four boats.

"Yes, well, it will be going well if we are moving along soon." Osshi looks up at the sky. The storm from yesterday has dissipated, but there's no guarantee that another won't appear in its place, especially not when the Miriseh can seemingly call them up at will.

Tsua and Chio said that's impossible, but even they can't offer any other explanation for the storms.

"Here." I pass Tessen his wardstones and watch him tie all six in place. The others only have three each. It's not enough to protect them from everything, but it might be enough to save their lives if the situation is worse than we expect.

Tsua's eyes are narrowed with concern, lines deepening at the corners and between her eyebrows. "I know how desperate you are to save Yorri, but you must be smart about this, Khya. You can't know for sure what you're walking into here." She doesn't give me a chance to respond. Instead, she looks at Tessen, spearing him with her intense gaze. "Do *not* let her sacrifice herself for this. Get her out of there if you need to."

I want to protest that I don't need her or Tessen to make my decisions for me, but the fear in Tsua's eyes is genuine, full of losses older than Itagami. I've become familiar with death, but I can't imagine how many lives Tsua has watched end. I can't blame her for not wanting to add more to the list.

So I don't say anything. I vault over the side of the ship and climb down the rope to the smaller boat below, bobbing on the cresting waves. Tessen follows me into the boat, and as soon as he's settled on one of the benches with the flat-ended pole in his hands, I untie the rope tethering us to the ship and push off, sending us into the ocean.

Imaku is a lump of shadow growing out of the water from this distance. Fighting the current to reach it won't be easy, but we have a better chance of sneaking in undetected this way. The current is in our favor now, each wave aiming us toward the shore. Difficulty comes in keeping the boat aimed for the *right* shore.

The tight grip I have on the pole rubs the skin on my calloused hands raw, and every muscle in my arms is straining before we're halfway to the black rock. The three other boats are spread in an uneven line between us and the ship. Nearly everyone left behind is standing at the railing, watching us and the island.

"Anything?" The word comes out as a huff of air, but Tessen understands.

His head tilts like a teegra trying to catch a scent on the wind. "There's definitely someone moving on the island. Two—maybe three."

"Can you tell who?"

He glances at me without moving his head, the curve of his lips more than a little grim. "It's nice that you think so much of my senses, but even I have limits." Switching his attention back to Imaku, his eyes narrow. "There's something odd, but I can't tell what."

I try to nod or do something to acknowledge I heard him, but I think if I move at all, the panic and fear bubbling under the surface is going to overwhelm me.

"Just promise me you'll be careful when we land," Tessen says.

The sharp slap of a wave against the side of the boat unbalances us before I have a chance to answer—a good thing, because I don't know what to say to that.

Promising to be careful feels too much like promising to abandon the mission at the first sign of trouble, and that's not a promise I can make.

"I feel like I'm being watched," I tell him once we're back in control of the boat.

He nods, attention still on the black island. That is not reassuring.

The sensation grows stronger the closer I get to the

island. Paranoia or truth? In the end, it doesn't matter. I push past the feeling, concentrating on guiding the boat toward Imaku.

I count time in strokes; there are more than two hundred between the ship and the moment Tessen leaps to the rocky edge of Imaku. The only openings we saw before were on the east and west ends of the island, so we landed on the north side where there's nothing but a solid wall of rock.

Within a few minutes, we've landed and tethered the boats. Two people stay to guard our escape, and Tessen and I lead the four others to the western end of the island.

The edges of Imaku have been worn mostly smooth by the force of the waves. My foot slips. My body slams against the rocks, the impact hard enough to force the air out of my lungs, but I tighten my grip on the tenuous handholds I found. Fingernails digging into the unforgiving rock, I keep myself in place by luck and willpower alone. A moment to reorient, to make sure of my footing this time, and then I continue to climb.

My hand lands on something slimy. My grip slips. My foot slides. I start to fall—

My foot hits something solid and warm, the impact jarring my leg and shaking whatever I landed on. I look.

Not whatever. Tessen.

He must have moved sideways fast to get his shoulder underneath me; somehow now I'm half braced on him. The muscles in his arms are straining to hold our weight. Gritting my teeth, I reach for a different handhold, hauling myself back to where I was.

Ten feet. Five feet.

Between the work of guiding the boat and the effort of climbing this slick, treacherous slope, my arms are trembling by the time I lift myself onto the ledge. I lie on my stomach and reach for Tessen to help him finish the climb.

"Check ahead," I sign as soon as he's safe.

Nodding, Tessen moves to the edge of the short passage between the chamber and the exterior of the island. Once Rai is there to help the others up, I move to Tessen's side.

"Something feels wrong, Khya." His voice is so low I have a hard time hearing him over the waves, but the worry on his face is more than clear. "I think there are two inside, but something is definitely different."

"We knew they'd change something." It'd be careless of them to leave everything exactly as it was. And it'd be just as stupid for us to rush in there. I tighten my grip on his arm, a physical fetter to keep me here. "Is there a ward?" I can't feel one, but we need to be sure.

"No." He places his hand on the rock, his palm pressed flat against the surface.

"I don't like that." A ward would've been the easiest way to secure this point.

"Would they bother if they know we can break through?"

"Yes. It'd slow us down and drain me."

"So, what? Do we retreat?" His expression pinches and his shoulders are tense.

I can't do that—I *won't* do that—and Tessen probably knows it.

Shaking my head, I draw the tudo strapped to my back. "Everyone just needs to know that we're likely walking into a trap."

I look behind me. Rai, Etaro, and the others are standing at attention. In a series of quick signs, I warn them to be braced for anything. Then I strengthen the wardstones they're wearing, and with Tessen off my left shoulder, I lead them into Imaku.

The dimness of the passage after the blindingly bright sunlight blacks out my vision for a moment. When it clears, what I see is worse than any blow I've ever felt.

The room is empty.

All forty-five black platforms are gone, leaving nothing but a wall of bare shelves and a massive empty chamber behind.

CHAPTER
THIRTY-TWO

ire explodes through the arch connecting Imaku
and the tunnel to Shiara.

I push my own ward out, creating an invisible
wall for the flames to crash against.

People rush through the fire, blades and eyes glinting
red in the light.

In the front of the pack are my blood-parents.

"What did you do with him?" I scream, strengthening
my wards and raising my weapon.

They charge forward, weapons drawn. Anda shoots
loose shards of rock at us like daggers, the island providing
her with a never-ending supply. Ono raises his zeeka, his
blow aimed for my head.

The kaigo and the nyshin aren't like the Miriseh. They
can bleed. They can die.

Tessen leaps in, blocking Anda's flying weapons, his
sword a blur in front of him.

I leave a long slice of red on Ono's thigh and step over
his body when he drops to the ground. Anda ducks under

my blade, grabbing Ono's arm and dragging him back a foot, behind the cover of the wards of a fykina. The *nyshin* fykina who trained me years ago.

This isn't just the kaigo. The nyshin-lu are here, too.

Gritting my teeth and bolstering my squad's wardstones, I fight forward inch by inch, moving ever closer to the arch. Rai lights someone's tunic on fire when they get too close to me. Daitsa punches a nyshin so hard they crack their head against the wall several feet back. If they keep anyone from sneaking up behind me, we can clear the way through the tunnel. We can search the city. We might be able to find him.

Tessen's hand closes around my arm, yanking me sideways. I stumble.

A white-hot bolt of lightning flashes inches from my head.

"We have to go! Now!" Tessen shouts.

Fire roars in a solid column on the other side of the chamber.

Iron clashes and stone cracks.

His hand still tight around my arm, Tessen tries to pull me back, away from the tunnel. Away from Yorri.

"No! I have to find him!" Breaking his grip, I bring my sword up. I'll fight my way past him if I have to. "Come with me or let me go."

"I will not let you die!" he bellows, his face dark with rage.

I try to lunge past him. He ducks my sword and locks my arms to my side, trapping me against him with my back pressed to his chest. Etaro and the others form a wall between us and the battle, their wardstones keeping them safe for now.

"Who'll save him when you're dead, Khya? Stop trying to kill yourself to save someone who *cannot die!*"

I gasp. Each word strikes my chest like a blow, one no ward can protect me from. I stop fighting, letting my weight fall back against him. Some part of my mind sees the hopelessness, but I can't... I have to...

"He needs me, Tessen. He needs me and I failed him." Again.

"He needs you *alive*." Tessen's voice is hoarse, and his grip around my waist tightens. He drags me toward the western ledge. "Throwing your life away won't help Yorri. He needs you alive. *I* need you alive."

Etaro swings eir zeeka up fast enough to leave a deep line of red on Anda's cheek, but then ey staggers, chest heaving. The wardstones around Rai's wrists flash, their energy deflecting a blow that might have severed her hand from her wrist, but the light is dimmer than it should be. Daitsa's are losing their glow, too. I've demanded too much of these stones. Everyone is tired and my protections are on the verge of failing.

They're going to die here if they don't leave now.

Slamming my elbow into Tessen's ribs, I break out of his hold. I move closer to the line Rai and the others have created and held. Gathering as much of the chaotically swirling desosa as I can, I funnel it into a ward as strong and solid as the rock walls around us.

"Go. I'll watch the retreat." They hesitate. I grit my teeth and shove my ward wall back, pushing Anda and the others toward the tunnel. "Go!"

Tessen's hand settles on my shoulder. Only *then* does anyone else retreat. Rai's arm is around Etaro's waist, helping em limp away. Daitsa and the other nyshin-ten look meaningfully at Tessen as they flee.

I almost laugh. They don't trust me to leave. I can't blame them.

I feel too much. I feel nothing. I pour all of it, the nothing and the overload, into my ward, shoving the wall and everyone behind it back.

Step by step, foot by foot, I claim Imaku.

The kaigo and the nyshin-lu shout and slam against the wall none of them can see. Nothing makes me lose more than a single step of ground. I force every single one of them into the tunnel. Each strike of a blade against my ward reverberates through my body. Fire thrown against the invisible shield brings heat to my skin, just on the safe side of burning.

They don't break through, though. Not one.

"Give—your wardstones." The words are mangled, spoken through gritted teeth, but Tessen reaches for the leather knots holding his wardstones in place. He offers them to me. I shake my head. "The floor—line them up. The edge of the passage. The arch above."

His eyes light up, and he grins as he follows my orders.

This would be so much better if I had an ishiji to sink the crystals into the black rock. I'll have to make this work without the anchor. It won't hold as long this way, especially if the stones Tessen shoves into divots above our heads don't stay put, but it should be enough to give us a chance to escape.

Once they're secured, I use them to fix my ward in place to cover the archway. It's like nailing a sheet of iron over the opening, closing it to anyone but me. For a while, at least.

I grab Tessen's hand and run. "It won't hold long."

"It's enough." His hand tightens on mine. He's still smiling. "We can get away."

We can get away.

Pain as sharp and stinging as kamidi venom rises from

the pit of my stomach, eating away at my insides and numbing my limbs.

We're getting away, but without Yorri—without anyone we came for. Tessen was right, though. To fight the kaigo back all the way to Itagami would be impossible for six people. It's impossible for sixteen.

Attempting it would be suicide, but running away from it feels worse.

I try to find the calm, disconnected, walled-off center I created the last time I left Imaku with only failure in my hands. It's there, but no matter how quickly I shove everything inside, it keeps leaking out. Instead, I focus on each step I take, making sure I stay on course.

Don't slip, don't fall, don't think.

In the boat, Tessen unties us while I grab the poles. Rai's shouted instructions guide us toward Osshi's ship, still off in the distance, out of range of Varan's mages. We're not out of range yet. We will be soon. Tsua will pull us in as soon as she can reach us.

Until then, I'll have to row while staring at Imaku.

No matter the cost, I'll come back. I will return for Yorri.

And may rot take anyone who tries to stop me.

CHAPTER
THIRTY-THREE

The only sound is the water slapping the sides of the boat and our harsh breathing. If we can reach Osshi's boat and I can get away from everyone else fast enough, I might not break.

"Khya, we couldn't—"

"We couldn't do anything?" My eyes snap open and I pin Tessen with a glare. "Or, no— It wasn't our fault? Was that what you were going to say?" I tighten my grip on the pole and force myself to look away from the frustrated hurt in his eyes. "Don't, Tessen. Whatever you think might make me feel better, just don't." My voice cracks and my eyes burn. I close them and pretend I don't feel it. I pretend I don't feel anything. "Please, don't."

He takes a breath, a long one like he's about to speak.

We lurch forward.

He cries out. My eyes fly open, and I grab for anything solid. His hand lands on my leg, like he could possibly hold me in the boat if a rikinhisu is trying to knock us out of it.

We're flying back toward Shiara faster than we could

ever row ourselves. There's a strip of land that juts into the sea just west of Itagami, and that's where the boats are aiming.

I swallow everything else down, concentrating on my thudding pulse and the danger looming ever closer. It's too far away for me to see who is waiting for us on the shore, but Tessen can. "What are we facing?"

His eyes widen and he breathes out a soft, "Oh, no," before he closes his eyes. "Varan and Suzu are there. And they're not alone."

Of course they're not. Anda was on Imaku, so the two Miriseh rikinhisu mages have to be the ones yanking us to shore. If Varan is trying to get to Ryogo, capturing these boats and then the ship would be the fastest way to make it happen.

And he doesn't need us alive to do that.

"I'm sorry, Tessen."

Tessen shakes his head, not a hint of defeat in his iron eyes. "Get your wards up, Khya. This isn't over yet."

But it is, I almost say. They moved Yorri and the others. We'll be back on Shiara in seconds. My wards will protect us for a while, but I can't hold out forever.

We tried, we fought, and we lost.

"*Wards*, Khya! Now!"

I grit my teeth and bring up my wards. Everyone but Tessen is wearing wardstones I made, so I reach out. Using those points as anchors, I extend my ward farther than I've ever tried to before. Maybe I can keep us from reaching the Miriseh for a while longer yet.

"Hold on!" I scream, praying they can hear me.

Our boat stops short. Like it's hit a wall. The flat front of the boat cracks. If I hadn't been holding on, I would've lurched over the side.

My ward extends a few feet into the water, well over our heads, and a dozen feet to either side of us. It's impermeable to magic and solid enough that it caught on the outcroppings of rock rising from the ocean, barring passage between them.

"Blood and rot, it worked." I exhale, tightening my grip on the boat.

My ward is so long it feels stretched thin. It feels like *I'm* stretched thin.

Rikinhisus batter the ward with stones from the shore. The ratoiji hit it with bolts of lightning that create burning spots of bright light across my vision.

This won't hold for nearly as long as we need it to. And that's only if I don't do anything but fuel the ward.

"What now?" Tessen had better have a second part to this plan.

"Just hold on," he whispers in my ear, so quiet I almost don't hear him over the waves. "The ship is moving closer. Just hold on until Tsua is in range, Khya."

I grip the boat tighter. Splinters of wood dig into my skin.

Tsua had better hurry.

"Impressive, Khya!" Varan calls from the shore. "You would have made an excellent nyshin-lu if you hadn't betrayed us."

Betrayal? I clench my hands around the edge of the boat so hard my nails break. How dare he accuse *me* of betrayal?

Then my heart stutters. I blink, trying to clear my vision. I can't be seeing this. Exhaustion and strain must be making me hallucinate, or Neeva is here messing with my mind.

"That isn't possible." There's disbelieving fear threaded

through Tessen's voice.

If Tessen sees it, too…

Varan is walking into the ocean. No, Varan is walking *on top of* the ocean.

The normally roiling, ceaseless waves are flattening themselves out before him, creating a path as smooth as the stone tunnels of Itagami. And apparently as solid.

His steps are as sure as when he's walking through the center of Itagami, but the ocean wind whips his tunic tight against his body, the bottom edges flying out behind him. The smile curving his lips is assured, as though he's condescending to play the game my way only because he chooses to. Not because I'm making him.

"An illusion. Neeva." I gasp, flinching when the ratoiji's lightning strikes a weaker point of the ward.

"Neeva was at Nasera. She can't be back yet," Tessen says. "This is real."

Rot take them all. "Is that Izujo behind him?"

"This is what Suzu and Neeva were talking about," Tessen says. "This is what they've been working on. A way to cross to Ryogo without boats. A path across the water."

"A bridge to Ryogo." That's what Varan had promised during the celebration.

Rai had been wrong. Varan was being far too literal that night.

On top of the attacks from the mages on the shore, there's something pressing against my wards. It's like the water itself has started fighting to break through.

"Etaro," I gasp to Tessen. Please let him understand. I can't say more.

He does.

"Etaro!" he bellows across the water. "Push us back. Everyone else, guard!"

The pressure against my ward comes from our side this time, a magical touch that I recognize. Etaro is straining to do what Tessen asked, but the effort is weak compared to the power that pulled us toward the shore. Like the ripples in the bathing pools next to the white-capped ocean waves.

It's not enough, and Etaro is the only rikinhisu we brought with us to Imaku.

Varan is approaching steadily, crossing the fifty feet at a swift march. The waves to either side of his three-foot-wide path batter against the sides of the flattened surface. They batter against my ward, not just the water but the desosa, too. All the energy in the waves and the air above them is changing, buzzing frenetically. Electrified. It prods at my wards in strengthening bursts. Each one sends a shock through my mind.

"Tessen— I can't— The desosa, it—"

Together, the ratoiji strike the ward.

Pain lances through my chest. My vision goes white. I cry out.

For a second, my ward falters.

"Khya!" Tessen. Afraid.

Someone screams.

Pain bursts through my link to the wardstones. Burning fire in the center of my chest.

An energy source vanishes.

Someone keyed to the stones dies.

Shouts of panic.

Two more bursts of pain. For a second, it's like the air has been sucked out of the world.

In the boat to the left, Rai is screaming and reaching toward the water.

Another two linked to the wardstones die.

No. No!

I close my eyes, grit my teeth, and force the ward back to full strength.

A moment. It was less than a moment. But it was enough.

Three dead. And it'll happen again.

My muscles are trembling. I'm sweating. My bones ache.

"Tessen…" The word barely comes out as a breath.

He moves behind me, one arm around my waist and his lips against my throat. "I know. Hold on. Please. You can do this. Please, just hold on."

"*Tessen*, I can't—" It hurts. Everything hurts. The air moving against my skin carries knives. The spray of the salt water burns like my body is covered in open wounds. I open my eyes; my vision is a blur of blue and brown and white.

I can't. I *can't*.

But somehow I do.

I draw from Tessen. From the wardstones the others wear. From the powerful waves beneath us. From Varan, who's getting closer every second.

Gathering more of the desosa than I thought it was possible to hold, I funnel it into my ward to reinforce the protection. My vision funnels to a single point, to Varan and Izujo watching us from the other side of my shield, waiting patiently on top of the waves for me to falter.

I won't. I will not give Varan that.

The boats jolt. I jerk forward so hard I nearly smack my forehead on the side of the boat.

I lose hold of my wards. Tessen's grip tightens.

"No!"

"It's okay! Khya, it's okay!" He holds me tighter. My vision begins to clear.

Varan is holding his shoulder, hunched like he's protecting a wound. And we're moving, but this time we're moving toward Osshi's ship, not back to Shiara.

Tsua is bringing us to safety.

Just not all of us.

Breathing deep, I try to stop the shaking. I don't want...I don't want to know. But I have to know. "Who? We lost— There were three. Who?"

Tessen's forehead drops to my shoulder. "One was Daitsa."

My eyes burn. I don't bother trying to stop the tears that roll down my cheeks. "How?"

I feel Tessen swallow. "Lightning. Daitsa pushed Rai out of the way and it struck her in the chest." A deep, shaky breath. "The others, they— The rikinhisu pulled them out of the boats and dropped them to the bottom of the bay."

Failed them. I failed them all.

I can't deny the swell of relief that if anyone was lost today, it wasn't Tessen, Rai, or Etaro. But that balm doesn't last long before it's burned away by doubt.

How long will it be before I fail them, too? Before I make a mistake big enough to break whatever it is that ties them to me? Until my quest to save Yorri leaves them in as much danger as I've left my brother in?

I can't let that happen.

The boat slows seconds before it bumps into the side of the ship and ropes are thrown down to us almost before we've stopped moving.

I tie off the two ropes to the front rings with trembling hands and let Tessen help me climb up the side of the ship. Rai, Etaro, and the others follow, grief on all their faces.

We stop near the center of the boat, and Rai takes a breath. Whatever word she'd been about to say becomes a bitten-off, anguished cry.

"We can't even pray for them," she says, choked and in tears.

I flinch when the implications settle, and I cover my mouth to hide my sob when I remember the last time I recited the prayer for the dead. In bits and pieces because I couldn't bear the whole thing at once.

"They won't ever go to Ryogo and we—" Rai gasps, her body shaking with the breath. "We can't even pray for them because it's all *lies*."

I open my arms and Rai falls against my chest, gripping my damp tunic and sobbing against my shoulder. Patting her back, I try to cry with her. My eyes are burning, but I can't push past the nothing that's filling my chest and chilling my bones. The instant she pulls away, I release her. Etaro is the one who steps in and takes my place.

Crying silently, ey wraps eir arm around Rai and guides her toward the door to the lower deck, the others trailing quietly after.

I shake my head when Tessen tries to guide me to follow them. Sitting in the underbelly of this ship with nothing but my thoughts would be the quickest way to make me lose my mind.

"Osshi," I mumble when he looks down. He doesn't look happy about the request, but he doesn't fight me on it, either.

Osshi isn't easy to find. He's not in the group loading the boats, and the front platform is empty. Will I have to go wandering the lower levels of the ship to find him? My heart beats faster. I need something solid to focus on or I don't think I—

Wait. There. He's standing on the rear platform with the ship's commander, Kazu, both of them watching the men loading the boats we'd borrowed and returned empty. And with three fewer people than we left the ship with.

Because I failed.

I failed to save Yorri, and now he's trapped somewhere on Shiara, locked away because of Varan.

I failed to protect Daitsa and the others, and now they've been devoured by the waves and tossed into whatever afterlife exists. If any does.

I will not fail again. I'll learn the magic of Ryogo, the magic of spells, cords, message balls, and spoken words. I'll go to the land of people who discovered a way to cage the immortal Miriseh and figure out how to use that to not only trap them, but end them. When I return for Yorri— because I may not be able to save the three lost to the ocean, but I *will* come back for my brother—I'll bring an army if I have to.

I will learn everything Ryogo has to teach me.

I will use all of it to tear Varan and his plans apart.

CHAPTER THIRTY-FOUR

Though Osshi and Kazu are watching the boats, their heads are tilted toward each other, the conversation moving quickly if the speed of their lips is any indication. As soon as Tessen and I climb up to the platform, though, they focus on me.

Without the drain of maintaining the wards, the trembling in my muscles is beginning to subside. Exhaustion will win eventually—sooner than I'd like, probably—but I refuse to sleep until then. If I sleep now, I'll spend the night watching my mistakes over and over again.

"I need to draw a map."

Confusion fills Osshi's face. "A map?"

"Yes." My voice is calm and even. Dead. Or maybe just drained. I can't tell. "Do you have charcoal and paper?"

"I— Yes. I can maybe be finding something if you would like." He looks at Tessen, whose face gives nothing away. Not even to me.

When Osshi translates our request, Kazu's eyes narrow, but he nods.

"Follow and I will be getting that for you, yes?" Osshi nods toward the stairs, traveling down the flight far slower than I climbed it moments before.

We walk through the door under the rear platform and down a short set of steps even steeper than the ones at the front of the boat. Unlike the wide, open room under the front platform, this leads us into a dark, narrow hallway lined with several doors. He stops at the second one on the right-hand side and turns to look at us.

"You will be waiting here for a moment?" Osshi tilts his head toward the door. "What it is you asking for is inside."

When I nod, the motion so stiff that it pulls my muscles the wrong way, Osshi opens the door and slips inside.

Above us, the men working shout back and forth over the scrapes and thuds of loading the boats. The waves are the only constant, a ceaseless sound that's not quite as steady as a heartbeat but still gives me something to count, to block out everything else in my head. I lean against the wall and close my eyes, ignoring the feeling of Tessen watching me.

The door opens and Osshi returns with several rolls of paper.

"This is very much like charcoal, yes?" Osshi asks, holding out the thin, dark stick. "It is—well, the word is not there, but this will be working for what you are needing, I think?"

One end of the stick has been sharpened to a point, and when I test it against the corner of the paper in his hands, it leaves a dark gray streak. If it's not charcoal, it's something close enough for me.

"Yes, thank you."

Looking relieved, Osshi hands me the papers. "Be coming with me. I will be showing you a room." He nods toward the end of the hallway, away from the upper level of the boat. "The voyage across the ocean to Ryogo, it will be many days," Osshi explains as we walk through the hallway. Tessen has to balance me down the next flight of stairs. "The ship is not built for being comfortable for so many people as we are having, but rooms here will be giving your people privacy and quiet from the deck above. It is small—cramped and quite very much sparse."

Halfway down the next hall, he grips a wide ring set in a metal circle and pulls. The door opens toward us and we step in. It's bigger than my room in Itagami, but it feels smaller; there's so much taking up space—a low table along the right wall, a large box as high as my hip along the left, and shelves along the rear of the room.

"Should you not be wishing for company, all you are having to do is lower this." Osshi closes the door and flicks a small catch on the doorframe with his thumb, releasing a thick piece of wood braced with metal from the frame. It falls smoothly over the closed door, landing in a metal loop extending from the wood. "But should you be needing anything, all you are having to do is ask me. If Sanii and the other ones bring back food and water, we will likely be being fine, but the ship is—" He winces and shakes his head. "There are being so many people. Our food and supplies are soon going to be low."

"Just tell the others to be aware of rations," Tessen says. "We're soldiers, Osshi, and we're very much in your debt. You don't have to worry about us."

Osshi says something else, but I stop listening. I slowly kneel by the low, rectangular table and unroll one of the sheets of thick paper. Whatever this is made of, it's not nyska.

Holding the charcoal stick in one hand, I use an anto and two wardstones to weigh down the paper's curled-up corners. Then I survey the empty sheet, trying to picture the city as I've seen it from the outer wall.

I close my eyes, visualizing Itagami. Every building, every street, every entrance and exit to every single tunnel I have ever traveled. I need to remember all of them.

My hands are still shaky. The lines won't be precise, but it will be good enough to start. If I begin at the northern wall on the far left side of the paper and then draw the city north to south from that point, then—

I tense, freezing with the tip of the charcoal inches away from the paper.

The door just opened and closed. Osshi leaving? Possibly Tessen going with him?

But no. Someone is still here. They're breathing with the deep, even pace of someone counting breaths. That pace doesn't change, and the sound of it moves neither closer nor farther, so I exhale and place the charcoal to the paper, drawing the rough line of the north wall.

I've finished the wall and the first line of buildings and barracks before Tessen clears his throat. I don't look up. Sighing, he speaks anyway. "You need to eat, Khya. I'm going to go look for food. Will you lock me out if I leave?"

My hand freezes again. Though I open my mouth to answer, the words get tangled on the back of my tongue.

Yes. No. Why would you want to come back? How can you stand to be around me when everything I try to do goes so wrong?

All I manage is to lift one shoulder, not promising anything but not denying it to him either. He moves closer, running a gentle hand over my short hair and pressing a light kiss to the back of my head before he murmurs, "I'll be back soon."

Don't leave, I want to say.

Don't come back, I should say.

The door closes behind him.

I brace my hands on the table, letting my head hang. For a moment, I stop trying to stifle the tremors running under my skin. I want to sink into complete unconsciousness. I want to dive under the surface of the ocean and stay there until it devours me.

The tremor gets stronger, strong enough to make my elbows buckle under my weight.

I fold over, my control cracking.

I'm trying to breathe. Trying *not* to think. I only succeed at one.

Eventually, I manage to pull myself up and keep drawing. The effort of putting memory into lines on paper occupies most of my mind. I construct each line with more care and exactness than it probably requires, telling myself it's to counteract the slowly fading tremor in my hand.

It's not.

Each street comes with memories that I have to push back. Of Yorri. Of Tessen. Of Etaro and Rai. Of Tyrroh. They're memories of everything we've all had to leave behind. They've all jumped into the unknown because of me.

On top of that, each building and alley and cave I map could be the place they're hiding Yorri and the others. This map could help us plan the next attempt. If I draw it well enough, it could be what pinpoints where he is.

Tessen is gone long enough for me to finish my first sketch of the upper city and begin on the main sections of the undercity. Long enough that the thuds of a smaller boat hitting the side of the larger one begin again.

Even with a full floor between my room and the upper level, I hear the commotion when Sanii and the others return. I hear the agonized cry, the pained disbelief, when someone tells Sanii that only eir half of the mission succeeded.

Ey should have heard it from me. It was my mission and my promise that was broken, but I can't. I don't dare climb the steps and emerge from the corner I've tucked myself into.

It's the most cowardly thing I have done in my entire life, but I *can't*. I can't face Sanii with another failure so fresh.

I mentally walk through the undercity instead, my hand tracing the paths I remember.

The mushroom farms connect through a west-east tunnel to the passage that brings the yonin to the base of the saishigi chamber, but if you take the opposite turn, it will bring you past the entrance to the mural caves...

When Tessen opens the door and quietly slips into the room, I press the charcoal against the table so hard a piece breaks off. He comes to kneel next to me, leaning over the table and scanning the several pages scattered across the surface.

"There's an alley between these two barracks, I think." His voice is barely above a whisper, and he moves slowly, reaching for the paper halfway across the table and bringing it closer. Pointing to a section in the Northwestern Zon, he says, "Here. There's a break."

I loosen my hold on the charcoal and raise my head. Hands braced on the low table, his shoulders are tense and high, and the muscles of his neck are so taut it seems like he must be using most of his focus to *not* look at me. It makes it easier to twist my wrist and open my hand, letting the charcoal roll to the center of my palm.

He takes it, the motion just as slow as his reach across

the table, as though he's afraid a sudden movement might bring out my claws. I wish I could say he was wrong; I don't think he is. Mind and body, I feel like I'm made of poorly fired clay, fragile and liable to shatter at the slightest touch.

But Tessen doesn't push. He barely touches, with words or hands, and for a long time—hours maybe—we work on building the maps of Itagami until our hands and forearms are coated in charcoal dust.

Eventually, if I want this representation to be as accurate as possible, we'll have to show it to Tyrroh and my squad. And to Sanii. None of us know the undercity as well as Sanii does, and eir knowledge of the paths only the yonin ever walked will be invaluable…but not yet. I don't have the strength to beg for that favor yet.

Our work fills both sides of every paper and the charcoal stick has been sharpened down to a nub. Only then do I let Tessen roll up the maps and place them on the waist-high box against the opposite wall.

I look around, my eyes flitting from one surface to the next and finding nothing. There's nothing familiar, nothing to do, and nothing to keep my mind from traveling the paths I've worked so hard to ignore.

Tessen steps in front of me, places his hands on my shoulders, and waits until I meet his eyes. There's a streak of charcoal across one cheek and a fresh scratch across the opposite side of his forehead. They're completely different marks, but he bears both of them because of me. Yet he's still here, looking at me with nothing but concern in his gray eyes.

He slides his hands from the curve of my shoulders inward until his thumbs can gently rub the bare skin at the base of my neck. "We *will* come back for him, Khya."

I don't move, don't blink or breathe or speak.

"I promise. Whatever it takes, I'll help you." He wraps his arms around my shoulders and leans closer, resting his forehead against mine. "We'll come back and we'll find him. Even if we have to learn how to work one of these boats and steal one to do it, we'll come back. I promise."

My breath stutters, my body shudders, and I can't hold myself together anymore.

All the tears I've fought back flood out of my eyes, blurring my vision and clogging my throat. Collapsing against him, my legs boneless, I don't resist—I can't—when he picks me up. I feel him moving. I lock my arms around his neck, hiding my face against his chest, and hold on. He sinks to the floor slowly, the movements as even and steady as he always is, until he's sitting with me held in his lap.

Curled in a ball tucked tight against Tessen's chest, I break the way I haven't let myself since the moment Tessen woke me up in the middle of the night to tell me that my brother had died. I shatter completely and then let go of the pieces, because for the first time, I trust someone will be there to help me put them back together.

I trust that there is someone who *can* put me back together.

CHAPTER
THIRTY-FIVE

I spend the first two days of the voyage in the room, sleeping through half of the first and working the rest of the time.

Osshi called it sparse and cramped when he first brought Tessen and me down here, and later he apologized for the lack of comforts, but I still don't understand what he meant. I don't know what to name half the things in this wooden room, let alone what to *do* with them. Even trying to puzzle out the use of the too-sweet-smelling contents of the jar on one of the few shelves or the various multipronged implements I found tucked in the box Osshi called a chest couldn't distract me for long.

My maps, though? My maps devour my mind.

I don't sleep much once I regain my energy. Partly it's because I can't seem to adjust to the motion of the boat. Instead, I spend hours going over the maps and adding to them, recopying the more detailed versions onto fresh pieces of paper Osshi brought after he saw my project.

Never having seen Itagami, Osshi can't help me perfect

the maps, but he offered invaluable advice on making the representation as accurate as possible. He even brought a map of Shiara that was more detailed than anything I'd ever seen before, full of bright colors and details of geography. It's wrong in certain areas—including, for example, a section of coastline that had fallen into the sea long before I was born—but the map itself is incredible.

Between his advice and the memories of the others, I create something that closely resembles what we left behind, something that may help me figure out where the Miriseh are keeping Yorri.

The others offer help when it's needed, and all of them tell me—far too often—that no one blames me for the losses on Imaku. For Daitsa and the others dying under what had essentially been my command. Rai and Etaro are the only ones who never offer that platitude. Instead they come with a story about the moment when my ward faltered, the moment Etaro took a chance and shot a shard of rock from Imaku at Varan—the cause of his apparent injury.

"You should have seen the look on eir face when it worked," Rai says. "I think ey was more shocked than Varan."

It's one of the few moments I smile.

Everyone else comes and goes; Tessen is the only one who stays with me. He's the only one I *want* with me, the only one who doesn't make me feel a breath away from screaming.

When the door to the room opens, I expect it to either be him returning with food he'll make me eat or someone who remembered some tiny detail they want to add to one of the maps that have taken over the room.

I look toward the door. It's not Tessen.

Sanii walks into the room and closes the door.

I hold my breath, unable to look away. I knew I couldn't avoid em for the entire voyage, but I can't... I don't think I'm ready to explain myself to em.

Apparently ey is tired of waiting. "I haven't seen you in days."

I nod; there's nothing I can say aloud.

"Etaro said you were trying to make maps of the city." Ey doesn't look away from my face, not even to peer at the very maps ey hasn't yet seen.

Another nod. It's not like I can deny it when the evidence is covering every flat surface of the room.

"Have you started on the yonin tunnels?" Ey still hasn't looked away.

I can't keep nodding as though my tongue is locked to the roof of my mouth.

What is this? Why isn't ey angry with me?

"There." I gesture to the forward wall of the room where small pins are holding up several pages detailing the layers of the undercity and the way the passages and main caverns connect to the yonin passages. The ones that I've seen, anyway.

Sanii moves to the wall and picks up a not-quite-charcoal stick lying on top of the chest. Then ey unhurriedly walks from one end of the room to the other. On some maps ey makes only small adjustments, explaining why with each change, but on others ey shakes eir head and adds entire passages, tunnels, and caves I never knew existed. I help em remove the pins from those pages and carry them to the table, watching over eir shoulder as ey continues to sketch out the yonin sections of the undercity with an eye for detail I envy.

It takes a long while before I relax and begin to speak without overthinking every word. Maybe we don't have to talk about the past at all. Maybe Sanii wants to do what I've been trying to do and focus solely on our next attempt at rescuing Yorri.

"I don't blame you, Khya."

My heart skips more than one beat, and my hands close into fists on top of the table. How can ey not blame me?

Bellows. Did I ask that aloud?

Sanii blinks and then looks at me with such pity in eir large eyes that my breath catches. "There are a lot of nyshin who never would've listened to me, even if I came to them with information concerning someone they cared about." Sanii shakes eir head, but I can't read the expression on eir face. "That night I came to find you, I thought you'd turn me away. You didn't. You followed me. You believed me."

"Yes, I believed you." I laugh, rubbing suddenly dry eyes. Dry—that's why they're burning. "How much good did that do? I failed to bring him home *both* times."

"No." Ey says it loud, strong enough that I look up, my hand falling away from my face. "You didn't fail any more than I did."

"It was my wards we were counting on to—"

Sanii puts eir hand over my mouth, shaking eir head. "To keep us alive. That's what I expected your wards to do, fykina. That's all." Ey moves eir hand to the back of my neck, gripping hard enough that I feel eir fingers pressing into the knots in my muscles, but not so hard that I couldn't break free if I tried. "You're the only one who expected more. There was no way…" Eyes filling with tears, Sanii's mouth keeps moving though no sound emerges. Ey stops for a moment, swallowing hard enough I can watch the muscles contract in eir throat, and then ey exhales a slow, shuddering breath.

"We were supposed to save him, Sanii."

"I know."

"We're *leaving*, and we didn't save him."

Ey winces, pain flashing across eir face. Eir hand tightens on my neck. "We'll come back." When ey opens eir eyes, determination fills every line of eir face. "We're going to where they come from. We'll learn everything we can there. Once we know how to break the Miriseh, we'll come back—we'll *steal* a boat to get back if we have to."

I smile. I can't help it. Tessen had promised that, too. The stupidity of the plan hadn't occurred to me at the time, but it does now. The three of us trying to run a ship? To do what an entire squad of well-trained Ryogan men are responsible for? We wouldn't make it a mile.

"Just stay with me, okay?" Smiling back, Sanii grips my face between eir hands. "You're the only one I trust to not forget why we started this. None of the others know Yorri like we do, and none of them will fight as hard as we will to get back to Shiara. I just need you to promise you won't forget, and that you won't leave me behind."

"I promise." It's an easy promise to make. I touch my forehead against eirs for a moment and breathe, so much of the tension that's plagued me since we left Shiara draining away. "You know I could never walk away without you. Besides," I say, lifting my head and trying to make my small smile more teasing than sad, "I don't think Yorri would forgive me."

Sanii's smile softens, growing almost fond. "I should hope he wouldn't."

The ball of guilt and fear that's been eating my stomach since the moment I plunged into the ocean without Yorri begins to fade. It doesn't disappear, and I don't think it will until I find him, but the edges lose a little of their sting. I can breathe around it without my lungs burning. I can contemplate walking the halls of the boat without my hands shaking. I can ask Sanii for help when I need it without being unable to look into eir eyes.

"We'll find him." I repeat it, needing to hear the words one more time. "I won't stop looking until we find him."

"I am so glad that you are everything your brother ever thought you were." Sanii grips my face harder, but eir smile warms. Pulling my head forward, ey kisses my forehead and then pulls back. "Thank you, Khya."

Eir hands drop to my shoulders, and ey squeezes one more time before leaving.

I'm still standing in the middle of the room staring at the door when Tessen comes in, a plate of food in his hand. After placing it on one of the only clear sections on the table, he closes the distance between us slowly, his fingers sliding up my arm, rising higher until he can tuck a strand of my short hair behind my ear. I lean into the touch and cup the back of his head, winding my other arm around his waist to pull him closer.

"Are you all right?" Tessen murmurs the question against my cheek. I feel his words in the shape his lips make and the gust of his breath against my skin as much as I hear them.

I nod, letting the tip of my nose draw a line along his cheek before I pull back to see his face. "Were you listening?"

"I—yes." His cheeks flush darker, but otherwise there's no remorse in his expression. "I was on my way back and I heard em in here. I wanted—I hoped that ey would make you hear it when ey said it wasn't your fault, since you wouldn't listen to *me*."

"You aren't Sanii." I draw away gradually, letting my

fingers linger against his warm skin. "It's not that you didn't want to save Yorri, but that isn't why you're here."

"No?" Tessen steps forward as I step back, keeping the space between us small. "Why am I, then?"

The scratch on his face from our last visit to Imaku is healed, but I remember where it was. My fingers trace the invisible line from his hairline, down the side of his face. "You did it for me."

Tessen smiles, the curve of his lips slight but the light behind his gray eyes near-blinding. "Finally figured that out, did you?"

"I knew. I may not have understood it—I'm still not sure I do—but I knew." I run the tips of my fingers across his cheek and begin to pull away, but Tessen catches my hand and brings my fingers to his lips, pressing a kiss against each one. His eyes never leave mine.

It shouldn't feel this good. It shouldn't rise up my arms like warm water, seeping into my bones and chasing away the harshest edge of the chill that has settled into my body since our first plunge into the ocean days ago. It shouldn't, but it does, and I close my eyes to enjoy feeling *warm*. Then his grip on my hand switches to press our palms together and intertwine our fingers. I open my eyes and instantly find his, the light that had filled them moments before undimmed.

"Come on, Khya." He tightens his hold on my hand and gently tugs me toward the cushions surrounding the low table. "You need to eat something."

"I don't know what we would've done if Sanii hadn't brought food back from the city," I mutter. He laughs, but I'm not joking. Considering the options available on Osshi's ship, I really don't know how much of it my stomach will be able to take when the stolen stores from

Itagami run out. There's something they call bread, but it's hard enough that I could likely kill someone with a sharply broken piece. The dried and salted meat is gamey and tasteless. Their wine barely warrants the name.

If this is the food of verdant Ryogo, I prefer the desert.

Tessen nudges me toward the side of the table closer to the wall and we sit cross-legged on the cushions, leaning against the wall behind us.

In the course of my life, I've been wrong more than I care to admit, but somehow I think there are few people who I've been wrong about more often than Tessen. So often, in fact, and for so long, that I don't even yet know of all the moments, for there are stories he's holding back — ones I hadn't been ready to listen to, according to him. Now, though, I think he might be willing to tell me the truth.

"Do you remember the day we found the ward guarding the tunnel to Imaku?" I slowly chew the pieces of dried ahuri fruit he brought me.

Without lifting his head from where it's resting on the wall, Tessen angles toward me. "It wasn't that long ago, Khya. Of course I remember it."

"Do you remember..." Do I want to know what he thought Yorri had been hiding from me, though? If I ask now, I'm positive he'll tell me, so I'd better be sure I want the answer.

But...I don't know if I do.

He's watching me closely now, waiting. I have to say something, something important enough that he would believe it could make me nervous. "Do you remember what I said when you asked if I trusted you?"

Though he opens his mouth like he's about to answer, he doesn't say anything. His expression changes, like a new thought has just changed his course, and he closes his mouth again, sitting up, turning his body toward me more fully.

"That's not what you wanted to ask," he finally says. "You want to know about Yorri, don't you? What I said about not knowing everything, right?"

How does he *do* that? I've never thought I was an easy person to read—I took pride in it—but Tessen always seems to reach into my head and speak my thoughts as though they're part of the conversation, as though he can hear them the same way he hears my breathing and my pulse and what I choose to actually say. Not always, but often enough. But he's right, as he usually is, and denying that will get me nowhere.

"This is getting ridiculous. Can you actually read my mind?"

Tessen laughs. "No. If I could, it would've made the last few years much easier for me."

"You always seem to know what I'm thinking. Guesses aren't right as often as you are."

"I didn't say I was guessing, either."

Oh, I hate it when he plays these word games. "Explain, Tessen."

He sighs, but he's still smiling when he does. "You've heard the stories about the basaku, right? That if their senses are all enhanced that much they have the power to pick thoughts out of the air like someone's speaking."

"Yes, that's why I'm asking—"

"Khya."

Lips pursed tight and jaw clenched, I nod for him to continue.

"It's true, but I can't read thoughts. You can feel it in the desosa when magic is being used, right? It ripples through the energy." He shrugs. "It works the same way with people's emotions."

"That can't be true." Or is it? The last basaku was so long ago. And what I sense sometimes could be considered close to what he's describing, I suppose. I never know what people are feeling without being able to read it on their face, but strong surges of emotion stir their magic, which stirs the desosa in the air around them. If I had a basaku's senses...

Could it be true?

"I promise it is. For most people I can only sense the strongest of feelings—like rage or joy. I have to be close to them, and I have to be concentrating on them, and to really have any idea what they're thinking about, I also have to know them very well." He swallows and holds my gaze for a moment before looking at the maps on the opposite wall. "For some people, though, if I'm attuned to the way they normally affect the desosa, I can sense subtler shifts."

"And you can do that with me?" My heart pounds. Intrigue or fear? I can't even tell, so what does Tessen feel?

He nods, watching me out the corner of his eye. "You're one of the few."

"Okay, well, fine." I look down, rubbing at a gray smudge on my palm. "Since you knew what I wanted to ask, tell me what I wanted to know."

Tessen smiles, the expression lifting the corners of his lips and the edges of his eyes. He nudges the plate of food toward me again—though most of it is gone.

As soon as I pick up a piece of teegra meat, Tessen says, "I don't know how they managed to do it, but Yorri and Sanii somehow created a sumai bond the night of his herynshi."

I drop the food. "They *what*?"

He winces. "Yeah, that's a version of what I thought you'd say."

"They... Blood and rot, that makes sense." I run my

hand over my hair, looking again at my memories of Sanii. "Ey never thought Yorri was dead. Not for a second after ey found out his body was missing. But...an *actual* sumai bond?"

"I felt it happen. I was in the undercity after the celebration when I saw Yorri looking like he was sneaking off somewhere," Tessen says. "I knew what you'd say if he managed to get himself in trouble the same night he was declared nyshin, so I followed him. I was going to try to talk him out of whatever he was planning, but when I heard him and Sanii talking, I..."

"Your curiosity got the better of you. Again."

"A bit. But when I felt the bond..." He shakes his head, a little awe in his eyes.

"Did they see you?"

"Sanii did. I expected them both to leave the way Yorri had come, and my options for hiding were limited." Tessen smiles at the memory. "Yonin or not, that ebet threatened me within an inch of my life if I told anyone, especially you, what they'd done."

"How is it possible? Haven't other people tried? There are stories, at least. No one but the Miriseh have been able to do it."

"But no one has ever been able to glow like Sanii, either," Tessen says. "I don't know. Maybe it was a combination of his Miriseh heritage and whatever strange magic Sanii has that made it work, but I promise you it *did* work."

"Why didn't ey tell me?" We've become friends over the past few moons. I can understand why ey wouldn't say anything at first, before ey was sure I could be trusted not to drag em before the kaigo and the Miriseh, but what about all the time after?

"You'll have to ask Sanii, but I think it was fear of how you'd react and maybe…" He tilts his head, eyes distant. "Sometimes it felt like ey thought I pitied em for the way things had turned out with Yorri. I think ey didn't want you looking at em the same way."

"True, I suppose." Varan would've killed them both for that. And Tessen for knowing about it. Yet I'd accused him of not caring. Of being in this for the wrong reasons. Of so many things that I hate remembering now. Eyes closed and chest tight, I let my back thud against the wall. I can't look him in the eye yet. "Why are you here? How can you possibly be here after everything?"

Fingers touch my chin, guiding me toward him. I turn with the pressure, but it's another moment before I open my eyes.

Impossibly, inexplicably, Tessen is smiling.

"Because of your skill. And because I remember what it was like when we were friends, before ranks and promotions got in the way," he says, his hand dropping from my chin to rest on my knee. "Because I saw you help people you didn't like perfect a skill you'd mastered in minutes, and I watched you with Yorri, how you loved all the traits and habits that made him baffling to the other doseiku."

My heart skips a beat and warmth diffuses through my body.

"I saw you, and I *knew* you. I knew exactly why you reacted like that and why you pushed me away. I didn't like it, but I knew why. And, besides…"

Swallowing, I place my hand over his, squeezing lightly. "Tessen, please."

He huffs a breathless laugh, like he's laughing at himself, and shakes his head. "I couldn't stay mad at you when all I wanted was to figure out how to earn the kind of blind devotion you gave Yorri." Glancing at me through his eyelashes, he curves his lips into a self-deprecating smile. "It wasn't exactly an easy task to set for myself."

"Tessen..." The words lock in my throat. That's probably good, because I have no idea what I was going to say. What *can* I possibly say to that?

"What you asked me the day we found the tunnel? I—" I swallow the lump forming in my throat and force myself to hold his eyes, to let him see the truth of the words. "I *do* trust you, Tessen. I think you may be the only person I trust completely."

Because the only thing I was right about was that trust needs to be earned, and Tessen has more than done that. I have faith in the others, of course—how could I not give that much to Sanii and everyone who followed me into this? But Tessen has earned something deeper that I'm not sure I have the words to describe yet.

"Khya." His eyes are wide, surprise, relief, and maybe a little confusion in his expression. "The *only* one? What about Yorri?"

And he *would* want to know everything, wouldn't he? Even the details that are only beginning to occur to me. I look down at my hand over his.

"I...I thought I trusted him, but—but I couldn't have." I move my thumb along the edge of his, taking notice of every line and ridge of his skin and the feel of the small scar just below his knuckle. "I kept trying to make his decisions for him, to guide his life in the direction I wanted it to take. It felt like I was protecting him, but I think...it was more that I didn't trust him to make the right decisions. I didn't trust him to be in control of his own life. I always saw him as—"

I take a breath, holding his hand tighter. "Do you remember the day I found my magic? When I stopped that blade from hitting his neck, it wasn't love that freed my wards, Tessen. Fear brought it out in me. Fear and the overwhelming need to protect what I considered *mine*."

But Yorri wasn't ever mine. No one can belong to someone else like that. Even a sumai bond isn't like that—it's about partnership, not control. Yorri was never mine, and Tessen never *will* be mine, because all we can ever be is our own.

"I know." The gentleness of his tone makes me look up. I relax a little when I see the warm smile on his face. "I just wasn't certain you'd ever see that."

"I might not have if all of this hadn't happened." If I were with anyone else, even Sanii or Yorri—perhaps especially Yorri—I don't think I would've admitted this, but Tessen has somehow become a safe place to fall. He's the only one I trust to neither judge nor try to change me. "The night they laid him in the saishigi core, I blamed myself. I thought that if I hadn't taken him out in the desert and forced his magic to appear, he might have been placed yonin, and he would have been alive and safe."

"You know it wouldn't have happened like that." Tessen edges closer, rubbing his hand up and down my arm. "Being placed yonin would've just made it easier for Varan to get rid of him. And neither you nor Sanii might ever have known he was missing."

"I know that—I *do* know that—but I was so sure it was my fault that..." I shake my head. "It's a hard feeling to forget, Tessen."

"No one's asking you to." His palm cups my jaw and his thumb rubs a gentle line across my cheek. "The only one expecting perfection from you is you."

Before I can answer, his expression shifts, determination and mischief making him look like the young doseiku I'd been friends with years ago.

"All I expect is for you to leave this room today." He frowns with obviously false severity. "You're becoming *far* too lazy, going days without training."

Smirking, I push the plate off his lap and straddle his hips, sliding my hands behind his head and holding his lips less than an inch away from mine. His hands land on my hips and his chin tilts toward mine—or it tries to; I hold him tight enough to resist the motion, smiling when he relaxes.

"*Or*..." I brush the tip of my nose against his and lightly run my short fingernails across his scalp once I'm relatively sure he won't try to move. "Or, instead of training, I could ward the door to keep everyone out, and we could stay here."

"We—we could, but..." He swallows, his eyes dropping to my lips before jumping back up to my eyes. "It's—well, Nyshin-ma Tyrroh ordered us to meet on the deck. I think... we probably only have ten minutes left to get ready."

I watch how his cheeks flush, his pulse point flutters in his throat, his lip *almost* gets sucked between his teeth. The signs—individually or collectively—could mean a hundred different things, but added to the way his eyes can't hold mine for long, the way they jump *up* toward the ceiling instead of down toward my mouth...

"You asked him for that order, didn't you, Nyshin-ten?"

"I..." After a slow exhale, his eyes meet mine. This time they stay. "I *may* have, yes."

Keeping our lips apart, I inch my knees forward, forcing him to back up against the wall and then using my body to hold him there. He moves readily, relaxing as soon as I have him pinned. He sinks into the moment as though he's been holding himself tense for hours waiting for this and now he can finally just *be*. To hold that kind of power over anyone is heady, but to have Tessen in this position, and see exactly how much he wants to be where he is?

That knowledge is intoxicating.

"Why would you ask him to do that, Tessen?"

His gaze darts to the maps on the walls, but returns quickly to my face. "I was worried about you, and you wouldn't leave the room on your own. I thought…"

"You thought that an order from our commanding officer would be the most effective option?"

"Possibly."

"Tessen." Loosening my grip on his head, I ease back enough to watch as I trail my fingers along the lines of his jaw and then up to trace the shape of his face. "If there's something you need from me, all you have to do is ask."

His lips part as though he's about to speak, but then his jaw clenches. What had he been about to say? In all likelihood, he doesn't believe me. I can't blame him if that's true. I'm not sure I'd believe him if the situations were reversed. If I had reached out to him for years and had my hand slapped away each time, I don't know if I would trust anything offered now.

"I promise." I place my fingers under his chin and tilt his head up to brush my lips against his, the pressure of the kiss as gentle as my touch. After I pull away, I wait until his eyelids flutter open, wait until his iron-gray eyes are focused on me. "Tessen, I promise. All you have to do is ask."

He nods slowly, his eyes searching my face. I don't know if he trusts it, trusts that it'll last or that whatever we'll encounter in Ryogo won't send us back to how things were between us. But like I told him weeks ago, trust has to be earned.

"Come on, then." I tuck my toes underneath myself and stand, extending my hand for his.

He takes the offered help, though it's awkward for him to get to his feet when we're both crammed into the foot of space between the low table and the wall. To stand without knocking me over, he has to slide his back up the wall. When he's on his feet, we're pressed together from thigh to nose. Luckily, it doesn't seem like he minds.

"Are you ready to go?" I glance at the door and link our fingers together.

"Go where?"

"Out of here." I take a step backward, careful to avoid the table. "Apparently we're supposed to be in a training session."

"But you—really?" He follows me toward the door.

"After you went to all the trouble of begging Tyrroh for training, it'd be rude of us to miss it."

"I didn't beg," Tessen quickly corrects. "I don't beg."

"No?" I smirk and take another step back. "That's a shame."

His jaw goes slack. He trips over the corner of the table and curses when I don't stop moving long enough for him to regain his feet, but he's smiling when he does, watching me with a particular light in his eyes that I'm beginning to grow very fond of.

I open the door and move backward into the hall. Behind him, in the room I've refused to leave since we came back on board, the efforts of two sleepless days and nights are spread out on display. The Miriseh and the kaigo still have Yorri somewhere.

But I have this ship.

I have Osshi and his men, who are taking me to Ryogo.

I have Tsua, Chio, and Zonna, all of them willing to stand against the plans that Varan, Suzu, and the rest of the Miriseh have been building for centuries.

I have Tyrroh, whom I've trained, worked, and bled with for over a year.

I have Etaro and Rai, both of whom deserve more trust and care than I've given them.

I have Sanii, the only other person on this ship who shares my relentless need to get back to Shiara and try again—to *keep* trying until Yorri is free or our blood has been spilled to feed the sands of the desert.

I have a small flame of hope. Hope that my maps will help me figure out where they've hidden Yorri. Hope that what we learn on Ryogo will help us defeat Varan. Hope that Etaro and Rai eventually forgive me for keeping secrets.

And I have Tessen, who will one day stop doubting me when I tell him that I trust him, and that he can trust me just as much.

As we step onto the top level of the ship, I listen to the mix of sounds, some already familiar and others that are becoming familiar. The crash of wind and waves against the language spoken by Osshi and his men, a language full of words I can't understand. Tyrroh's booming voice mixed with the orders called out by the ship's leader, Kazu.

"I was beginning to think we'd never see you in sunlight again," Rai yells at me from the edge of the forward platform where everyone has gathered. "Come up for air at last, have you?"

I know she's still angry with me, mistrustful, but she's smiling. It's enough to give me hope that, angry though she is—and understandably so—it's a wound that has already started to heal.

Nothing I am capable of doing will be able to stop Varan if he makes it across the ocean. Nothing I know will help any of us navigate Ryogo, a land we grew up hearing stories of but that no one actually understands. Nothing I see ahead of me will help me accomplish the task I have failed at twice when I try a third time—because I *will* try a third time.

Today, though, we train, because unlike the typhoons that batter Itagami every year, the storm that's brewing on Shiara, the one aiming itself for the shores of Ryogo, is one that can be bested by skill and iron and magic.

As long as we're ready when it lands.

GLOSSARY AND INDEX

RANKS OF SAGEN SY ITAGAMI
Highest rank listed first

Miriseh
Kaigo

Nyshin-lu
Nyshin-ri
Nyshin-co
Nyshin-ma
Nyshin-pa
Nyshin-ten

Ahdo-na
Ahdo-mas
Ahdo-sa
Ahdo-po
Ahdo-li
Ahdo-va

Yonin-na
Yonin-mas
Yonin-sa
Yonin-po
Yonin-li
Yonin-va

MAGIC OF SAGEN SY ITAGAMI

SOYIJI MAGES – ELEMENTAL MANIPULATION

Ishiji – Stone Mage – Ability to reform, lighten, move, and meld stone

Ryiji – Earth Mage – Affinity for plants and soil that helps these plants grow in the desert

Kyshiji – Water Mage – Ability to find, clean, and sometimes manipulate water

Myiji – Weather Mage – Extremely rare ability that can manipulate wind and detect or, sometimes, call up storms

DESOSA MAGES – ENERGY MANIPULATION

Assistive:

Dyuniji – Kinetic Mage – Ability to use their own kinetic energy, or sometimes someone else's (for example, blows landed during battle) to augment their own strength

Zoikyo – Augmenter – Ability to boost other people's powers by funneling desosa to them

Hishingu – Healer – Ability to use the desosa to heal themselves and others

WARD MAGES:

Sykina – Ability to use their own energy and the universal desosa to shield themselves from other magic

Fykina – Ability to shield themselves and others from both magic and the physical world

Offensive:

Kasaiji – Fire Mage – Ability to use the desosa to create sparks and/or fire

Ratoiji – Lightning Mage – Ability to use the desosa to create lightning

OKAJIN MAGES – ENHANCED HUMANITY
Physical Abilities:

Kyneeda – Enhanced strength, stamina, and endurance

Ryacho – Enhanced speed and ability

Kynacho – Enhanced speed, ability, strength, stamina, and endurance

SENSOR MAGES:

Uniku – Enhancement of a single sense, usually either vision or hearing

Oraku – Enhancement of three senses: sight, smell, and hearing

Basaku – Enhancement of all senses, plus the ability to sense magic, and, rarely, the impact emotions have on the desosa

SHINTE-KINA MAGES – PSYCHIC ABILITIES

Rikinhisu – Telekinesis – Ability to move objects or people without touching them

Rusosa – Mental Manipulation – An uncommon ability to create, among other things, illusions in other people's minds

Akuringu – Scrying – Ability to use a reflective surface to see across great distances or, rarely, a short period of time into the past or future

GLOSSARY OF TERMS

AHDO – Second citizen class of Itagami

AHKIYU – A longbow

AHURI – A fruit of the desert cactus that is eaten and used to make wine

ANTO – The style of dagger used on Shiara

ATAKAFU – Headscarf worn in Itagami as protection from the desert winds

BIKYO-KO – The armory and the barracks for the two councils within Itagami

BYKA – A caffeinated bean given to those on long missions to help them stay awake

DENHITRA – Clan that lives in the southern mountain range on Shiara

DESOSA – The ambient elemental energy of the world

DOSEIKU – An Itagamin clan member under sixteen who hasn't faced the herynshi yet

EBET – The sex designation for those neither male nor female

GASUREN – A sugar-like sweetener extracted from the desert plant of the same name

GENSU – A woman's monthly menstruation

HERYNSHI – The trial undergone by all Itagamin citizens the moon of their sixteenth birthday

IMAKU – The black island off the northern coast of Shiara

ISAGYSU – A formal greeting of respect and deference

KAIGO – The council that serves directly under the Miriseh

KAIGO-SEI – The candidates chosen from the nyshin as potential future kaigo council members

KAMIDI – A large lizard with venomous spit

KHAI – A relationship chosen specifically to produce children

KUJUKO – The empty realm between our world and the afterlife

KYIWA – The run of mountains and cliffs that border the eastern coast of Shiara

MIRISEH – The immortals who lead Itagami

MYKYN – A large bird with sharp teeth and vicious claws

NIORA – A mountain lion

NYSKA – One of the tallest shrubs on the island, which bears pods that can be dried and used to make grain; the plant itself is also used to make cloth, bowstrings, paper, and other useful items

NYSHIN – The highest class of citizens within Itagami

PATSU – A lacrosse-like game with two teams in which each player wields an iron pole with a net on one end and a blade on the other

PIRA – Vicious, sharp-toothed fish

Ryogo – Although Itagamin citizens believes this to be the name of a paradisiacal afterlife, it is the name of the country from which Varan, Suzu, Tsua, Chio, and the other Miriseh came

Sagen sy Itagami – The easternmost city on Shiara, it was created by carving out the center of the largest mesa on the island; the name is often simply shortened to Itagami

Saishigi – The last rites for citizens of Sagen sy Itagami

Shiara – What those from Itagami call the island itself

Suesutu – The pass southwest of Itagami between the larger of the Kyiwa Mountains

Sukhai – A bondmate/lover

Sumai – A deep bond/partnership/love; can be anywhere between entirely platonic or very sexual

Suraki – A weapon with a blade on one end, a weighted, sometimes spiked ball on the other, and a five-foot chain connecting the two

Surnat – A date-like fruit that grows on low bushes on the island

Teegra – A large, scaled cat

Tokiansu – The fighter's dance

Tsimo – Westernmost clan on Shiara

Tudo – A long, curved, narrow sword

Ushimo – Someone who is asexual or falls on the asexual spectrum

Yonin – Lowest citizen class of Itagami

YAJITU – A flat iron recurved bow with slicing blades affixed to the exterior surface

YUGADAI – The system of khai bonds the Rohko have used to enhance the strength of their clan

ZEEKA – A slightly curved short sword with a narrow blade

ZEKIYU – A short bow

ZON – A district or zone within Itagami

THE RYOGAN CHRONICLES

SEA OF STRANGERS

ERICA CAMERON

CHAPTER ONE

The ship rocks to the side, swaying so violently that Tessen and I have to grab the rope stretched down the center of the deck to keep from sliding to the edge and over. Straight into the dark, angry ocean.

Lightning streaks across the sky, making the three red cloth sails glow as if on fire. For an instant, the world is thrown into stark relief:

The wave cresting several feet above the ship.

The Ryogan crew fighting through wind and rain to keep us upright.

The purple-black storm clouds obscuring almost the entire sky.

It's been too long since this storm started chasing us. Maybe a day and night. Without being able to see the sky, I can't be sure.

What Tessen had spotted through the small window of our room on the lower deck could get us out of the gale winds and out of the drenching, chilling rain.

As we haul ourselves along the deck, I scan for Osshi or the ship's commander, Taikan-yi Kazu. The rain is too heavy. I can barely see the rope in my hands.

Someone is shouting; the words are lost on the wind, drowned in the crash of a wave slamming into the ship and washing over the deck.

A hand grabs my elbow. The touch sends an unpleasant shock up my arm. I don't dare shake it off, not without risking my balance.

"Get below, Khya!" Osshi screams. His eyes are wide, but his square jaw is set and determined. "You can do nothing here. Go!"

"Look! There!" With the hand not gripping the rope, I point to the horizon, to the strip of shining, bright blue almost invisible at this distance. His gaze follows my finger, but it takes a moment of squinting into the driving rain before he sags with relief.

"Thank the Kaisubeh." The drop of his shoulders lasts only a heartbeat; although safety might be on the horizon, we're not there yet. He pushes me toward the lower deck. "Go! I'll tell the captain if Kazu doesn't already know."

Of course he doesn't. Taikan-yi Kazu, the commanding officer, is on the rear platform of the ship, steering us through the massive waves and—hopefully—focusing on making sure the storm doesn't overturn the massive ship and drown us all. I'll be shocked if *any* of the crew has noticed it yet. I wouldn't have if not for Tessen, and Tessen did only because his basaku senses are far stronger and more discerning than anyone else's on this ship.

Tessen tugs on my wrist. When I meet his gray eyes, they're pleading, almost begging me to return to the dry safety of the lower deck. And he's right. We passed along the guidance; there's nothing else we can do here.

I follow Tessen across the deck, both of us holding the rope tight. The fibers scratch and aggravate the skin of my palms. I grip harder. That abrasive texture means I'm attached to the deck. Not even my magic will save me for long if I fall into the ocean.

I can't swim.

Tessen reaches the door first. A flash of lightning illuminates his straining muscles under his soaked, clinging nyska and silk tunic. The wind must be holding it shut. It shouldn't be this hard for him to open.

Yanking myself the few feet, I wrap my left arm around the rough rope and grab the handle of the door to help Tessen. For a breath, it doesn't budge an inch. Then the wind shifts or slows or changes course. Whatever it is, it's enough for us to haul open the door, rush inside, and let it slam closed behind us.

The walls of the ship aren't nearly thick enough to eliminate the howling wind or the crash of each wave against the wooden hull of the ship, but for a moment, the world sounds silent to me.

Then Tessen's pained, and poorly stifled, groans register.

"You shouldn't have come with me, Tessen."

He grunts. Was that supposed to be a word? Maybe, but if he tries to repeat it, he might start throwing up again.

It's probably because he's a basaku that he's reacted like this. The rise and fall of the normal sea he handled fine, but the extreme dips and climbs of the storm-tossed waves infused his terra-cotta skin with a gray tinge and seemed to turn his stomach upside down. He hasn't been able to eat much of anything since it started, he's been achy all day, and he seems weak now, like the short trip took up all the energy he had left.

I put out my hand, waiting for him to take it. I'd think the rain was what chilled his skin, but no. I was out there, too, and his hand feels cold even against my own cooler-than-usual skin. He's still sick. I urge him on, trying not to listen to the ominous creaks and groans that echo through the hull with each wave. Each one sends a shuddering chill over my skin; it seems like all of Osshi's assurances that the ship can withstand storms are about to be proven wrong.

Of course they are.

How can any structure not reinforced by magic survive a continuous assault like this?

The ship tilts. I stumble left and lose my hold on Tessen. My shoulder slams against the wall of the narrow hallway. From the thump and the pained, nauseous groan behind me, Tessen lost his footing, too.

Bellows and blood. It's not a long walk between this deck and our room one level below, but it takes us several minutes, and we collect close to a dozen new bruises on the way. Tessen has to stop twice. I stay with him, one hand pressed to the center of his back and the other braced against the wall.

"I know I promised...we'd steal a ship to get...back—" He has to stop again, breathing deeply several times before he can continue. "Back to Shiara, but we might have...to steal a crew...too. I don't think I'll be much use...running the ship."

"You were fine before the storm." I rub circles on his back.

He groans, resting his head against the wall and peering at me through half-open eyes. "And with our luck, there will be storms the whole voyage."

With our luck, it would be—*will* be—exactly like that.

Moving my hand to Tessen's arm, I guide him away from the wall. "Let's get you sitting before I have to drag you the rest of the way."

Tessen pushes himself off the wall. Another ten feet, and we reach the door to the room we've been sharing with Rai, Etaro, and Sanii.

"Please tell me they're taking us toward the end of this," Rai says with a groan as soon as Tessen and I enter. Though her stomach isn't faring as badly as Tessen's, she's not exactly enjoying this new way of traveling.

"We pointed them to it, but they'll be able to head that way only if the wind lets them." I hover over Tessen long enough to make sure he doesn't collapse completely, and then I sit against the wall next to him.

It's warmer in here with the closed space containing everyone's body heat, but I'm soaking wet; I shiver. Tessen is starting to shiver, too.

Rai must notice, because she shakes her head and says, "No. Can't. Don't have the energy for fire. Change before you both catch a chill and die."

"We're not going to die from a chill." But I do as she says. I should have before I sat down.

"I might." Tessen lifts one of his arms as though thinking about taking off the sopping-wet tunic stuck to his skin, but he quickly drops his hand back to his lap. "Dying would probably hurt less than this."

"No one is dying. There's been more than enough of that already." Sanii unpacks changes of clothing from the bags we stored in the chest along the far wall. When ey holds out the pieces of cloth, Etaro—who hasn't seemed affected by the storm at all—uses eir magic to float them across the room and make them hover just slightly out of my reach, waiting patiently while I strip myself and Tessen out of the soaked cloth we're wrapped in.

The ship rolls again. Tessen's head smacks against the wall. I fall forward, my hands landing on Tessen's chest. Sanii almost tumbles off the low table ey'd been sitting on. Etaro and Rai slide a few feet before they manage to brace themselves.

"I *hate* that," Sanii moans when the ship has righted itself once more.

"Oh, really?" Sarcasm is practically bleeding from Rai's tone. "I'm sure the Miriseh will call the whole plan off, then!"

"We don't know this has anything to do with the Miriseh," Etaro says.

Rai glares, but it's Sanii who says, "We don't know it doesn't, either."

It's an argument that's already been beaten to death from both sides, especially since the storm hit, but they keep coming back to beat it some more. I can't blame them. If there were any way discussing whether or not the Miriseh could create a storm and send it after us would give us an answer, I'd bludgeon the conversation again, too.

But we can't know for sure. We didn't know when we were on the same island—in the same city, even—as the immortal leaders we all spent our lives serving. How could it possibly be easier to figure out now that hundreds of miles separate us from them?

With another groan, Tessen's hand lands on my knee, flopped there without any of his usual grace. I bite back a smile at the pathetic-ness of his expression as I sit down in front of him, placing his upturned wrists on my thighs and applying pressure to the points three finger widths below his wrist. Our healer, Zonna, helped ease Tessen's agony until the ship's crew started collecting injuries more life-threatening than an upset stomach. Pressure-point relief is a poor substitute for Zonna's magic, but it'll have to be enough. I'm no hishingu. My wards may be able to keep someone from getting hurt in the first place, but they can't do a thing to help anyone who's already in pain.

"We were supposed to arrive today." Sanii is looking out the small window, eir narrow face tense. Most of us have to duck or bend to look out the window; ey's so short it's at a perfect height for em to peer out into darkness broken only by lightning. "Or yesterday, if it's past midnight."

"Who can tell?" Etaro stares at the small black stones dancing in midair above eir palm, tokens from our last day on Shiara. From Imaku. From the barren, black island that was once my brother's prison.

No. I close my eyes for a second and press my thumbs deeper into Tessen's skin. I can't think about that now, not until I have some idea how long it'll be before I can try to rescue Yorri.

Try. Again. For a third time.

"Horizon was…too bright," Tessen manages to say. I open my eyes; his are still closed. "Not night. Sunrise, maybe."

"Maybe we'll find land today." Etaro bites eir full bottom lip, eir already concave cheeks sucking in deeper. The words are almost hopeful. Eir expression is far from it.

"Do you really want to get there?" Rai's question is the one I've been thinking but haven't asked.

We're headed to Ryogo—a land we believed we'd see only after death—and so much of it isn't going to look or feel anything like we expected it to. It's not going to look like *I* expected it to. The realization hit in bits and pieces over the past two weeks, like the sporadic grains of sand and rock at the beginning of a dust storm. And like those small strikes, it's become more uncomfortable—nearly unbearable—the closer we get to the reality of Ryogo.

"Even with what we stole from Itagami, we're going to run out of food soon." Sanii doesn't look away from the window. "Either we find land or we starve."

Sanii's pragmatic reminder makes me look at the empty plate sitting on the floor in the corner of the room. A few hours ago, those of us who could stomach food at all shared a meal that might have been what *one* of us ate back home; the kitchens in Sagen sy Itagami had only ever stinted us when drought forced rations on our desert city.

The city where the clan we abandoned still lives.

Where Yorri is hidden somewhere.

Where we all thought we would live our entire lives.

ACKNOWLEDGMENTS

As ever, I have to thank my family for always backing me up no matter how far-fetched my aspirations may sound. My mom especially is more epic than I can explain, and I owe her more than I can ever repay. Love you to the moon and back, Momma.

My beta readers, critique partners, and friends are always invaluable, but with a project this big it becomes more important than ever to have people there to encourage me and ask the right questions. Haley, Katrina, Tristina, Cait, Lani, Olivia, and Brett, you guys are amazing. Thank you *so* much.

Many thanks go to Katrina Spade and the Urban Death Project for A) taking the time to answer my questions about human composting, and B) not thinking I was a potential serial killer for asking those questions. I sincerely hope you like how I've used the concept here!

Even as I write this almost a year after it happened, I'm still a little in shock that a convoluted conversation with Kate Brauning about the fantasy world I invented in college turned into a request for my draft, which turned into the series with Entangled. Kate, you helped me shape this story into something complex and enthralling, and I am so happy we happened to sit next to each other at lunch that day.

To everyone at Entangled Teen who has been so wonderfully supportive, especially Ashley Hearn and Bethany

Robison for their early (and gleeful) enthusiasm for the story! I'm so grateful that this series has become part of the Entangled catalog.

And finally, to all the readers who have followed me from my previous series and all the ones who are picking up one of my books for the first time: hello and thank you. All of you are awesome.

GRAB THE ENTANGLED TEEN RELEASES READERS ARE TALKING ABOUT!

LOST GIRLS
BY MERRIE DESTEFANO

Yesterday, Rachel went to sleep curled up in her grammy's quilt, worrying about geometry. Today, she woke up in a ditch, bloodied, bruised, and missing a year of her life. She's not the only girl to go missing within the last year...but she's the only girl to come back. And as much as her dark, dangerous new life scares her, it calls to her. Seductively. But wherever she's been—whomever she's been with—isn't done with her yet...

REDUX
BY A.L DAVROE

Their domed city is in ruins. With nowhere to go, prodigy hacker Ellani "Ella" Drexel and a small band of survivors escape the wasteland *she* unknowingly created.

But malfunctioning androids and angry rebels make sanctuary hard to find. Worse, the boy she loves is acting distant, and not at all like the person she first met in *Nexis*.

Ella needs to turn back and make a stand to reclaim her home. She's determined to bring a new—and better—life to all who've suffered.

Or die trying.

INFINITY
BY JUS ACCARDO

There are three things Kori knows for sure about her life:

One: Her army general dad is *insanely* overprotective.
Two: The guy he sent to watch her, Cade, is *way* too good-looking.
Three: Everything she knew was a lie.

Now there are three things Kori never knew about her life:

One: There's a device that allows her to jump dimensions.
Two: Cade's got a lethal secret.
Three: Someone wants her dead.

TRUE BORN
BY L.E. STERLING

After the great Plague descended, the population was decimated...and humans' genetics damaged beyond repair. But there's something about Lucy Fox and her identical twin sister, Margot, that isn't quite right. No one wants to reveal *what* they are. When Margot disappears suddenly, Lucy is forced to turn to the True Borns to find her. But instead of answers, there is only the discovery of a deeply buried conspiracy. And somehow, the Fox sisters could unravel it all...